BARRY E WOODHAM

Genesis
search

BARRY E WOODHAM

Genesis
search

MEMOIRS
Cirencester

MEMOIRS
PUBLISHING

Published by Memoirs
25 Market Place, Cirencester, Gloucestershire, GL7 2NX
info@memoirsbooks.co.uk www.memoirspublishing.com

First published in England, August 2012
Book cover design Ray Lipscombe

Hard copy ISBN 978-1-909020-88-7
eBook for Kindle ISBN 978-1-909020-90-0
eBook for all other readers ISBN 978-1-909020-89-4

Printed in England

DEDICATION

Once again I dedicate this book to my loving and patient wife, Janet, who even now listens to the strange ideas that I still bounce off her practical mind. I also again dedicate Genesis Search to Emelia Hardy (USA) who has read this book as I produced it to look for any mistakes.
Her enthusiasm for my writing keeps me continually searching for new ideas.

List of Characters

Human and Ape

Larse	First to make contact with alien nannite.
Thomas	Larse's friends and comrades
Alexander	Leader/mayor. Telepathic gestalt achieved with Gnathe and humans
Frederick	Giant/warrior
Hannah	Scientist. Fredrick's lover
Joom	Chimp
Nannites	Original crew that landed on Jupiter of the Red Sun.
Kamiel 637 Nannite	Weapons expert, psychologist and historian.
Asue 637 Nannite	Nano-tech expert and Astrogator
Sharn 637 Nannite	Medical/biologist/geneticist
Minns 637	Nannite (Medical/biologist/geneticist)
Minnis	Nannite battle suit. A.I. Built from reclaimed Minns and programmed by Kamiel. Can kill! Controlled by Fredrick
Solace	Nannite. Re-programmed to join Search

Gnathe

Link-soo-shan	Once Tyrant. Builder of the Gate
Suzzan-link-khann	Brood - daughter of Link
Trann-link-khann	Brood - daughter of Link
Ender-whann-soo	Telepathic adept. First brood-mother to contact Humans
Azander-link-whann	Brood - mother, Daughter of Ender, (Part human mind - Alexander's)
Marren-link-whann	Brood - mother, Daughter of Ender, (Part human mind - Alexander's)
Khann-link-sool	Grand Brood-mother of Ender

Trans-sentients

	Co-ordinator
	Deep-thinker.
	Archive
Thipdar	Primm. First of family Smelch

Foreword

Humanity and the Gnathe have entered into a multi-alien society since the confrontation with the Goss. A time of peace and co-operation has endured for hundreds of thousands of years.

Preface

Over nine hundred-thousand years after the defeat and incorporation of the Goss into the fabric of the Galactic society a survey ship is sent to examine a possible reason for the imminent collision of the Andromeda galaxy with ours. The event has been speeded up to take place within a thousand years. By travelling back in time the survey ship finds that the alteration of the movement of Andromeda coincides with the time Gnathe and Humans moved the Earth and moon to orbit Icarus, to escape the expanding sun. A decision is taken to travel back through time to bring back via cloning and mind transference the original team that altered the Goss. Kamiel 637 is directed to take charge of the operation.

Acknowledgements

Thanks are given to those of my loyal band of readers who e-mailed me to say that they enjoyed my story.

There will be more email barry.e.woodham@btinternet.com for more information.

CHAPTER ONE

The 'Vogb' (Violet/Orange/Green/Black), or Conic, manipulated the instruments so that a stream of data filled the screen that the Thipdar was watching intently. The tendrils of the Conic twisted the tiny knobs of the equipment while the electrically charged one, fed small trickle charges into the scanning device. The pile of donut rings shivered with anticipation as the bottom ring anchored itself to the floor. All eyestalks swivelled round to stare at the screen, while the inverted 'vee' of the head remained very still.

The Goss watched fascinated, as the mental chatter of the two aliens were fed through its mentality. It had never regretted accepting the offer that the nannite Guardian, Kamiel 637 had made to it, when it had given up its ability to dominate all sentient life for the endless wonder of being a telepathic bridge for all aliens to use. The universe had become a far more interesting place since it had relinquished control. The two aliens were not the only ones on board the Toarvak who were training their instruments upon the swiftly approaching galaxy. There were a large contingent of insectoids with five queens and their attending males forming a very strong group mind, while the sterile females manipulated their scanning apparatus as well.

Toarvak 12,402 had brought the scientific expedition far out of the galaxies edge to make their observations. Out here the wormholes were few and very scarce. The Toarvak crew had maintained an open wormhole behind the vessel and were forcing it to stay open. It would not do to lose it this far out in the intergalactic darkness. Long before the ship could return, the stars would have ceased to shine and the event they were tracking would have overtaken them.

1

Blue/orange/green finished the final adjustments and let loose a rainbow of colours across the top ring while the rest of the rings went a dark blue.

He fixed his gaze on the Thipdar with all six of its eyestalks, before it spoke through the Goss and said, "It seems that we were right! We must correlate all the previous results with all of the others that our esteemed colleagues have gathered, but there is little doubt in my mind that our suspicions are correct. There can be no other answer!"

"I fear that you are right 'B-o-g' old friend," the Thipdar answered and stood back on her third leg, waving the two lesser arms about under the still, strong ones. We will check with the others first, but I fear that they also will have the same results."

The trip'o-dal swung round on one leg and planted the other two firmly in place to stare unhappily at the other scientists. Her eyes closed for some moments as the vertical lids met, so that she could concentrate her mind, looking for any flaw that she could. The Conic was very thorough and the equipment that the two of them had designed together was a very accurate rangefinder. She opened her eyes again and opened her mind to the Goss.

"My colleagues have you all finished? Shall we leave this life forsaken place?" the Thipdar asked.

There was a welter of affirmation as each group finished taking their individual instruments apart and stacking them away.

"Toarvak," she asked, "Please take us home."

"Madam scientist I shall be only too happy to do so. I can hold this wormhole together for a very little longer, if necessary, if you so wish."

"Thank you Toarvak, but it is time to go," she answered and watched as the silver coated Kresh concentrated their combined will.

All that could be seen of the Kresh were their faces, as the substance of the Toarvak vessel engulfed the rest of them. They were sat in a five-bodied cone that was tilted so that they were touching each other by their heads, with their huge ears overlapping each other. The body of each Kresh sat at a sixty-degree angle and all arms were crossed over each chest. They were very still.

The Thipdar smiled to herself as she recalled the human she had met, once refer to them as giant rabbits. Out of curiosity she had researched the term and found a picture of the animal that did live wild on the human's original home world. If you dressed them up it was true, they did look like miniature Kresh except for those huge ears. Still she thought to herself the human did admit that the Thipdar with their three-legged body and four arms did make them far more outlandish than the Kresh.

She was Family/Smelch; - 'Primary of group', known as Primm, matriarch to her clan and at this moment wished that she were lower down the family tree looking after the young, instead of being here as 'First Scientist'. The observation port closed, signalling that they were travelling back through the wormhole and back amongst the stars.

"Goss! Call them together and blend thoughts," Primm instructed the symbiont.

The alien scientists blended the information that each of them had obtained from their different instruments. This was not a group mind but a blending of information. Each of them remained an individual in their own right except the insectoids who reverted back to five queens and their own males to be five independent minds.

The Kresh in Toarvak with the ship, applied their collective will to the time distorting crystal carried in the heart of the vessel. They had been so far out beyond the galactic arm to do this study that subjective time had passed in hundreds of thousands of years. Toarvak 12,402 had also travelled back in time millions of years to the beginning of the phenomena. The collective mind fastened upon the anchoring crystal set in their own timeframe of the present, as viewed by the civilisation that had sent them and opened the wormhole around them to speed upwards in space-time. They had an incredible journey to take, of hundreds of thousands of light-years in distance and more than six million years in time.

Using this same method, the Kresh had retrieved their world before its willed destruction and replaced it in orbit around its sun, placing it in the same timeframe as the 'Three Worlds' and the Jupiter society. It had taken quite some time before the old type Goss had been totally eradicated and the new symbiont introduced. The input of the grateful Kresh, whose highly scientific culture had surpassed the efforts of mankind in the area of interstellar travel, had boosted the new wormhole connected society to new heights. Over nine hundred, thousand years had passed since the war with the Goss had taken place and the new blended civilisation spread throughout the Milky Way galaxy. The Gnathe, Humanity and the Kresh had fished through time to retrieve every alien race that had been used and destroyed by the Goss when it was in its parasitic state.

Great care had been taken not to cause any paradoxes and all the aliens were taken at just before the point of death, so that their disappearance would not change history. Their minds were stored in crystal and enough living cells taken, to be able to clone the individuals. Enough beings were taken and given a second chance at life to create a viable gene pool.

Once the crystal-mining project had turned up enough very large and powerful time distorting gems, other options had been looked at.

Project 'Time Fisher' was instigated by a consorted agreement of all the alien races gathered in. Now the Toarvaks could travel far back through time and twist the Gnathen wormhole system, as well as their own method of travelling through space. It was possible to gather in all alien sentient species that had died out due to suns exploding, warfare or natural disasters removing them from the universe from the very far past. Worlds were relocated to orbit stable stars in this time frame, leaving behind whatever disaster had threatened them. There were plenty of spare suns without planets orbiting the 'Goldilocks' zone (an area where water did not freeze or boil). All of them were exposed to the genetically altered Goss and were able to understand each other without any problems. This was when the memory of the Goss that had existed for over a million years had presented a strange anomaly to a researcher in ancient astronomy. At one time due to the records kept by a long dead race, the Andromeda galaxy and its family had been in a system of stasis with the home galaxy. At some time in the past, the whole galaxy and its family of smaller star clusters had altered its relationship with the Milky Way and was now heading on a collision course instead. The Toarvak expedition had gathered enough information to find the date when this had occurred.

The information gathered had alarmed the scientists on board the Toarvak vessel as all the indications pointed the same way. The collision was determined as a deliberate action. Some 'Thing' or sentient life form with almost infinite energy had turned the galaxy's direction around and had even managed to accelerate the speed towards them.

This was the information that Toarvak 12,402 was taking back to the home world of the Kresh and the confederation of worlds on Toarvak Prime. Whilst they were out of phase and traversing the wormhole it was not possible to communicate with the scientific elite that had sent them. The emergence had been set to coincide with a time two weeks later than the time that they had started from and the anchoring time crystal would not be activated until then. The crystal was split from the same master gem as the one carried on the Toarvak and once switched on would home onto the crystal coming forward through time and space.

During the time-span from the defeat and changing of the Goss, the Toarvak ships of the resurrected Kresh had explored every arm of the Milky Way galaxy. In the nine hundred, thousand years or more that had been passed since Link-soo-shan had risked her sanity and life to fool the Goss, thousands of intelligent alien people had been found, contacted and infected with the symbiont. Many had been approaching the point of extinction due to their sun becoming unstable. Again, those worlds had been moved into orbit around suitable suns and relocated. Of the others, those who were developing interstellar travel by using wormholes were quickly assimilated into the loose federation of worlds. The more primitive societies were monitored and watched for the point that they could be contacted without destroying their culture.

Peace had now reigned in this galaxy ever since the war with the Goss had ended and under the 'Guardianship' of the nannites all alien races had prospered. The telepathic link-up by the symbiont Goss, made it impossible for any act of aggression between alien races or themselves. Any potential sentient species had been 'up-lifted' by genetic engineering into full members of the Federation of Worlds by those members gifted in this area of knowledge.

It was to this Federation's headquarters located on a world purpose built for this enterprise that the scientific expedition was headed. It was known by the Kresh name of Toarvak Prime that translated as 'The Great Collective.' This planet had been chosen with great care. It had been found orbiting its sun too far out for the water on this world to ever thaw and life come into being by any action. It was a truly sterile world, but of the right size to be able to encourage life to continue once it had been moved closer to its sun. The Kresh and the Gnathe had moved it to 'the Goldilocks Orbit' where its water could freeze at the poles and not become steam at the equator.

The nannites descended onto the planet's surface with as close to the emotion of joy that they possessed. Drawing on their knowledge of the thousands of different sentient species and their independent needs they proceeded to separate out the common habitable areas that as many sentients could co-inhabit. Containing them with the people that required their coexistence solved any problems with broadband lethal microorganisms. Mountain plateaus were built and sculpted to suit those who needed lower pressure air to be comfortable, while artificially deep canyons were forged for those who needed the opposite. The seas were seeded with aquatic life and the lands with plant life to suit all alien sentient creatures. The nannites selected a moon to produce tides and other smaller moons to be used as stopping off points and the Kresh placed them in orbit around Toarvak Prime.

The Gnathe and Kresh moved two gas giants closer together so that they became a binary set of worlds, so that they would mop up any large comets that might accidentally drop towards the sun. The chance was slight as the nannites established a copy of the civilization that they had built in around the Kuiper belt at the fringes of mankind's original home. From here they would be able to keep a keen observation on Toarvak Prime and its development. The original programming by Alexander McBald had easily been adapted to encompass all of the alien races brought back and established in the present time frame. Nannites were integrated into all societies and the term of Guardian suited their purpose exactly.

It was to this sprawling civilization that Toarvak 12,402 was traversing the wormhole in time and space. The permanently engineered star-gate was anchored to one of the outlying moons in orbit around 'Prime' and resembled a giant ring made from spider webs. Thousands of equally spaced command crystals with telekinetic ones riding piggyback were located around the ring, interconnected by gold wire circuits fed by solar panels. The star-gate was kept permanently open as it took a massive amount of traffic. The indication of its impending use was signalled by the void across the gate showing an orange glow that lit up the anchoring moon.

Two weeks after the Toarvak ship had left, the star-gate signalled orange and the vessel emerged into present space-time. The ship dropped down towards 'Prime' and made its way towards the common landing point for the species on board. As 'First Scientist' Primm had the responsibility to report the amazing and disturbing findings to the representatives of the council of worlds. Although she could as easily debriefed on board the Toarvak ship to the council, she preferred to do so from the quarters assigned to her amongst her family. Once down and anchored to a stable point the scientific colleagues all made their way back to their own areas to enjoy the benefits of living in their own custom built accommodations.

Family 'Smelch' greeted her with affection and joy. Her husbands and junior wives clustered around her and the younglings all required attention. Primm had plenty of time to correlate the results from every alien scientific result on the journey home and now that she was back amongst her family, it was time to contact the Council of Worlds.

She locked her legs into the comfortable tripod position folded all four arms at rest and opened her mind to the Goss.

"Goss! Contact all members of the Council of Worlds and inter-link their minds with mine. Establish privacy over the link. What I have to report will need to be passed on to each and every alien in the confederation, but it will need delicate handling," Primm commanded.

The Goss separated part of itself and joined to only those spores that the council members were host to and signalled Primm to begin.

"Members of the council I have grave news to impart," instructed Primm. "As you remember, we have known for eons that the Andromeda galaxy is set to collide with ours. Once this was in the exceedingly far future, as our earliest records show. Recent observations have shown that this once remote in time disaster, has been speeded up! Instead of billions of years in the future it appears that the whole galaxy has altered its shape to form a more closed configuration so that collision with a multitude of stars will take place."

The clear bell tones of the 'Co-ordinator' replied in question, "This could not be a natural phenomena?"

Primm mentally shook her head and replied, "No Co-ordinator! It is not possible for stars to move in this way unless an intelligence is responsible."

The great globe inflated the air bag above its body and lifted into the air with alarm. Her tendrils hung down and thrashed in a dance of anxiety and she opened all of her eyes along the perimeter of her body. Tran-sentient Ones were from the earliest time that sentient life forms had developed in this galaxy and were an airborne life form with no natural enemies. On their own world they lived a hunter/gatherer existence without any technology. They had an incredible life span and were almost immortal, being very slow growing. They mated infrequently with a policy of deliberately restricted numbers. They were philosophers and thinkers with broad ranging telepathic abilities. 'Co-ordinator' was named for her ability, as were all the 'Trans-sentient Ones' and so she linked up with 'Deep-thinker' for advice.

"What else did your instruments tell you," Deep-thinker asked.

"The date at which this action was initiated," Primm replied.

"And this was?"

"As we who decided to undertake this expedition through space and time had feared! The alteration of the galaxy's movement away from us, to towards our position, coincides with the moving of the Humans' world away from the expanding sun and the relocation of the Gnathe! Since then our combined civilization had spent its time removing inhabited worlds away from unstable suns and relocating them in time and space to become members of our federation," the Thipdar declared and waited.

The thousands of representatives of every alien civilisation remained quiet. They were reflecting that they too were many of them refugees, from yellow stars about to go 'Red giant' or nova, thus destroying their home world.

Deep-thinker conferred with Co-ordinator for a few moments and addressed Primm and all other aliens in the 'loop', "We have also been fishing through time and space and relocating ancient civilizations that were doomed to the fire of their expanding sun. We now share this time-span with every intelligent race to evolve in this galaxy and that includes us. Were it not for the translocation of our world, from the very beginnings of the first stars to settle down and produce life-bearing planets to this time and space, we too would have died when our star went nova."

Primm accepted this fact and questioned Deep-thinker, "What relevance does this have to the problem that we have verified?"

"I possess vague race memories that are not clear that may shed light upon the subject. We need 'Archive' to join the loop. She is the oldest amongst us and her memories are vast. Her years number the millions and are beyond counting. I will awaken her and ask her to remember her beginnings."

A thousand and more minds respectively waited as Deep-thinker and Co-ordinator gently woke the immense giant of their kind. 'Archive' was the largest of the Tran-sentient Ones and massed over a hundred tons including the gasbag that kept her aloft. She was the size of a shuttlecraft with tendrils thicker than most of the aliens, where they sprang from her body in groups of ten. They were a hundred feet long at least and even in her sleep they constantly ripped vegetation apart and fed it into her maw. Her eyes wearily opened as she awoke and focussed her mind on the insistent clamouring of the two others of her kind.

"I am awake! What is it you need from me?" 'Archive' asked and concentrated her mind on the problem presented.

She experienced surprise at the request initially and then analysed the data that Primm had brought back from far out from the galactic arm. Every mind was concentrated upon her answer and remained quiet. 'Archive' had stopped eating and sent her mind inwards and back to the farthest reaches of her long existence.

'Archive' spoke finally to the assembly, "Long ago when the first stars were cooling and planets being formed, life evolved upon a few worlds. We were able to register this fact across the vast distances from star to star. Something moved amongst these new worlds spreading the primitive life and leaving it to mature. We became aware of it, as time went by, but remained hidden from its sensors. Our world developed independently and we the Tran-sentients, kept ourselves hidden from this thing. To our horror our minds became aware that when the life forms on each world became many, a catastrophe would be engineered by the life form to wipe out most of the life on each world. Whatever the thing was, it fed on the life energies of dying creatures. We named it 'The Harvester' as it seeded worlds from the natural life that it found and spread it. Then it would reap the harvest from the life it had nurtured. As time went by intelligence developed after the successive engineered disasters and 'The Harvester' found a taste for intelligent life. Some aliens managed to develop interstellar travel and the moment they did so, 'The Harvester' would explode their sun and feast upon the life force of the race before they could escape. This went on for millions of years and we went unnoticed or so we thought. Our star was just starting to go unstable when the Kresh and the Gnathe moved our world through space and time to the here and now. 'The Harvester' did not get its meal and I suspect that the timelines have been changed in our universe so that it has remained unable to feed here, since the beginning of sentient life in this galaxy. All this time it has fed on the life forms in the Andromeda Galaxy and now it has run out of life force. Now I believe that it is coming here!"

There was a stunned mental silence from the assembly as these facts were assimilated.

At long last 'Co-ordinator spoke to all of them, "We

must ask more of Primm. What other knowledge can you bring to this assembly? Do we have point of impact and timescale?"

Primm's mouth went dry as she correlated the other results of the measurements taken in the empty gap between the galaxies.

She instructed the assembly the facts as she knew them, "We have but a few thousand years before the onslaught begins, as this thing 'Archive' refers to as 'The Harvester' has speeded up the stars' movement towards us. The whole galaxy of Andromeda is accelerating towards us and the stars at the front have been brought closer together so that they will impact our stars."

"What would be the effects?" asked 'Co-ordinator' and settled her specific gravity so that she hovered closer to the ground.

The Thipdar had studied the effect of the impending collision and replied, "Within a thousand years the masses of stars would begin to excite each other and vast cosmic flares would erupt from the nearest suns. Long before the stars collided the whole area of the galactic arm that faced Andromeda would become sterilised of all life, no matter how primitive. Once some of the more massive stars got close enough they would rip open and congeal together, become unstable and either explode their matter into the void, or contract into 'black holes'. As more and more singularities formed they would spit out a lethal storm of X-rays and plunge into each other to form a super-black-hole to rival the one at the galactic centre. This would unstable the star-fields of the incoming stars and the home suns. The impact would cause a ripple effect all across the spiral arms sending the stars at the other side of the Milky Way into unstable orbital paths around the centre.

After all of the stars settled into a new configuration

combining the two main galaxies and the satellite ones, a super galaxy would be born. It would take billions of years to settle down before new planets would form and with them new life. For the life that lived here now however, there would be no escape."

The knowledge that this carnage was intentional and deliberate filled the research scientist with fear. What type of being could have that much power? What could be done to avoid this mega-death?

CHAPTER TWO

Some of the very early alien races that developed interstellar flight had found that on empty worlds with free water and viable land, life would suddenly appear where none had been before. The oddest thing was that much of the basic DNA was compatible with the first interstellar visitors. The few alien races that met each other found that no matter how unalike they were to each other, they shared the same type of DNA. This was so right up to the present day. All across this galaxy the life was related in some bizarre way. They deduced that something was seeding life wherever a possible life-bearing world could be found. To their horror, they also found out that for no apparent reason some suns would go into their next sequence early and expand, while others seemed to be timed to coincide with a civilization at its peak. Every one of the interstellar cultures were wiped out by their suns going unaccountably unstable. When this happened there were too few star-ships left, to start again with the crew on board.

These were the actions of the being that Archive had named as 'The Harvester' and only now did these findings make sense to the ancient members of the council of worlds. It was an ape, one of humanities closely related cousins that provided a small glimmer of hope.

"I am Jondar, citizen of Daedalus Two of the Three Worlds and representative of my kind. It seems to me that we cannot defeat this creature and so I propose that we move our worlds out of the way!"

Deep-thinker considered the proposal and spoke to all, "We need do more than that! I have considered the problem and I agree with the member for Daedalus Two, but it is not just planets we need to move, but the stars that they orbit also! We must contact the Kresh, the Gnathe, Human and Ape stellar engineers. In fact we must involve every sentient race of beings conversant with the relocation of planets through space and time. We have been given a time frame in which we must mobilise our talents and efforts. This galaxy must be left empty of every sentient being before this destruction is visited upon us."

The clear tones of Co-ordinator rang through their minds, "There will be another necessity. While we mobilise ourselves and relocate all worlds from the area of impact, first a force will be needed to keep 'The Harvester' busy and occupied. Otherwise, should it become aware of what we are doing it may step up its attack."

An insectoids' hive mind spoke up, "We have lost the art of warfare. There are none in this timeframe that could think in this way. The Hive has considered the problem and has had an idea."

"And your idea is?" answered Co-ordinator, bluntly.

"Those who defeated the Goss when it was a parasite, were the last of their kind to think in this fashion. These are the ones that should be re-created or time-fished from their time to ours," the hive mind answered. "Look to the records and find them. Give them a second chance at life in return for their services. Ask the Kresh and their Toarvak ships. They will know who they were. Contact the Humans and the Gnathe as well, they will have records."

"An excellent idea," replied 'Co-ordinator' and sent her thoughts to those representatives concerned. "Do it and do it soon" she instructed. "This extraordinary meeting is closed. Those closest to the place of impact will be the first to have their world moved to the opposite end of our galaxy. Stellar engineers will move suitable stars into a globular cluster outside of the galactic plane and shielded from the Andromeda galaxy by the mass of the Milky Way.

Obviously this will take all priority from any other projects. Primm!"

"Yes 'Co-ordinator' I am here," replied the Thipdar.

"You did well as first scientist on the information retrieval. I am pleased with your efforts," the Tran-sentient told her. "I would ask you to take charge of the time-fishing team. Gather all the sentients that you think you will need. Do you feel that you can do this?"

Primm locked all three legs to prevent toppling over in stunned appreciation of 'Co-ordinators faith in her managerial abilities. A surge of pride and a balancing feel of doubt opened her mind to the Tran-sentient, with a voiceless affirmative.

"I will be there if you need me. You will have my authority in all that you instruct. I warn you though I do foresee a possibility that you and your family may end up as an integral part of the group that you assemble," 'Co-ordinator' sadly told her.

"I understand, 'Co-ordinator," Primm replied. "If it necessitates, I will not be coming back to this galaxy or time frame. The saving of all of the Council of Worlds is of more value than my family or me. They will go where I go and we will not be alone."

The Guardian fixed its eyeless stare at the Thipdar for some time before answering. Primm knew that it was communicating with others of its kind. What she had asked would take some effort amongst the 'silver ones.' It was wearing the Vogb shape out of courtesy to the beings it was visiting, but without the six eyestalks at the top of its head. The top ring flashed a medley of colours to the group that it was teaching and it fashioned a tympanum on the side facing Primm.

"The nannite you seek was known amongst us as Kamiel

637. As we speak the Guardians are sweeping a search through our archives. The search is in machine time so it should not take long," the nannite said with a measured finality.

Primm locked her three legs into a stable position and waited as patiently as she could for her answer. A sequence of rapidly different shades of colours imparted to the 'class' that the session was over and the young conics replied in kind and moved away from their teacher. The multitude of hidden feet carried them out of the classroom and down the corridor to their thinking quarters. 'Teacher' rapidly reformed the conical body into a semblance of the Thipdar form, but again without the vertically slit eyes and the fringed mouth. Primm soon found herself looking at a similar shape to herself, locked also into a trip'o-dal form while the silver being gathered the information fed to it by its colleagues.

Primm could sense the surprise emanating from the nannite as it spoke to her and said, "There are no records of this individual! We have swept through every available list that we possess and cannot find him. His partner, Asue 637 is missing also!"

The Thipdar's mouth tendrils writhed in disappointment as she replied, "We need him! In fact we need both of them. What can we do?"

"We are scanning our records again for the last time that they were both recorded as being in this universe. They are registered during the war against the Goss, this is certain. From that point we are running the records forwards."

Primm stared at the nannite as the obvious solution came to mind. She shut her vertical eyelids to concentrate her mind on the only possibility and its consequences.

The nannite spoke, "First scientist we have come to a point in time that both nannites are in existence and then not! It is several centuries after the war with the Goss and its alteration into a symbiont."

"We retrieved them from their era," Primm said with certainty. "You will accompany my team to that time and assist in the retrieval of these two nannites. There will be no time paradox as it must have been done and it is already history. Your kind keeps meticulous records and there can be no other answer."

"The nannite community has already sent my replacement as teacher to the Vogb, so I shall be only too pleased to go with you. A chance to meet the most famous nannite that has ever come into existence and his partner is an opportunity not to be missed. He is unique! My mind has been reminded that there are others who you will need and Kamiel 637 will know who they are," replied the nannite. "Extra programming has been downloaded into my neural networks to enable me to assist you in a better capacity. I have been upgraded from teacher and have been given a name. You may call me Solace for I shall support you in every way that in can."

"What makes Kamiel 637 unique?" asked Primm thoughtfully.

"He died during the first attempt to travel back through time and was destroyed by a Gnathe. When time was run back, he was recreated without the programming restrictions that all nannites have ingrained into our electronic souls. He alone can do more than defend; he can destroy. He is governed by his own state of ethics, as is Asue, who experienced the same effect that also took away those safeguards," Solace explained to the Thipdar.

"He would seem to be the key to open up a viable list of those we need for this venture. How do we go about acquiring him?" asked Primm.

"The first thing we need is a time-travelling Toarvak and

crew," the nannite declared. "I would suggest the one who took you through time and space to observe the phenomena that has inspired this interview!"

"Toarvak 12,042 was the name of the vessel that carried the scientific expedition. It was most helpful and the crew were Kresh. Who or what else do we need?"

"Archive!"

"What! That's impossible, you know it is. She is larger than a Toarvak! Besides which she is too old. We cannot ask this thing of the Tran-sentients!" exclaimed the Thipdar as she rocked backwards and forwards on her three extended and ridged legs.

"Ask Co-ordinator if she has any young, or if not, will she mate to produce one? Whatever she remembers and knows is passed on to her progeny," the nannite insisted. "You will need her or her memories, to persuade both Kamiel 637 and Asue 637 to leave everything they have achieved behind and travel to our time and space. You will also need her to track the 'Harvester' as they are the only life form that is sensitive to its thoughts."

Primm calmed herself and thought it through and realised that the unemotional nannite was right. She composed herself and extended her will.

"Goss!"

"I am here as always."

"I need to speak with Co-ordinator. Please find her for me," the Thipdar asked.

"I am everywhere and in everyone," the Goss replied. "She is here!"

Nervously Primm outlined the requirement the Solace had put to her about Archive.

Many miles away from where Primm and Solace were in conference, the Trans-sentients had their grazing grounds. It was an area of abundant vegetation with the meat animals also living there for the necessary dietary requirements of the floating giants. Co-ordinator shot into the air with such shock that she uprooted the tree that she was feeding on. Every eye around her body opened wide and her bunches of tendrils thrashed and spasmodic twitches sent bundles of leaves and branches flying through the air. The Transentient vented gas to bring her specific gravity down and returned to a position where she could anchor to a large tree.

"What you ask is impossible! 'Archive' is the oldest among us. She has not mated for more than a million cycles around our star! I cannot ask her to do this thing, besides the gestation time is hundreds of your years."

Primm screwed up her eyes and thought it through and said, "She must have offspring. I know that what she knows, her progeny will also carry in memory. Let me speak to her and explain."

Co-ordinator sent her thoughts to the eldest and respectively entered into conversation with the giant amongst her people.

Primm was aware of being scrutinised by an amazingly amused presence.

"Mouthful! What you ask I would gladly do if I were able!" The mind shook with mirth and tinges of regret and spoke to the Thipdar, "I have had many, many young in this immense lifespan, but all are also millions of years old and far too large to fit inside a Toarvak! There is a way however. In the way of our kind there are young and impetuous youth who would be glad to go with you when you search for this abomination of consciousness. They will be sent to me and I will imprint my memories into these young Tran-sentients. By the time you return from your time-fishing project I will be ready and you will find that you will have many of my kind going with you. One per Toarvak will suffice, as they will still be a great deal larger than you!"

"Madam Archive you are wise. We thank you for your wisdom", Primm replied.

"Little mouthful I was aware of Co-ordinator's shock." Again, the mind of the ancient shook with laughter, as Archive floated to her friend's massive frame and laid a consoling tendril around one of hers. "I have not been so amused in hundreds of thousands of years. Now go about your business and leave us to ours!"

The nannite waited for Primm to recover from her mental efforts before speaking again.

"Have you sorted out the requirements with the Tran-sentients? Will Archive comply?" asked Solace.

"She will, but not quite in the manner that you suggested. She will impart sections of her mind into willing younger Tran-sentients who will be of a size that we can take them with us," replied Primm and relaxed her legs from the locked position.

The nannite rocked forwards towards the door of Primm's office and before leaving said, "You should visit with your family and tell them your news. I have business with the Gnathe. There are things that I will need to find out in your name. Get some rest in the meantime while things come together. I have already signalled that Toarvak 12,402 and its crew will be needed. They are still in orbit and will approach when needed."

The Thipdar watched the nannite disappear through the door and wondered what the future would bring?

Solace made her way towards the living quarters of the Gnathe. The giants had genetically adapted themselves to cope with the stronger sunshine of the yellow star that Toarvak Prime orbited and permanently lived on this world. Preferring a red sun the Gnathe had spread out and colonised a great deal of planets in partnership with the genetically altered humans and apes. The human race was now firmly separated into two entirely different species, the Jupiter born and those of the Three Worlds who had retained their unaltered lineage.

The nannite had changed shape to that of the birdlike aliens, but no larger than one of the females. She was met by a male Gnathe, who took her immediately to the rooms of the Gnathe ambassador.

Shan-link-khann eased herself down on the perch so as not to be too overpowering to the smaller nannite. The triangular head stared down at Solace and both pointed ears were cocked in the nannite's direction. She had tucked her tail underneath the perch and folded her backward facing knees.

"What can I do for you?" she asked directly.

"I have been given the name of Solace, madam. I am now part of the time fishing project and I am gathering information," the nannite replied. "There are things that I need to know that are far back in the history of the Gnathe."

"How far back?"

"I need to know the names of those Gnathe who assisted in the 'restraining' of the Goss. I also need to know whether you have any of those minds saved in crystalline fashion and their genetic patterns. If not I require the assistance of someone trained in these skills to assist me in what needs to be done," Solace replied and waited.

"That was over nine hundred thousand years ago! We have no minds in storage from that time! As for genetic patterns of any of those Gnathe from that time, their genetic structure has been absorbed into the Gnathe of today. I cannot help you with this part of your requirements, but we do still have experts in the art of crystalline storage of minds. You will find them on the home planet orbiting the human's original sun. You will have to go there and ask. I will ask the Goss to contact the institute where they practise."

Solace relayed the information to Toarvak 12,402 and waited for the Gnathe to use her telepathic link with the symbiont.

"Goss!"

"I am here!"

Shan-link-khann collected her thoughts and asked, "Would you connect me to whoever is available at the 'Institute of Crystalline Studies'. Someone of authority it must be!"

The Goss did what its unique structure had evolved to do and expanded its consciousness across the light years separating Toarvak Prime from Jupiter. The mind was spread across the galaxy from spiral arm to spiral arm. Millions of conversations were taking place between alien individuals who all carried the genetically altered spores of the Goss. Using the intelligence of the Gnathe that had requested its help, it examined the minds at its disposal that were awake at the institute. The Goss selected one that carried overtones of authority and connected Shan, after making its presence known.

"Ambassador! To what do I owe the honour?" asked the Lecturer in crystalline studies.

"Forgive the intrusion, Professor Whann-sool-lin, but I have a pressing need to ask you for some information. You are conversant with the knowledge gained by the expedition that travelled beyond the galaxies rim?"

"I am indeed. How do the results concern me?"

"I have been visited by the nannite concerned with altering the outcome. The name of the nannite is Solace. She had need of someone skilled in the downloading of minds into crystalline storage. Do you have such a one on your staff adventurous enough to assist and travel and I do mean travel. Because I believe that the nannite will be going back in time to collect minds that fought against the Goss."

"What!"

"I should also think that a great number of clones will be needed also for these minds to be downloaded into. I reason that if Solace is preparing to travel back in time to collect minds, then she will also be collecting genetic material to grow as clones! It might be a good idea to alert our human allies to the possibility that they will also become involved."

Shan let go of the link and stared thoughtfully at Solace.

"These are extreme times, 'silver one' and I feel that there is much to be done. I have heard that your kind can receive thoughts from biological sentients such as myself if you touch us?"

"This is so, but many consider it an unwarranted intrusion," the nannite replied.

"I feel that this may be a time to put such things to one side. I have much to tell you and it would be easier to impart the information straight to your mind from mine. So touch me and enter my thoughts."

Shan-link-khann felt a sharp sting as Solace made contact with her body and spread filaments right into her living brain. She felt the nannite accept the information and her suppositions that she had agreed with the institute professor.

A cold voice whispered, "Thank you Shan-link-khann. You have courage! Now forgive me, as I must leave you and prepare others."

Solace retrieved her nannite filaments and turned and left and the Ambassador sat on her perch watching her go.

She quietly marvelled at what the nannite was planning to do and what the other members of her gathering team would see.

Solace now reached out to the Toarvak ship and asked it to pick her up. She needed to speak with the Kresh as independent minds and not as part of the collective. The nannite made her way to the top of the building that was home to so many different types of alien. From the outside the structure looked similar to a vast pyramidal skyscraper reaching into the sky for two miles above the countryside. Inside the building, were located thousands of command crystals, linking the places inside with landscapes to suit each individual race of beings by their own wormhole. There were even Stargates that located this world to others throughout the galaxy. Toarvak Prime was a vast terminus as well as home to thousands of alien species.

At the top of the tower was a hollowed out area for all beings to briefly rest until boarding the Toarvak ships that docked there. From up here it was possible to gaze over the sea and watch the many flying creatures diving into the waves below to capture the fish. In every other direction the variegated landscape stretched out to the horizon showing hills and mountains covered in trees and vegetation of all kinds. Solace felt a twinge of nannite pride that her kind had made all this possible.

The sky darkened as Toarvak 12,402 hovered over the basin and extended a boarding tube towards the nannite below. Solace found herself rising into the substance of the interstellar, time travelling ship. Having no need to breath she was fully encased in the different molecular mix that the Nano-technology constructed ship was composed of.

"We have not met before Toarvak. I greet you and expect to get to know you much better," the nannite communicated to the immense form that housed the artificial intelligence.

"Knowing you better I will expect, nannite, now known as Solace. Much we will have to do with each other in the future I am expecting. My collective waiting they are and eager to hear your instructions."

Solace was ejected into the presence of the clans of Kresh who ran the Toarvak ship. The five who blended into the collective with the artificial intelligence known as Toarvak 12,402 were waiting to greet her. Around them stood the extended families of each 'First' in various stages of maturity and sex. What the nannite had to say would involve the whole family of each represented 'First' and would require that all agreed with her proposal.

Solace morphed into a similar shape to the Kresh, but without the eyes, preferring to keep to the optical band with its three hundred and sixty degree range. She also altered the tympanum's frequency so that it would operate in the ultra-sonic range that the Kresh used.

"Let me introduce myself," Solace said to the silent Kresh. "I have been selected by the Guardians to be of assistance to the Thipdar that you all know as Primm, who ran the expedition far outside the rim of this galaxy. You all know of the purpose of that fact- finding mission and the results. There are people that we will need and we will have to find them deep into the long past. I mean the time of the defeat of the Goss! The one personality we need most is not organic. He was one of us: - a nannite. I speak of Kamiel 637 and also Asue 637. Once found and inducted into this mission, they will be running it and I shall be the one who is told what to do. I need you to find them both and bring them back to this time. They will also know who else to bring back that will benefit this ultimate venture. The question that I must ask of you all is this; - are you all willing to risk yourselves in this venture? For once you give me that assurance there can be no turning back as the future of our combined civilization depends on those who are willing to risk their lives!"

The Kresh remained silent as they telepathically grouped to discuss the situation. This was not just a matter for each 'First' but involved each family member. The Toarvak was home to the Kresh on board, as now the entire crew's family travelled with them wherever the 'Collective Five' went. There was a complete viable breeding compliment that lived in the ship and could settle any empty world that they chose. This was the result of the demise of the Kresh, when the Goss infected their world and those on the ships grew old and died fighting against the parasite without any young to carry on instructing the artificial intelligences. The original nine Toarvaks had fought on without their biological counterparts and had almost entered madness. The search for the Goss had taken hundreds of thousands of years alone, before Toarvak 6 had found the humans and Gnathe on Daedalus One and Two, making them 'New Kresh.'

First of clan Silver/Black spoke simply, " Solace, it would be an honour to assist. We pledge that wherever you require this ship to go, we will go, in time or space."

"Thank you, all of you," Solace replied to the collective. "Be ready. I will now waken Primm and call you from there."

CHAPTER THREE

Co-ordinator had called a meeting with those races that were skilled in stellar engineering. These were the wormhole experts of the galaxy. They numbered amongst them the Kresh, Humanity (all types), the Gnathe, some of the Conics or Vogb, the Thipdar and some of the older races from the rescue zone who had learnt the ability to manipulate wormholes from the Gnathe.

The mind of the Tran-sentient reached out in tandem with Deep-thinker to speak with them all and said, "You have been briefed on the reason for this assembly. It will be necessary for you to use your collective talents to remove all the inhabited worlds and whatever stars you will need from the impact site of the galactic arm to the far side of the galaxy. Your aim is to design and maintain a globular cluster that will be hidden from the Andromeda side. When finished, it will be projected towards the Greater Magellanic Cloud. Here we will make our new home away from the attentions of this feeder upon life. We have but a few thousand years to accomplish this matter at the point of impact, or perish eventually at this abomination's hunger. Those suns and worlds on the Magellanic side will have a great deal more time, but none are to be missed, so do your best! We intend to send a task force into the Andromeda galaxy to distract this thing and prevent it from finding out what we are doing. Some of you will be required to go to be part of this expedition. I will let you know just how many, when we have time-fished the controllers of this exercise and brought them back to this time period. This is in place as we are speaking."

The Goss spread the thoughts of the Tran-sentient

throughout the minds of the scattered beings involved and marvelled at the size of the daunting task in front of them all.

Primm was wide-awake and organising the members of the time-fishing expedition while the Kresh began meld together to become the collective mind with Toarvak 12,402. On board were a conic scientific team including B-o-g, who had assisted Primm in the initial fact finding exercise. There were also included, the full hive of insectoids that had also participated with the Thipdar. The Bazantii had also sent scientists of their own, so that they could experience time travel and check the sophistication of their own instruments. There was a constant hum of inter-Goss chatter between the assorted aliens.

Solace called the leading members of the expedition together and said, "People of the Federation, we should be on our way. I have the space-time co-ordinates of the last seen and recorded positions of the nannites that we need to start this expedition. Because of the interaction of myself the Toarvak and yourselves, I have been fitted with an organic sack, carrying the spores of the Goss. As long as I can keep this organism alive, I will be able to meld minds with you all, instead of one by one with contact to your flesh."

With that spoken knowledge given, the nannite sent her mind into the mental communication system of the Goss and fed into the collective, the last known designation of Kamiel 637.

Kamiel stood leaning against the pillar of the homestead entrance in a very human gesture. He was watching the young humans, apes and Gnathe playing a complicated game with sticks and a ball. It would have been very similar to the ancient game of hockey except that the apes operated the goals, while the humans battled the Gnathe for possession of the ball. Flicking the ball past an ape with a bigger cleft stick and a catcher's mitt took some doing, whether it was done by humans or Gnathe. Also two more apes working at the left and right flank defended each goal. Occasionally blood was spilt, but without loss of temper. He reflected on his lot and found that to his surprise he was bored! He did a systems check and diagnostic. Nothing wrong! Not satisfied, he did another with the same result. He almost whished that he had found something to rectify, but realised that would be ridiculous!

Although his counterparts Sharn and Minns were always busy, he could not say the same. This world had been his responsibility for centuries and he could not fault the fact that he had succeeded here. Not only here, but across the emerging civilizations that he had helped free from the Goss, his name was legend. The re-born Kresh had rescued their world from their intended plunge into the sun. With the alterations in the DNA of the Goss spores, so that it became a symbiotic rather than a parasite, a telepathic union had descended upon all sentient species of alien. The Kresh world had been cleansed of its infection by the Nano-probes and re-seeded with the altered spores. Now they were leading expeditions to find new alien races and traces of alien races from the past. Partnering them were the Gnathen adepts and those strange human aliens that had evolved due to Toarvak 6's insertion of its substance into their infant brains. The human race was no longer just human! There were the genetically enhanced human and apes with Gnathen genes interwoven through their living tissue living on Jupiter under the red sun. Elsewhere there were the 'Pure stock' human and apes living under the domes of Jupiter and on the Three Worlds. In amongst the people of the Three Worlds were Humans, Apes and Gnathe, all carrying a silver ball of the wrecked Toarvak inside their brains that constantly improved them.

The nannite mused to himself, "Alexander McBald, 'Old Maker', you certainly started something when you dreamed up the Genesis Project! I still wonder what potential I have left, to develop beyond the programming you laid down. Mind you," he thought, " you never thought about what being disrupted and rebuilt by reversing time would do to me and Asue!"

The silver figure straightened up and his optical band flashed as he detected the approach of a strange nannite walking towards him with Asue as company. A shiver of uncoordinated curiosity went through his Nano-circuits. Was this a visitor from the nannite community spreading throughout the Kuiper belt of frozen comets and why the silence over their communication bands? Anything different would be welcome from the constant routine and endless monotony of the challenge-less civilization that was flourishing without his help.

To his continuing surprise, Asue spoke to him using sound waves, "Kamiel, do not use the communication band. What we are about to speak about must remain secret from the other nannites!"

Kamiel adjusted his hearing to an acute sharpness, so that the conversation could be held at a frequency that the biological players of the games could not hear.

"I am listening," he said and patiently waited.

"This nannite is from the far future," Asue said. "Apparently they need our help!"

Immediately Kamiel was alive with a burning curiosity and an unfamiliar emotion of relief.

He directed his full attention to the strange nannite, "Speak," he commanded.

"Kamiel 637, in orbit and out of phase is a Toarvak time-ship waiting to pick you up. We will walk away from this area un-noticed to the top of that hill overlooking this complex. When we get there both Asue and yourself will not be heard of again in this time period. The survival of every race of sentient beings in this galaxy and there are now over one hundred thousand sentient species, will rely on you and your guidance in this matter," Solace replied.

"McBald programmed me to look after the human race, not every intelligent species of alien," Kamiel retorted and laughed.

Asue swung round to the nannite and said, "Suddenly our responsibilities have grown larger. I have seen the records that Solace carries in her memory banks. We do not exist in this time frame from this moment. Come, we need to get to the top of that hill. It is time for us to go. These people do not need us any more and those of the future do."

"I agree, my dearest companion and sometimes conscience. I would know a lot more about the future that will unfold from our beginnings and the nature of the threat these people have to face. As the only way for us to go forward in time is to go with someone who has travelled back, then this opportunity will not be missed," replied the nannite and strode off unhurried to the top of the hill that had developed a distinct shimmer.

Unwatched and un-noticed, Asue and Kamiel disappeared from the history of the beginnings of the Council of Worlds and into the interior of Toarvak 12,402. Once they were inside, the ship translocated back to its own time frame and into orbit around Toarvak Prime.

Both Kamiel and Asue had been gifted with an organic sack each, which was maintained by them with an independent life support. For the first time both nannites could communicate with any alien race, without a one on one contact with their flesh. The amazing spores of the Goss were present and permeated the meat fibres of the biological construct. Kamiel had spent a great deal of time accessing and speaking with alien sapient creatures from all over the galaxy. The mind of the Goss was colossal and beyond belief. What a legacy he had left behind to the many peoples of this sprawling complex! Both nannites had explored the communication skills of the Goss symbiotic to the utmost. The closest that Kamiel could understand the working of the organism, was that its mind somehow existed inside and outside the wormhole system that filled this galaxy universe. Yet on its own, the symbiotic had no mind or consciousness of its own, but used the minds of its hosts. Its personality remained the same non-dominating presence that the Gnathe genetic engineers had produced, linked to his Nano-probe design.

Kamiel had dug into the ancient memories of the old Goss mind that was still present and marvelled at the variety and scope of the races of people who had lived long before the Earth had cooled. Through the organism he could search through the racial memories of those species that had been brought forward in time to escape the depredations of the Harvester. Now he needed to speak with the eldest of them all, Archive of the Trans-sentients. Out of respect for an organism that was purported to be millions of years old, Kamiel had insisted that he meet her in the flesh, so to speak.

Both nannites had decided to go and Co-ordinator had met them at a large balcony towards the top of the pyramidal tower. She had coasted towards the edge of the balcony and seized hold of the tethering rings to draw her down to the same elevation. Asue and Kamiel extended their optical range to take in the size of the alien. A multi-coloured gasbag shaped somewhat similar to the hull of a sailing ship supported a loaf shaped organism that had tentacles in groups of ten at the both ends and the centre. A ring of eyes around the bottom edge of the loaf stared out in all directions. They were coloured a brilliant blue with a dark slit, allowing the creature to adjust the light input. Each eye was larger than the nannites stood in the afternoon breeze. A mouth was situated at the leading edges of both ends of the loaf. What could only be two anuses were shown as a puckered area midway between each bunch of tentacles.

Co-ordinator extended two tendrils towards the Guardians and curled them around the silver figures, lifting them into the air.

"Welcome my friends and allow me to thank you for your contribution to history. Without your rescue of the Kresh and defeat of the Goss, none of this would have been possible," the bell clear tones of the immense organism's mind projected to the nannites.

Kamiel objected, "Co-ordinator! There were far more involved than just we two! I protest!"

"I have studied the periods that lead up to the defeat of the Goss. You were the prime instigator who involved humanity with the affairs of the Gnathe. It was due to your decisions and acceptance of sacrifice that altered the course of history. I know that many more were involved, but you were there!

"So was an old man's programming," Kamiel wryly answered.

A feeling of amused respect suffused them both from Co-ordinator and she replied, "That's why you are here!"

The Trans-sentient opened up two flaps in her side to catch the breeze and released the balcony tethering rings. They sailed over the variegated landscape towards the area set aside for the aliens to live and feed. As she sailed over the ripened, fruiting trees below, the tentacles extended and tore off complete branches loaded with fruit. Occasionally she also let rip almighty farts and clouds of excrement down over the vegetation below. The areas had scars from the Tran-sentient's feeding patterns and in these places new life was busily growing towards the light, exposed by the gaps in the forest below.

At last another Trans-sentient came into view. Where Co-ordinator was huge, this creature was colossal and it looked 'old' beyond belief, by the condition of its skin. The colours had faded from its gasbag and the loaf like body was covered in warts. Some of the eyes had sealed over with rheum, but those that had not, remained clear and the light of intelligence sparkled within them. Great stains and chunks of dung remained clinging to the warts around her twin anuses and two very much smaller versions of the trans-sentient, were rubbing wet branches over the area to help keep her clean. Others were hovering around the sides of the creature and tending the odd splits in her skin that sun and age had put there.

Kamiel sent forth his mind to greet the 'ancient one' and said, "I am overwhelmed by your presence!"

The answer came back swiftly, "Kamiel 637, I have studied what is known about you. You intrigue me! You are different to other non-living beings that I have met amongst your kind. All others have a conditioning that prevents them from doing any more than to defend. Quite bluntly, you are different; - why?"

"I once died and was resurrected. The experience seems to have altered or removed my conditioning to the extent that I can run to my own set of rules. Asue is the same, but gets troubled by conscience," Kamiel wryly expounded. Now I need to know first hand, your memories of this abomination you have named 'The Harvester' and everything that you can remember."

"For this, I believe that the Goss will be insufficient. You will both need to touch me and enter into private communication with my mind," the giant replied and extended a tentacle hundreds of feet long towards Co-ordinator for the exchange. The swap over took place high in the air above the tops of the trees and both nannites soon found themselves entering another world as their minds opened up to Archive's.

They were floating across a forested continent, ripping the tops off of the trees below and feeding. There was a feeling of newness in the air as if the very fabric of existence had just come into being. In fact it was, as the new star settled into its long stable phase, warming the planet below. The universe was new and most of the emptiness was still filled with the coalescing gas that one day would become the stars that would shine on Earth, billions of years into the future. New giant stars, very unstable, with mighty gravitational forces, were cooking the very atoms that would one day become life. Their life spans were short, maybe no more than a hundred million of years before they imploded. The resultant constant series of nova explosions constantly enriched the soup of worlds waiting for a star to form to swirl about and become solar systems.

Amongst this maelstrom of events, pockets of life slowly evolved on scattered worlds orbiting more long-lived stars, only to be snuffed out by the star becoming abruptly unstable. These events fed the hunger of an energy pattern that wrapped itself around the emerging planets. As the life on the world died, the emerging life form flourished.

The long minds of the Tran-sentients travelled across the interstellar reaches, listened to its slow forming thoughts and grew afraid. They watched in horror, as on several worlds after eons of time, intelligent life evolved to the point of leaving their world and exploring others. At this point their sun would go unstable, engulfing the living world. The thing fed as it had never fed before! Some races had managed to travel the great open reaches to other worlds, but before they could establish themselves, the Harvester struck the home world leaving them stranded. As time went by the Trans-sentients masked their thoughts, hiding their abilities and intelligence from the abomination that crept around the galaxy in fear that they would be next. Where it had come from and what the nature of creature this was, they could not guess, but they knew what it did.

Kamiel watched the events build up as the abhorrent living energy field became aware of the floating giants' planet. It did something to its star that caused it to wobble and retreated from the area to wait. The star developed streamers of fiery plasma that expanded millions of miles from the surface of the sun. Great ugly sun spots, large enough to swallow planets the size of gas giants began to develop and darken ominously. The star began to reach out towards the living world as the surface expanded and the view in the sky changed. A fleet of Kresh time-ships had manipulated a massive wormhole, controlled by a thousand on-board Gnathe and swept up the Trans-sentient world. They placed it in orbit around another star, in the same time period as the Council of Worlds. After contact with the sentient giants had been established and the locations of the other early emerging civilizations determined, the time-fishing Toarvaks departed to rescue these as well.

Asue and Kamiel marvelled at the logistics that this civilization managed with such consummate ease. The galaxy was filling up with sentient beings from all past time periods that had at one time fed this creature with their life energies. In that first reach back into the past and retrieving the Earth from annihilation, the realisation of the Gnathen blood debt had changed the time-lines and created a parallel universe.

"McBald's Genesis Project had more far reaching consequences than the old man ever dreamed of," Kamiel said to Asue in amazement."

"We still have much to do to make it all come to fruition, my companion," Asue remarked.

Kamiel thought for a moment and sent his mind to connect with the floating giant, "Archive!"

"I am here!" The trans-sentient answered.

"We need access to these memories when we hunt for this thing. We will need your sensitivity to this thing's mind to find it. You are too large to get you into a Toarvak and we could never find enough food to keep you alive. What do you suggest?"

"There is a way to accomplish what you require. When you have need of me, I will have done what will be necessary," the giant replied. "Make your plans to include me and return when you are ready to go. I have the feeling that it will take many cycles before you are ready to pit your wits against this abomination."

"You are right Archive and we still do not know or understand the nature of the creature that we must defeat. We know nothing about where it came from and nothing about its construction. The only thing we do know about it, is its awesome power to influence a complete galaxy of stars to change direction and the fact that it feeds on life! I must give this matter a great deal of thought," Kamiel answered and connected to Co-ordinator. "Take us back to the central administration building and arrange a meeting with the Kresh High Command. After that I will need to return to Jupiter by way of the Three Worlds."

The Kresh listened to the nannite's thoughts as Kamiel unfolded his immediate needs to them. They were not accustomed to his direct way of thinking, but they had been told by Co-ordinator to obey his every wish. The 'First' of each orbiting Toarvak collective family, had come to the large assembly hall to listen first hand to what Kamiel had to propose. The Goss linked up to the home world of the Kresh and fed the thoughts towards the other leaders of family, until hundreds of millions of the Kresh were tuned in.

"First I need to know how to retrieve a Toarvak from the heart of a star at the point that it goes back into phase," Kamiel asked.

"This has never been done before, Great Kamiel! The Kresh replied.

"Then find out how and do it as soon as you can," the nannite snapped, "and will you stop calling me Great Kamiel! I am Kamiel 637 and nothing more!"

"The Toarvak builders are giving the problem their full attention, 'Gr' um, Kamiel," the Kresh replied. "May I ask why this is necessary?"

"I need Toarvak 6. I know where she went and I know what she intended to do. She must be retrieved at all costs!"

"It is a Toarvak! You called it she! Toarvaks do not have sexual gender. They are artificial intelligences that are designed to mesh with biological units," the Kresh protested.

"Do you question me? Are you not aware that although I am incapable of reproduction, my mind is as male, as Asue's mind is female?" Kamiel replied and reduced the Kresh, 'First' to shocked silence.

Kamiel knew that interwoven in the personality of Toarvak 6 was a small part of his own mentality that had hived off from Minnis, when she had brought the destroyer down onto Daedalus One.

The unique mind of the Kresh ship was able to think in ways that no other Toarvak could and once Kamiel had reunited her with the others that had been her crew, he would have the fully functioning collective back in command. Toarvak 6 was a killing machine. She was re-designed to be that way after the Kresh world had fallen to the Goss. Now in this peaceful universe the 'art' of warfare had long gone. There were millions of Toarvak ships in existence at this time frame, but they were all research and carrier ships. Every space-going alien species had fleets of them given by the Kresh for their use. None of them had ever been used in war since the defeat of the Goss. Of the ones at Kamiel's disposal, Toarvak 12,402 had proved to be very adaptable.

'First, of Brown, Dappled Silver,' stood and waited for the next instruction from the slightly built humanoid figure before her. He/she knew that this was not all that the nannite required. The Kresh stood much taller than the Guardian and with ears erect and cheeks puffed out to display the formidable whiskers, 'First' was at high alert.

"I want you to run a check on the whereabouts of the other eight original Toarvaks. Where are they now and if, as I suspect they cannot be found, when were they last heard of? I have a suspicion that certain individuals may be missing through history if we check the records," the nannite instructed.

"It will be necessary to send back through time a number of agents to within a thousand years after the conflict with the Goss. From there they will be able to access records that will be fresher than those that exist now," 'First' replied, "And work backwards from there."

Asue interrupted the Kresh's thought flow and added, "I will direct this part of the exercise, as you will need someone who can access the records at machine time speed. All you

41

need to do is to take me back in time to those periods that I indicate and I will do the rest."

Solace had found that associating with Kamiel 637 seemed to inspire her way of thinking to new heights. As teacher to the Vogb young, she had been fulfilled as any nannite would be and had run her neural nets to the extremes of her programming. It was what she had been programmed to do! The extra upgrading that had been inserted into her artificial intelligence enabled her to explore facets of her personality that had hitherto remained dormant. She realised that she now operated at Guardian level, with a far greater range of responsibilities to the biological entities that she willingly served. To her inner amazement, she was experiencing the emotion of excitement and constantly analysed her most inner neural pathways to try to understand herself more. She was aware of an amused presence gently intruding into her mind and Kamiel projected a feeling of assurance.

"You will experience many more emotions as this enterprise takes off. We are going to meet the most amazing biological minds that are off the scale as it were, compared to the people that live in this time frame. These people had to fight or die! This oncoming catastrophe will require sacrifices and bravery from those who are involved. I felt privileged to be part of their lives, long, long ago. Some of them are dead and will have to be resurrected," Kamiel remarked. "It will mean finding them and imprinting their minds into crystal receptacles before they die and taking a DNA sample at the same time."

"I have been in contact with the Gnathe on the home world of Jupiter via the ambassador and an expert in this field has volunteered her services. A professor Whann-sool-lin will come with us and expedite the mind transfers,"

Solace replied. "Cloning chambers have been activated. All we need is to go back in time and find them!"

CHAPTER FOUR

At the direct instruction of the 'Kresh High Command', Toarvak design engineers had considered the problem that Kamiel had sent them and had reached a verdict. 'First' of clan, 'Black Bars on a Dappled, Brown Background', sent his/her mind into the busy telepathic world of the Goss.

"Goss!"

"I am here. What do you need?"

"Connect me to the nannite known as Kamiel 637."

The symbiotic searched through sub-space and wormhole until it found the nannite who was stood alone at the Cheyenne complex on Earth. He was surveying the incredible view from the mountaintop in the dawn's early light and was looking out over the beautiful town laid out at the foot of the Cliffside. It was a mixture of trees and buildings set out in such a way that the hand of man was not intrusive. Nine, hundred thousand years of mixed alien civilization had mellowed this world, rather than exploited it. The whole world had been blended into a living paradise for those who chose to live here. It was difficult to accept, that without the plans he had agonised over that had destabilised Link-soo-shan's empire, nothing of this would have come to pass. The twist of fate that had projected the tyrant's mind into his, when he had journeyed back in time and totally altered her mind-set, had made her a staunch ally.

Kamiel felt the weight of the years that had passed since he had stood in the Director's office on Greenland and outlined the incredible plan of the Gnathen adepts. They had formed a group mind so powerful, that they had been able to wrench the Earth and its Moon from orbit around the increasingly unstable star, and feed it down a colossal wormhole to here. 'Here' was Icarus, a gas giant with two planet sized moons and a collection of minor ones all orbiting a stable sun. Earth had become a teaching world for new alien species and many had settled on the two moons, Daedalus One and Two with humanities' joint children. From here, humanity had spread right out into the empty reaches of this galaxy, with both aliens and Jupiter human help. Woven into the fabric of all societies were his own people, the Nannites who had been created by human beings, who in turn had lost the science of bringing them into being. The shape shifting nannites were totally integrated into all alien societies wherever they were needed. Now with the addition of a living biological unit installed inside their bodies forming a home to the Goss spores, they were also able to easily enter the telepathic gestalt of the biological aliens. Even the mighty Kresh had not quite accomplished the nannite identity with their Toarvaks, but the self-aware ships were as adaptable as Kamiel and his people.

From the impossible idea of moving a world, the natives of this galaxy were now contemplating moving complete solar systems out from the edge of this galaxy that faced towards Andromeda, to form a globular cluster on the opposite side. Once this was done, the entire cluster would be ejected from the gravitational pull of this galaxy and sent on its way towards the greater Magellanic Clouds. The journey would take at least a hundred thousand years or more depending on the wormholes available. So far the project was to build the cluster first, while a number of Toarvaks surveyed the accessible wormholes to join the cluster to the 'Clouds' one, hundred and seventy thousand light years away. If they succeeded and he was sure that they would, he and his task force would never see it, as they were headed into the opposite direction, straight at Andromeda.

The Goss made contact and spoke into the nannite's mind, "Kamiel! I have someone here that would speak with you."

"You are?" Asked the nannite.

"Kamiel 637, we are the Toarvak design engineers who were set the problem by the High Command. I am first of the team," the Kresh answered.

"Do you have an answer for me? It is crucial to my plans that you do!"

"We do indeed have an answer. By calculation, it is understood that we will need a thousand Toarvaks enclosing the vessel that you require, all touching and partially impinging the substance of the suicidal ship. The timing must be precise and the outer Toarvaks must keep the energies of the star at bay when the ship comes back into phase. I will go with you and co-ordinate the exercise. This team has also decided to be part of your task force and have volunteered to go with you wherever you decide to go. You may have need of us to defeat this abomination that seeks to live off our life energies."

"Tell Co-ordinator of your needs and she will arrange things and meet me here. From here we will need to go back in time and find our quarry. At last things are on the move!" the Guardian said and launched himself from the mountaintop, opening his shape into a gliding form. He next directed his thoughts towards Toarvak 12,402 in orbit above him. "Pick me out of the air, it is time for me to be back at my place on board."

The Toarvak dropped out of orbit, scooped the nannite up with an extended pseudopod and put them all out of phase. It then entered the Earth, accelerated through its core and shot out the other side to re-enter orbit.

****

Ten years had slipped by before Kamiel and the Kresh engineers were satisfied that the original idea would work. During tests, several ships had dissolved inside a star because the timing was out. It took precious Nano-seconds for the fields to overlap and latch onto the ship in the centre to prevent the pressure of the sun squashing it out of existence. In the end Kamiel himself became the over-riding controller of the ships, by using the organic, spore infested, piece of meat that he kept alive inside his chest as a telepathic link. He became the master of the collectives, using his mind in machine time to slow everything down to that speed of reflection. So it was that Toarvak 12,402 found itself used as a conduit to all one thousand ships, by entering the Guardian into the rapport of five to make six.

Kamiel's mind had now expanded to the level of a thousand Toarvaks and just as five biological units plus one machine intelligence made a group mind more powerful than the minds added together, this combination went off the scale. The Guardian now had an appreciation of how it had felt to Azander when she had directed the group mind of the Gnathe and humanity to reposition the Earth. The power at his command would have been addictive, had he not exercised an iron control upon his own ego. He willed the fleet back through time to his own era and scanned the space-time of the 'now' for the signature of Toarvak 6. He was looking for a piece of the universe that was walled off from existence and was travelling towards the star that Icarus orbited. He had scanned the records of the Toarvak ships for the moment that she had disappeared and had materialised just before she had gone out of phase. It was important to retrieve her at the moment that she re-materialised inside the star so that no time paradoxes took place.

All of the journeys back in time had the same constrictions placed upon them and that was why the planets were snatched away from the expanding or unstable suns just before they were about to be destroyed. The alien races that lived on those worlds were then transported upwards through time to the current 'here and now' that the Council of Worlds existed in. They could not travel any further forwards in time, as the future had not come into existence. Items and sentient beings could be taken forward to a time when the takers existed, but not beyond.

What the multi-civilisation did not realise was that in the taking of these populated worlds to a place of safety, a different time-line had been mapped out for the entity known as the Harvester. One reality abruptly ceased to exist and a different one was being mapped out and it had started with the relocation of Earth.

The grief maddened Toarvak 6 began her headlong drop towards the sun carrying the cooling body of Larse in stasis, to a joint oblivion. A thousand Toarvak ships in perfect global formation enclosed the suicidal vessel and dived into the star with her. The outer rings stayed out of phase, while the next internal globe remained out of phase also in a state not related to this universe, but the inner surfaces slightly in phase. Inside the second layer, was a smaller globe in a transition effect with this universe and the out of phase outer envelope, with the surfaces of each ship integrated with the others. The final inner globe had its inner surfaces totally in phase and ready to latch onto the outside of Toarvak 6 and weld it securely to the giant envelope that totally surrounded it.

Kamiel hovered and waited like a bird of prey for the Nano-second that the joining could be attempted.

He felt the grief of the mad Toarvak soar into his mind

and replied, "Your task is not done. It is just beginning."

The complete multi-Toarvak collective tore itself from out of the star's internal nuclear fires and away from its destructive power. Once they were well away from the massive gravitational pull and in orbit around the outer gas giant named as Tantalus, the outer rings began to disembark back to the time of the Council of Worlds until there were only Toarvak 12,402 and Toarvak 6 left joined together.

Kamiel transferred himself onto Toarvak 6's communications deck, dropping through the floor and studied the stasis chamber that the old, yet still powerful body of Larse, laid naked on the dais.

"Is he dead?" asked Kamiel.

"Dead the body is, Kamiel. His mind does not exist. Lost to me he is! Grief do I suffer now that he is gone. Why, my death did you not allow?"

"Simply this my friend; - we need you and we need Larse. In fact there are a lot of people that are living or are dead at this time-span that we need. Larse will be the first that we will retrieve, for with him will come your full co-operation and skills."

"If Larse you would retrieve from history then Emelia you would also need. He would not give you anything that you need without her by his side. If anyone could know this, then it would be me! The time has come I think, for you to tell me the reasons behind my rescue and the need for the people of this time-frame," Toarvak 6 answered and allowed Kamiel to fill her memory banks with the missing knowledge.

Kamiel waited, to know that Toarvak 6 fully understood all the ramifications of the problems that the future civilization faced, before he asked for the help of locating Larse from some point in the past. As he had died on board this vessel it would be fiendishly difficult to get a crystal record of his mind without altering the timelines. This was something that the nannite dreaded more than anything else. Do something that reverberated through time and the future could change to another parallel universe leaving everything that was planned so carefully in ruins. The most difficult thing he had come to terms with, was the awareness that he would never know. His past and the future he trod would cease to exist and the unique talents that he searched for would never be called upon to aid the Council of Worlds in their bid to avoid the Harvester.

"Kamiel, The facts I have studied and agree with your analysis I do. I have a small part of the problem solved for you."

The nannite responded to the mental communication with curiosity and waited for the Toarvak to speak to his mind. *"I lied to you. Larse is not quite dead. I have his mind stored away in unending sleep deep within my consciousness. We into oblivion were to go together. Alone, I found I could not go!"*

"The very fact that you could lie, tells me that I was right to come back in time for you and the unique way that you think! There are no other Toarvaks with a mind like yours. You are female and have a mind of a hunter/killer," the nannite declared. "All other Toarvaks are just servants to the collective minds, but you add something more."

"For Larse, to keep him safe, there is nothing I would not do! He killed for me and kept my mind and substance alive when we wandered the world of Daedalus One. He reunited me with the rest of my substance with the aid of the others in my collective."

"It is for that predatory nature that you have, that I am here. The people of the far future have lost the ability to kill. Here in this timeframe there are many who can fight and contemplate death with the ability to avoid it. There are a thousand willing Toarvaks who risked their very existence to retrieve you from your suicidal impulse. Of them all Toarvak 12,402 has become the most adventurous and will absorb all you can teach it. Asue has gone in pursuit of your companions that fought against the Goss. What we face far in the future is I fear, much worse than the Empire of the Goss. This thing that sprawls across the star fields, feeds on the life force of living things on a far grander scale than did you, when you were separated from the majority of your substance. From the memories that Archive showed me, it can manipulate wormholes to destabilise stars. It can spread life to fallow worlds and wait for it to climb the evolutionary ladder. After systematically sending the early life to almost extinction, it allows the creatures left to evolve further until it starts the process again. Eventually it has a world with sentient life ready for the great leap into space and then it harvests them without pity and feeds upon the improved life force. It is beyond evil!"

"A worthy foe we have to take down! My Larse you will need and those who pitted their lives against the mental strength of the Goss, also I would commend. My crew may I pick?"

Kamiel stood thoughtful as he weighed the behaviour of the rouge Toarvak in his mind and asked, "Whom would you recommend? You are the first Toarvak to consider this idea and I am intrigued."

"I mentioned that to get Larse to co-operate to the full, you would Emelia need by his side. The human females, many qualities she has and difficult I found it, to get them to allow my presence in their minds. Find this one and allow me to insert a small silver ball into the growing foetus of her clone, as I will do the same for Larse. Ruthless you will find her when her mate is threatened! I would also ask that you find Thomas and I will do the same for him. To balance the scales I would ask for Link-soo-shan and Khann-link-sool.

51

The Toarvak mind that will evolve from this mixture will be a hunter/killer the like of which you will not have seen before! Toarvak 12,402 will need an addition to the Kresh that make up the identity. I recommend Link-soo-shan's daughters, Suzzan and Trann-link-khann be added to the collective and two Kresh to stand down. Their worth I am aware of as we worked together many times."

Kamiel did something that distinguished him from other nannites and laughed!

"Toarvak 6," he said, "You are without doubt well worth the risk of becoming part of a star! Your perceptive nature is a bonus to my planning. We will need to go fishing together you and I! Our next stop will be the cloning laboratories of Jupiter to meet the Gnathe who have the skill of storing minds in crystalline form."

Kamiel considered the situation and brought on board a full temporary working crew to blend with Toarvak 6 until the rest of the full working crew of the future had been found. The next thing he did was to send Toarvak 12,402 forwards in time to sit in orbit awaiting Asue's return with the other original Toarvaks. Its purpose would be to go back with the date he could safely return and join the cluster of ships, couriering   Asue back to him. They could then both engage in the tricky business of locating the other members of the hunting expedition and ferrying the necessary DNA and mind carrying crystals to the cloning laboratories of Jupiter.

Asue had checked the records regarding the first nine Toarvaks to find where they had dispersed to in space and time. T 6 was Kamiel's problem to solve, so it was down to her to find the others. After the Goss incident had been determined, there had been a manufacturing explosion of

Toarvak ships and they had been shared out amongst the space-going races. The Lagdoo, Thipdar, Insectoid hives and the Vogb or conics had renewed their exploration of the empty worlds that they could use as new homes.

It would be several centuries before the Bazantii would venture out from their home world, but eventually they did and settled other worlds.

Meanwhile the Gnathe had started an expansion drive from their home orbiting the red sun looking for other star systems that could be adapted and seeded with new life taken from Jupiter and transferred. In the expansion of stars that had finished their existence as yellow suns and altered into red giants, many gas giants had their dense heavy atmospheres stripped away. Underneath the once impenetrable cloud cover were large silicon rocky worlds with small iron cores. Many of them had abundant water and little, bar microscopic life, that would never develop during the briefer life of a red sun. These worlds were eagerly seeded with more complicated life by time travelling into the their past, left to go fallow and re-seeded at a later date with more up to date plants and animals taken from the home worlds. It was to one of these worlds that Asue had tracked down two of the original Toarvaks 3 and 5 who were working as carriers from the home world of Jupiter and had not returned from a trip back for more living seeds and animals. Asue intercepted them as they warped into phase at the edge of the solar system and made her offer of a more demanding task. Each Toarvak vessel and crew with a full breeding complement needed little urging to be refitted with the more sophisticated time travelling crystal systems. Asue sent them to the prearranged waiting area in time and space and went on to the next hunt, leaving them in orbit around Toarvak Prime.

Eventually Asue tracked down each Toarvak prior to

the date that they had disappeared. Now all the original Toarvaks were patiently circling Prime in orbit waiting for the arrival of Toarvak 6 and Kamiel. A date had been set in the future for their arrival one month after the last Toarvak had been found. Asue had handed over to Primm the organisation of the supplies and the old Toarvaks' crews had been taken down to T Prime's surface for rest and induction into the current state of affairs. She now needed to return to Kamiel's side. With a feeling of total confidence in her partner's abilities, she instructed Toarvak 12,402 to return to the time era a week after the proposed retrieval of the grief stricken ship. Before doing so, she had imprinted into her mind, the abilities of a working Sharn's geneticist background and years of experience. Over the hundreds of thousands of years the four basic types of nannite had been replicated over and over again. All that was different about the later models were their experience with the thousands of alien cultures and body types. This was another part of Kamiel's planning, in so much that Asue would get a re-mind in this area so that she would be able to work with and monitor the scientists at Jupiter after the samples had been retrieved. She would carry the genetic codes and cells forward in time to the cloning vats at the university that the Gnathe professor, Whann-sool-lin's team were waiting for.

Kamiel watched the approach of the Toarvak as it winked into phase and suddenly appeared half a light year away. His mind reached out to Asue's on the nannite band to welcome her.

"You have what we need?" he asked.

"All of the other eight Toarvaks have been found and are now in orbit about T Prime. You I can see, have been successful," Asue replied. "I can see and sense Toarvak 6, but what about Larse? Is he retrievable?

"Inside my walls, he sleeps in unending suspension. To board me you must

and tell me how to resurrect him you will."

Asue felt the undercurrent of menace in the deranged Toarvak's mind as she answered, "I will pull him back from death if I can! This will depend on what you have left me to work with. Do not threaten me! I felt it in your mind. The personality of Larse and those who shared the fight against the Goss, are as important to this exercise and to me as they are to you!"

"Sorry am I! Care for this human I do! Fear, have I, that he will not return to me. Die would I, if this universe does not contain him!"

Kamiel's mind came thundering in with great overtones of anger and exasperation and drummed into the Toarvak's quailing consciousness like a pneumatic drill!

"I will lock your mind into a tiny box and punish you beyond your limited imagination if I hear one stray thought from you of this again. You and those who you hold dear are necessary to my plan. BUT! I will tell you now and remember this; - you and I are totally expendable in the fight to defeat this creature that feeds on intelligent life energy. The entire population of this galaxy will depend on us and whatever sacrifices we have to make, for them to live free of this menace! Now extend a pseudopod towards Toarvak 12,402 and get Asue safely aboard."

The orange-clouded gas giant dominated the sky that the two Toarvak ships orbited and would have been more than twice the size of Jupiter. The planet was streaked with white and red swirling vortexes, large enough to swallow worlds. Tantalus was much further out from the sun than Icarus and was surrounded by frozen moons covered with hard ice that shone with reflected light from the distant sun. Just the same as Icarus, the gas giant also had large moons the size of planets. These were a possible extra bonus if and when they could be moved towards the sun. There was plenty of time to contemplate this at a later date. This would be one of the star systems that would be moved completely to form one of the anchors of the globular cluster that was planned to travel to the Greater Magellanic Clouds. The Gnathen and human 'God Mind' had selected well when it had moved the Earth to its new home.

The Toarvak ships gently 'kissed' and Asue came aboard Toarvak 6. She was propelled at some speed to the living quarters of the Kresh crew where Kamiel awaited her. Here in the living space deep inside the Toarvak lived the Kresh who would be giving over the control of Toarvak 6 to the new crew, once found and inducted. On board as well were contingents of other races, including the Thipdar, Insectoids, Vogb and Bazantii. They were taking the opportunity to study the time frames that Kamiel needed to operate in. Solace greeted the returning nannite with a sense of awe. She was in the presence of the greatest artificial intelligences of all time and felt great respect for these two Guardians. They of course paid no heed to this hero worship and ignored it as of no consequence.

Asue opened her mind to the ship and asked bluntly, "Larse; - where is he? I would need to examine him for a few moments out of stasis. I need to know how soon you encapsulated him in the time field."

"The moment the heart stopped, Larse I put in stasis. He is neither alive, nor dead while I keep him that way. His mind I took and placed it safely asleep in storage until we would have died together."

With that statement ringing in her mind, Asue found herself sinking through the floor and conveyed to Toarvak 6's stasis chamber. In the centre of the cavity, protected from time, lay the body of a once tall and strong man who had become bowed with age, laid naked on a raised dais. His face was lined and his hair had turned to snowy white. The once strongly muscled body had retreated into a heavier smoother form with the layers of fat concealing the once taut sinews. The nannite approached the apparently sleeping man and signalled Toarvak 6 to release the time stasis field. She extended filaments into the body to find that it was still warm. He had been presented into stasis, the very moment that the heart had stopped. This was better than Asue could have expected. She rapidly removed the top of his head and extracted the brain from the casing. Next, she whirled the brain around in a specially designed mesh until everything had turned to pulp and she was able to extract the RNA from the bloody mass. She then took a DNA sample from the cooling body and encapsulated it with the RNA.

"My Larse! What have you done to him? This body dead must be! This I did not expect," Toarvak 6 cried, in an agony of uncertainty.

"Simply this Toarvak 6," replied the Guardian. "I have removed from his still almost living brain, all of his memories stored in the ribonucleic acids of the brain cells. I have all that I need, including enough DNA to enable the cloning tanks of the Gnathe at Jupiter to recreate him. Now activate a new stasis field for these items and expel the rest of the body. We do not need it any more. All we need is to download Larse's mind into a crystal and let The Brood-mother, Whann-sool-lin re-animate the clone she will grow from his DNA and inject the RNA into the brain to help retain all of his memories. Next she will pour his personality back into the living body. This will be done eighteen years before the 'here and now' of the future timeline so that all of the resurrected ones will be brought back at the same time. Now my friend we need to find Emelia!"

"Thanking you Asue, for what you have done for me this day. In your debt I am and in your debt I will stay," and the Toarvak filled the mind of the nannite with her grateful emotions.

CHAPTER FIVE

At the very beginning there was no time or space, only an emptiness, waiting. The universe had yet to be born.

There was nothingness. A timelessness that had endured an existence beyond thought.

It was not darkness, rather an absence of light.

The universe began.

A rift appeared nowhere and everywhere. Energy poured through in every direction, at many times the speed of light, in a globular fountain. In a trillionth of a second obeying a form of physics unlike anything in the now, the universe expanded to an incandescent ball of energy a hundred, thousand times the temperature of a star. Within the first millionth of a second all the forces of energy were the same.

Gravity separated from the other three forces that remained united.

At less than a hundredth of a second Quarks and anti-quarks dominated the universe as the strong forces separated from the weaker ones. A period of rapid growth ensued and the temperature dropped rapidly until protons and neutrons formed. At this point all four forces had become distinct.

At 1/100 of a second, electrons and positrons formed, as the temperature fell to 100 billion K. at this point the building blocks of atoms were in place. Now the ball of energy began to really expand, cooling down in the process to where our laws of physics began to be formed, as energy divided by the speed of light began to generate mass and with it gravity. A full second after the Big Bang, the universe became transparent to neutrinos. Now it was darkness.

After 3 mins with the temperature at 1,000,000,000 K protons and neutrons had combined to form the nuclei of helium and other elements.

It was during this blend of what was, into what will be, that an energy field came into being, linked to the creation of dark matter. In the abundance of energy loose in this primordial soup, it translated energy into its form. In the expanding universe the energy field began to spread itself thin and as yet had not emerged into sentience. By converting some of the abundantly swelling universe's seething potential into itself, it became self-sustaining. It was not aware, it just was!

300,000 years later the universe had cooled to 3000 K and the first atoms came into being.

The universe became transparent to light, thereby emitting cosmic background radiation. During this time the energy field had prospered and had learnt how to convert the plentiful radiation to maintaining its integrity. Dark matter had produced the warping and twisting of space and time to produce the wormholes that criss-crossed the light-years and the Matrix was formed.

After 1 billion years with the universe at a temperature of 20 K, galaxies began to take shape. The early stars were large, hot and unstable, cooking the elements inside them before they exploded, scattering that most valuable atom of all, the carbon atom, along with silicates and metals. Supernova after supernova ejected trillions of billions of tons of mass into the cosmos, to be scooped up by new stars and made into planets.

Thereafter more stable stars with solar systems and planets came into being with liquid water, where living matter could exist and evolve. A time of stability had arrived.

Fifteen billion years later, at the time of the Council of Worlds, the temperature of the universe had fallen to 3 K and would continue to very slowly diminish.

At the beginning of the formation of the galaxies, finding the kind of radiation that sustained the creature was not difficult. Long thoughts that spread over hundreds of thousands of years began to take shape, directing the energy hungry being to where the feeding would be best. It would be another one hundred million years before the first unstable stars would form.

At last, there came that time, when the early galaxies began to coalesce, two to three billion years after these events. The unstable suns had exploded, after cooking the elements in their hearts and filling the cosmos with exotic matter. After five billion years planets began to form in orbit around the new and still unstable stars. Primitive life evolved on some and soon perished, as the new stars exploded, adding new elements to the young galaxies. New, more stable suns would soon begin to form with cooling planets, ripe for the development and spread of life over a longer time-span.

The event had yet to take place that gave the evolving being an alternative form of energy.

Kamiel and Asue had studied the records very carefully. They were sure that this was the time prior to the last moments of Emelia's life. Toarvak 6 had taken them to the homestead that Larse and Emelia had lived before the Goss had been defeated. They went out of phase and dropped down submerging below ground level and remained completely out of sight. Above them, at last alone in this 'time-space' a hundred years or so afterwards, Emelia lay dying, still waiting for the return of Larse.

It was a prosperous small holding that had been lovingly planted and tended by the family. The house was of the standard nannite construction and had been added to as the years had gone by. Banilik trees had been also planted so

60

that they could be coerced into the type of living house that the Gnathe preferred and several Brood-mothers and their kindred did so, as extended family. The children of Larse and Emelia had settled and stayed here over the years, also bringing back their children from their partnerships. Now there was an aura of impending grief, as the incredibly old lady still waited for the return of her love, unaware that he was prevented from doing this. She had carried on, refusing to be put into stasis; so that she could watch her children grow and be there for them, driven by the knowledge that he would return to her side as he had promised.

He was destined to do this, but one hundred years too late. Loved by her children, grandchildren and great-grandchildren, they had all stayed close, believing that Larse would return within the time left to her. After the defeat of the Goss, the expedition had to find another way back, after the parasite had sealed off the wormhole. It had taken too much time and centuries had passed for the Three Worlds while they had made their way back. When Larse returned, even his own grandchildren were mostly dead and he had become a legend.

Toarvak 6 extended a pseudopod from several hundred feet below the building, still out of phase, until it broke through the floor, next to the old ladies bed. A pale light illuminated the bedroom and fresh flowers were placed in a vase by the bedside table. The remains of a meal had been put to one side, as one of her great grand daughters had left the room to get the old lady a cool drink. The two of them realised that they had five to ten minutes, no more, before she returned. Emelia was uneasily asleep and her once blondish hair was now a snowy white. Someone had brushed and tied away the locks of hair away from her face with a ribbon. There were a few stray crumbs scattered across the front of her nightdress that had fallen open. Her hands were clasped together with the thumb and fingers of her right hand turning the wedding ring round her third finger.

Asue swiftly went to Emelia's side and checked that she was still breathing, while Whann-sool-lin placed a crystal upon the wrinkled forehead. The Gnathe entered her mind and bridged the way into the storage crystal. The old lady's eyes fluttered open to see the Gnathe and the nannite beside her. They opened wide in shock and she drew in a terrified breath to scream.

Asue placed her silver hand upon the thin withered arm and rapidly entered her body, connecting to her brain.

"Emelia! It is Asue. I have come to take you to Larse if you are willing. We will be travelling to the future and you will be young again."

Emelia understood the nannite and released herself to Asue's promise.

The Guardian felt the aura of implicit trust from the old woman.

She commanded her, "Now sleep!"

At the nod from Whann, that she had transferred the mind into crystal storage, Asue shut down the heart and all the systems of the aged woman. She then opened the top of her skull and removed the still warm brain and spun out the RNA and replaced the empty mush to the cavity. Storing the precious RNA in a stasis chamber with the wedding ring and a piece of flesh containing Emelia's DNA that she had removed, Asue then sealed up the broken skin to remove all traces of her presence. The nannite took off the wedding ring, knowing what it meant to Emelia and replaced it with a hastily made copy, made from her own substance. The two of them stepped back into the pseudopod and Toarvak 6 took them out of phase, returning them back underground to where the ship lay hidden. The whole operation had taken less than five minutes.

Kamiel was exultant on their return and ordered the ship to drop through the planet's crust and go into orbit on the other side of the planet.

"That's two of T 6's designated crew accounted for, Solace," he said to the enhanced nannite, as Asue returned. "Now we have to find the difficult one."

Asue carefully placed the nannite ball containing Emelia's RNA, DNA sample and her mind in crystalline storage in its separate stasis box, next to the remains of Larse. She keyed in the combination that sealed the contents and named each preserved identity so that each would be attached to the clone during its reanimation. The wall of the Toarvak had been altered so that each stasis box could be stored under each person's name. There were potentially, thousands of them, all waiting for their occupants.

"Which is the difficult one that you speak of, Kamiel? Solace asked.

"Thomas! He was the first to join with Larse and Toarvak 6 and was with him right up to the discovery and conversion of Toarvak 7. You see, young Solace, he became part of Toarvak 7's crew during the conflict with the Goss. I know that all the fleet made it back to the Three Worlds, but I have no idea what happened afterwards. Once the new civilization was up and running, we returned to Jupiter to fulfil our duty to our own people. That's where we will locate Link-soo-shan and Khann-link-sool and all of the Gnathe and humans willing to come forward to our time-line. The records show that a great number of the population of Jupiter left during this era, to relocate to other red sun systems. It is my belief that quite a lot of them came with us. That is something we can leave to do for another time period."

Asue turned away from storing the potential personalities

and said, "We should go up-time minus eighteen years and start the clones. Let us be sure that the eggs are in the basket before we do anything else. The Institute of Crystalline Studies at the 'Life University' on Jupiter will need to be visited a year or two before that so that things are ready and a wrap of secrecy placed around it. I fear anomalies in time! Whann-sool-lin will exist in that time, so she must not in any circumstances meet herself. We have no idea what could happen."

"Remember when the first experiments in time travel were done," Kamiel replied. "Khann was sent back to the earliest times of the Empire of the first Gnathen tyrant, Shan-mace-soo. During that epoch she was a young Brood-mother raising a homestead. She avoided the areas that her younger self had trod and returned without any trouble. We must just be very careful, as the two of them should not be at the university at the same time."

"Then the important thing we have to do," interjected Solace, "is just to keep her on the ship. The transference of the crystalline stored minds will be done eighteen years later. The project will have to be kept from the younger self. She will remember the areas of the university that were not visited by her younger self. All we need to do is ask her!"

"Well done my young apprentice," Kamiel laughed and added, "You are proving your place on this project. Sometimes the obvious eludes us. We have been activated a long time! There is one other personage that I would like to find, but it would have to be done discreetly."

Asue gave her partner an eyeless stare and remarked, "You mean Minnis!"

"Yes!"

"What do you need her for?" Asue replied uneasily.

"Why is Minnis so important?" asked Solace on their private communication band.

Kamiel answered, "She had a great personality, brave and courageous, a nannite not quite like any other. I built her from the ruins of another partially destroyed personality, without the constraints that bind you to obedience. She is a well-kept secret from the Guardian's civilization. She has the ability to kill sentient life and as much free will as Asue and myself.

One of the people that we will need is a petite human being called Hannah. Where weapons are concerned and innovative science, she is of genius level. She designed the first time-travelling device with the help of two incredible Gnathe. Just like Larse and Emelia, she would not be any use without Fredrick and where Frederick is concerned, Minnis is also part of the equation. For the mind of Minnis also contains part of his personality. I designed her with free will and to be partially sentient. Paired with Fredrick as a battle suit, she was able to evolve and the two of them could work together as one. She has a composite mind!"

"It may have been a secret in your timeframe, but all nannites are fed the knowledge of how she helped to defeat the Goss. She is known about, but has never been found," Solace replied.

Kamiel nodded in a human fashion and replied, "Nor would they. Where Fredrick and Hannah lie side by side in their graves, Minnis sits in a cave nearby in stasis waiting for the day she may be needed. I know just where they are; I was with them before they died and had their personalities recorded in crystalline storage. As they are among the first re-activated clones to be brought into being on Jupiter's harsh environment, we still have their DNA patterns on record. All I need do is to retrieve the crystals, switch off the stasis field containing Minnis and return. I also need to reactivate an old friend who lies close by. He and I are of a similar mind. I speak of Alexander McBald the elected leader of the humans and apes that settled Jupiter at the beginning. He was re-cloned many times and his mind transferred to the new body, so he has a thousand or more years of experience. His telepathic abilities are off the scale, similar to Link-soo-shan. Our original creator gave me the mind of the original Alexander, blended with many more to make my mind. Alex is Alex! We will need him, along with some of his colleagues to crew fighting Toarvaks. This I will do when we return to Jupiter at a more localised timeframe. Now we need to find Thomas!

After the altering of the Goss into a symbiotic life form, Thomas had roamed the star-lanes, as a component of Toarvak 7, doing his part as a member of the gestalt crew. Fernando had returned to his father, Lord Francisco Samovar and took up his position as the ruler's son. There was much to be done in ferrying colonists to new and empty worlds and Thomas had been content to be part of this new age. He had met and befriended many of the alien peoples he came in contact with during the time that he had spent as Toarvak. The time came however to leave this wandering life and head for home before he died of old age. He was now approaching a hundred and forty something standard years. Although his hair was silver and his body aged, due to Toarvak 6's alterations in his basic genetic makeup, he was still fit. The alterations in his brain and neuron linkages had given him an advanced mental ability that had stayed with him. All the psychic abilities had remained throughout the years, as sharp as during the times he had ridden through the adventures he had experienced with Larse on Daedalus One, hunting down the Algarie with Jon and Samuel at his side.

Thomas had left the company of the changing gestalt that had become Toarvak 7 and joined a family of Gnathe who had decided to settle a world in orbit around a similar sun to the one that had warmed the 'Three Worlds'. Here on this fertile world were a scattering of the Insectoids and Conics who were settling by a natural harbour. The insectoids built boats that sailed out to sea on three hulls with the masts on the centre hull. At the back of the boats raised up and straddling the three hulls was the nest site. It looked like a loaf of bread with holes in the top. The decking divided into four levels, open at the sides. Along these edges the Vogb dug themselves into place and extended their stinging tendrils into the space that the fishing nets were drawn up. The insectoids hauled the nets up to the surface and the Conics did the sorting and stunning with their electrically charged tendrils. Although the Gnathe were fond of fish, they were never very good sailors, so Thomas was the one who sailed with the aliens helping them with his abilities. He could sense the shoals of fish far beneath them and would instruct the insectoids when to cast the nets. By the power of his mind he could 'persuade' the shoals of fish to come to the surface. For his help the ship would allocate part of the catch to him and the Gnathen family he helped to support. It was a good life as long as you enjoyed the company of aliens rather than humans.

The time came that he felt the urge to go home to Daedalus One and to be among his own kind. He had broached the subject with the Brood-mothers, Choappa and Lingstron-sooom-shantic several nights ago. In the pale light of their glow crystal he had explained his needs and talked to them about his home world. He had agreed to sail with the tri-marine for another trip to gain a harvest of fish for them before he put in a request to travel on the next Toarvak that visited the world they called Morning Glory. He had sent a mental massage by the Goss, to his old ship Toarvak 7 to find him and provide passage if it could. As it happened, his old friend was indeed going to be in the area of this world in the near future and was looking forward to becoming 'one' with him.

That morning he walked down the path that led to the harbour and watched the sun climb out of the sea. The insectoids were already busy trimming the ship's sails and finding the wind while the Vogb settled themselves onto the stanchions overlooking the hold where the fish were to be stored. They were waiting for him to come aboard before casting off. Thomas stepped onto the deck and held onto the rail, while the insectoids cast off. The harbour mouth was ringed in white caps, with a heavy swell. "This was going to be a rough passage out to sea", thought Thomas and grinned as he remembered that the Conics were not good sailors when it got rough.

They were well equipped to withstand the bumps and roll of the trimaran with the number of tentacles they had to hold on with. It was the up and down movement of the boat when it had to cross the waves at ninety degrees that they found difficult to manage. Thomas had no problems with rough weather and quite enjoyed it. The insectoids built amazing boats that were fast and stable in the roughest conditions. He had sailed with them for years whilst he had lived on Morning Glory. The queens that had settled here had soon found out about his abilities and rotated his presence around all of the boats to be as fair as possible to each hive. The one time-consuming passion that they had, was their love of playing chess. This game that humanity had created fascinated them and each queen would invite Thomas to play against them in the evenings. His individual way of playing would be studied by the other queens while he pitted his wits against the one who had come to her turn. The males found the game too complex to play against the queens unless they grouped their minds together.

The trimaran's sails caught the wind and pulled steadily

away from the quay heading for the harbour mouth. The insectoids raised the mainsail at the last moment and the boat shot through the gap into open water. Now they really began to move as more sails were dropped into place and tightened by the wind. The sea's swell lifted the trimaran high onto the crest of the wave and they slid down the slope to face the upsurge of the next wave. Already the Vogb were suffering from the motion of the trimaran as it crossed the waves.

After several hours of this the boat tacked to the side and Thomas signalled to the insectoids using the Goss, that they were over a good shoal of fish. Like a well-oiled machine they went into action and shot the nets. Soon the rhythm of fishing took over and everyone was busy at their tasks, oblivious of anything else. It was while the nets were up and the Vogb were sorting, that Thomas lost his grip on the rail, as the trimaran dropped into a big swell. As he slid down the side of the hull towards the water he caught the back of his head on the edge of the deck. Unconscious and unable to levitate out of the sea's reach, Thomas slid beneath the waves as the boat sailed on.

Toarvak 6 had followed the trimaran out to sea and out of phase waiting for this moment. The records had shown that Thomas had gone to sea and never returned with the insectoids to dry land.

As the trimaran fought the wind, it was taken further away from where Thomas had entered the water, unconscious. In the confusion of lifting the nets and stunning the fish neither the conics or the insectoids noticed Thomas lose his grip on the rail. It was not until the fish had been stowed away that the human's role of fish finder was needed. Immediately the Goss was summoned to locate him and make the mental link, but there was no trace of him.

Several hundred feet under the plunging sea, Kamiel and

Asue were examining the body of the human. The blow to the head had been quite extensive and the skull had been fractured badly, causing extensive bleeding into the brain. His mind was on the point of expiring, when Whann-sool-lin placed a crystal upon his forehead and brutally entered his mind to make a bridge before it shut down. She rapidly stored the fading mind away, before Asue opened the skull and removed the brain to extract the RNA. Once again she became a centrifuge and spun out the memory retaining substance. A time stasis capsule was inserted into the wall with its label until it would be required.

"That was close! Said Solace in dismay and turned to the other nannites.

Kamiel asked Asue, "Are you sure we got all of his mind saved before it was damaged?

"Quite sure," Whann answered for her. "I made the bridge in time, so that I was able to drain his mind into the crystal storage and save it there. He will have some strange memories when he regains consciousness in a new cloned body. We will have to make sure that we are there to bring him into the new world.

Kamiel looked at the wall with its precious cargo secreted away and said, "Well my companions, we have made a start. Toarvak 6, take us to Jupiter and the time period we require. It is time to harvest the Gnathe and for me to walk down a path that I never expected to have to travel again.

CHAPTER SIX

The energy field was in the vicinity of an exploding star that scoured all the life force from the orbiting planet and the energy that was released from the mega-deaths, more than sustained it with a new vibrancy. Intuitively it looked for more and in the looking became aware of itself for the first time. The old energy that had sustained it for billions of years was fading away, as the cosmos cooled and matured. The galaxies were getting further and further apart as the millions of years went by. It found that it was marooned in a group that were endlessly orbiting about a common centre and settled down amongst the swirling spiral, elliptical and globular clusters of billions of stars. Instinctively using wormholes to travel from star to star, it began to spread the new life amongst the planets that were favourable to biological growth. It began to learn how to manipulate stars to expand and go unstable, bringing the life on the world orbiting to a quick end and replenishing its energy stocks.

Thus it was that 'The Harvester' came into being and once it had tasted the life energy of sentient creatures, its hunger and appetite became its driving force, as each mega-death increased its awareness of the part of the universe it ruled.

It learnt to farm the worlds and direct evolution into diverse patterns. When the planet under its 'care' was full to capacity, the Harvester would cause a large enough asteroid or comet to precipitate a mega death, by directing it at the world. It became skilled at doing this many times to the same world, so that it could collect the life force each time without totally destroying the planet and the life upon it.

When it came back to the replenished world, it found that the surviving creatures had evolved to more complex forms, each time to a stage higher. Each feast became more complex and satisfying, until at long last intelligent beings evolved. Then and only then, did it realise that the feeding from these life forms was richer than from any primitive type of life. It took many millions of years between feeds, sometimes hundreds of millions of years and the farming kept it busy.

The long thoughts became adjusted, so that for a limited time at least, it could speed its thoughts up to the mayfly existence of the creatures that had evolved. When it did this, it found that it could influence the lives and purposes of the intelligences that had developed. Sometimes it was able to enter and control the flesh and spirit of an individual person, until its presence burnt out the nervous systems of those it turned into puppets.

It allowed and encouraged the creatures to create diverse religions, centred round its meddling interference. By doing this, it engineered wars between the factions that disagreed with each other and killed hundreds of thousands to feed its gross appetite. As the sapient creatures developed science, it found that it could get them to kill millions of their own species by applying its techniques. The Harvester would allow them to develop to the point of interstellar travel, disrupt their sun and finish the meal. The Andromeda galaxy became rich in sapient life and developed the beginnings of interstellar travel all across the spiral arms. Many civilizations developed the ability to send out self-replicating probes to pave the way for further exploration. Before they could join them, the ancient, alien life form, would de-stabilise their sun and destroy their worlds, feeding on the rich, life energy.

The Harvester became very busy in the Andromeda

galaxy due to the number of different life energies that had matured. The pickings were rich and satisfying and the spreading of life for its future took all of its attention. So it was that the Harvester began to miss the races that had developed much further than usual in the neighbouring galaxy, while it was about its grisly harvest.

It missed the rise and development of the Kresh with their war against the Goss. On re-entering the home galaxy of the Kresh and all the other races of interstellar travellers, it found the Earth had gone from its orbit, around the star it had purposely destabilised millions of years ago. It was in time to see the sun change from a yellow star to a red giant, long before its time, but to no advantage to itself. Its next meal was no longer around! While it was puzzling this out, it became aware of a fracture in time and space. Reality changed! It now found itself in an alternative universe.

A raging hunger swept through its vast corporeal existence, instead of its usual sated feeling. Every final meal of life energy from this galaxy had disappeared from its past. It was as if a wave had surged forwards from the beginnings of this galaxy, taking every intelligent race of beings with it! This immense sweep of stars was empty of intelligent life from spiral arm to spiral arm, at this moment in time. Try as it might the Harvester could sense nothing in any direction. It travelled the matrix across the light years, speeding down the wormholes and exiting into each spiral arm. Hungrier and frustrated beyond its comprehension, it searched in vain for intelligent life. All the pickings it could take were the lean energies of lowly life forms that recently emerged. A few dinosaur worlds kept it nourished as it smashed comets into life devouring impacts, but this was not enough.

The one ability that the 'Harvester' did not have was an ability to travel in time, forwards or back. It could only move forwards at the pace that time moved. The great mind considered and came to a decision that the previously harvested intelligent life had moved there away from its grasp. The how was not important! What was the main fact, was a vast meal awaited it millions of years in the future.

It re-located to the Andromeda galaxy and manipulated the wormholes at its command to generate an accelerated movement towards the empty at this time, Milky Way. There would be a reckoning in the millions of years to come in the future and the feeding would be good. What was the Harvester's prey, would be prey again. It turned its attention to the untended 'farms' it had left, to see which would furnish a ready meal.

Although Link-soo-shan was old and her body was beginning to fail, her mind was still sharp and her thoughts were clear. All of her contempories had long gone to their graves and she was the last of her generation of Gnathe left, who had defeated the Goss. Even her Brood-mother daughters, Suzzan and Trann were showing signs of extreme age. She had determined that her last days would be held on her planet of origin. The old Gnathe had travelled around the galaxy with her daughters, in one of the many willing Toarvaks that the grateful Kresh had put at her disposal. With the alteration of the Goss to a symbiont life form, that was uniformly spread throughout all the intelligent aliens scattered around the spiral arms, communication was universal. She no longer needed the telepathic enhancing crystals to send her mind on a journey, although she still used the combination of telekinetic crystals to use the wormholes or gates as the humans called them.

This evening however she regarded the two matching crystals that lay, one in each hand and concentrated her mind. All of her life she had used the enhancing abilities of the crystals to open doors in mind and space. The Matrix was as a second home to the aged Brood-mother and she constantly strained to understand it more before she died. Link-soo-shan had worked within the planetary Matrix in her youth and had expanded the sphere of influence to the empty reaches between the stars, during the building of the bridge to the Three Worlds from her home on Jupiter. What she could recognise were the threaded paths of the wormholes linking up the distortions of space and time that the dark matter had laid down at the very beginning of the universe.

From time to time she had sensed something out there within the Matrix, huge, powerful and full of hunger! She had never contacted it, as the thoughts that powered the thing were so very slow. Now and again the vastness of the presence impinged upon her consciousness, without her being able to connect to it. It was her pastime during the many quiet times that she had to herself, to try and reach out to it, but it seemed so much further away now than when she had sensed it in her youth. Her sister Chang had never felt its aura, so they had never discussed it together, as running the Empire had taken all of their attention.

Empire!

The elderly Gnathe had given up all thoughts of Empire, when she had shared her mind with the nannite Kamiel, for decades, as they both fell towards the yellow sun in the deep past, her consciousness held in storage in his nannite brain.

Memories of the titanic struggle she had initiated against the humans and their ape partners in those early days floated up from long ago. Her part in the building of the interstellar bridge, after the relocation of the Earth to a new sun and before the war against the Goss, gave the old Gnathe a feeling of satisfaction. The Kresh had honoured her for how she had fooled the parasitic life form and enabled

75

them to retrieve their world from their induced plunge into their sun. Indeed she had lived a long and eventful life and had been a pivotal force in the events of her galaxy. Even now she was aware of the actions of the Kresh, in rescuing alien civilizations from unstable stars, using the knowledge she had freely given. It was rumoured that they were even fishing through time to rescue earlier intelligent settled alien worlds from the same fate.

The Lady Jennet, as those who did not know her real identity called her, reached for a toasted pod-vine fruit and crunched it between her back teeth. Her concentration lost, she nibbled at the plateful of dainties her daughters had left her.

"Goss!"

The voice in her head answered promptly, "Yes Lady Link, what can I do for you?"

"Connect me to my daughters Suzzan and Trann," she replied.

"They are not here, my Lady," answered the symbiont.

"What do you mean, Goss? Be more specific," she asked with concern.

"Exactly that Link-soo-shan. They do not exist! I cannot connect with their minds. I fear that they are dead, my Lady. I cannot find them."

"Nonsense! They are my daughters and I am much older than them. If anyone was going to die amongst my family it would logically be me," Link replied and considered the conundrum.

After some thought an idea made its way into her mind.

"Goss, are my grand-daughters alive and well and all the kindred?"

"They are my Lady," answered the symbiont, as it

stretched out the field of awareness from the elderly Gnathe.

A sensation of excitement, long gone from the humdrum existence, electrified her thoughts. Something was about to alter her life again. She could feel it coming as sure as the rising of the sun. All she had to do was wait. She stretched out her tail and stood tall on her perch in anticipation. The hairs on her arms stood up and her ears swivelled to pick up the slightest sound. All her senses came onto maximum alert and a prescient anticipation took control of her very being. It was now late evening and the household would be settling down to sleep. She would not expect to be attended to until morning, so any visit to her chambers would occur around this time.

A hazy cylinder rose from the floor in front of her and a familiar silver form stepped out of its influence.

"Kamiel! I have been expecting you," Link-soo-shan laughed. "You have taken my daughters, Suzzan and Trann so it was only a short matter of time before you came for me."

The nannite gave the Gnathe a shrewd eyeless stare, before he said, "Link-soo-shan, you still have the ability to amaze me! I will not bore you with pleasantries. The future has need of such as you and I. Open your mind to the Goss, as I carry a living piece of organic material within my nannite body, host to the living spores of the symbiont."

Link-soo-shan linked her mind to Kamiel's amazing personality and took into her consciousness all the knowledge that the Guardian had gleaned about the adversary. It took some time for her to be satisfied that she had a complete understanding of all the factors. The old Gnathe had lived for more than a thousand years. This was split between her first existences as the Tyrant, followed by the survival of her death by transferring her mind to that of her female daughter. She had genetically altered the host into the third sex, to once more become a fully functional Brood-mother and pursue her revenge against the humans. After Kamiel had taken her into the future, he had preserved her mind as her body expired in the hard vacuum of space. Her third period of existence occurred when Kamiel returned her mind to the new pattern that she had designed and had grown in the cloning tank. This body had endured time's ravages well, with all the improvements that she had designed into it, but it was beginning to fail.

"Well, Kamiel you had best get on with the transfer and I will join my daughters in crystal storage until the new body is ready. Take enough genetic material, so that I get the same body type as I designed and store my mind with care! This will be different than when we shared your nannite body. Will you be resurrecting Khann as well? I feel that she will be just as needed, as you and I will need as many killers and ruthless minds as you can find. Before you send this body into inert meat, let me tell you of something that happened many years ago when I was the ruler of the Gnathen Empire. It was something that only I experienced when I was questing through the Matrix. My sister was not quite as adept as I and when I asked her, she said that she had never felt this strange echo of a vast mind. I only felt it a few times and it was far away from the planetary confines of the Matrix that we used. I felt an ancient hunger for only an instant that changed to a feeling of satisfaction. I think that this thing was the entity that has been named as the Harvester!"

Another silver humanoid shape exited the hazy cylinder, followed by a Gnathe carrying a box of crystals and a nannite container. Link eyed the two with a twinge of apprehension. Whann-sool-lin approached the aged Gnathe with reverence while removing a crystal from the selection in the box.

"Great Lady Link-soo-shan, I feel privileged to meet you. We will meet again in the far future," she said as she moved forward to make the mind meld.

Link turned her head to stare at the silver companion and asked, "Asue is that you? Are you responsible for the transference?

"We really do not have the time to talk," Asue replied. "I take it you are coming with us or am I wasting my time? We only have a few minutes before we will be interrupted and I need to remove your brain, take a DNA sample, make it look as if you have died naturally and get back to Toarvak 6! Don't worry old friend, I have done this many times before."

Link protested, "But not to me!"

She felt the characteristic sting as Asue made contact, the cool feel of the crystal on her forehead and the mind bridge secured before her consciousness blacked out.

Asue rapidly did what was necessary and they all retreated to the hazy area projecting through the floor. Toarvak 6 took them out of phase and dropped further down into the planet's crust. Over and over again they tripped back and forth in time collecting Gnathe, human beings and apes for the project. None took the other option of oblivion and all of them pledged their lives to the success of the proposed venture.

The time had now come to finding and resurrecting the other main participants, to be specific, Alexander, Hannah, Frederick and Minnis.

Toarvak 6 had become very adept at moving through a planet's crust and interior by taking all the molecular structure out of phase. As matter is made of atoms and there are vast spaces between the nucleonic structures, going out of phase took the ship between the spaces. In this out of phase existence there was an absence of gravity, temperature and molecular pressure. It was a unique discovery by the Kresh and gave the Toarvaks their power to travel through stars.

Combining this ability with the manipulation of wormholes by their own method and also the mind control of the Gnathe gestalts, enabled the self-intelligent ships to go anywhere in time and space. It was those crystals mined from the bottom of the gas giants' atmosphere that enabled them to travel through time and construct Stargates locked into planetary orbits.

Kamiel had Toarvak 6 travel through the inside of Jupiter's crust, until she had taken up a position directly underneath the tomb where Minnis sat in a time stasis field. The crypt had no doorway to the outside world and backed onto a natural cave. Inside the vault of grey stone and nannite fixings were three coffins raised on a large slab of granite. Each one was constructed from pure nannite and had a glowing crystal embedded in the headstone. One was a lot smaller than the other two and was almost a child's size. By its side was a coffin that dominated the dark slab by its size. Hannah and Fredrick lay side by side with the heads of the coffins touching. The other coffin lay at right angles to them with one side fused to the heads of the other two. Etched into the small headstones placed at the feet were just the three names of the deceased; Alexander McBald, Fredrick Branski and Hannah Branski. The layout of the coffins made the mathematical sign of Pi.

Kamiel stood for a few moments with his optical band on full power in the clammy darkness. A small chimney to the outside world let in sufficient light for him to see and allowed sunshine to feed the crystals with energy when they were illuminated. He stretched out his silver hand to depress the hidden switch that sealed Minnis away from the world. The end wall slipped smoothly into the floor revealing a cone of force, behind which a silver form could be seen. Fused to her chest were three nannite boxes containing pieces of living flesh that carried the DNA codes of the genetically altered human beings. These contained the alterations that Khann had wrought when they had first been able to breath Jupiter's atmosphere. All three people were no longer totally human as they also carried Gnathen genes in their cell structures. Imbedded into each one was a mind storage crystal, keyed to the container with the name etched on the side.

The Guardian shut down the underground power source that powered the time stasis field and watched as Minnis turned towards him.

The mind of his creation entered his, "This must be serious or you would not be here. You have need of my precious and secret cargo and my abilities. Take me where you will and tell me everything that I need to know. You must have arrived here by an out of phase Toarvak as I see the walls have not been breached."

With that the two nannites stepped into the cylindrical pseudopod and Toarvak 6 sent them out of phase and dropped them down inside her substance twenty feet below the crypt. She momentarily matched phase with the planet with certain areas of her skin and allowed Jupiter's spin to take her out of its gravitational field, by immediately going out of phase again.

Now that Kamiel had collected the most important members of the expedition it was time to head up-time to the date eighteen years before they made final preparations to head towards the Andromeda Galaxy. The cloning tanks nine hundred thousand years in the future were going to be busy and Whann-sool-lin would have much to do. The tanks were in a sealed wing of the university and were underground. There were five thousand units that had been built and shipped in from different technical worlds. All they needed were the living cells, carrying the DNA, to produce perfect clones of all the personal that the searching Toarvaks and crews had brought back from the time after the confrontation with the Goss. Once they had grown to their mature size in about eighteen years for the humans and apes, the RNA containing all their memories would be drip-fed into the dormant brains and then the minds stored in the crystalline matrixes would be reintroduced to their new homes. As a bonus to the volunteers who were ready and willing to risk their new lives against the coming struggle with the harvester, all of the clones had the aging gene removed. This would mean that they would continue to live as matured organisms, just as the first settlers inside the Jupiter domes had done. Barring accidental death, their life spans would not be curtailed for centuries or even thousands of years. The only thing that the females would be unable to do would be eternally fertile. The Gnathe clones would be ready much quicker than the humans and apes as their growth to maturity was a more rapid process. There were also nearly a thousand cloned Kresh suspended in the tanks who had followed Alexander and Link-soo-shan's plans during the defeat of the Goss.

Kamiel and Asue had engineered a staggering process so that all the clones would be activated to emerge from the tanks at around the same time over several months. The nannites that were encoded with the personality and skills of the original Sharn and Minns were called into action to oversee the implementation of the collected cells and the creation of the embryos from the DNA. Over the gestation period the tiny groups of cells multiplied and diversified and soon recognisable arms and legs began to take shape. The heads began to develop and the empty brains were kept in a receptive state. Each foetus took on the characteristics of the pattern skilfully inserted into the stem cells by the nannites. Month by month the embryos kept growing and continued to develop into recognisable unborn babies. As the time of birth arrived each was put on standby. The artificial wombs were placed next to the growing-on tanks where the babies would be placed onto breathing machines and feeding tubes.

The time finally came when the babies came of 'age' needing to be born and severed from the umbilical tubes linked to the artificial wombs. Once they were breathing and all dependency finished, they were allowed to kick and wriggle about in the cots while the next stage was brought on line. They were fed by the nannites for a week or so until they were readied for the next stage. Tubes were inserted down into the tiny stomachs and the lungs inflated with pure air from the machines. The babies were suspended in warm antiseptic fluids and would spend the next eighteen years growing into the cloned receptacles for the crystal-stored minds to be inserted. Muscles were kept flexed by inserted electrodes and the bodies strengthened. At the age of twelve, each human an ape had a small silver ball, donated from the Toarvaks, inserted into the brainstem. The next six years would be devoted to improving the neural systems so that upon awakening each person would have the abilities that they had 'died' with. A great deal of them would gain mental powers that had only been developed by those who had been 'taken' by the Toarvaks. Amongst the crop of the reborn were Kresh, Conics, Insectoids, Lagdoo as well as the Humans, Apes and Gnathe. Each type of alien had a different gestation and maturation period, so a great deal of planning had been done by the nannites and the Gnathe overseeing the project. All of them had been injected with the spores of the Goss. The symbiotic life form would monitor the crossover from the crystal storage and the Gnathe forming the bridge.

Hanging in geo-synchronic orbit over the University, far below, Toarvak 6 made her presence known. She had done this by constructing an avatar along the lines of Minnis, so that she could be at the side of the tank when Larse was transferred to his body. Next to this tank had been placed the one that contained Emelia. Each body had been given a light sedative before being disconnected from the life-support and lay in mindless sleep on a low bed.

The storage crystals had been brought the side of the bed and Whann-soo-lin indicated that she was ready. The Gnathen Brood-mother given the charge of bringing them back placed the crystal containing the mind of Larse onto the brow of the sleeping youth. She was conscious of Toarvak 6's mind lurking in the background and chased her off with a reprimand. A day before, a nannite had injected the RNA directly into the brainstem and she had allowed the memories contained in the fluid permeate the brain. Now the minds were ready, but inactive and the next stage was ready.

Now she made the bridge from the crystal to the once empty brain and allowed the mind to flow into the perfect sleeping receptacle. A shudder went through the naked man and the hands clenched into fists. His eyes opened and focussed onto the giant poised over him. He felt the mind open and explain what had happened. Larse lifted his young hand to his eyes and looked in wonder.

The familiar mind touch of Toarvak 6 entered him and said, *"Not dead you are, my son. Much to find out you must. Know this, Emelia lies beside you and will be the next to awaken. Not dead the both of us, but so much we must do!"*

Larse rolled unsteadily over onto his side and saw a young and beautiful naked woman by his side. His breath caught in his chest as he realised who she was. Her head had been shaved as had his, but her nose and lips in profile were just as he remembered them. She was fast asleep. He watched as the large three-fingered hand of Whann-soo-lin delicately placed the storage crystal upon her forehead and concentrated on perfecting the mind bridge. For a few moments nothing happened. Larse began to panic a little and then the young woman gasped. Her hands clenched and her whole body shuddered as the impact of awakening took over. The Goss opened the link from her mind to his and she turned her head and smiled.

The full impact of mind-to-mind contact, made her eyes open wide with astonishment.

Larse wept, as the full impact of her long wait washed through his consciousness as the century moved on without him.

She felt his agony at finding the wormhole closed, after the defeat of the Goss and finding that so much time had elapsed when he eventually got home.

They felt the absolute joy of re-union after all hope had gone.

Larse dragged his reluctant body of the bed and over to her side. They entwined their arms about one another, he on his knees beside her, while Emelia rolled towards him and pressed her naked breasts against his chest. They kissed each other, oblivious of the noisy activity about them as others re-awoke into this new world.

Some distance away, Alexander and Link-soo-shan also became aware of their new life and greeted Link's daughters, Suzzan and Trann. Fredrick and Hannah were sat with their arms around each other while Minnis stood by.

The day of awakening had arrived. Soon the armada would be formed and the journey to the Andromeda galaxy would begin, but first Kamiel would have to renew his meeting with the huge Tran-sentient known as Archive.

This time he would be bringing his long awaited associates from the conflict with the Goss. He wondered what the giant had in mind for going with them. They needed its abilities to locate the entity that had labelled the Harvester, but how they could share a Toarvak with such a large creature was beyond his capability to reason.

CHAPTER SEVEN

Once again a world played host to sentient beings. On a far-flung arm of the Andromeda galaxy, a trip'o-dal species very similar to the Thipdar had evolved under the watchful senses of the Harvester. Several generations on from the last series of wars, there were now two major powers about to sign a peace treaty and trade agreement, allowing both factions to join forces. The minor factions would pledge allegiance to their more powerful neighbours and agree to the joint exploitation of the oil reserves buried deep under the ground.

At last religious differences had been settled between those who believed that the three-legged God with four arms, was a different manifestation of the God with two arms cherished by the proud trip'o-dal species of the North. Those that believed that the four-armed people of the South were an abomination had reluctantly been brought round to the idea that both four and two armed were variants of the same species and the God they worshipped was universally the same.

The flying machines were grounded and the dirigibles were all tethered. The armies of the North were on low standby during the negotiations, as were the hoards of the South. Both Northern and Southern Continents were enjoying the longest period of trade and peace for many generations. Numbers of two and four armed trip'o-dal people had slowly crossed the intervening seas and settled in each other's neighbourhoods. Eventually the differences in the number of arms had no significance and inter-breeding took place, producing the fact, that two arms or four, they were all of the same species.

The Harvester increased the speed of its thoughts so that it could become aware of the day-to-day happenings of its livestock. At this level of existence it could infiltrate the minds of its subjects and turn them into puppets. The energy being began the process of spinning itself around the world beneath it, into the latticework of a giant sticky net. When the killing started, the harvest would begin. The commander of the Southern air force found himself giving the orders to scramble the long-range bombers and protecting fighter planes. The trip'o-dal wept as he gave the co-ordinates of the peace conference to the invading force. The flyers would never think to inquire why; they were trained to obey orders!

In the North, radar sweeps of the air space over the peace conference picked up the waves of planes heading for the meeting and the incredulous watchers gave the alarm. Orders were rapidly given and the invading forces were met with dogged resistance as they tried to get to the conference that would soon lay in ruins. Down came the bombs! The life energies of the fallen rose up to the sky, where they met the sticky strands of the web and fed the Harvester's need.

Years passed and the conflict grew even fiercer and scientific progress increased as it always did during conflict. Millions of the trip'o-dal people died, fighting a war that should never had been started had they been given the choice. As the enduring war hit new crescendos, more of the life force was gathered, until the awful hunger of the being was sated. Now was not the time to reap the ultimate harvest, as there were enough survivors to re-build a new civilization.

The Harvester sped up its thought processes and once again began to influence individuals. This time they were influenced to exhort a peaceful means to end the conflict.

This civilisation was just pre-atomic at this stage. The next war would probably be final and the energy being would have to start again somewhere else. The other alternative would be the breakthrough in science that would give the trip'o-dal people the science of wormholes and interstellar spaceships. That was one thing that the Harvester would not permit at any cost. The answer to that would be the un-stabling of the natural forces binding the sun together or a 'world-killer' asteroid intersecting this world's orbit. Sometimes this would cause a new evolution of life to take place and supply further meals in the future, of increasing complexity.

Leaving the sensitive web behind to catch the stragglers, the Harvester spread itself through the wormhole system and searched the part of its universe that it dominated, reaching out for indications of more sentient life force energy to feed upon when it hungered again.

Thomas gasped and arched his back, as the air filled his lungs instead of salt water. He awoke dry, instead of being soaked and clenched his fists, opened his eyes to see a Gnathen, Brood-mother stood over him. Her mind was inside his mind, giving reassurance. The Goss connected him to his friend Larse who was stood by the side of his bed. By his side was an impossible sight. Emelia was stood with him, naked and bald as he realised he was, but they were both young and so was he! As everyone who had been awakened did so, he examined his un-wrinkled hands and marvelled at the change.

"The last thing that I remember was falling off the side of an Insectoid trimaran and choking in seawater," he said. "I hit my head as I fell and everything went black. Now I find myself here, wherever 'here' is?"

Larse gripped his old friend's hands in his and opened his mind explaining all he had been told by Kamiel and

Toarvak 6.

Thomas sat quietly and digested the information that had been fed to him. He looked around the chamber and the rows and rows of beds. Some contained sleeping figures, yet to be awakened, while more held men and women like himself that had been raised from the dead. He stood unsteadily for a moment on his own legs and flexed his muscles.

"Have you eaten?" he asked them. "I don't know about you, but the experience of being raised from the grip of the sea has given me an appetite. I shudder to think how they fed these bodies of ours while they waited for them to grow, but my stomach feels empty!"

Larse and Emelia laughed, while Thomas scratched his crotch and smiled.

Toarvak 6's avatar had returned to the side of the bed with three full length tunics folded over its arm. Two of them were blue in colour and one was in pink.

"Clothes have I brought you. Dress you must, so that comfortable you will be," Toarvak 6 remarked as she passed them around.

Emelia reached for the pink one and slipped it over her head while the other two men wore the blue ones.

Larse remarked, "It looks like one size fits all!"

"The one thing I did not expect was to be wearing a dress in company," Thomas laughed and pulled the hem of the bottom of the dress down to his knees, only to see it wrap around his legs and form a set of trousers.

"Well that's an improvement," he said with relief and looked around.

In the distance could be seen a vast canteen with all sorts of beings eating food and drink suitable for their different natures. The lighting was diffuse and shone down from the walls and ceilings in such a way that shadows were non-existent. Buried under the university a thousand feet down, the whole complex remained secret from the day-to-day affairs of the surface dwellers. Only those involved in the project even knew of the cloning tanks and crystal storage banks stored deep underground.

"Attention all of you! By now you will have been told the basic reason for your resurrection. Know this! You will have sufficient time to re-orientate yourselves before we meet in conference one week from now. I am the Guardian that you came to know during the conflict with the Goss known to you as Kamiel! We have contact through the Goss, as I have a small piece of organic flesh kept alive inside my body that is host to the symbiont. All of you have been given the spores of this creature and can extend your telepathic range clear across the galaxy. Do not be too ambitious at first in how you use the symbiont. Much has changed in this galaxy since you all last lived and died. Appoint leaders to take on the responsibilities of relaying information from the ruling council. You will soon get to know who these individuals will be. For now, enjoy yourselves and make yourselves comfortable. I will contact you all again closer to the time of departure."

The precise tones of the nannite faded from the minds of the resurrected beings and a hum of conversation rose in the chamber. Many of the different alien species were familiar with each other and settled down at the tables laden with food. There were quite a lot of couples that had something other than hunger on their minds. Kamiel, in his understanding of the biological needs of the many aliens, had planned the resurrection centre for just this need. All along the outer walls of the chamber were private rooms with adjustable furniture.

Many of the different aliens who were male and female in gender and even those who were bisexual made for the sanctuary of the private rooms. Those such as the Gnathen

Brood-mothers that had no interest in sex, preferred to make their way to the tables of food, where they could talk amongst themselves and renew old associations. Gnathe did not feel the need to oversee new kindred coming into existence at this time. This was something that could be attended to after the mission was over. There would be ample male and female Gnathe shipping out when the time came.

The same could be said of the Kresh who would need to grow into maturity and generate several sex changes from male to female. The minds of the resurrected Kresh were in a strange state as they had all the memories of adult clan leaders and existed in young bodies. A place had been set aside for them to grow to maturity, fifteen years ago at the Kresh reservation, on the nannite-constructed world called Toarvak Prime. Soon the resurrected Kresh would be ferried into the past and left to mature there.

The conics indulged in-group sexual activity within their clans and many of the trip'o-dal formed new family groups integrating into existing clans.

Among the mass of humankind, two people moved swiftly towards the private rooms located at the perimeter of the vast chamber with little thought for food. They were with an influx of re-united couples holding hands with one thought in their minds.

Larse pulled an un-protesting Emelia rapidly into the privacy of the small intimate room. Inside the room were a table, two chairs and a bed. The lighting was soft and the door closed behind them as they lay down upon the bed. Within seconds they had discarded the tunics given to them and were in each other's arms.

Emelia had never had the gift of telepathy as a natural born, but now, as she had grown inside the tank with Toarvak 6's silver ball inside her brain, alterations had been made. Far different to the communication by the Goss that was open to all, this ability was the same that Larse had mastered. Each mind was bound to the other so as they kissed so they both felt the pressure of each other's lips upon their own. As the blood pumped into Larse's penis, she could feel the increased sensitivity that flowed into it as it extended, as Larse could feel the desire for him mount in his wife's body. He felt the juices flow to accept him as he penetrated. She felt the joy of his penetration and he hers to receive it. As the rhythm built up between them both felt the other's impending orgasm and were joined in ecstasy as they both exploded with the culmination of desire. She would not let him go. They remained joined together as they explored each other's minds and told each other's stories.

Emelia's told of the century of waiting for Larse to return and he explained the frantic search for a way home via new wormholes, joining the narrative together. The loneliness that both of them had endured and Larse's wish, to live no more, combined with Toarvak 6's realisation that without Larse neither could she. The joy of the choice that been given after they had been brought back to live again filled them both. As they lay together kissing and sharing tongues gently around the lips and tips, the blood began to pound and flow back and they both felt the change. This time without speed or haste they gently built the rhythm back and in the slipperiness of their renewed union the two of them were transported again into a double being giving and receiving pleasure. Finally the pressure mounted and with both of them knowing when to match each other, Larse gave a final shudder, as Emelia's orgasmic vagina clamped down on him.

This time they pulled apart and wept tears of joy as they lay together upon the bed. Now, they felt hungry and after a while they sat at the table and asked the room for some food. They smiled at each other, as bread buns with cheese, cooked meats and fruit appeared, rising up from the middle of the table.

As they ate, they also stared at each other, measuring the differences in the bodies that that had been given. Both of them were of a body age of about eighteen years of growth. Larse had been in his thirties when he had met Emelia, who had been in her early twenties and living with her parents. This was before the final conflict with the Goss had taken place and many of the taskforce had settled down until the time came to mount the assault. They had lived on a smallholding not far from her father's headquarters. Lord Francisco Samondar was one of the ruling council of the Three Worlds and a close friend of Suzzan-link-khann, brood-daughter of Link-soo-shan. He had not been resurrected, as he had no experience in combining his mind as a member of a Toarvak crew.

Larse stretched his arms out to Emelia and held her hand gently and said, "Do you understand why we have been resurrected?"

"No! And do I care? All I care about is that we are together again and both young! I remember being so old! Whatever it is that Kamiel wants us to do, I will willingly do it. If it costs our lives then so it will be," Emelia stated and laughed. "We have an amount of time to be together before the reason for being here is realised. Let us not waste any of it!"

Larse laughed and swept her into his arms again and ran his fingers over her shaved head. He could feel a fine stubble beginning to form under his fingertips.

"Soon you will have hair," he whispered in her ear "and be even more beautiful than you are now."

Emelia giggled and slid her hand down his thigh and

gripped his stiffening penis, giving it a squeeze.

"I have waited over a hundred years for this," she said and bit his earlobe.

Alexander made his way to his old Gnathen comrades. Fredrick and Hannah had disappeared into one of the many private rooms leaving everything going on without them. Link-soo-shan had found her daughters and was talking to Kamiel, Asue and Solace.

Link turned as Alexander came into view and swept him off his feet and held him aloft with her great three fingered hands to the level of her sharp-toothed mouth. She flicked out her tongue, delicately touched him on the eyelids, nose and lips before effortlessly tossing him up into the air and catching him before he got beyond her eye level.

"Alexander! My friend and once mind companion, inside Kamiel's nannite skull! I am so very pleased to see you again. Ender-whann-soo has also been resurrected along with those strange brood-daughters of hers with partially human minds, Azander and Marren. The great Khann-link-sool and Trann-link-khann have also been chosen to be part of this escapade. My brood daughters Suzzan and Trann are here too! In fact old friend and one time enemy, practically everyone who stood against the Goss is here in this time-frame," the giant Gnathe's booming voice exultingly informed him.

"Put me down you overgrown, overactive bunch of nerve ends, before I find something for your strength to be used on, such as shovelling the dung from out of the Bazantii stables! Youth does not become you! We seem to have been granted a another chance at life by Kamiel", the human said, "but as we all know my nannite friends gifts come with a price! What is it Kamiel?"

As Link-soo-shan carefully put Alexander to the ground Kamiel gestured to a round table that had mushroomed from the floor. Rows of seats of various heights were one side of the table with a row of perches on the other.

"Goss!"

"Yes Kamiel," the symbiont answered.

"Multi link the members of the Andromeda council only and divert all other minds from this conference," Kamiel ordered.

He stood on the tabletop with Solace, Asue, Minnis and another silver figure. This one was much larger than the other four and had the shape of a human female in her middle age. It was the avatar of Toarvak 6. She was taller and her body shape was fuller than the other nannites. All of the female-minded nannites were slim built, as were the male personalities. This shape was the shape of a mature mother with the illusion that she had bourn many children. Recognisable features could be seen in her face and strands of silver hair were plaited back into a ball. Unlike the nannite Guardians she had given herself a humanoid face instead of the featureless silver ovoid with the optical band. Also, unlike the sexless nakedness of Kamiel and Asue, she had added the impression of being clothed in sweeping folds of silver cloth.

Toarvak 6 was beautiful in a most un-earthly way. The shock to come however would be when she shared her mind with the assembly.

Kamiel stood still for a moment and waited until he was sure that he had everyone's attention. Within the stored memories of the Goss, he drew upon the scientists of the Kresh and the mind adepts of the Gnathe to explain project 'Time Fisher' that had rescued every intelligent race of beings that would have perished by their sun becoming unstable, long before its time. All of these civilizations had been brought forwards in time with their world to this period and placed in orbit around a suitable star. This had become a vast undertaking involving many alien races.

The nannite allowed some time to elapse to allow this information to sink in and added the flat statement, "There are consequences to this altruistic action! There would seem to be an ancient form of life made of pure energy that has existed since around the beginnings of this universe. To put it flatly; - it feeds off biological life! This thing has been known to the Trans-sentients who existed at the dawn of time, as a single being they call the Harvester! In a nutshell; - it creates the conditions conducive to life and transports it around both galaxies, until through manipulation of cosmic events, intelligent life is formed! When it achieves this situation it partially destroys the emerging life forms by encouraging warfare and feeds off their life energy. Whenever the alien intelligence achieves the point of interstellar transport this abomination destabilises the sun and finds itself with a final meal. Project 'Time Fisher' has deprived this thing of the many meals that it once had in this galaxy and that is why it has sent the Andromeda galaxy on a collision course for ours. We are going to stop it or at least distract it so that this galaxy-wide civilization can build a globular cluster and escape the mega-death this thing has engineered! These are already under construction on the outward fringes, facing toward the greater Magellanic cloud."

Kamiel manipulated the devices set inside the walls of the chamber and projected the two galaxies into the air above them. He started the scenario at the moment of time when the Gnathe with the Jupiter born humans and apes, formed the first great gestalt of mind. With this power they were able to wrench the Earth away from the expanding sun and place it in orbit around another stable sun. Some centuries later after the confrontation with the Goss the surviving Kresh went back in time and retrieved their world from the induced plunge into their sun. They put it back into orbit around their sun, but into the same time period as the emerging galactic civilization. Soon after, project Time Fisher was instigated. Early civilizations that would have perished by being swallowed up by their de-stabled star were brought forward in time and re-settled by having their planetary home put in orbit around a different sun. Some of them had been put into Trojan orbits around the same star with two other worlds so that all three benefited from cultural ties. The emerging galactic civilization had soon noticed that amazingly similar types of alien species had the same DNA. It was as if life had been started from the same building blocks of life on similar worlds around different suns at dissimilar times.

Certain types of intelligent life were quite common; - such as the Insectoids, who emerged at the beginnings of evolution of their world and colonised the land first when the oxygen content was high.

The reptilian Lagdoo were also widespread on different, heavily forested worlds and came in slightly different types. In some the intelligence was greatly enhanced against the other cultures. One of them had developed interstellar travelling space ships. These were the ones who had discovered the Goss dominated world and had unwillingly spread the parasite.

The Conics or Vogb were found in every spiral arm at all stages of development. These people were artists and natural electronic experts that used electricity as part of their natural makeup. All conics could store power in internal batteries similar to that used by electric eels, inside their bodies and control the amount delivered by their 'stinging' tendril.

Spread across the galaxy were great numbers of a trip'o-dal race of beings known as the Thipdar. They stood on three legs and had four arms at their disposal. These were known as great craftsmen, sculptors and musicians. Strangely these were a people that seemed driven to war over and over again in all their different histories. What was so odd, was once they were removed from their resident time period, all warlike feeling disappeared. Now they held positions of trust in every kind of post all throughout the Federation of Worlds. The question they asked over and over again of themselves, was what had driven them to slaughter each other in the past.

The intelligent species that were unique throughout the galaxy were the Tran-sentients, the Kresh, the Gnathe and Humanity that alone did not seem to be duplicated, although the DNA of the Gnathe and Earth creatures were compatible with each other. Of all the telepathic creatures in the Milky Way galaxy, only the Tran-sentients could 'overhear' the thoughts of the Harvester. They put this down to their incredibly long life spans and the slowing down of their thoughts during times of meditation.

Kamiel began to move the galaxies onto the collision course that had been predicted by Prim and her scientific team. One of the spiral arms began to ripple as it entered the fringes of the home galaxy. Stars collided with each other or passed so close that the insides of the smaller stars were sucked out and produced a fountainhead into the larger one. Those planets in orbit around any of the stars lost their stability and were cast off into the dark reaches or sailed into the stellar flares to be consumed. The Guardian sped up the time path further into the future and showed the second Andromeda arm interacting with the next section. Now rogue stars from the last encounter were added to the next cycle, increasing the carnage. As time went by the pinwheel shape of each galaxy merged into an amorphous mass of stars. In the raging fires of cosmic radiation all life in both galaxies would be extinguished except for those stars well out on the periphery at the back end of the Andromeda galaxy. This small oasis of stars would form a small globular cluster and wander off away from the stellar conflict.

Kamiel once again contacted all the members of the Andromeda council and spoke simply to every mind, "That is why Prim and the Tran-sentients have fetched us to this time. This is why you have all been given a second chance at life. What I have shown you is the deliberate action of a sentient being. As I said before, we are going to the Andromeda galaxy to this creature's own turf as it were. If nothing else we will distract it and allow the many civilizations of this time period to escape via the globular cluster they are building on the fringes of this galaxy. If we can, we will destroy it. How we do that, I cannot tell you as yet. We need to think and think hard! I have allowed a week for those amongst you to acclimatise to their new bodies and renew old relationships. After that, those of you here will need to inform the many who are not here now, of the situation. When that time comes we will all make our way to Toarvak Prime, where others who are needed will join us."

CHAPTER EIGHT

The Harvester had fed well and had excess energy to spare, so it budded off a few hundred more of its information system components. Their shape was similar to a long fuzzy vee supporting a central cylinder topped by cluster of optical bands. The extended vee spread out and supported the body by wings of force. These caught the solar winds that gushed from the stars. Like birds made of pure energy they soared over worlds, sending back information through the wormholes to the parent energy field. From time to time they would hurtle through the Stargates back to the Harvester to be re-absorbed and give up a more detailed report. Each component was a small part of the massive energy field that gave the thinking part of the Harvester life. For a short time each would be independent of its master and have some sort of free will as it gathered information. The great search was a continuing quest for life-bearing worlds or worlds that could be seeded with primitive life from others. Once the life density made it worthwhile for the Harvester to gather in the new crop, a one-way journey through the wormholes commenced and the information-gathering sibling returned.

The other galaxy had been empty of useful life-stock for hundreds of millions of years and the Harvester was in no hurry to expend its energy to look for life energy while it had so much to do in this one. The rupturing of the wormholes to force the galaxy to reverse its direction towards the other one had happened long ago. No more needed to be done by the energy being, but wait. It never occurred to it to send an emissary to spy upon the life forms that had abruptly disappeared from its time frame. Eventually they would all coincide once more. It was supreme in its universe and unchallenged. In the far future this was going to be changed.

Deep underground at the hidden base under the university, time had passed and the newly re-born alien people were on the move. Eventually tired and happy groups of couples rejoined the throng and learnt the reason for their resurrection. None of them thought that the price was too much to pay.

Toarvak 6 had once again decided to wear the shape of the person that she identified herself to be. The offshoot of her identity was being questioned by Alexander, Hannah and the senior Gnathe, headed by Link-soo-shan. They were particularly interested in her early wanderings with Larse, when she had nourished herself with the life-energy of those that Larse and the others had killed.

The shimmering woman, shaped of silver nannite, was uncomfortable about that aspect of her early struggle for existence, as a symbiont carried by Larse and later by his friends. She had fed on the life force of any flesh and blood creature, but had benefited the most by the energy she had taken from sentient creatures. Designed by the Kresh and fashioned by events unforeseen, she was unique. Each time she had fed on these, her mass had expanded so that she could allow more hosts to carry her inside themselves. Bit by bit she had increased in size until she was split into two groups of five. She had become a true symbiont and had redesigned her carriers to increase their abilities, by altering the neuron structure of their brains. She had connected up dormant areas of the brain-lobes to increase memory ability and explore the dormant psychic abilities of both human and Gnathe. Telepathy, telekinesis, levitation and teleportation had been endowed with the humans and improved by the Gnathe who were used to the crystal-induced powers. Precognition was the one ability that had not quite been achieved.

Kamiel was relentless in his questioning and probed the mind of the Kresh designed nannite further. Riding piggyback upon his questioning thoughts, were the senior minds of both human and Gnathe.

"What makes the life energy of a sentient being so different from that of an animal?" Kamiel demanded of Toarvak 6.

"An animal exists in the time of now. Energy there is, for the time of being here is all it has. No knowledge of tomorrow does it have. Only the now! Hard it is to explain, but a sentient being knows of tomorrow and has energy to spare in its 'soul' to keep it in existence for the future! Energy from lower forms of life will nourish, but from a thinking being, growth can be channelled from that energy. Power from the exploding atoms of the sun can sustain such as I, but compared to the energy that sentient life can provide it is insufficient. Fragmented was I and desperate for survival when into the light I came. Until that first death of the tiny mouse creature fed me energy, unaware was I of this means of feeding. Each more complicated animal I fed upon gave me more until I took the life force of the Algarie soldier. It was then, that capable of real growth was I."

Kamiel allowed the minds in concert with him to examine Toarvak 6's explanation, while he pondered on the difference of the Kresh design to the human design of himself. His type of nannite was unable to go out of phase without the Toarvak ships doing it for them by encapsulating everyone and altering the very parameters of space. Similarly until the Toarvaks had met the human designed nannites they could not produce independent avatars such as the shape that stood before him. The mind of Toarvak 6 stayed inside the ship and the silver shaped woman before him, was just an extension of the artificial intelligence. Also another factor had shaped this artificial intelligence and that was the merged mind of Minnis, when she had entered the Toarvak and stopped its swathe of destruction long ago.

Link-soo-shan leaned forward and projected her mind into the alien thought pattern, using the silver ball that rested in her living brain, with a hundred thousand filaments connected to her neuron network.

"What happens to the mind of the sentient that is taken to feed your needs?" she asked.

"Absorbed it becomes and dissipates into mindlessness," Toarvak 6 answered.

Alexander seized onto the next question and asked, "If this is so then does the mind carry nothing on to the recipient?"

"Nothing! Ceases to exist it does!"

"In that case, I believe that this abomination would have absorbed nothing of the knowledge of the races of beings it has used to keep itself alive! If so, we may plan our attacks upon this energy being and hope that it is unaware of us as an enemy," Suzzan added. "It will know only of our existence when we attack it. In all the eons of time that it has existed, the creature has never known fear. We will bring this emotion to its attention!"

"The bitter irony is that this creature is responsible for scattering life spores throughout both galaxies. It created us by its own selfish actions and considers us as cattle or livestock to be harvested! It has no awareness of us, as beings in our own right," Alexander sadly added. "It would appear that many alien races of creatures including our ancestors have worshiped this thing as a God, even as it fed upon them! Without its interference none of us would naturally exist. By using evolution as a long tool, it has continually brought this leverage to bear, by wiping away the early primitive life forms, forcing the life that was left to adapt."

Link-soo-shan hissed with anger and retorted, "That may be so, but it does not have the right to take sentient life to keep alive. We must find a way to damage this abomination that it has become and stop it from doing this any more. If we can destroy it and take its influence away, then it can no longer be a threat and our kind of life can flourish, without being wiped out by a sun going untimely nova!"

The mind of Ender-whann-soo, a thinker not a killer, interjected, "Could we not build a group mind powerful enough to communicate with this 'Being'? Once we moved a world and its moon to an orbit around another star and travelled through time using the collective will of thousands of linked minds."

Trann-link-khann answered, "What if this communication alerted the Abomination to our presence? This thing has caused a galaxy to stop in its tracks and aimed it at our homes. It lives off death! It has no idea of compassion and does not comprehend that we have a right to live! I rule that we do not even think of communicating with it. We keep our presence secret from this thing until we rise against it. It must not know about the construction of the globular cluster that this galactic civilization is aiming at the Greater Magellanic Clouds."

Kamiel agreed and said to the assembly, "The most important thing that we must do is to make sure that the globular cluster is launched and the 'being' never knows about it. We must cross over to the Andromeda galaxy and distract this thing. The next thing we need to do is to return to Toarvak Prime and re-establish contact with Archive. I have tried to communicate with her via the Goss but without success. She may be sleeping too deeply for me to awaken her. The other Trans-sentients are also very quiet. What we need to do now is to board the waiting Toarvak ships and those who are to merge with the Toarvak mind should do so and re-acquaint themselves with becoming a small group mind integrated into a new personality.

These new gestalts will be the first hunter-killers loosed in this galaxy for hundreds of thousands of years. Whatever takes place between us; contact between this new force and the civilization that assembled us must not happen. Cross contamination of the violence that we are capable off must not be passed on. Telepathic silence will be held at all times between the new Toarvak group minds and the thousands of 'normal' Toarvaks that are serving the galactic civilization that is fleeing this inevitable conflict."

"What if the combined civilization needs to be able to fight for their position in the Greater Magellanic Cloud system?" asked Link-soo-shan.

"That has been thought of and duplicates of those who have been judged necessary have been formed and placed in stasis," replied Kamiel. "That subject is now closed!"

The thousand Toarvaks took flight and made their way to Toarvak Prime. The new gestalts were not the placid minds that had replaced the galactic exploration ships. These were the honed and battle hardened ship's minds that had fought the Goss, based on the original nine that had fought for hundreds of thousands of years. Leading them all was Toarvak 6 and Toarvak 12,402.

At Toarvak 6's suggestion her gestalt was the combined minds of Larse, Emelia, Thomas, Link-soo-shan and Khann-link-sool. Link-soo-shan's two brood-mother daughters Suzzan and Trann-link-khann had replaced the Kresh who had been part of the combined mind of Toarvak 12,042. All throughout the fleet, two or three of the crew had stood down to be replaced by the time-fished personnel that had been re-grown and re-created. A massive change took place in the gestalt minds that now ran the Toarvaks. All of these were hunter-killers and were as unalike to the other Toarvak ships, as wolves to sheep.

Emelia had never been part of a Toarvak's gestalt mind

and was more than a little apprehensive. She approached the control mound with a reluctance that was noticed by Larse and the others. Already Link-soo-shan and Khann-link-sool had settled into a comfortable position and were completely covered in silver nannite, as they sank into the embrace of Toarvak 6. Thomas had sat himself down and was relaxing into a reclined, seated position, sinking into the mass.

Larse turned and held Emelia's hand and said, "Do not fear this. I have done this many times. Once you have surrendered your mind to the Toarvak, all will fall into place. I will be there with you."

"Emelia, chosen you were by me to join with me. Expanded you will become. A necessary part you will become of a unique personality. Welcome you will be!"

Next to her stood the mature figure of a beautiful middle-aged woman in shining silver that had risen from the deck of the ship. The words had come from her directly into her mind, where it was impossible to lie, so Emelia sat herself down and sank into the mound with Larse. As she closed her eyes she became part of a new personality. She was linked to Larse, Thomas and the two Gnathe. Wrapped around the five minds was the artificial intelligence of the Toarvak. The mind expanded! Six minds became one mind to the power of 6. As two squared is four and three cubed are nine so the mind expanded to forty-six thousand, six hundred and fifty-six. When Kamiel took control of the thousand Toarvaks plus the ones that the nannites crewed he would have at his disposal the mind power of a god, as he had when he had plucked Toarvak 6 from the heart of the sun.

Emelia felt the power running through her mind as the gestalt reached out into the great dark and found the wormhole that led to Toarvak prime. She and the others twisted space and winked out of phase, entering the conduit. Subjectively faster than the speed of light in a timeless state of being the ship sped on, followed by the rest of the fleet. The string that united that part of the universe with their destination vibrated with their passage.

Kamiel remained on board Toarvak 6 and ran the fleet from there with the other nannite companions, Asue and Solace. Also on board were thousands of the recruits who had joined their minds together to move worlds and suns into different times and places for the galactic civilization that they had served. Also heading for the same rendezvous were some different type Toarvaks, crewed by the nannite civilization that has spread throughout the galaxy from the outer reaches of the old solar system to the cometary clouds that orbited the fringes of all planetary systems. The Kresh designed Toarvaks had amalgamated with some of the human designed nannites and produced hybrids. The original programming by both designers had been bent a little by both artificial intelligences, but the main directive still rang out; - to protect and defend organic life wherever it could be found and intelligent life most of all. By choice, millions of nannites throughout the galaxy had decided to accompany the expedition to the Andromeda spiral. Without the organic minds' creative abilities, none of them would have been built. They owed a debt to the humans and the Kresh that would be honoured by them come what may. Creatures of pure logic, yet driven by electronic emotions, they sought an empathic relationship with their organic creators.

Some of them had become hosts to packets of organic material kept alive, so that the Goss spores could live and prosper within them. These became conduits and stations to broadcast the telepathic relays across the light years that set them apart. The immortal Goss now inhabited the whole of the Milky Way Galaxy, as a willing partner to every organic sentient creature that existed. None had refused to become hosts to this incredible life form that gave telepathic communication to all intelligent beings.

Project 'Time Fisher' had made this civilization possible and had deprived the alien energy being of the meals it had once enjoyed. By their actions the Kresh and the Gnathe had altered the timelines of this small part of the universe, isolating the 'Harvester' inside the Andromeda galaxy. Its revenge would have produced a massive meal of life energy if the interstellar and time travelling civilization had not realised what had been set in motion.

Toarvak 6 shot through the great star-gate and into orbit around Toarvak Prime while the great armada coasted to a stop and orbited around the binary gas giants further out. On board the sentient ship were Alexander, Hannah and Fredrick along with a full compliment of Gnathe and Kresh as well as the nannites. With them also were Prim, the trip'o-dal and B-o-g the Vogb conic with their families.

Prim gestured to the observation window that Toarvak 6 had provided and said, "Come here and see the wonder of the galaxy. This is Toarvak Prime, the great collective. From here, are all the important decisions made by every species of intelligent life in the Milky Way. The nannites made this world to suit all forms of sentient life. It is here that the Tran-sentients live that help to guide our life. This is where you will meet Archive, the oldest living creature in the known universe. Her species existed at the dawn of time when the formation of stars and planets were still in its infancy."

Alexander and his friends stared down at the planet below in awe. This was indeed the fabled artificial world had been designed by nannites to house all the many different types of aliens who filled the ruling council. The gestalt crew had relinquished control of the ship and had returned to having independent minds.

It took a while for Emelia to recover from being part of such a powerful group mind. It had been an incredible sensation joining up to the human and Gnathe minds with Toarvak 6 surrounding them all. She had been able to think on a level far beyond that of her natural ability and had been part of a group control. To say that it was to be likened to a tight family would not do the effect justice. The gestalt had been able to twist space and navigate wormholes with ease. This was something that Toarvak 6 was designed to do, but enabled by combining with the others, took it to a higher level. What was not understood was that the universe they knew was only one of a number of different dimensions. Gravity was the 'weak' force because it kept the multi-verse stable and dissipated throughout the dimensions. The wormholes were the strings that held all dimensions together. All realities were separate from each other and existed beyond time and space. The dark matter created when the multi-universe was Nano-seconds old pervaded through each reality. The Harvester existed in this dimension, but was part dark matter and was in turn twisted throughout the wormholes. A giant spider with a hundred thousand legs, each one tapping into the strings that held the multi-verse together; - it travelled through its natural element with ease.

One life form could sense the great slow mind of the Harvester and that was the giant Trans-sentients. Kamiel had spoken to the ancient and revered being at Toarvak Prime and she had assured him that it would be possible for her to travel with them to Andromeda. This statement defied the laws of logic, as Archive was larger than a Toarvak ship. It was with some misgivings that Kamiel gave the order to land near to the place where he had last left this amazing being. She was the oldest living thing in the universe and numbered her years in millions.

Toarvak 6 hovered above the countryside near to the building of administration and extended anchoring pseudopods, lowering herself gently to the ground and sinking partially into the rocks. Coming to meet them was the massive forms of Co-ordinator and Deep-thinker floating above the land and towing themselves along by their tentacles. Alexander and Kamiel walked through the walls of the ship to meet them.

The bell-clear tones of the Tran-sentient known as Co-ordinator entered the minds of human and nannite with overtones of immense sorrow.

"You are welcome, Alexander, to Toarvak Prime. The being that you expected to meet is here in a sense. Archive solved the problem of her size in a way that we had not expected. I will carry you both to where she is. Be prepared to see something that may shock you. I realise that you came from another age entirely and have only seen a fraction of this civilization."

Tentacles dropped down from the floating behemoth and curled around the two forms and lifted them gently into the air. Both Globes caught the prevailing wind by opening the flaps on each side and swung round to float over the forest below. The tree tops sped by underneath them and Alexander shivered in the cold wind. Kamiel noticed his friends discomfort and detached himself from Co-ordinators grasp. He flowed over Alexander's body, making sure that his own piece of living flesh was safely tucked away in a secure bulge of nannite. The nannite skin needed to be only a few molecules thick to shield Alexander from the cold. Kamiel directed some solar energy to heat the second skin as well and formed a helmet over the human's head. What remained of the Guardian's body stayed attached like a Siamese twin by his side.

Kamiel spoke into Alexander's ear and said, "This is strange. The last time I met her she was most mysterious about her accompanying us to Andromeda. She was adamant that she would come and she is larger than even these two creatures."

"We will soon know old friend. Our travelling companions are slowing down. They are grasping the treetops and deflating the floatation bags," Alex replied.

The tentacle holding Alexander unrolled and gently deposited him and Kamiel onto the shingle bar at the edge of the forest. In front of them was a wall of decaying flesh that stretched away into the distance. What was left of Archive lay in puddles of her own juices that were leaking out of the open pores of her body. The smell nearly paralysed Alexander with its power. Suddenly the flesh in front of them quivered and parted and a bunch of tentacles thrust through into the air. Wriggling into view came a young Tran-sentient with its floatation globe hugging its body. As they watched fascinated, the young creature climbed to the top of the mountain of flesh and filled the floatation globe with hydrogen. It was followed by another slithering out of the hole and then another until ten of the Tran-sentients were aloft anchoring themselves to the corpse.

Kamiel detached himself from Alexander and widened the field of his optical band into the infrared and scanned the corpse. Deep inside the cooling flesh there were more spots of heat, moving around and burrowing into the light. A new hole ripped open and more of the young Globes wriggled from the dark and stinking hulk, making their way to the top of the immobile, ancient Trans-sentient. A steady rain began to fall, washing clean the young creatures and causing the smell to drop back to a more acceptable level. Alexander knelt and retched dry heaves and lifted his face to the heavens, letting the rain wash his skin. Kamiel helped the human back onto his feet and walked him away from the revolting scene into the shelter of the trees. Only now as the two of them had stood away could the whole of the panorama be seen.

Hundreds of young Trans-sentients were taking to the air and attaching themselves to the bodies of Co-ordinator and Deep Thinker. One of them began to drop towards the human and the nannite.

"I wish to greet you, Alexander and Kamiel. I am Archive; - 'Small Portion' that will travel with you to Andromeda!"

The young Tran-sentient hung from its flotation bag at eye level to the human and fixed the two of them with its encircled blue eyes. He was approximately the size of ten Gnathen Brood-mothers and his loaf shaped body rippled with health. The eyes were clear and the tentacles supple, unlike the two giants still anchored above them. This was a young male of this unique race of creatures. Yet there was a hidden maturity in its manner.

Alex stared at the Tran-sentient in dismay as the creature extended its tentacles toward him and telepathically stated, "Prim instructed me that I would meet Archive here and she would have the solution to the problem of her size. I did not expect to find her dead! What have you done?"

"We have taken into our minds, her memories in the only way we could, by eating her brain while she was alive!" The young male continued, "Archive gladly gave up her life to a greater purpose. Now all of those who have dined upon this great being can carry her memories to use in the struggle to come. It was the only way that she could aid the civilization that saved her race from the Harvester's hunger! We can now travel inside the Toarvak ships, scattered throughout the fleet."

Alexander and Kamiel were stunned by the information

so freely given in such a matter of fact manner. It was true that each resurrected being from the past had been given the RNA from the brain of their deceased predecessor, to assist memory transference, but the way that the Trans-sentient had chosen to pass on her memories shocked them both.

Kamiel chose to communicate with Alexander privately by inserting a nannite filament into the human's brain and said, "Order the Toarvaks down using the Goss and take on board one of these amazing creatures for each ship until they are all accounted for. What a sacrifice to make!"

"When you think about it, we are all willing to give up our lives to rid the universe of this soulless destroyer of intelligent life," Alex replied. "Archive was just the first one to do so!"

Alexander reached out to a tentacle and grasped it in acknowledgement and thankfulness. He could feel the heat of the alien's touch as the tentacle wound around his arm and lifted him from the shingle with the aid of the others. Kamiel was also treated in the same manner and Small Portion lifted them effortlessly into the air until he was able to attach himself to Co-ordinator. The Guardian once more encapsulated his friend and Alex reached out with his mind, as all around them hundreds of young Trans-sentients grasped onto the two giant creatures. Below them lay the putrefying mass of the dead Tran-sentient already being attacked by scavengers, but tucked away in the hundreds of young were the memories of the telepathic touch of the Harvester.

"Goss!"

"I am here, Alexander!"

"Contact all the Toarvak ships that have organic crews to make rendezvous here at Toarvak Prime. They will have additional crew to take on until all of the young Trans-sentients carrying Archive's memories are accounted for," Alexander instructed and watched the forest underneath them undulate beneath.

.

CHAPTER NINE

Some time after the beginning and after the first unstable galaxies had torn themselves apart; the first giant stars went supernovae. Some of these unstable suns condensed afterwards to become neutron stars and developed into black holes. Over the billions of years after coming into existence, they became of monstrous size, as they reached out to any star that came within their gravitational grasp. Long before the stars entered its embrace, their outer substance was sucked down into the gravity well. These became the anchors for the new stable galaxies to form around. The billions of stars orbited around this greedy centre gradually stabilised. Many large stars in the spiral arms fell to the same destiny and became equally dangerous to their neighbours, but in time an equilibrium of balanced forces came into being.

One such singularity had come into existence in the spiral arm that held the star systems of the early confederation of worlds. It was positioned deeper into the centre where the stars were much closer together and the cosmic radiation was high. Those stars that had planets orbiting around them would never be host to any forms of life this close in to the galactic centre. After the war against the Goss, the Kresh, Gnathe and Humans had held council about the fate of the last Ark of the Goss. On board was an ancient weapon that the Goss had used to close off the wormhole that the Toarvaks had used to get to the Bazantii world. It had been considered that the ability to do this was so dangerous, as it put a permanent kink into the strings of force that held the universe together, that they had decided to put the Ark in quarantine.

Using the mind of Link-soo-shan as the controlling

influence, the Gnathe had built a group mind that included the Kresh and all the free humans and apes. The gestalt spread its telekinetic feelers into a local wormhole to drop the Arc towards the black hole's event horizon, where the intense gravitational force would bend time itself. Once there the godlike power at Link-soo-shan's disposal would twist it into a mobius ring. This meant that it had infinite length and existed outside of time. She blended the Kresh's knowledge of wormhole technology with the Gnathen method of bending space-time, using the enhancing power of the crystals. Link took control of the gestalt and twisted the ends of the wormhole into a ring, imprisoning the Ark to endlessly fall within it, until the very end of time itself. On board were the Lagdoo that had controlled the Ark and its weapon systems. The reptilians had decided in their coldly logical way that if the Ark were to be needed then a knowledgeable crew would also be a necessity.

Nine hundred thousand years later Link-soo-shan would have to collapse the ring and direct the Ark away from the singularity. It would not be easy!

Alexander ran his fingers through his hair and over the brow ridges of his forehead. The leader of the humans and apes no longer looked totally human with his enlarged forehead, cat's eyes and thickset body. To some extent he looked more like a tall Neanderthal than the basic human frame. Gnathen genetic structure had been melded into his DNA patterns. It gave him the additional psychic power from those extra lobes of brain that all Brood-mothers had. Hannah also had the same characteristics enhancing her small physique. She was perfecting her new crown of crystals, similar to the one that she had worn during the defeat of Link-soo-shan's endeavour to destroy the first attempt to wrest the Earth and Moon away from the expanding sun. It would give her a localised influence on time. It was also a telekinetic booster once linked to an electrical generator. Once again she had shaved her head so that a perfect contact could be made.

The new crew of Toarvak 6 were sat around the table that the ship had made to raise from the floor. They were watching Hannah as she began to increase the amount of power into the crown. The Gnathe perched at one side while the humans sat at the other and watched. Prim the trip'o-dal anchored her three legs in the locked position while B-o-g the Vogb rested the base of his cone shaped base firmly by her side and observed with all six eye-stalks the tableau before him. Kamiel, Asue and Solace had tuned their optical bands to all the visible and non-visible spectrums.

Hannah gave them all a cheerful smile and disappeared from sight.

She stopped time for herself, leaving those around the table frozen where they were sat, stood or perched. Carefully she left the table and cautious not to touch anyone she left her chair and walked away to the other side of the room. From there she manipulated the controls and brought herself back into the time-stream.

"That was a localised effect," she said and returned to the table. "I stopped subjective time for me only and it appeared as though all of you were frozen solid!"

"What was it you did when you defeated me at the laboratory when I nearly destroyed the project?" asked Link-soo-shan.

"I ran subjective time back for just the area of the room that we were in," Hannah answered. "It was sufficient to alter the timelines back onto their course before the ripple effect would have totally destroyed us all. I think that I could expand the field with extra power, to the size of the

Ark. It is big enough to hide all the Toarvak fleet inside if necessary, out of phase. I believe that if I am incorporated into the Toarvak when we hunt for the Ark it will give us an extra edge in wresting it from the endless trap that Link-soo-shan placed it for safety."

Alexander turned to Fredrick who was once more wearing Minnis to re-acquaint himself with the nannite and asked him, "Can you do the same trick?"

"In a word, no," he replied. "But Hannah, Minnis and I can combine ourselves and become a unit. By doing that we can board the Ark outside of time if placed inside the wormhole by a group mind. It will require a massive collection of Kresh, Gnathe and any other sentient minds that can come on board."

Link-soo-shan called a mental reminder to the group, "I was the controlling influence for the gestalt in placing the Ark into the mobius shaped wormhole by fusing it together. Doing it in reverse will require an intuitive grasp of the situation. The slightest deviation in the breaking of the wormhole's exit could shoot it down the black hole's throat. The gravitational pull will mash you into soup!"

"Not if we are out of phase," answered Minnis. I have never told the nannite collective, but during the time that I was part of Toarvak 6 I found the secret of slipping out of this universe! I can expand enough of my substance to envelope Hannah and Fredrick by several molecules thickness. Inside this container I can easily slip into the Ark's control room where the main drive can be activated and the time stasis crew warned about what we intend to do. Hannah can extend her grasp of time to encapsulate the entire Arc in the field and revert it to mainstream time."

"Is this possible, Hannah?" Alexander asked. "Can you be sure that what Minnis advises is a viable answer?"

"We will have one chance at this, my friends. This crown

can be worn by only the one who designed it and that is me," Hannah answered. "I will need a Toarvak mind at my disposal linked to mine. Fredrick, Minnis and I will group together. No, that will not do! We need an intuitive understanding of electronics at our disposal and a Kresh for stability."

A clear mental voice entered into the telepathic discussion as the Vogb said, "My race is born with this ability. First of spectrum, Blue/Orange/Green will be part of this group mind."

All of the assembly turned to face the conic. 'B-o-g's tendrils were agitated and the top ring of his upper cone radiated colours at a fast rate. His eyestalks fixed upon Alexander and Hannah's faces as the lower part of the inverted cone anchored down to the floor.

"Toarvak mind that will into the wormhole enter will be mine," added the powerful mind of Toarvak 12,402. *"Experience have I with wormholes more than any other Toarvak. Kresh have I on board that would be compatible to the others of the group mind proposed. Settled it is! I go! Those that are to go will transfer to me when the time comes."*

Thousands of light-years away from where Toarvak Prime used to orbit its star, Co-ordinator and Deep-thinker were contemplating a changed sky. It was twenty years since Archive had released her memories into the young Trans-sentients and they had boarded the Toarvaks to begin their journey towards the Andromeda galaxy. The Kresh stellar engineers had relocated the nannite created world of central government away from the collision area with its sun and all the other planets including the nannite civilization on the fringes.

All of the gas giants in the system had been mined for their crystals before the moving of worlds had taken place. An endless train of out of phase Toarvaks had made their way to the bottom of the turbulent atmosphere to the strange area of the crystal rich strata. Here they scooped whatever they found from the murky depths and stored them on selected moons placed in orbit around the newly moved worlds. The globular cluster was beginning to take shape on the fringe of this spiral arm. So far there were more than a thousand stars, locked in orbits that kept them stable with each other. The amount of cosmic radiation suffusing the cluster had been carefully monitored by the vast group minds that were in charge of the globular assembly. The distances between the stars were dictated by the living spaces requirements.

Some of the steadily burning suns had planets that bore life to the same species and were placed in Trojan orbits, so that all three worlds were locked into a steady state system like beads on a necklace. These were the ones that project 'Time Fisher' had found over and over again at the point of harvest by the energy being. All of them had the same DNA, although they had been rescued from different time periods and different suns. So called treasure planets had been placed in positions further out on the bitter cold fringe of the 'Goldilocks' orbits so that they could be mined for their ores.

In a few hundred years, it would be time for the greatest group mind of all to be assembled from every sentient creature in the globular cluster, to wrench it away from the parent galaxy. A wormhole big enough to swallow a mass of stars 200 light years across would be needed to send it on its way. Hundreds of thousands of crystals were being positioned to build the greatest star-gate that had ever been attempted. Stars had been moved and positioned to become an outer ring to the globular cluster. Placed in orbit around these stars were multiple Stargates anchored to these suns waiting for the command to open up a wormhole large enough to swallow the entire cluster. Each gate would twist space around itself and join one to another like a giant necklace across the void. The very strings that held the universe together would be plaited together and would rip the fabric of space-time asunder, sending the globular cluster on its way.

Deep-thinker focussed his eyes onto the great darkness, searching for the point of light that the Greater Magellanic Cloud was situated.

"Can you see our new home?" he said to Co-ordinator.

"In the great scheme of things it will be temporary, as the cloud will interact with the amalgamated galaxy of Andromeda and our own millions of years in the future. With a time span of that nature however, I feel that we will have little to worry about," Co-ordinator replied. "If you scan the eastern horizon you can just see the edges of the cloud rising above the hills."

"I find the blackness disturbing when we are looking outwards, knowing that each point of light out there is a galaxy housing billions of star systems," Deep Thinker replied. "Any one of them could contain a life harvesting entity, just as unable to realise that organic sentient life has a right to exist in its own right."

"I would judge that we would be far enough away that if so, they will never be aware of us. There are times that I spend thinking about those brave souls that have remained behind to distract or destroy the entity that has been prevented from feeding off our life energies. I feel a sense of remorse and shame that we brought these people back from the time of the Goss to die for us."

Deep Thinker wrapped his tentacles around Co-ordinator and brought her close and replied, "They were all given a choice to stay in this time and come with us. None took that choice! Every sentient being decided to go to Andromeda and do what they could to prevent the Harvester from finding out that we had gone. Soon the invading arm will start to impinge the edge of the spiral and start the destruction. Before that happens the time exiles will have to be inside Andromeda and do whatever they can. They are not like us! They are not the result of nine hundred thousand years of peace. There could never be a place in our society for hunter/killers. With each sentient species connected to the Goss in telepathic harmony, the idea of conflict will never occur for us, nor could we practise it."

"They are going to retrieve a weapon that was used against them at the time of the conflict with the Goss," Co-ordinator replied. "It is beyond my imagination or comprehension how they will accomplish this. The Gnathe, Link-soo-shan parked the last Ark of the Goss in some kind of orbit around a singularity when she was in control of an immense group mind. Even now with the stellar engineers as accomplished as the Kresh and present day Gnathe have become, such a feat of spatial engineering would not be tried."

Deep Thinker sighed as he tried to reassure his lifelong mate and companion. He gained height and let the wind take him for some distance until he was over the top of a grove of fruit trees. He stripped the fruit laden branches and inserted them unto his mouth and crunched them into pulp. A grazing animal leapt out from underneath the base of the tree and the Tran-sentient snatched it up with his front set of tentacles, broke its neck and sent it on the way of the fruit pulp.

As he ate, he sent his feelings to Co-ordinator's mind, "The future of us all and I do mean every sentient being that will relocate to the cluster, rests in their abilities. I have been inside the minds of the humans and the Gnathe who were brought back. I have shared the consciousness of the

Kresh who built the first Toarvaks that fought against the Goss when it was a parasite. I have spent time delving into the rainbow world of the conics who were also retrieved from the past. All of them have a ruthlessness that you cannot imagine and I will not share with you, lest you also dream the dreams that torment me. They are not of our time and I believe that they will do all that they can to make sure that we escape to our new home."

Co-ordinator shuddered as she lifted up into the wind to join her mate in feeding, accepting his counsel and said, "I miss Archive and her store of the past. She showed a bravery that shames me in the choice she took in going with them. She too was of their time and will travel wherever they go and our race of Trans-sentients will colonise another area of the universe if all goes well. It has been a long time since we had youth in our species."

On the other side of the galaxy, some ninety thousand light years away in the spiral arm that once housed the Earth, before it had been plucked out of the void complete with the entire solar system, a Toarvak fleet had stopped and was orbiting a star. Many gas giants orbiting around their suns had been mined for crystal and a series of wormhole manipulators had been built with focusing abilities. These were constructed to be inside each other so that similar to a telescope they could be extended from the base. That base would be the Ark of the Goss. The main part of the fleet concentrated on this task while Toarvak 12,402 and Toarvak 6 prepared to drop towards the singularity where Link-soo-shan had 'parked' the last Ark of the Goss. To do this they needed a special crew.

During the twenty years or so since the awakening of the time-fished sentients, the Gnathe had instigated a selective breeding program. A major alteration of the Gnathen male and female type had taken place. The Brood-mothers has instigated the growth of the extra lobes to the brain of their kindred so that they would be more receptive to the same psychic powers as the Brood-mothers. This was so they could be drawn into the group minds as an extra power-base. The Kresh had become very interested in this enhancement and had urged the Gnathe to attempt this measure on their genetic structure.

Khann-link-sool had immediately volunteered her services as an instinctive genetic engineer and transferred to another Gnathen Toarvak. Once Kamiel had removed some living flesh samples from a number of mature Kresh, she had inserted the living cells into her brooding pouch to study. The hermaphrodites had a fascinating double helix genetic structure that had both x and y-chromosomes hinged together so that the Kresh fluctuated from male to female. What triggered the change was mating and maturity. After carrying young the female stage would retreat from dominance and the Kresh would become male. After mating several times the Kresh would again drift towards being female. Once all the eggs carried by the ovaries were used up, they stayed male and remained this sex until death. The psychic abilities of the Kresh had been bred into the race from centuries before they had built the Toarvaks. Each Kresh with the 'talent' had been sought out by others of the same abilities and slowly the entire race became telepathic. Those without the ability had been refused the right to procreate until the old genetic framework had almost disappeared. The ability to form group minds came later with the construction of the first artificial intelligences that the Kresh found that they could blend with. If the parasitic Goss had managed to infect the whole of the race of the Kresh and incorporated them with the Toarvaks, then the whole galaxy would have fallen to its domination. This is why they had thrown their world into its sun, rather than let it fall into the reach of the Goss. Their rescue had made them fanatical about rescuing those civilizations that would have fed the Harvester's hunger.

As she had done with the living cells of the humans after her rescue from Link-soo-shan at the early part of the Gnathe/human relationship, Khann sent her mind inwards to the brooding pouch. Here she discovered the basic genetic makeup of the Kresh. She scanned the double helix for similarities to the Gnathe base structure and found certain 'anchor' points. Here the recent change in the age-old pattern where the psychic mutation had occurred branched off from the main sequence. There was a similarity to the Brood-mother's genetic twist that they had installed recently into their own males and females. Lost in a studied trance the ancient mind in its brand new body began to insert some of the genetic characteristics of the Gnathe into the Kresh genomes.

She felt the mind of her granddaughter, Ender, slip into her consciousness with the addition of the analytical personality of Link-soo-shan. The twin minds studied the changes and in admiration they called into the group the minds of Suzzan and Trann. Ender's daughters picked up the invitation so Marren and Azander merged into the group. Now a genetic expert composed of seven blended minds led by Khann, considered the situation in a depth unique to the Gnathe. All of them were more than instinctive genetic engineers and had taken the 'art' to a higher plane. The living cells were reprogrammed to be changeling activators and reduced to a soup, fed by the environment of Khann's breeding pouch.

Satisfied that they had accomplished the enhancements desired by the Kresh the guiding minds withdrew, leaving Khann to play host to the increasing, living cells. All seven of the Gnathe realised that they were more than just hungry! Three days had been spent locked into the genetic study of the Kresh and only now were they aware that they had been kept clean by attentive kindred as they had voided bodily functions.

As they ate at the table provided by Toarvak 602, Khann reached out with her mind, "Goss," she said.

"Yes Khann-link-sool. I am here as always," the symbiont answered.

"Find me the mind of the First of Clan, 'Dappled Grey' and tell him/her that I have the answer. Ask those who are willing to chance the change to make their way to Toarvak 602 where I am residing at present and make the crossing. First I must eat and drink, then sleep for a while."

The billions of the spores of the Goss had been genetically modified from parasite to symbiotic by the nannites and were present in all the sentient creatures that travelled inside the Toarvaks and all settled worlds. The mind of the Goss extended right across the galaxy and lived in all of its hosts. The Milky Way galaxy stretched around one, hundred, thousand light years across its spiral arms and was seven hundred light years thick. Throughout the one hundred, billion stars, those that bore life-sustaining planets had been settled by the galactic civilisation. Many had been set aside for development. Every sentient being was 'inoculated' at birth by these spores and grew up in a telepathic community. The unique mind of the Goss was instantly aware in all of its hosts, by infusing itself throughout the wormhole systems of the galaxy.

It was an amalgam of every sentient thing that existed, yet had no mind of its own other than the combination of species that hosted it. The Goss was a telepathic phone system that enjoyed being what it was. Its limitation was that it could only be a carrier to the hosts. Outside of the galaxy across the void, the colliding Andromeda system was silent. It teamed with life of all sorts similar to the life forms of the Milky Way, as the same DNA had been spread over and over again by the Harvester in its hunger for life energy.

First of 'Dappled Grey' was currently male again and was in the upswing of his male aggressive mood, when the summons via the Goss came through. His female days were now over as the ovaries he had once carried were now being absorbed into his body. He would now continuously dominate the clan until he died. The domination would take the form of ultimate decision maker and receive the occasional sexual advance by the females to spread his genes into the clan.

"Toarvak!"

"I hear you, 'First'.

"Take us to impingement with Toarvak 602. There will be a number of the clan disembarking. They will be returning soon, so stay adjacent to the vessel. I too will be boarding and transferring for a while. I am to be part of the group mind, retrieving the last ark of the Goss. You will place me onto the flight deck of Toarvak 12,042 and leave me there."

"Wait shall I, until return you do!" the Toarvak replied.

First of 'Dappled Grey' smiled inwardly at the artificial intelligence's remark and answered, "A new 'First' you may need to help chose. I cannot say with any certainty that I will return. The only thing that matters is the retrieval of the Ark!"

The two Toarvaks were almost ready and the crews had been selected with care. Each combined mind of sentients and Toarvak had practised some of the manoeuvres that would be necessary. Toarvak 12,402 would plunge towards the singularity and enter the closed mobius loop of the wormhole. Toarvak 6 would hold back to become an anchor point. A hundred light-years back, one hundred Toarvaks fully crewed and carrying contingents of different aliens all with their own special skills would begin the mind meld that would be controlled by Link-soo-shan. They began the headlong plunge towards the black hole's event horizon.

They were entering an area of space that had been swept clean of all matter. It was a void empty of stars. Those whose spatial orbits had intersected the reach of the singularity had been sucked in and absorbed. With each stellar mass added, the reach of the black hole increased. Behind the Toarvak a mantle of stars scattered across the skies, blazing intensely all across the spatial arm.

In front of them were the densely packed star-fields of the centre of the galaxy bright with stellar radiation. In the centre hung a warping influence. The stars rippled around a hungry mouth that could not be seen, only the distortion of its effect. It had a reach of light-years and close to its event horizon, time and space were warped and twisted in such away that reality become redefined.

The one-time Ultimate Ruler of the Gnathen Empire drew on the strength and power of the combined minds far away at the edge of the singularity's reach. As the group mind built, the power washed over her and her awareness increased exponentially.

Working with her, the small group mind of the Toarvak put itself out of phase with the dimensions of the universe and out of reach of the singularity. She scanned the complicated strings holding the universe together searching for an anomaly. Somewhere in the tangle of wormholes would be an endless circuit, twisted into a mobius strip of a two dimensional object in a three dimensional universe. Riding this strip would be the last Ark of the Goss, endlessly caught in a fraction of time, forever in stasis. The mind reached out and found it.

CHAPTER TEN

Link-soo-shan reached out and felt for the twisted wormhole that she had sealed off, over nine hundred thousand years ago. On the edges of the wormhole she had left some key features that she could latch onto should she ever need to reopen it. This close to the hungry gravity well of the black hole, even out of phase it was possible for the collective mind to feel its siren pull. The whole of the Kresh gestalt that was the backbone of the mind-meld reached for the Gnathen contingent to hold it together. By her mental side was Alexander, channelling the power at her disposal. Out in the void hurtling towards the intersecting orbit of the closed wormhole, Toarvak 12,402 and its collective mind dropped out of phase.

Inside the Toarvak the punishing gravitational attraction abruptly shut off and reverted to normal. The immense pull dropped away as the ship hung suspended in a dimensionless void intersected by thousands of threads; - all wormholes connected to the singularity and some looped around it. First of Dappled Grey extended his will and the other four organic minds linked with the Toarvak did the impossible in concert with Link-soo-shan. They flipped into the endless, infinite loop of the closed wormhole that Link had pulled shut, with the Ark trapped inside it. Sensors at maximum, the Toarvak collective reached out to find the Ark and found itself alone in its own time encapsulated bubble.

Hannah joined her mind to Fredrick's and then to the cold mind of Minnis. The three reached out and added the mind of the Vogb. Blue/Orange/Green's intuitive knowledge of electronics added to the collective. The next mind produced the stability of the Kresh and linked them to the Toarvak. First of Dappled Grey could not exist both inside the collective Toarvak and the bubble that Minnis would create. He would need to transfer from the Toarvak and hand over his position to another unit. This would be Link-soo-shan's Brood-mother-daughter, Suzzan. She would provide both beacon and linkage back to the God-mind that her mother controlled. As the silver, nannite material of the Toarvak released 'First of Dappled Grey' it oozed up and over the Gnathe.

Minnis swept the Kresh into her embrace and encapsulated them all.

Toarvak 12,402 increased her sensitivity and linked herself to the miniature Toarvak that awaited her instruction.

"Minnis-Hannah, reach into the time barrier and twist us into the same timeframe as the Ark," the Toarvak collective instructed.

The augmented Hannah mind reached into the crystal Matrix and fed electricity into the crystal crown to increase its reach. The conic inserted his charged tendril into the lattice surrounding Hannah's shaven head allowing her to access his stored charge. Fredrick gave her his strength, while Minnis added to her logical systems. 'First of Dappled Grey' provided his knowledge of stellar engineering and wormhole control.

The time field swelled out to encompass the entire limits of Toarvak 12,402 and they winked into the same timeframe as the Ark. All around the silver ship they were aware of a twisted ribbon that seemed to be both flat and yet touched the sides of the ship on all of its surface. The Toarvak sped along this mobius dimension, searching for the last Ark of the Goss. Hannah-Minnis increased the amount of power she was taking from the conic, Blue/Orange/Green. She slowed up the time frame and the mass of the Toarvak accelerated along the strip back towards the time-frozen artificial moon.

The gestalt that was Toarvak 12,402 rapidly gave the orders, *"Now! Hannah-Minnis disengage! Link-soo-shan remove us from the wormhole!"*

The mind of the massive collective, headed by Link-soo-shan, reached out and plucked the Toarvak out of phase from the twisted wormhole, leaving Hannah-Minnis alone. Power was fed into the framework that Link was strapped into, activating the crystals built into its structure. Next to her, sat strapped into his, sat Alexander directing the psychic power at their disposal and working as a channel. Throughout the Toarvaks positioned in a far orbit well out of the reach of the raging furnace of the black hole, thousands of Kresh and Gnathe were lending their minds to the collective. Threaded into this gestalt were the Thipdar, Vogb and humans including the apes that had all been fished out of time. This mind was far greater than the Gnathen and human construct that had torn the Earth away from the expanding sun and put it in orbit to form the three worlds civilization.

Held in reserve were the Lagdoo's reptilian logic and the entire nannite combined mind, including the Toarvaks. Kamiel had insisted on this arrangement to run this operation. He could not forget that when he had taken a thousand Toarvak minds into a great collective, to pluck Toarvak 6 from the heart of a sun, he had felt the awesome power. The lure to repeat this exercise lay constantly at the edge of his mind. When they finally entered the Andromeda galaxy and confronted the entity that ruled there, he felt that it would be better to have something in reserve. He stood in the observatory on the flight deck of Toarvak 6 and strained his optic band's visual ability beyond the natural vision of his flesh and blood companions. Seeing into the energy realms beyond ultra-violet and infra-red he was able to appreciate the massive amounts of radiation that were being warped and twisted by the pull of the collapsed star. Somewhere close to the energy-sink his friends were going to wrest the super-weapon away from the safe place that Link-soo-shan had placed it, hundreds of thousands of years ago.

Asue reached out and touched Kamiel on the shoulder and said, "They are on their way back to us. I reached out to them using the Goss! Toarvak 12,402 is safely on its way back to this position. This small piece of organic living material we all carry and keep alive that is host to the Goss spores, enables a true mind melding of nannite to organic. Through this gift I can appreciate what it is to be alive in an organic sense."

Kamiel turned suddenly to confront his nannite friend and companion and replied, "Asue! Do you yearn to be organic? Have the long centuries of endless awareness left a mark upon you?"

"No! What I am is all I wish to be. I am Guardian to these beings. My function is fulfilled far beyond Alexander McBald's original programming. All that I meant was that my appreciation of what it means to be organic enables me to understand them far more than in the past," she answered.

Kamiel reached out and took hold of her silver hands and joined her nannite substance to his in a bond beyond the senses of organic possibilities. He projected his warmth and feelings for the creature of Nano-technology that had stood by him for thousands of years.

"We still have much to do and our responsibility has

increased beyond our maker's imagination," he said and released Asue's hands.

The deck beside them swelled up into a pillar that transformed itself into Toarvak 6's adopted form. The silver woman adjusted the folds of her dress and fixed the long flowing hair into a plaited bun at the back of her head.

The combined minds of her crew were in control of the avatar, but it was Emelia's mind that was in control of the gestalt.

"Kamiel and Asue be assured that our sister ship Toarvak 12,402 is about to enter our universal state. The collective Hannah-Minnis has launched themselves at the Ark. Link-soo-shan's great group mind, stands ready to realign the wormhole. Stand ready to receive the Ark, as in their universal dimension, no time has passed. Only here will time pass as it does," the collective advised them. *"We are ready!"*

Outside of time and space the nannite shell of Minnis was about to enter the flickering mass of the last Ark of the Goss. Inside her and out of phase with the universe, encapsulated in a bubble of time were two humans, a Kresh and a Vogb. Using the methods of propulsion unique to the Toarvaks, Minnis swam through the substance of the moon until she was able to enter the control centre of the Ark. Here she disembarked the crew by reabsorbing the several molecules thick cloak that she had spread over her 'guests,' while Hannah maintained the time bubble.

There were ten of the Lagdoo stood at their crew positions, frozen in time along with the rest of the ark. Braced around them were the support bars and framework that they were strapped into. They were similar in build to the Gnathe with large heads, sharp teeth and the same type of bird-like knee joints. Their prehensile tails were wrapped around the bars as an extra anchor point. The scales along the back were coloured in iridescent blues and greens, while their chests and bellies were a dappled cream and grey. All of them were slightly bigger than Fredric and were dressed with crossed bandoliers carrying a multitude of pouches.

Hannah and the Vogb remained coupled together so that the human could draw on the electrical energy of the Conic's stored charge. She enlarged the time bubble to nullify the effects of the stasis field that kept the entire Ark from being part of the universe's time scale. With practised ease the collective mind reached out to include the Lagdoo. Within them all lived the spores of the Goss and an information exchange ensued as Minnis took their minds into machine time to avoid any accidents with the controls.

The Lagdoo flight controller and crew accepted that hundreds of thousands of years that had passed, in their usual logical fashion. Minnis then released control of the group mind to allow independent thought in real time. As the controls had not been altered since the boarding party had come aboard, the Lagdoo left them on standby.

Hannah brought the Ark's crew into the picture and explained what they had to do when Link-soo-shan and the combined group mind at her command ripped open the twisted wormhole. Maximum lift would be needed to exceed the black hole's gravitational pull. A possible immediate relocation to another wormhole leading away from the singularity might need to be chosen, or it would mash them to the walls of the control room. As soon as they recombined as a group mind they would have to reach out for the greater collective and trust in the once Ultimate Ruler to warp space and bring them in.

The Ark's group mind reached out and made contact with the godlike power watching out for them.

Link-soo-shan increased the amount of power running through the telekinetic crystals and wielded the ability like a precision axe, cutting the twisted wormhole. At this precise time, Alexander fed the mental energy into her augmented consciousness and linked up the many different alien species that gave this mind its power. He called upon the massed Vogb to release the pent up energy stored inside them and directed it into the crystal lattice. The telekinetic crystals increased the extent of the field as the electrical discharge flooded into them and Link-soo-shan untwisted the wormhole by diverting it out and away from the black hole in the direction that the Ark was travelling. She fractured space-time and opened a star-gate in a safe proximity to Toarvak 6 and linked the Ark's velocity to theirs.

Half a light year away a distortion occurred and the hollowed out moon shot out of the wormhole into the hard vacuum of space. The two Toarvaks edged closer to the Ark and touched the surface of the vessel and welded themselves in place. The Lagdoo engaged the warp drive and took the combined ships away from the safe orbit that the Toarvaks had maintained and headed out to where the rest of the armada were parked. The combined minds began the process of regaining their individualities and first the Vogb withdrew, disengaging their electrically charged tentacles from the crystal lattice surrounding Link-soo-shan. They had surrounded the framework hiding from sight the Gnathen mind-master from the sight of the rest of the crew. Each double-coned body had gripped the Vogb next to it by the rest of their tentacles so that they resembled a nest of snakes. Across the void the rest of the aliens also left the group mind and became once more a definite individual.

On board the Ark, the Lagdoo were doing a diagnostic check of all the systems while the 'rescue crew' began to take stock of what they had achieved. Minnis had plugged herself into the main computer and was doing her own system check to re-acquaint herself with the vessel. Fredrick was helping Hannah to pack safely away the crown of crystals that allowed the scientist to control localised time into his haversack.

Alexander, Link-shan-soo and the rest of the crew of the Toarvak 6 and Toarvak 12,402 exchanged their positions to the command centre of the last Ark of the Goss. Kamiel, Asue and Solace represented the nannite contingent scattered throughout the armada.

The Guardian sent the request to the symbiont, "Goss! Connect all the minds that are part of this expedition."

The Goss connected its spores to link to only the minds within the Armada and shut down all links with the rest of the galaxy wide civilization allowing Kamiel to speak to them all.

"Sentient beings all! We have retrieved the weapons and living space that are part of the last Ark. Now we will have somewhere for the organic members of our taskforce to rest and live. What we are about to achieve, has never been done before by any sentient being apart from our adversary. We will need to travel to the edges of our galaxy and search for wormholes that connect this one to Andromeda. We know that they exist because this abomination has been able to cross over from time immemorial to feed upon us in the past. As you know, the Kresh and the Gnathe have changed history by collecting up all those civilizations that were to be this thing's life energy, thus creating an alternative universe in this area. Whatever awaits us in Andromeda will have never come against such as we. We will have the element of surprise on our side, but that will only work once! All Toarvaks will attach themselves to this hollowed out moon and provide a shield so that the whole moon can be taken out of phase when required. The telescopic star-gate will need to be fitted along the equator during the long journey to Andromeda. To be used, it would need to be disengaged and carried by six Toarvaks away from the moon and reset after use to be repositioned back along the equator for travelling. For this to be done a number of support pylons would need to be built straddling the equator. This will be a construction task to be undertaken by the Guardians, as only nannites would be able to withstand the conditions inside the wormhole while we are travelling."

All Toarvaks controlled by the nannite Guardians made their way first out of orbit around the black hole and positioned themselves around the equator of the hollowed out moon in a double ring. The rest of the Toarvaks followed suit until every sentient ship was anchored down onto the surface of the Ark and touching each other. A silver skin now enveloped the moon's surface so that it resembled a giant silver ball. Immediately the nannites began to transport material from underneath the Toarvaks to form a central mountain range, that would be constructed as a giant flange with a turned over lip. Each Toarvak would be left anchored onto a mushroomed spike as the material was wasted away beneath them and altered into inert nannite to begin the formation of the flange.

The Lagdoo ran up the searching system to engage the nearest wormhole leading towards the edge of the Milky Way galaxy and found a suitable string. They opened the hole and let the moon be pulled through. Space and time ripped apart as the giant craft dropped through the rift in space.

Weeks turned into months as the Ark negotiated the wormhole, travelling ever faster towards the nearest edge in the direction of Andromeda. Inside the Ark the eco-system had long since come on line and the different life forms had settled in and spread out along the gravitational limits of the spinning moon. Once more the Insectoids made use of the higher and lower regions with the lighter gravity and built their hives just below the poles. The rest of the living space soon became a mixed race area with every sort of alien specie making its home next to another. Suspended in the centre of the moon was the artificial sun. Rotating around this was a chequered ring of transparent and darkened panels in a cross-sectional shape of a 'U'. This allowed night and day to follow each other, as the dark squares cut off the light at intervals.

Prim and the family Smelch had taken over a clear flattened area under a shelter consisting of a roof on stilts. There were many of these areas to be found, some with furniture and some without. When the artificial rain fell from the 'skies,' shelter was a necessity. Inside the Ark were woods and ploughed, crop bearing fields with grassy plains. There were small seas that abounded with fish. Mountains rose high enough into the skies for ice to form and then melt as the temperature fluctuated. It was an artificial world with a landmass equal to a normal sized planet but with much smaller seas. The whole system was a self-sustaining eco-system that could maintain itself for many thousands of years between planetary stops. The Ark had been built by the amalgamation of all the science open to the Goss. Some of it had not been studied by any other race of sentient beings since it had been put together.

Prim's people had once helped to run this world when they were hosts to the Goss. It had faded into legend as the hundreds of thousands of years had passed. She was fascinated by the workings of this artificial world and was constantly eager to learn more. The trip'o-dal concentrated her mind and contacted the Goss.

"Goss!"

"Yes Prim?"

"Can you locate the human beings and Gnathe known as Alexander and Link-soo-shan?"

"I can," answered the Goss and provided the telepathic bridge.

Prim entered the minds of the people she needed and said, "I need to meet with you, face to face. Can you come here?"

There was a 'pop' of displaced air as the human and the Gnathe appeared in front of the trip'o-dal.

Link-soo-shan leaned forwards to bend down to Prim's height and lightly ran her tongue over the trip'o-dal's forehead while Alexander placed his hand upon the top shoulder of the prime female of family Smelch.

Upon flesh-to-flesh contact the telepathic bond was private between them.

"Why the need for secrecy?" asked the Gnathe.

Prime shuddered under the mental scrutiny and replied, "It is the genetically altered Kresh that bother me. I feel that Khann-link-sool and the collective mind may have altered those Kresh that received the genetic enhancements beyond what their species were meant to achieve. These strengthened abilities may not be beneficial!"

Alexander dug into the Thipdar's mind and viewed her worries and concerns.

"You feel that there is an imbalance amongst the Kresh!" thought the human.

"My family have been amongst the Kresh for generations. We have a long association with them," insisted Prim. "There is talk of a restrictive breeding program to eliminate those 'natural born' Kresh by the enhanced ones. We need all of these people knitted together as a united front if we are to carry out our task. So I came to you as the leading figures of the defence council to voice my misgivings."

"I will see Khann," declared Link-soo-shan and promptly disappeared leaving Alexander with the trip'o-dal.

Khann-link-sool was settling down to her 'morning' meal as the dark square rotated away from the artificial sun high overhead. She had a pouch full of young kindred that would soon be born onto this artificial world. The genetic enhancements had borne fruit and they would be all capable of greater psychic abilities than the kindred had been able to draw on in the past. She was quietly confidant that her efforts would be an asset to the upcoming struggle and had settled down to breakfast when Link-soo-shan arrived out of the empty air.

"Greetings Khann! I see you are doing your bit for the confrontation, by the size of your pouch," she said and hopped onto the vacant perch beside her old adversary.

"What brings you here, Tyrant! I feel this is hardly a social visit," the geneticist replied.

"A mistake we all made when we modified the Kresh!

You have lived too long with humans," Link scoffed. "It has given you their dreadful sense of humour! Tyrant! That was so long ago and several body shifts and still you manage to get in a dig about the past. It is a good thing that I put such childish things behind me. Just remember if it had not been for me and my ridiculous need for revenge at the time, we would not be here now!"

"At the time you would have killed me! I well remember that! Still we have done much together, you and I in times past, so tell me what is the problem with the Kresh?"

"Simply this, my meddling friend; - megalomania has set in. Those that are enhanced feel that they are the way of the Kresh to be," Link stated and reached for some toasted pod-fruit. "Leading the faction is our old friend 'First of Dappled Grey'"!

"But all of the enhanced ones are males who have achieved the last sex change," Khann replied as she ate. "They can only breed as males! The enhancements are passed down through the female line when the Kresh are female. It is the females who are genetically the designers of the next generation. They know that!"

"That is why the situation has become ridiculous. You and I need to pay a visit to the Kresh and remind them of this with our Brood-mother daughters. We will take with us a shielding crystal each and teach them a lesson in Gnathen physical restraint. The cure for megalomania is humiliation in front of their own people!"

"Just remember that we will need them as an anchor when we form the group mind to take on the Harvester," Khann replied so they must not be too damaged!"

"There is ample time for them to recover, Khann," Link

laughed and flexed her young body's muscles. "We could do with a work out!"

Kamiel gave his friend a long eye-less stare from his optical band and said, "Alexander! I find it difficult to believe what you have told me. I have enough to do outside this vessel without behaving as referee between the Kresh and the Gnathe!"

"It is an organic thing, old friend. We need challenge and locked inside this artificial world there will come from time to time the need to resort to physical means," Alex replied to the silver form that stood next to him. "I know that you are building the 'ring' around this world to launch the star-gate when we need to in the future, but you must heed my words. We need Asue and whoever you can spare from the project, to recreate a shielded dome with an amphitheatre."

"I will accept what you say," the Guardian said and walked away towards the connection to the outer surface.

He stopped abruptly and walked back to where Alexander stood.

"Tell me," he said, "Did this idea come from a certain Gnathe?"

Alexander laughed at the expressionless silver face that was inclined towards him and replied, "Yes and no! Link-soo-shan and I have thought about the solution to the Kresh problem and have agreed that this idea could have many uses. Even Khann and many others agree that some things need more than logic to resolve them. If you and Asue are agreeable to providing medical attention to prevent the occasional serious injuries turning into deaths, then we can begin once the amphitheatre is built."

Asue had changed her many of her attitudes throughout

the long centuries that had followed the defeat of the Goss. She, just as Kamiel, had endured death at the mind onslaught of Link-soo-shan during the attack on the time laboratory. When Hannah had spun time back and re-created her, the action had wiped out all the defensive programming that Alexander McBald had made sure was integrated into her personality. She was now her own person and no longer subject to the basic programming that all other nannites were created with. Kamiel's construction, known as Minnis, was also free willed. They were the only nannites in the galaxy who could kill a sentient creature. The responsibilities of this ability remained a heavy duty amongst the three of them.

The female minded Guardian had modified the inside of the artificial world and had added to the original design. Now, a network of monorail systems stretched around the inside, connecting all of the different eco-systems peculiar to the alien species who lived and farmed the landscape. Because of the spinning moon's artificial gravity by centrifugal force, no right-angle turns could be designed into the system. Clover-leafs were instigated at crossover points and the rails angled out to connect with other systems and junctions. It was possible to get around the inside of the moon, but as Lars once observed, it could be a white-knuckle ride! She selected a terminus that was built over a spare area of ground and began to construct the stadium there. She had to keep in mind the different resting places for each alien being. Some had to be flat, while others needed perches and seating arrangements. Over the top of the arena was a nannite bridge that carried a master shielding crystal controlled by Asue with a similar system to the Habitat's dome on Jupiter that had kept Link-soo-shan out.

Once switched on and fed power, all psychic abilities were turned completely off. The only telepathic power that worked would be supplied by the Goss, which did not seem to be affected by the shield. Now the games could begin!

CHAPTER ELEVEN

A week or so later, the Kresh had at first reacted to the Gnathen way of settling the dispute with disbelief. The fact that each Gnathe had taken a shielding crystal with them that 'turned off' the enhanced psychic power of the genetically altered Kresh, forced them to reconsider the situation. The basic telepathic connection of the Goss made it possible for them to communicate one alien to another.

"You are interfering with our species and the right to enhance ourselves," First of Dappled Grey insisted.

Khann was insistent in her rebuttal and replied, "Your argument is flawed. You asked *me* to look at the prospect of genetic enhancement of your species. Now you are flying in the face of logic, by insisting that the abilities be genetically passed on to your offspring. As only 'last change' males have been given the genetically altering serum, you know full well it is not possible! You must understand that the unforeseen side effect to this enhancement is megalomania! We have a cure for that."

"Hand to hand combat in an arena! How civilized is that?"

"You will lose," the Gnathe replied, "and in doing so it will burn itself out of your system!"

"Lose!"

The Kresh let fly with an ultrasonic screech of rage and a swinging fist that was caught by Asue before it reached the taunting Gnathe. She flowed into his nervous system and paralysed his muscles.

"Not here," she said. "I have prepared a place for this to take place. Now listen to me and I will not have any dissent amongst you. All genetically enhanced male Kresh will make their way to the monorail system and make their way to the arena. The rest of the Kresh will attend if they can. Those that cannot will view the events by way of the Goss. Do I make myself clear?"

"You do! Please let me go now," replied 'First of Dappled Grey' and relaxed his muscles.

Asue released the Kresh from his state of paralysis and motioned the Gnathe away by a wave of her hand.

The Gnathen delegates left the Kresh to make their own arrangements and made their own way to the arena.

All across the inside of the artificial world anything other than essential work had stopped. Harvested crops had been stored away in silos and all meat animals had been turned out to fields or locked securely inside stables. Every alien species had found a safe place to rest and watch the proceedings through the eyes of those at the arena through the telepathic reach of the Goss. The enhanced Kresh had been quarantined from their families and penned into an enclosure with a full view of the proceedings.

Likewise the Gnathe had decided to occupy a vacant area directly opposite their opponents. The shielding generator was at full power and was being monitored by Hannah, who was sat overlooking the arena from a balcony just under the bridge. The arena was shaped as a circular pit with a bridge spanning the combat zone. Around the arena Asue had built a tiered stadium so that those who came here could watch the proceedings safely. In the centre of the bridge was a large shielding crystal being trickle fed a pulsating electrical charge. While it was activated all natural physic powers were effectively cancelled.

The only telepathic power that worked was the symbiotic linkup using the Goss. As all the sentient people were carrying the spores, they were all mentally joined together, as the mind of the Goss lived in them all. As the many sentient aliens that lived inside the Ark were all connected together it made the combined mind of the Goss a formidable creature and an excellent librarian. Having no real mind of its own the Goss was a combination of minds. New additions to its composite mind were the many components of Archive that were scattered all over the inside of the artificial world. The young Tran-sentients had at Archives' insistent consent, eaten her brain alive to ingest her mind and distribute the ancient store of knowledge into themselves. The floating creatures were the only life form that could 'listen in' to the thoughts of the Harvester and recognise it and know where it was situated.

Inside the arena and standing against the walls of the stadium were a number of nannite medical specialists who would rush into the melee and prevent death from occurring by mischance. Kamiel had insisted upon this safeguard, as each mind would be necessary some time in the future. In extreme cases it might be more practical to download the mind into a crystal and re-grow a new clone. This had yet to happen, but Asue had made sure that she had covered all possibilities.

'First of Dappled Grey' stormed out of the enclosure to the centre of the ring. Waiting to meet him was Khann-link-sool balanced on her toes with tail tucked to one side.

The Kresh crouched forward and flexed the muscles of his double elbowed arms and splayed out the three fingers and opposable thumbs ready to grip. 'First' puffed out his cheeks extended his whiskers and flattened the giant ears down his back. His large splayed feet dug into the sand with his toes.

Khann watched for the signs of a charge, as the Kresh flexed his knees forwards and dropped into a crouch, shuffling forwards as he came. 'First of Dappled Grey' was a heavily built male, still very active after his last sex change. Up against the giant form of the Gnathen Brood-mother he still presented a formidable challenge. His head would still come up to her chest when she stood up and his body weight was a match for hers. Her advantage was that she was not insanely angry and could fight in a more logical fashion. How long that would last would remain to be seen!

First abruptly hopped swiftly towards the Gnathe and reached out for her arms with his extensively wide grasp. His plan was to get to close quarters and throw the Gnathe to the ground.

Khann wasn't there!

She had bird-hopped to the side and swung her tail into the side of the Kresh to send him spinning across the sand. 'First' lost his air-supply to his lungs as the tail cracked a rib and he sank momentarily to his knees.

Wheezing, he got to his feet and clenched his fists. All he could see was the taunting figure of the Gnathe to his side who had sat back onto the sand by flexing the backward facing knees and squatting. Now she was the same height as himself. Slowly he advanced towards her, opening one hand and keeping the balled fist ready.

Khann waited for the Kresh to come within her reach and stretched out her hand towards his open one invitingly. 'First' snatched hold with both opposable thumbs closing over the bigger hand of the Gnathe and brought the balled fist towards the chest of the Brood-mother. Khann grabbed the fist, twisted to one side and lifted the Kresh from the sand by swinging his body over hers. As 'First' lost contact with the ground he let go of the Gnathe. As he hung for a fraction of time, he could not avoid the tail that followed his flight through the air. Once more it crashed into his ribs. This time he felt some ribs go and his chest flooded with pain. This time he lay bemused in the sand, his breath coming in sobbing gasps. A large foot placed itself upon his head and held it down upon the sand. He felt the weight of Khann as she lowered her knee and sat down beside him pressing against his 'good' side.

"Had enough old friend? Have you got it out of your system? The Gnathe asked gently.

Something deep inside the Kresh shifted and his mind seemed flooded with light. A change of attitude ensued that Khann could pick up via the Goss and she let him go. Standing up she waved the nannites forward and watched as one of them touched the Kresh and rendered him unconscious. She walked back to the Gnathen area of the arena and looked at the ready throng.

Speaking aloud she said, "Watch out for the next one. Remember that they are watching us fight. Every one that goes out there will need something new. We must not lose! Just as I thought, the act of losing has jolted the Kresh mind back into sanity."

"Well done Khann! Watching you out there revived memories of the rite of succession," Link-soo-shan remarked with glee. I will go next!"

Khann-link-sool swung round and faced her once greatest enemy and replied, "There are times that I sometimes see in you the remains of the old Tyrant that ruled the Gnathen Empire! You sometimes worry me."

"Ha! My dear Khann, had you spent the length of time that I did enclosed inside Kamiel's mind and sharing it with Alexander, you really would not think that way," Link answered. "What I achieved and wanted in the long past has no relevance today. This is a far more satisfying life I lead now. It has real purpose!"

Link-soo-shan made her way towards the centre of the arena and eyed up the Kresh who was making his way towards her. She mentally chuckled.

151

"Do something different," she thought to herself. "I'll give them something different."

Link suddenly picked up speed and sped across the arena in ground devouring hops, sailed up into the air and came down onto the unsuspecting Kresh from above him. There was a muffled snort of pain and a grunt of expanding air as both feet came down onto the back of the Kresh forcing it onto the sand. Link dragged the winded 'First of Bars of Silver' towards the waiting nannites. She dapped his head up and down onto the sand and twisted his leg over his back to immobilise him.

She felt the change in the Kresh's mind as the sickness left him and gave him to the tender mercies of the nannites. She made her way back to the centre of the arena and beckoned the next Kresh onto the sand.

"Bring a friend," she insisted via the Goss and two Kresh made their way towards her.

Link-soo-shan watched the approach of the insane Kresh towards her and decided on a different tactic. She shuffled towards them dragging a leg, as though injured and tripped to lay full length on the sand before them. The Brood-mother drew on ancient skills honed in the sands of the old Imperial City's arena. She had been the greatest fighting Gnathe ever genetically produced. Since then she had redesigned herself several times when her clone had been grown in the human's life vat. Long gone were the deadly claws that could be extended similar to a cat's and with it the hearing crest that had been replaced by pointed ears. A better sense of balance went with the new ears and with it a much better co-ordination. This new body was young and immensely strong. She had taken possession of it as a newly grown adult and had plenty of time to acclimatise to its youth. Link had lived more than a thousand years, when she had been offered a new life. She remembered well the feeling of being old and weakened. Not so now!

The two Kresh both jumped at the same moment with huge fists drawn back for a crippling blow. Link dropped to the ground, dug her fingers into the sand, spun around on her side and cut the legs from under both of them with her tail. She continued the spin and pressed down into the sand with her hands, springing back onto her feet. The Gnathe rapidly bent forward and seized hold of the heads of the two Kresh and slammed them together. She loosened her grip and grabbed the long ears instead and once again dragged the Kresh towards the waiting nannites.

Link-soo-shan's hearts beat steadily and in perfect rhythm and her breath came easily. The old fighter felt the blood course through her as she warmed up and as she looked behind her she could see her daughters enter the field. A large shadow passed over her shutting out the light for a moment and she looked up. Floating above the arena were a large number of Trans-sentients with most of their tentacles tucked up out of the way. The rest they used to join to one another and anchored themselves to the bridge. They were acting as suspended cameras, projecting the fights to the rest of the aliens scattered around the artificial world.

The enhanced Kresh had taken enough of the single combat and all now entered the fray. Old Gnathen formations came into play, as the Brood-mothers formed a fighting wedge against the undisciplined crowd of Kresh. Slowly and steadily the Kresh body count mounted up and more of the rabbit-like aliens were left to the tender care of the nannites. The speed and dexterity of the fighting Gnathe had totally overwhelmed the slower bipeds. There were quite a number of broken bones, mainly ribs, suffered by the Kresh, but apart from some bruising; all of the Gnathe were quite unscathed.

Hannah powered down the shielding crystal and the dampening field evaporated. Only now did she notice Alexander had sat down by her side and was staring thoughtfully down at the arena.

"I think we have something here to alleviate the boredom of the long journey to the edge of our galaxy! Growing our own food and farming the Ark is all very well, but we do not want to go down the same path we all faced at the habitat on Jupiter. The reason we are here and not the 'galactics' is that we are capable of being aggressive creatures and they are not. What we need to do is to create contests of martial skills one alien specie against another," declared Alexander.

"I have a better idea than that," replied Hannah. "Team up two alien species together and teach the idea of teamwork between them. We could allow minimal weapons, such as padded clubs where one alien was disadvantaged to another."

Fredrick had been listening to the conversation with interest and his face was full of anticipation.

"This is something that I can get to work on," He said. "Ye gods, it will give me something to do! Give me some time to sound out the attitudes of the other alien species and I will get back to you."

With that comment Fredrick disappeared through the doorway and made his way to the Bazantii compound. Alexander called Asue on her frequency and put the idea to her. To his surprise she immediately agreed and began to make arrangements through the nannite systems for medical backup in the future.

Leaving the 'organics' to organise themselves, Kamiel once more directed his attention outside the Ark's surface. This had been modified from the rough cratered exterior of a normal moon to a smooth nannite surface anchored deep into the substrata. All around the moon's surface, an equidistant set of hollow tubes projected outwards that were big enough for the various aliens to travel through them. Secured to the tops of these, the spherical Toarvaks totally enclosed the moon's surface anchored to the moon by these tubes and touching one another so that they were fused together, leaving enough room for the nannites to work inside the sandwich. Sprouting from the moon's new silver surface on universal joints, were hundreds of thousands of solar cells ready to point at any star they encountered and soak up the energy. This was fed into capacitors situated deep under the regolith and stored. All of these capacitors would feed power to the crystal systems when required. Many thousands of nannites duplications of his and Asue's design were busily engaged in constructing the giant flange around the moon to support the 'star-gate' ring that they had brought with them from Toarvak Prime. This had been reduced in size to fit the moon's circumference and the spare crystals cannibalised to make a concentric ring that would fit inside. At the same time other crystal rings had been made encircling the moon and fitted into the flange as spares.

Rearing out of the Toarvak cover was the flange, which stood well over a mile high and was built as a latticed trellis. The top of the 'T' was a quarter of the height and was sloped so that each smaller ring sat beneath its neighbour on a ledge. Flying buttresses extended a third from the top down to the moon's nannite surface.

Filling the 'sky' above the construction in more colours than the rainbow was the inside 'surface' of the wormhole.

The nannite construction team had soon learnt not to look up for too long, as to do so was to lose their identities and descend into nothingness! Never the less it was a consistent

155

siren song that they could not disregard continually. After more than a hundred of the artificial intelligences had been sacrificed, Kamiel had made it a rule that all nannites worked as teams of five with one of the team watching the others and closely monitoring any signs of mental fatigue. All the nannites had narrowed the optical band around the top area of their heads and turned off the all round vision that they normally used. The nannites increased their safety by adding an additional visor that projected around the sighted area, to shield them from the sight of the inside face of the wormhole. During the shaping of the inserts along the flange it was difficult not to occasionally glimpse the sides of the tunnel. Once this happened the nannite would find itself fighting a losing battle not to stop and stare. This was when the fifth Guardian would drop a nannite bag over the head of the mesmerized builder and shut off the view. Needing neither sleep nor rest, the nannites had to spend a limited time away from the exposure of the wormhole to remain sane.

The work got done; as the single-minded artificial intelligences knew that when they entered normal space, they would be at the fringes of their own galaxy, ready to do the big jump. They would have enough time to orbit a useful star, soak up enough solar energy to fill the capacitors, before the Ark was closed down and put into stasis. Kamiel had joined up his controlling mind to the rest of the Guardians to consider the necessary alterations to the Ark of the Goss to turn it into both host and killer. The outside of the hollow moon was his natural element, but after a while he found that he missed the company of the 'organics' and after a satisfied inspection he returned to the internal world.

The first thing that he needed to do was to replace the fist size piece of living organic material that was host to the Goss spores. Outside the contained artificial world, the radiations criss-crossing the inside of the wormhole would be lethal to any other life form than a nannite. Every Guardian replenished the telepathic link when they returned, to enable themselves to connect to the people that they voluntarily served. Renewing that link gave the artificial beings a greater sense of purpose. As with the Toarvak entities somehow the link to flesh and blood creatures inspired all artificial intelligences beyond the original programming.

Kamiel soon found his way to the new 'life vats' that the nannites and the Gnathe set up on the inside of the Ark. The instinctive gift of genetic manipulation by the one-time masters of Jupiter had increased over the years. Not content with manipulating their own genetic blueprint they had studied every sapient alien species that had joined the galactic community. It was the Gnathen Brood-mothers that had combined living cells from every race of beings to produce a living construct that grew no bigger than a human fist and did not age. Every blob was a clone of the original experiment with a multi twisted DNA and each globule was host to the Goss spores.

The technique that the nannites employed to attach nannite strands to living nerve ends and communicate mind to mind with organics was adapted. Kamiel was expected and a Sharn type nannite had selected a new spore host for the Guardian. It floated in a nutrient solution, dormant, yet the surface rippled as living pulses allowed it to ingest the food and expel the wastes. It was a miracle of genetic engineering that allowed the minds of the artificial intelligences to connect telepathically to any organic creature.

Kamiel expanded his chest towards the jar that Sharn extended towards him and formed a bowl for the host's new home. The nannite geneticist poured the blob and its liquid medium into the cavity and Kamiel closed himself over it. He then rapidly connected his neural net into the living flesh and set up the parameters to keep the host alive.

"Goss!"

"Yes Kamiel," the symbiont answered. "I am here!"

The Guardian wasted no time and projected his thoughts to the network spread across the Ark and said, "Listen to me all of you. The work outside is reaching its conclusion. Also we will soon be reaching the end of this extended wormhole. When we do, we will need to orbit a sun and store as much energy as we can. Also, if a planet is near that sustains life; it will be necessary to replenish organic supplies from its raw materials. If we are fortunate to find one nearby, we shall plunder the whole system, as this area will be the first to feel the effects of the Andromeda collision. For the time being enjoy the games and remember the purpose of them is to find out about each other's strengths and weaknesses!"

Emelia gripped onto the Bazantii's top shoulder harness and shifted her position so that her feet were between the second set of shoulder blades. She was crouched down with her legs hunched, ready to spring from the centaur like creature. Droose was a young female Bazantii born from the life vats, as were the majority of the dwellers inside the Ark. Built like a six legged cat, her upper torso could lay flat or rise up from the second set of shoulder-blades. She was from a time not long after the defeat of the Goss when life was hard, as the Bazantii reclaimed their world. It had taken centuries to repair the damage done by the Goss. It had turned her world into a production plant to mount an attack against the civilizations that opposed it. Vast tracts of land had been left poisoned by strip mining and the use of industrial techniques without any regard to pollution. In comparison, the inside the Ark was to be transferred into a living paradise!

They had been allowed the use of a stave each with padded ends and Droose, in keeping with her size, had been given a staff thicker than Emelia's arm and eight foot long. The pads on the ends were six inched wide and a foot long. Droose carried it in a lance posture while her 'rider' held her smaller version under her arm, ready to drop it into a two handed position. She was ready to swing it with as much force as she could muster against their 'foe'. Both of the fighters were a golden blond colour, but Emelia had her hair plaited into a bun at the back of her head. A chest harness to protect her breasts, leather gloves and a small pair of breeches were all that she wore. The Bazantii had made sure that any long hair from her mane had been cropped too short to be of any use as a handhold.

The foe were two Vogb surrounded by a set of insectoids. Mounted on top of a six foot high plinth was a bright orange ball. The trial was to take possession of it and take it back to an identical plinth at the other end of the arena.

Already the Vogb had extended three of their tentacles and was resting each one on top of each of the insectoids and looped around it. A queen controlled the six workers and used them as an extension of her mind. She was positioned between the two conics and sat on top of a cradle made from a loose nest of tentacles that joined the two together. Coiled like a spring alongside the conic was the electrically charged, stinging tendril. With their all round vision it was impossible to creep up on them from a blind side. The six eyes rotated on their stalks to face the oncoming challenge and colours flashed around the top ring as they communicated with each other. At the same time they were mentally in tune with the insectoids through the Goss.

Slightly behind Emelia rode Larse, dressed similar to Emelia. His Bazantii host was a magnificent male called, Janssen who was as black as darkest night. Larse was also poised to jump from the back of his mount when the time was right. Having spent the majority of his life on the back of a horse, the Bazantii were very strange to ride as he was riding behind Janssen's back and hanging onto the back of the Bazantii's chest harness. As they approached the two Vogb, their minds joined in an intelligent rapport and they fought as one creature. The Bazantii extended his hind claws for a better grip and passed Droose to the left aiming for one of the Vogb. He drove the lance at an insectoid aiming to put the padded end underneath and tip it over.

The Vogb lifted the insectoid and hurled it up the lance towards Janssen's chest.

Larse leaned over the Bazantii's shoulder and flipped the insectoid off the heavy staff. He stood up and leapt towards the plinth, only to be caught by two tentacles and held aloft in triumph! The insectoid queen received the bundled human and wedged him into the cradle she was standing in and placed her pinchers around the human's neck. At this same moment Emelia made her effort by somersaulting into the air above the other insectoids as Droose charged into the melee. Her lance knocked over the right-hand conic completely onto its side. The cradle of tentacles came undone as Emelia dropped into it shaking Larse loose, as the queen let go of his neck. As the stinging tendrils uncoiled they both grabbed them in the insulated gloves that they had worn and placed them on the opposing Vogb who stiffened as they both endured an unexpected electrical shock. The queen had been knocked out of the cradle and was now directing her workers towards the two humans to immobilise them. Too late, she saw Emelia direct the stinging tendril in her direction and stiffened as the shock rendered her unconscious as well as the Vogb. The workers stopped and froze for a moment before wandering aimlessly off.

Janssen lifted Emelia up by the hips, for her to retrieve the orange ball from the plinth. She threw it to Droose and they made their way back to their end of the arena mounted up again, leaving the tangled Vogb to return to consciousness in their own time.

The Bazantii reared up and placed the ball onto the plinth letting Emelia slide off onto the sand. The massed aliens, humans and apes cheered the victory of the mixed team from the parapet of the arena. It never mattered who won with what team in the trials, only that each alien species worked with each other to exploit strengths and weaknesses.

From the bridge over the arena, Kamiel watched satisfied during the rest of the day, as combination after combination were tried and tested. The only ones not to take part were the Trans-sentients, who were content to float over the games and convey the controlled mayhem to those who were busy elsewhere with their own telepathic powers.

CHAPTER TWELVE

Time passed on board the artificial world and at last the Lagdoo gave the signal that the end of the wormhole was soon to eject them back into the universal real time. The wormhole collapsed and the last Ark of the Goss entered normal space at the edges of a stellar system that turned out to be a binary star. Locked into the Lagrange position was an Earth sized world with water and abundant life in its seas. The main star was a yellow sun of a size comparable with Toarvak Prime's and it was orbited by a red dwarf.

Looming in an even closer proximity was an Andromeda star, the first of many to begin to invade the Milky Way galaxy. At the moment it was less than several light years away and dominating the sky, but behind it were thousands more beginning the intersection paths that would destroy both galaxies. Already there were alterations in the symmetry of the two suns and the locked planet. A wobble began to insinuate itself in the path of the lightest body every time the orbit took it ever closer to the invading star. As the rogue star got nearer, the planet would tear away from the balanced orbit around the yellow sun and start the long dive into the interstellar night or plunge into the new star.

Before that happened the inhabitants of the Ark would harvest as much organic material and anything else of value that they could. Already the Toarvaks were fully crewed and lifting away from the moon. Now the solar panels twisted to catch the full power of the yellow sun and began to store the electrical energy into the capacitors below the regolith. Inside the Ark all living food animals were being collected up and put in stasis chambers as well as all of the many different crops being stored away after harvesting. The artificial sun was being powered down and the wheel that gave night and day by rotation had been stopped. Soon the inside of the moon would return to bitter cold darkness.

Using Thomas's memories Toarvak 6 had fashioned herself into a giant trimaran shape once she had made contact with the sea of the doomed world. Sweeping underneath the hull were miles of nets, terminating in a giant bag. Outriggers kept the nets opened and swept the fish into the bag at the end. The aliens had named the planet 'Bounty' and were plundering it as fast as they could. The outward sky was empty and black except for the edge on 'Catherine wheel' of Andromeda and the rag-tag collection of the outermost stars. The rogue star could be seen every night and was the brightest star in the blackness. Spears of brightness erupted from the surface as the binary system began to also influence the other star. Weather patterns began to alter on the surface and storm systems began to brew across the tropical seas.

Larse, Emelia, Thomas, Link-soo-shan and Khann-link-sool were the designated crew to forge the Toarvak mind meld with T6. At the moment Thomas was the controlling influence as he had the most experience in the running of a fishing trimaran. On board were a complete family of conics with several hives of the insectoids. The Thipdar family Smelch had made Toarvak 6 their adopted home along with the Gnathe associated with Link and Khann. Those that were born from the life vats had not aged and those that had been born naturally had been treated by the Gnathen genetics masters to retard the aging process. Every new mind was added to the pool when they came of age and schooled in the mental disciplines that would be needed in the future. Every alien was well aware of the conflict to come and what the outcome would be if they failed.

Thomas called a halt as the holds filled up and raised the

ship into the air, absorbing the nets back into the Toarvak's substance. The vessel winked out of phase and drifted out of the atmosphere until it entered orbit. Allowing the part facing the ark to phase back in for a moment, the Toarvak closed the gap, relying on gravitational pull to bring her into range of one of the hollow tubes. Once contact had been made, Toarvak 6 disgorged its load of fish into a stasis chamber and anchored down.

The silvery material of the ship oozed away from the organic crew and allowed them to stand up and resume natural bodily functions.

Thomas said to the others, "I quite enjoyed that. It took me back to the years that I spent fishing with the Vogb and the insectoids. I must admit though that the boats were considerably smaller!"

Emelia shook her hair out of the plaited bun she had arranged and answered, "I have never fished in my life. I was a farm girl and harvested crops, until I met Larse."

"The Gnathe do not fish! The water and our people were never great companions," Khann replied and stretched her arms out, flexing her fingers.

"Its as well that one of us had the skill then," Thomas laughed, "or our holds would be empty. Surely we have been here long enough? If those storms increase in severity it will be no use at all going down to the surface."

"This is true."

They all heard the voice of Primm in their minds and watched as the trip'o-dal ambled over in her three-legged gait. She stopped, anchored down and stared back at the Toarvak's crew. The tendrils at her mouth were agitated and her eyes kept opening and closing in her sideways fashion. Her pointed ears were angled forwards from each side of her globular head. Some of the dark spots on her golden coloured skin had faded and it was obvious that she was agitated about something as the top pair of arms had locked over her chest while the bottom set were agitated.

"We must leave this world immediately! Some of the outer scouts have picked up a distortion in energy patterns coming towards this world from the direction of Andromeda. Whatever it is we must treat it with caution. The Tran-sentient ones feel that it is something to do with the Harvester although on a much smaller scale. If it is, we must stop it going back with knowledge of our expedition. Kamiel is certain that we must have the advantage of surprise when we meet the abomination. The Ark is breaking orbit as we talk and Kamiel is placing the rings. We may need a distraction until we are quite ready."

The five organic components of Toarvak 6 settled back into the silver mound and allowed the nannite substance to entomb them once more.

"Tell all that are inside me to anchor down! This could be rough!"

The Toarvak released the port on the docking tube and rose from the hollow moon, smoothed her surface to polished silver and opened a nearby wormhole. She flashed down the inside until she was well away from the Ark. Toarvak 6 emerged and contacted the scouts to get the position of the incoming energy field. It was indeed on its way from the Andromeda galaxy. The composite intelligence opened and closed another wormhole to get closer to the invader.

Scouting the fringes of the invading galaxy, the Collector had noticed the first affected planet in the new system had life. If there were enough life energy to gather, it would oversee the disruption, as the incoming star caused the planet to die. It raised its wings of force and began to brake, by digging its energy constructed hooks into the inside surface of the wormhole. The shape of the Collector was similar to an inverted arrowhead or giant 'Vee'. In the centre of this was the sensory body of the energy pattern that housed the nervous system. An optical band ran around the 'head' giving it an all round view similar to the nannites preferred method of gathering information.

If the life were of a low order, it could feed off it itself and search for more along the fringe. The Harvester would not want to waste energy pushing itself this distance unless there was intelligent life to feed on. The Collector put its sensing abilities on long range and picked up conflicting results. The planet had only plenty of advanced and rudimentary life in its seas, with the land sparsely settled by organic life, but there seemed to be intelligent life here! It fluctuated on and off until there was nothing at all. Yet the Collector knew that the strong pulses of intelligence had been present and it had been varied. There had been many more than one identity of alien. Some it had recognised from earlier collections, but some were completely new. The greater part of its collective mind would want to know more about this, so the Collector grated to a stop and collapsed the wormhole around it to exit. It left the passage behind it intact so that it could easily return.

A pattern of immense beauty hung in empty space. The 'vee' of its wings of force spread out from the main sensory body and swept golden sparkles from the white framework of their structure. Lightning flickered along its energy patterns, illuminating its shape. Giant fingers extended from just underneath the 'head' to make a frill that expanded outwards into a huge light sail. Soon it would be able to fly on the solar winds and travel to the life-bearing planet.

In front of it hung the yellow star and its red dwarf companion. In a rapidly unstable triangular orbit spun a living world with the rudimentary life it had sensed. There could be no intelligent life here! For the first time in its billions of years lifespan the Collector sensed the emotions of doubt in its own abilities and questioned the situation.

Kamiel had the Lagdoo take the Ark at right angles to the triangle of binary stars and planet by half a light year. The nannites had shed the rings from the flange and had twelve Toarvaks in hexagon formation tow two of them away from the hollow moon. He had them tilt the rings to face the intruder where it had stopped while the other ring was lined up with the star. This was taking a little longer than anticipated.

"Goss!"

"Yes Kamiel," the symbiont answered.

"Connect me with Toarvak 6," the Guardian replied.

"I hear you Kamiel. What is it you wish me to do?"

"Delay that thing for a few moments more while we align the rings. Then go out of phase and stay out of phase! Do not show yourself for long! The Lagdoo are about to close the wormhole."

In front of the Collector, space shimmered and several tiny moons appeared and with it the strong pulse of intelligent life. Instinctively the Collector reached out to feed on the compacted and varied life forms within its grasp. They winked out of sensory range and were ringed around it instead. The Collector reached out again for the one closest to the yellow star and touched a group mind of immense power. Three more reached out for its mind and memories before they all winked out of existence. One was not so fast and the Collector stripped it bare of all organic life force. It felt something scream with unbearable loss and vengeful pain, deep within its thoughts. Something cold and alien ripped through its consciousness.

"Kamiel! Stripped of life I am. Insane am I. Focus the beam upon my signal and the crystals that I carry," came the signal from the life stripped Toarvak.

The next thing the Collector was aware of was the collapse of the wormhole behind it. The moonlet it had stripped of life was coming straight at it under intelligent power and lodged itself inside its sensory systems. The collector could not eject it, as the edges were not in phase with the universe. Detonating around the edges of its being were atomic explosions ripping through its body with floods of neutrons and gamma radiation as the remaining Toarvaks bombarded the Collector before going in and out of phase.

Kamiel fused himself with his Lagdoo host, gripped the command crystals tightly and sank his personality into the gestalt of alien minds. They all surrendered their identity to his and he gave the order as leader of the group mind. The power of the collective mind twisted space open using the rings of crystal. The ring closest to the yellow star opened a hole in the centre of the flaming ball of atomic fusion. The other gate twisted space around the Collector and fed the collapsing star into the space that it occupied, centred on the crystal signal coming from the crewless Toarvak.

The Collector felt the power of fusing atoms for long enough to know it was about to die. The complex energy patterns came apart under the onslaught, as the unstable atoms at the centre of the star rushed through the star-gate under immense pressure. For some while Kamiel kept the two gates opened until he was sure that the thing was destroyed. A new sun shone where the collector had been for a few minutes more until it evaporated. The Guardian let go of the gestalt and returned to his own single mind, leaving the Toarvak 'tugs' to replace the rings onto the Ark's flange.

The Ark's control room was ringing with noises of congratulations amongst the normally taciturn Lagdoo. The reptilians were coldly logical beings and not given to emotions.

"Well done my friends," the nannite said, "but bear in mind this thing was just an off-shoot from the main body of the Harvester. When we meet the abomination I have the feeling that we will need a bigger sun!"

The nannite reflected on the significance of what he had done and thought to himself, "Ah McBald, little did you think that when you created me, the power I would have and the responsibility it would carry. I have just destroyed a being of pure energy that was probably unique to this universe. Whatever it was part of, has to be our enemy, as it prefers to feed on organic sentient life. My duty is to protect that same organic life that created me, along with all other forms of sentient life! It is a heavy burden old friend and one you did not completely program into me. This I do through free will, something that you never thought of! Now all nannites are carrying that defence command except Asue and I, who lost that strict code when we died under the power of Link-soo-shan's mind. My newfound ability to destroy, weighs heavy on what you would call my soul! I have to constantly remind myself that for over nine hundred thousand years this galaxy knew peace without the Abomination's influence."

He was aware of Asue's mind in his as she reassured him, "What you have done this day was necessary for our joint survival. Minnis and I both agree that the ends do justify the means!"

"There are only three of us in the known universe without programmed governors, that are of artificial intelligence, discounting the Toarvaks and they are incomplete unless they are merged with organic sentient life! I made Minnis to be the way she is. Because we died, the experience altered the two of us permanently. Do you realise that the other nannites fear us because of that difference?"

"They also respect what we are and will follow you to wherever you lead them, Kamiel," Asue reminded him.

"As I was created without any of that moral nonsense, it doesn't bother me at all," Minnis replied.

The three nannites felt the presence of Alexander in their minds, as the Toarvak he had been part of the collective driving force, landed and anchored down over a transport tube. Alex opened and closed a portal and appeared in front of the Guardians. He had with him Link's two Broodmother daughters, Suzzan and Trann who had been part of the gestalt controlling their Toarvak.

"Well done, Kamiel," he said to his old friend. "That was not a moment too soon. The speed of that thing caught us unawares and its size! It was half the size of the Ark, when it extended those incredible 'wings' and yet its mind was relatively simple. I managed to extract some information from it before it burned out."

"What did you pick up, Alex? Was it anything we can use to locate its master?" the nannite asked.

"The Trans-sentients were able to read a great deal of its thought patterns before it perished. Using them as direction finders I was able to get knowledge of where it is at the moment. It appears to be feeding along the far edge of the spiral and is in a satisfied state at the moment. It has no feeling that one of its collectors has been destroyed, for one thing we were able to understand; - it has thousands of these 'collectors' working the Goldilocks zones around those stars that have them."

"Areas where water neither freezes solid nor evaporates," the nannite mused. "Maybe we should inspect a few of these star systems for ourselves and check them out. There may be intelligent life there that we can wrest away from the Harvester's clutches."

"I will call the Toarvaks back to the Ark," Asue declared.

"It is time we battened down the hatches and prepared for the long drop to Andromeda. We need to get everyone not necessary to opening up a wormhole, to file into the stasis chambers located in every Toarvak and have them activated."

Suzzan stood erect and flexed the muscles of her arms and said to the small assembly, "Its good to be alive and to be doing something worthwhile."

Trann laughed and answered, "Mother always said that the universe belonged to the strong and to those who were prepared to die to keep it!"

Link-soo-shan's mental presence echoed in all of their minds, "It would be a courageous death! We would all earn our positions in this abomination's hall of power."

"Lady Link! I for one," Alexander retorted, "Will do my level best to hang this thing in my own trophy room."

"Big room," said Suzzan, "judging by the size of that thing we just destroyed!"

"Never mind all this," Kamiel insisted, "Those of you who entered the things memory banks during the conflict, I want you to form a small group mind and examine what you have collectively found out from this part of the Harvester and report to me."

The last Ark of the Goss became once more covered in Toarvaks and the majority of the inhabitants settled themselves into the stasis chambers while the crewmembers readied themselves to form a large group mind. This would be necessary to search for and open a 'gate' into a large and steady wormhole that connected to the Andromeda galaxy. Before then, Kamiel called a meeting of his 'war council.'

The leaders and members of the prime positions among all the sentient species of the expeditionary force had gathered together in a large 'bubble' above the big control room of the hollow moon, built by the nannites. Unlike the variable situations that the Toarvaks could do, the Ark of the Goss had been built from the moon itself to accommodate the Lagdoo. The additional piece of new apparatus was the crystal chair that Kamiel had sat inside when he directed the conflict with the Collector. The chair had been designed to suit the large frame of the reptilian species that had helped to build the Ark. Kamiel had flowed over the Lagdoo and entered his nervous system to operate the crystal amplifier, as it needed organic life to make psychic contact. It was from here that he controlled the group mind of the expedition.

"On board each of the Toarvaks that engaged the Collector was a Tran-sentient, that in the brief time that it existed in our presence, was able to extract quite a large amount of information. All the other aliens that picked up telepathic images were also able to add their information to the pool," Kamiel stated via the Goss. "I have shared that information and I will now pass over the edited version for you all to study in your own minds. Open up your thoughts and I will imprint the information."

Kamiel broadcasted his interpretation of the Collector's background to the waiting throng and waited for them to accrue the secrets gained at the cost of one Toarvak and all of the many different aliens that were a part of it.

Into the minds of the assembly, a vision of ruined worlds and broken civilizations unreeled. In this unclean thing were memories of Trip'o-dal, Vogb, Insectoids, Lagdoo, Bazantii and many other alien sentient creatures unique to this galaxy. All of them achieving levels of civilization only to have their way of life crushed by warfare. Again and again on worlds orbiting different stars, they would start the expansion into space only to be destroyed and reduced to survivors. None of these people had managed the step to the stars. Some had sent probes to exploit the new worlds without ever getting the means to follow them. Those that had resisted a final war had perished in the flames of their sun, once they had been harvested over and over again. This had been the pattern since the first intelligent life had evolved here in Andromeda. The collector had also spread life by transporting it through the wormholes at the bidding of the Harvester. In its memory were the times that it was reunited with the main body of its being and drained of accumulated energy to be remade and sent out again and again. It had been both a 'Seeder' of worlds and also a destroyer of organic life. There was no record in its memories of Human, Kresh, Gnathe or the Trans-sentients. These four sentient life forms were unique to the Milky Way and it was the combination of their sciences that gave them the means to travel through time and space. The two artificial machine intelligences of the nannite Guardians and the Toarvaks were also unique to this galaxy and had never been developed in any of the Andromeda civilizations other than large computers.

Kamiel's audience marvelled at the beauty of some of the buildings and the blending of great parks with cities that vibrated with life. Around one particular star there orbited two habitable worlds, one insectoid and one inhabited by the Vogb. They had built a twin civilization between them, blending the best of both cultures. Somehow they drifted into warfare at the Collector's bidding. The great 'Hives' of the insectoids had been flattened by aerial bombardment while the pyramid cities of the Vogb had been over-run and the citizens slaughtered by the workers of the insectoids. The Collector had stored the life energy and returned to the Harvester with the crop, only to be sent back again to lift both cultures to a higher level and to encourage them to breed in great numbers. This time they had managed to almost attain interstellar travel before the Harvester paid them the ultimate visit and caused their star to go nova.

It was some time before any of the aliens communicated through the Goss.

A Bazantii female ran her hands through her hair and mane and broadcast, "This is why we came here. We destroy this thing or we die trying!"

A Vogb anchored its conic body down to the floor and while a multitude of colours played around the top ring, he said, "It must die! It has fed off organic life for far too long. It belongs to a far-gone age and has outlived its natural span by using its power to move amongst the stars and harvesting the life-force of our relatives."

From out of the multitude of minds came the thoughts of 'First of Dappled Grey' tinged with a great sorrow, "We cannot go back in time and rescue these poor souls as we did in our own galaxy. If we did, we would change the timelines that brought us here. That makes my heart heavy and my determination greater. The impending collision between the galaxies will still have to take place and the ruination of both homes to organic life will still happen." The Kresh stood tall and surveyed the aliens around him and reminded them, "If we can destroy this abomination there will be time to organise a rescue of the doomed worlds away from this planned death. We have enough stellar engineers to see to that problem. Some of the far spiral arms will pass through empty areas of the Milky Way and would be unaffected by the collision for millions of years. That should give our descendants enough time to sort something out!"

Kamiel stood quietly for some time before he said to them via the Goss, "My friends, you have given me the reaction that I needed before I committed you all to the next part of the plan. I want you to return to your Toarvaks and ready yourselves for stasis. Before that I shall call upon you to weld yourselves into the most powerful group mind at my disposal. I have to find a wormhole through the empty void that will take us across the Andromeda galaxy and somewhere in the vicinity of the Harvester. On the way we will find any intelligent life that we can and prevent their destruction. There will be other Collectors to destroy and new allies to co-opt into our force. What we are about to do is dangerous and some of us will die. But there is no going back now my friends. The only way is forward!"

CHAPTER THIRTEEN

Once again, the control centre of the Last Ark of the Goss was fully manned by the Lagdoo. The nannite's host had strapped himself down into the cradle and was gripping a command crystal in both hands. His feet were also naked and his hind-claws were curled around two more. A large telekinetic crystal was fixed between the two command crystals and a time distorting crystal was placed where he could make contact to the other three.

Next to him anchored to the base of the unit was a large Vogb. The conic was connected to the main power supply in such a way that she could draw extra power from the capacitors and direct it via her charged tendril into the time distorting crystal at Kamiel's telepathic bidding. The rest of the tentacles were wrapped around the Lagdoo and the cradle.

The Guardian opened his mind to the waiting throng scattered outside in gestalt with the Toarvaks and said, "I am ready. Let us cross the great void!"

Kamiel flowed over the Lagdoo and the Vogb, settling himself into their nervous systems. He reached out to the Lagdoo in the control centre adding them into the building gestalt. Already the collective was beginning to reach out and it gathered in the minds of the Toarvak crews complete with the artificial intelligences that the Kresh had designed. Thousands of free nannites blended into the greatest collective mind that had ever been constructed. It was greater even than the combined minds of the Gnathe, humans and apes that had moved the Earth from its perilous position in orbit around an exploding sun, to orbit the gas giant, Icarus. This time the group mind was a mixture of organic and artificial intelligence.

The gestalt opened up its perception and searched for a strong wormhole leading between this galaxy and Andromeda. It could sense the remnants of the wormhole that the Ark had closed and sought others that spread in that direction. Like tangled spaghetti, strings of gravitational force tied the two galaxies together. Inside these bundled ropes of force were tubes that formed and evaporated. The collective discarded those and centred on the stable ones that were anchored at both ends. Amongst these were Stargates that opened far too close to unstable suns so that emergence would be risky, even if the whole moon were out of phase. Kamiel had taken a thousand Toarvaks into the heart of a star to retrieve Toarvak 6, but underneath the cover of the blanket of the Kresh interstellar ships lay the Ark. He could not know for certain if the phasing out of the universe that the Toarvaks could do, would extend deep enough into the hollow moon to be completely safe. The mind was vast and drew heavily on the stellar engineering knowledge of the Kresh, as it reached out into the tangle of tubes. Several were examined and discarded until the collective made its choice. Kamiel/gestalt opened the strings around the gate and thrust the Ark into the wormhole and plunged into it, taking them to Andromeda, a third of the way in. From this position the Ark could establish the star fields and begin to map the area of Andromeda that it was parked and take stock of the situation. They had a reasonable idea where the Harvester had fed last in a general direction and this they meant to improve upon.

As the walls of the wormhole closed over the Ark, the Lagdoo opened up the drive system and collapsed the wormhole behind them using the ancient weapon. Moments later the Toarvaks took the hollowed moon out of phase and the acceleration took the vessel beyond light speed in the confines of the wormhole. Kamiel activated the stasis field from the Vogb's electrically charged tendril and everything froze except the mind of the nannite. This was a slowly evaporating stasis field that would be triggered to collapse just before they exited the wormhole. Whilst every other life form on and around the Ark would experience basically no time shift at all, Kamiel, the Lagdoo and the Vogb would be aware of time passing, but at a slower rate than normal. To prevent insanity taking over his two hosts, Kamiel sent their minds to sleep while he kept watch as the centuries passed in the external universe. Inside the wormhole, time stood still in bursts and would become variable depending on the crossover points or intersections that the wormhole ran through. An organic mind would go insane.

Over one hundred thousand light years from Kamiel's expedition to Andromeda, Deep thinker and Co-ordinator watched them go from the very extremity of the perceptions of the Goss. The moment that the greatly modified Ark had entered the wormhole, the Goss had been cut off from telepathic communication. Now to all intents and purposes for the fist time in its history, the Goss had been divided into two distinct entities.

Deep-thinker curled his tentacles around the fresh top branches of a 'tree' and ripped off the luscious growth. He stuffed the wet leaves into his mouth and tilted his body to catch the rain and direct it along his flanks and into his mouth as he spun gently onto his back. His mind was full of the leaving of the time fished people and the bravery of each soul. During their journey across the galaxy and their retrieval of the last Ark of the Goss, the galactic civilization had been very busy.

The globular cluster consisted of more than several thousand stars, all orbiting a medium sized black hole. Each star had been ferried across the galaxy with its life-bearing planet. Gas giants with moons had been added to the mix with extra worlds of reasonable gravity to be terra-formed. Storehouse planets were placed into orbits at the edge of the 'goldilocks' zone where water remained frozen. These were for mining and exploiting. Slowly at first and constructed with care, the globular cluster had been built and added to as time went by. Every star and settled planetary system had been moved away from the collision site. After this had taken place the galactic civilization moved the rest of the settled worlds out to the growing cluster. What was left behind would not be missed!

This entire organisation had occupied the Trans-sentients minds until now and the leaving of the expedition to Andromeda had alerted them to the situation. Already the first collisions and wrenching of orbits had taken place. In the next few hundred years exploding stars in that area would begin to destabilise the ones that were receiving unwelcome guests. Radiation would climb to higher and higher intensities unsettling the internal 'clocks' of high mass stars and causing them to go nova. The proximity of so many stars moving together could form new black holes that would in their turn swallow even more stable suns.

Co-ordinator burrowed into Deep-thinker's mind, "They've gone," she said.

"And so must we," answered her mate. "Send the signal via the Goss. Connect up every mind on every world. We have the largest ever star-gate to activate, to open a wormhole big enough to swallow the Cluster!"

A shimmering hole in space occurred at the far side of the Milky Way galaxy and the artificially constructed globular cluster called by the inhabitants; 'Transit' disappeared inside it. The gate closed and all gravitational anchors dissipated within that sector of the spiral arm. Without that stasis in place stars began to wobble out of their balanced positions and took up new orbits around the central black hole. Now this side of the galaxy began to disrupt into chaos as a variation on the Harvester's planned collisions took place on the opposite side. There would be no chance of returning to this reforming galaxy for millions of years until long after the Andromeda system had amalgamated with this one.

Kamiel switched off the stasis field and brought the entire Ark and Toarvaks back into play. Once again the gestalt swept out and studied the new 'home' from the position of the wormhole's end. To the vast mind, no time at all had been taken, only Kamiel had been aware of the centuries that had passed. He quickly surveyed the space around the wormholes edge and found it empty of any threats and bid the Toarvaks to bring the Ark back into phase. The blackness of space was a welcome sight to see with the millions of stars spread across the heavens. As luck would have it they had materialised on the edges of a solar system consisting of the usual gas giants that were spread out from the star's central gravitation pull. This system had seven of various sizes, some with rings and some without. All of them had moons in orbit around them. There were smaller planets made of similar materials that all inner worlds coalesced into. At this distance out at the edge it was impossible to find out by long-range sensors whether or not the inner ones were life bearing. Kamiel sent Toarvak 6 to find out.

This star was twice the size of Earth's sun and was a bright yellow with constant flares erupting from the main body, only to be sucked down by the insistent gravity. The first three planets from its furnace-like conditions had been long ago crisped and burnt. The forth one out had a boiling atmosphere of sulphur dioxide similar to Venus.

The fifth world was far enough out for water to form and freeze at the poles. Volcanic action had thrust high mountain ranges along the tectonic plates where they collided and here the ice settled in great glaciers. There were four large continents sat along the equator, one of which stretched up to cover the North Pole and down the other side. This planet was larger than the Earth by a factor of two, but was of about the same mass. The two moons that orbited this world would only pull tides when they were together in the planet's sky. When they were in opposition on either side of this world the seas would remain calm and steady. The inner moon was caught up by the outer moon every two months and during this time massive high and low tides would occur.

Toarvak 6 primed her sensors and relayed the information back to Kamiel, *"This planet has life abundant, Kamiel. There is intelligent life here, as I have intercepted radio traffic. There are two moons orbiting this world, so I will enter the nearest one out of phase and observe. Bring the Ark and park it behind the outer moon while we investigate the civilization that lays claim to this world."*

The collective mind switched the state of reality of the Toarvak to that alteration that allowed them to fly through the empty spaces between the atoms. Unseen and seemingly undetected the vessel approached the inner moon.

On that moon was the first outpost of the civilization that lived on the world below. Sheltering beneath the regolith were tunnels that connected to domes built under the surface. The tops of which were the only things bathed in the radiation of the parent star. It was these searching antennas and radio tuned discs that had picked up the brief appearance of the Toarvak. A large blip had shown up on the screens and had been recorded and had abruptly vanished. Its direction and velocity had been noted with some alarm.

The trip'o-dal viewing the screens hit the panic button and woke the senior members of the watch.

"The independent Colonists could have got a missile into space," the operator informed them. "They must have managed to launch it beyond the outer moon, 'Theyus' and have sighted the thing onto our position!"

"Steady down, watcher. Steady down," advised the scientific director. "We have no records of the Southern colonists launching from their site below the equator. You did the right thing to call us. Let us examine the information gained. Remember we are the only ones up here and we of the Instrumentality have the only operating space ships. I will radio the master base at City One and check on their knowledge. For the meantime treat this as secret and try to find out more about whatever this thing was. Maybe it came apart!"

The military commander twirled about on the rear leg and settled the other two front ones so that he faced the director and remarked, "We are not on a war footing as yet, my old friend, but we can be at a moments notice. I have ordered the missile silos to break caps, just in case! It may have come to that glorious time to take down the independent rebels who broke away from our protection, several hundred years ago."

"Commander! Those 'rebels' have no interest in dominating our affairs; they merely want to lead their own lives," the director argued.

"What you are talking is treason, Director! I would be very careful about to whom you speak to in this manner."

"My Lord Commander, I just wanted to make it clear that they are no threat to us! If anything can be said, it is our people that are armed to the teeth and are looking for some excuse to bring them down," the director explained.

The Commander's mouth tendrils went ridged with rage and his face began to swell as the blood pounded into his cheeks. His eyes opened wide and he fixed the director with a baleful glare. He reached forwards with the top pair of arms and shook the director by his shoulders in the light gravity.

"Your mouth is sealed! If I hear one more word of this sedition I will have you put outside the airlock! Enough!" he shouted at the scientist and threw him to the side and stalked out of the watch room.

Toarvak 6 settled herself down into the moon's surface until only a periscope peeked out of the side of the mountain where she remained hidden. From the periscope a number of antennas spread out upon the ground and changed form into dishes pointing at the world below. From these information points massive amounts of information began to return to the Toarvak and was displayed onto the main screens. Below them was a world on the brink of war! The main continent had armies spread across the upper shoreline obviously waiting for a massive low tide when a land bridge would appear. Hopelessly outnumbered and dug into trenches were the defenders waiting for the attack. From the state of the land on each side they had been there for some time. Large cannons had been dragged into place on high ground overlooking the crossing area. Concrete shelters had been built on both sides with supply tunnels deep underground. Anyone above ground would be in a theatre of death once hostilities started. It was a position of madness!

"They are all going to die! It is like a page out of our history," Primm explained. "Long ago, before we were taken over by the Goss, we suffered moments of madness just like this. It was not until the Kresh and the Gnathe began time fishing and removing trip'o-dal worlds away from the influence of the Harvester that we realised what had been done to us. Something has set this up. Either there is a Collector hiding somewhere nearby or it will soon be paying this world a visit."

"I agree," answered Emelia and took a cool drink before adding, "What are we going to do about it?

A silver female shape rose from the floor and said, *"Something else there is to consider. My detectors can a web of force sense, laid over this planet from pole to pole. A collector's net I feel it to be and to a nearby hidden wormhole some strands do enter! Also not far from where we hide, a moon-base have I detected. Inside are no more than twenty individuals. "*

"Tell Kamiel this instant," Link-soo-shan replied. "We must do nothing drastic until the Ark arrives and hides behind the outer moon. First, I think we will pay a visit to this scientific outpost and introduce ourselves!"

Fredrick laughed and said, "Minnis and I will go and look inside, out of phase. We can look around and find the airlock, learn how to operate it and let in whoever wants to come. Lets shake them up a bit and see what we can achieve. Is everyone OK with that? So who's coming?"

Primm answered straight away, "These are my people! They look the same and I'll be willing to bet they have the same DNA! I will go with you and enter the base when you have had a good look round. In the meantime those who are going will get ready to suit-up at Fredrick's signal."

The Gnathe looked at Primm's size and all agreed that if the base were built to her size then they would not be able to navigate the corridors. Blue-orange-green was the same size however and the conic would probably negotiate the underground base quite well."

B-o-g was adamant and relayed through the Goss, "I will come too, just in case you need me to sting someone!"

"A tunnel already I have constructed close to the base," the Toarvak

explained. *"Fredrick and Minnis can be on their way as soon as they have combined. Enter here!"*

A hole in the floor opened up and lay waiting for Fredrick and Minnis to enter.

Minnis flowed over her friend and became his battle suit once more. She expanded a transparent globe over his head and produced a re-breather set-up over his chest.

A familiar voice spoke into his ear, "Ready Fred! Shall we go old friend?"

Fredrick dropped through the hole and slid through the darkness towards the moon-base. Within a few minutes he was ejected slowly out of the tunnel and stood outside the establishment. Minnis had brought the soles of his feet back into phase so that he could walk over the regolith without sinking in. To anyone who was watching that area it would just seem to have a disturbance in the surface dust. Now that he was closer, Fredrick could make out a central dome with an entrance onto the moon's surface. The rest of the base was deep underground. Dominating the sky was the blue and green world above him. Over to the sunset was the reflection from the second moon as it orbited further out. Behind him were the jagged peaks of a range of mountains that he could see over the tops of the crater wall that surrounded the base.

"Well Minnis, shall we go in?" he said, walking to the door set into the side facing the sun.

Minnis altered the state of the soles of his feet, leaving two small piles of dust outside the door and Fred walked through. Once inside he examined the mechanism that opened the door. Two large prominent buttons stood out from a box on the side of the wall. There were no other signs of controls except what was obviously a lift button. Minnis sent the visuals through Toarvak 6 as Fredrick dropped slowly through the floor and down the lift shaft into the lift compartment. Here again were two buttons with an arrow pointing up and one pointing down! He smiled and walked through the door into a hall with a number of tunnels branching off, all with airtight doors.

Minnis did a scan and decided to look along the left hand tunnel as the life-signs were prominent here. Again she altered the composition of the soles of his feet so that he could walk easily. The tunnel broadened out into what could only be a barracks as a dozen hammocks were suspended from stands and occupying some of them were young trip'o-dal males doing what all military personal do when not killing each other; sleeping. Along one wall were what could only be weapons stacked in a rack. They were very clean and well cared for! Fredrick took Minnis over for a better look and Minnis altered the firing mechanism on all of them by fusing them shut. Now they could only be used as clubs!

Again, all of this was relayed back to the visiting party for debate and decisions while Fredrick continued to survey further into the base. It was just around the corner that the Commander's room was situated and the human and nannite had a good look round. Again they found a weapon's rack fixed to one wall and Minnis rendered them all useless, particularly the small handguns. On the wall was a picture of what Fredrick surmised was a female trip'o-dal with others who were much smaller. Other places were taken over by maps and what must be a computer placed on a desk. Also on the wall were sets of buttons with lock-down levers over them. Something about them seemed very ominous to both human and nannite.

"Check the wiring connections to these, Minnis and see where they go. If they go where I think they do, disable them," Fredrick ordered.

"Ok Fred, you will have to step out for a while and lose

my protection while I do this. One shaky move and I could set off what I am examining!"

Fred emerged from the back of the nannite as Minnis connected to the wiring to trace where it led. He still had the re-breather and globe over his face with a molecule thin suit covering his body. It was not enough to prevent the heat sensor from registering his presence. A light began to flash on the wall and the sound of a siren started up. Minnis found what she needed and traced the missile controls to their deadly cargo. She disconnected them and fused them beyond repair. Within a Nano-second she opened the air-lock door to let the rest of the boarding party into the base.

The commander smashed the door open to be confronted with something from out of a nightmare. A large biped with a silver globe over its head stood next to the weapon rack while a silver creature larger than the other flowed away from the missile controls. These were alien creatures from somewhere else and they were inside his control room! Bipeds! Not trip'o-dal. They had only two arms and legs instead of four arms and three legs, his instinct was to reach for the weapons on the wall only to find they were welded to the fixings. He was aware of the silver thing flowing up his arm towards his head and screamed in terror. He felt a sting on the side of his head and then blackness.

Fredrick laughed and said, "I think that went well, Minnis! Have you let the others in?"

"They are in the lower corridor my old friend and making their way here. I have disconnected this base from its weapons and communications to the world below. We need to do something that will prevent a world war.

At the bottom of the lift shaft the conic took the lead and his many tiny legs sped the Vogb in front of the others. As he glided along, his electrically charged tendril sought out the panicking trip'o-dal soldiers while his forward

187

tentacles reached for them. As they fell out of the sleeping hammocks, those at the front were sent straight back to sleep by the sting. B-o-g had studied trip'o-dal physiology at some length and surmised that these would be no different from his studies. Each sting was just enough to render the unlucky nearest into instant sleep. The rest tried to operate the weapons on the wall, only to find them useless. Now a real panic set in and they scrambled over one another to escape, only to fall one after another onto the floor in shuddering paralysis. Some of them were able to glimpse a female of their own species walking behind the weird alien creature before they were rendered unconscious.

Each soldier was secured to the weapons rack by a nannite-stranded set of cuffs around their necks. Once sealed together it would require another nannite to undo the restraints and remove them.

Primm made her way over to Fredrick and Minnis and asked, "Which way now? We need to find the scientists on this base. These types I will be able to talk to."

Minnis pointed to the corridor on their right and said, "Lady Primm, the observatory is there. I have the map of the place now taken from the computers. There are five life signs."

The Thipdar thought for a moment and directed her thoughts to the symbiont, "Goss" she said.

The ancient voice echoed in her mind, "I hear you Lady Primm."

"Are you concentrated enough to set free spores?"

"I am always ready to increase the collective! I understand and will do as you ask," the symbiont replied and allowed the always surplus spores to detach themselves from the skin of the hosts.

The air-conditioning sucked the free spores from out of the area and spread them throughout the base while the invaders made their way to the main control room and observatory. Fredrick had passed the military commander to Minnis's tender care so that she could drag him along to the control room. Already the spores had found new hosts and were multiplying inside the brains, connecting up synapses and neurons to facilitate the telepathic network. Inside the control room the director and chief scientist had opened the door ready to receive the new visitors, not knowing just what had invaded them. The only logical train of thought dictated that whatever was coming was coming anyway! They were all feeling dizzy as the spores multiplied and they began to here voices inside their heads.

Primm tried a direct link to the chief scientist, "Goss! Connect me to that one," she said pointing at the eldest Thipdar, "and screen us from the rest."

The trip'o-dal opened his eyes wide as Primm entered his mind, "Greetings, Joecata! You are the Director and chief scientist of Moon-base One, leader of family Chador, we have come here to stop a war and save you all from needless death."

CHAPTER FOURTEEN

Kamiel had the Lagdoo take the Ark into a wide orbit behind the larger outer moon and matched velocities. As the artificial world of the Ark was hollow, its mass was not enough to cause the outer moon to wobble in its path around the living world beneath them. He had watched the events unfold inside the inner moon's base through the link with Minnis.

He concentrated his mind and called upon the symbiont, "Goss!"

"I am here, Kamiel."

"Connect me with Primm."

Kamiel looked out of the Thipdar's eyes at the terrified trip'o-dals facing the mixed alien crew who were examining the observational equipment with interest.

"Have you made contact, Primm? Can they understand us yet? Judging by events down on the home world we do not have much time to stop a war happening," Kamiel worried.

"Give me a little more time, Kamiel. This is all too new for them. They think they are going mad! Let me try again with this one. He is the director of the establishment."

"I will ride behind your mind," the nannite replied. "Do your best!"

"Joecata! I know that you can hear me! Use your mind not your voice," she implored and held out the lower arms in supplication so that she did not seem a threat.

Sweat broke out on the forehead of the director as he concentrated his mind to answer, "Yes! Yes! I can hear you inside my mind. Who are you? What are you? You look like us, but these other ones! What are they?"

"We are your salvation! In fact we may be too late unless

you are willing to work with me to defuse the situation down on your home world. You at least seem capable of peaceful thoughts, which is more than I can say for this one," said Primm, pointing at the Commander. "Is he sane?"

Joecata shrugged and answered, "Sometimes I wonder? His name is Simi and he is the head of the military presence on this 'scientific' base. These people seem to want to dominate everyone on our world."

"Would you be amazed if I told you that they have been brainwashed into this frame of mind? You have much to learn. The first thing you must do is to trust me. With this gift we have given you, you will find that you cannot lie! Open your mind and let me and my friends enlighten you," Primm asked.

The commander was beginning to awaken from Minnis's nerve clench and began to struggle in the nannite's grasp. The Guardian fashioned a leash around Commander Simi's neck and fixed it to the wall. She then stood some small distance away and observed the Thipdar's ineffectual struggles with the unbreakable nannite strands.

Something cold and deadly slipped into his mind.

"Stop your struggling. It will do you no good," Minnis entered the Thipdar's mind through her own contact with the nannite strands. "When I deem it fit to let you go and only then, look, listen and learn. The continued existence of your race will depend on such as you breaking away from old habits! Believe me when I tell you we are not here to harm you. Your mind will change for the better. My friends have forever joined you to the Goss. It is a symbiont that will enable you to speak to any other sentient being; - mind to mind as it were! You will find that you can no longer lie and neither can anyone else that is host to the Goss. Reach out with your mind and ask for connection."

The Commander anchored his three legs down and

realised that there was a difference inside him. There seemed to be something else in his mind besides his own thoughts. It was faint, but it was there and quite unlike the cold steely presence of the silver thing that had him tethered.

The Commander reached into his mind and found a strange warmth just under the surface, "Goss?"

"I am here, Commander Simi. I will always be here. How may I serve you?"

The commander shook with the shock of hearing another's voice inside his head.

He did as he was conditioned to do and asked, "Can you connect me to my men? I wish to take away their fear."

He was immediately conscious of a multitude of questioning voices, all terrified of the situation.

The Commander made contact with them all and relayed the situation to them in an instant and immediately understood the silver thing's statement about lying. Whatever he knew, then so did they! They understood all his worries and doubts and they knew each other's hopes and problems. All of them now quietly anchored down on their tripod bases and waited for the next thing to happen, or the next order.

Primm and Joecata opened the channels to include the Commander and the rest of the scientific staff. Within moments the reason for the aliens being here was shared with every trip'o-dal on the base as the telepathic link spread out to the soldiers tethered to the walls of the barracks.

The mind of the Commander recoiled for a moment, as Kamiel entered his mind and said, "I understand you Commander, more than you can know. I also understand your doubts and the fact that this first contact goes against all you have believed to be true. I want you to signal the home world that you have had some technical difficulties, with a meteor striking your signalling antennae that has put you out of radio touch for a while. Better repairs have to be made and there is no reason to panic. Then I think you should come and visit me, where I can enlighten you further about our visit. If I tell you too much all at once, it will overwhelm you."

Minnis dissolved the tether to the Commander and he was free. He immediately operated the signalling equipment and relayed Kamiel's message to the anxious world below.

He then turned to the Director and said, "I owe you an apology, Director. My previous behaviour was beyond reproach! You were right in what you said about the forces down below on our home world. My mind is so clear now. None of the events down there make any sense at all. What possible threat could the people of the independent rebellion be to us, that we need to send armies against them?"

"My dear friend, we were all misguided and misled. The family Chador would welcome the family Axis to their hospitality on the home world below, but not before our new friends have explained what they wish to do and why. We have been told to watch the main observation screen. Their spaceship approaches."

The Thipdar watched the main screens in amazement and awe as a silver globe appeared on their screens. There would have been room inside it to have placed ten moon-bases and still not be totally full. While they stared at the screens, the globe changed shape, extending anchoring feet as Toarvak 6 released herself from the crust of the inner moon and rose out of the mountains behind the base. The trip'o-dals watched in awe at the size of the globe of silver that filled the view screens. She floated with majestic purpose across the ink-black sky until she settled into a position by the side of the airlock. There she sunk into the regolith and anchored down. Next she extended a pseudopod into the base out of phase to make an easy exit for Primm and the others. Fortunately the observatory had been constructed with a high ceiling, as the first new alien through was Link-soo-shan.

The Thipdar were very aware of a new sharp intellect amongst them as the Gnathe swept into the chamber. These were aliens indeed! The giants had to stoop a little as they walked from the out of phase tunnel and into the observatory. Link-soo-shan leaned forwards towards the Director and the Commander and place her immense three fingered hands around their upper arms.

"I have been asked to take you to Kamiel. This will entail travelling through space with me. Do not panic," she warned them as she concentrated her mind through the Matrix and opened a door into the main control room of the Ark.

Now at least she could stand upright as she released the two Thipdar into the presence of Kamiel. The two trip'o-dals were transfixed as they looked around the room at the reptilian Lagdoo stood at their posts! Other Gnathe were in evidence as were the Vogb placed in groups and studying the big screens. Several creatures shaped like very big cats with four legs and two arms with an upright torso were busy selecting results from a computer. The creatures that nearly put them into madness were the insectoids. The creatures did everything in unison as if controlled by a single intellect. They were black and came up to the Thipdar's hips with huge reflective eyes and formidable pinchers at their mouths. Walking through all these were more of the biped beings that had stormed the moon-base. Stood observing them was an un-impressive looking silver biped that was a slim copy of the organic bipeds. There was no mouth to be seen or eyes, just an optical band around the top of its head.

An ice-cold intellect slipped into their minds.

"I am Kamiel," the silver creature projected into their minds. "Welcome to the last Ark of the Goss. All that you see around you are to become your friends. We have come a long way to find you and to be truthful (what else!) we have only just begun our mission! If you are fully recovered I have to show you something and demonstrate to you what danger you are in at this very moment. I am sorry to be blunt, but we do not have the time to be gentle!"

"What are you and the other silver one that detained me? I have never seen the like of you before," said commander Simi.

Kamiel paused for a moment and answered, "I am an artificial intelligence built by the ancestors of the bipeds that you walk amongst. You have computers on your moon and below on your world. Think of my kind as a very advanced type of computer. Enough questions for now! Follow me."

He led them through the alien throng, who after a good look at them, ignored the two Thipdar completely and carried on with their work. On the wall was a flat viewing screen that was showing a picture of their home world, taken during the Ark's journey to hide behind the outer moon. Superimposed over the beautiful planet was an ethereal network that pulsed as they stared at the screen. Strands spun away from the net and disappeared into a shimmering opening in space. They found that they could not look at it for too long, as it made them feel dizzy and ill.

"The world below is our Shandon! It means Mother of Life," the Director exclaimed. "What is that net that surrounds our world? Did you put it there?"

"No! We did not place that abomination around your world. Something that feeds on life energy and promotes killing to get its sustenance, placed it around your world," replied Kamiel. "That is why we are here! I will ask you both to open up your minds while I enter them and give you some of the background."

The two Thipdar readily agreed and felt the cold logical mind of what they both now realised was an artificial intelligence, slip once more into their minds.

The Commander stared at the screen with increasing horror and said, "You are going to destroy that?"

"It's what we came to do! A collector will visit this world soon and tidy up what it has begun. Before that we must seed your world with the spores of the Goss and destroy the conditioning that you have endured for centuries. You are all sentient creatures! Sentients do not kill sentients. Ever! As we speak there are thousands of Toarvaks seeding Shandon with the symbiont. A new age will arise. Your profession is now obsolete Commander, but we will need the discipline behind it! After a while, this hollowed out moon is about to cause an eclipse of the sun to demonstrate our presence here and thousands of alien beings will orchestrate an information exchange with every living thing on your world. Your armies will all go home and your weapons will be thrown down and the metal reused. When everything becomes stable we will proceed to the next stage and destroy the web."

The Commander stared at the Guardian and replied bitterly, "So instead of destroying ourselves, this thing will do it for us? You have given us little choice!"

Kamiel gave the Thipdar a cold eyeless stare and said, "You have no choice at all! Had we come any later we would have found a ruined world with only survivors living amongst the wreckage of your civilization. Billions would have died here to feed the Harvester. We have destroyed one of these things before. What we did we can do again!

I cannot tell you to not fear this thing that collects life force for a greater entity, but I can ask for courage! There is much for you to learn about the psychic skills that as a race you must develop, that we may need to draw upon."

Over the next few days crossing the surface of Shandon, the invisible Toarvaks spread the spores of the Goss across the settled areas of the landmasses, concentrating on the cities and towns. As the Thipdar began to hear each other's thoughts they stopped what they were doing and listened to each other. Traffic drew to a stop and machines were switched off for a while. Those that were in positions of power found that all their secrets were now known by all of the people that they led. Some could not cope and went mad. Most of the trip'o-dals began to think in a different fashion and rapidly adapted.

As things settled down and the Thipdar began to pick up the pieces of their lives they heard voices in their minds that told them over and over again "Do not be afraid. Look to the skies. We have come to stop the killing. No more of your friends will need to lay down their lives for a cause that someone else tells them needs to be imposed."

In the skies over all major cities appeared the Toarvaks as they came back into universal space-time. Thousands of giant silver globes that reflected the sun's intense glare just hung in the sky motionless. High above them passing in front of the sun's light and causing an eclipse to many of the Thipdar cities was the Ark of the Goss, as it manoeuvred into a synchronistic orbit over the main city of the dominant continent.

The city of Anton had guests, the like of which had never been imagined before in its thousand-year history. As the weeks turned into months, the 'New Friends' began to be seen all over the planet called Shandon. The 'Mother of Life' was found to be one of many potential life-bearing worlds in Andromeda. The Toarvaks had been busy and had joined together to produce ten more of their kind that were donated to the Thipdar with accompanying Kresh. A forced maturity became the order of the day. All the time Kamiel had observers surrounding the opening to the wormhole to keep a watch for the coming emergence of the Collector for this world. The Tran-sentients extended their telepathic reach to set a watch for the Collector's arrival.

Their first contact with the scientific director, Joecata and the military Commander, Simi had been a useful way of opening doors, both in government and the scientific circles. The trip'o-dals had evolved a military style government that had endured by birthright for hundreds of years. Those that had risen to the top of the hierarchy kept their positions due to talent and behind the scenes manoeuvrings. The new ability of reading minds had shook the governing body to the core. Now it was impossible to lie or cheat without it being known. It only took one rash killing and the participation of every Thipdar connected by the Goss, in the death of the unfortunate prince, to make a profound change. Animals taken to slaughter for food were killed in as merciful a way as could be done, so that the 'killer' did not endure the creatures death. The society of the trip'o-dal people underwent an irreversible and profound change.

Kamiel called the meeting to order in the 'Great Hall' that dominated the great city of Anton. By using the Goss he was able to reach a great many more than the Thipdar stood in the hall.

He stood at the top of a sweeping ramp overlooking the assembly.

"By now all of you are full of the knowledge of where we came from and why we are here," he said to the assembly. "Soon a collector will come, when we break the force net that holds all the life energy of this beautiful world. When that happens, every person on this world will join up his or her mind to become a worldwide group mind. When this hungry abomination comes out of its hole you must stop it dead in its tracks. This is the point at which we will destroy it. Until we have disposed of its master, you will have to be vigilant for the rest of your days as others will come for your life energy."

"We have had to alter our entire way of life to do this thing that you say is necessary," the leader of the Thipdar said. "We have no quarrel with that as we have been re-educated as to the real nature of things. What of the far future? What time have we got left if you can defeat this energy being?"

Alexander took the lead and projected the facts, as the Nannites had foretold to the council of worlds from Primm's expedition outside of the home galaxy.

"You will have a good few thousands of years yet, being this far away from the point of impact. Sometime you and the other members of Andromeda will have to do as our people have done and build a globular cluster on the fringes of this galaxy to escape the collision. If we live, we can help you do that. Our knowledge is yours to keep! There are other civilizations out there being preyed upon by the abomination that need our help. The more we can save, the greater the group minds we can bring to bear on the problem."

"Just to remind you," Kamiel stated, "this thing destabilises stars when it finds any race of beings capable of leaving their own planetary system for another one. Destroying another collector will not stop this thing, so be quiet, be very quiet after this thing is done. Now we must leave you and cut the web!"

Toarvak 12,042 hovered over the Great Hall and extended a pseudopod down through the building until it covered the Guardian and his human friend. It took them out of phase and retreated into orbit. High above the world of Shandon the Toarvak took them to the Ark and placed them both into the control room.

In Kamiel's absence, once again the great stargate rings had been placed into position and tuned to focus onto the open wormhole that the threads of the net around Shandon entered. The Toarvak ships that had the responsibility of manoeuvring the second ring had attached themselves to it and were ready. This time the first burst of sun power would be focused on the energy carrying nets to blast them out of existence.

Kamiel settled himself over the Lagdoo and the Vogb hosts and became as one with their biological neural systems. He reached out to the willing minds and once again led a vast group mind to open the stargate and twist space in the centre of the Thipdar's star. He funnelled the expanding fury of fused atoms down onto the myriad threads that disappeared into the wormhole and felt them rip apart. The net unravelled around the world below and Kamiel felt the added strength given freely from the millions of trip'o-dals below.

Many light years away at a wormhole junction a very large collector spread itself over many threads leading to numerous worlds. The recoil from the severed threads to the Thipdar world shook it out of its slumber and woke it into real-time. The Collector budded off a small portion of itself to hold the strings together, while it went to investigate this unique phenomenon. In the billions of years of its existence as a collector of energy for the giant harvesting entity of which it was a small part, nothing like this had ever happened. The Collector did not have the capacity for worry and the closest emotion it possessed was a vague feeling of curiosity and a need to find out what had severed the signal strings. Swiftly it manipulated the wormhole to send it on its way to the Thipdar world. It had been a good feeding ground in the past and was approaching maturity once more. It was close to the harvesting point on several worlds and would soon do its work in collecting the life energy from these and returning to its absorption and re-birth. Maybe this world had ripened in its absence and was ready now. It would soon find out and was content in the anticipation of that knowledge. The Collector sent scouting probes of its energy base slightly ahead to relay back if the gathering net was still in place, in case it needed to spin another one.

These small extensions of the Collector's will, eased out of the wormhole's mouth and spread out to form a telescopic cubical hollow pyramid. Eight tiny suns appeared to shine in a truncated, pyramidal pattern.

Kamiel had sensed these intrusions and kept the fleet of Toarvaks out of phase. Only the Ark's observatory section of the main control room remained in normal time and space, the rest of the hollow moon was placed out of phase, contained by the remaining Toarvaks. It was from here that Kamiel controlled the group mind and the telekinetic crystals dotted around the focusing rings of the stargates. The main command crystals were tuned and open. All it needed was for Kamiel to unleash the fury of the stars heart through the gate and out of the other one close to the wormhole's exit.

The information relaying back to the Collector showed that the gathering net had unravelled, so the entity reached down into itself to bring the complex web into being to send it to encompass the planet below. As it emerged from the wormhole's exit it felt the accumulated life energy from its repeated visits swell, as billions of Thipdar minds registered on its consciousness. The other collector had been half the size of the Ark. This inverted arrowhead was four times the volume of the hollowed out moon. The wings swept out from its body to overshadow Kamiel's battle craft. Bolts of lightening pulsed between the tips as the Collector slowed its velocity until it hung in the skies above the Thipdar world.

"Time to harvest indeed! The 'Great One' will be satisfied with this," it thought to itself and felt the wormhole shut behind it.

Kamiel marvelled at the size of the energy patterns floating in front of him and released the locks on the gates.

The internal mass of the sun exploded into its centre and removed a great deal of its consciousness. For a brief time there were two suns in the skies of Shandon. As an automatic defence mechanism the Collector erected a force shield from the wings to deflect the rest of the incandescent energy away. A fiery stream of fusing atoms licked across the skies of Shandon and vaporised a major city in its passing.

The Thipdar planetary mind reached out to the Collector, using the telekinetic crystals in the rings to twist space around the energy being and thrust what was left into the sun. The psychic scream of death stayed in the collective consciousness for some time after the event. It would be something that the people of Shandon would remember for many years.

Kamiel withdrew from the telepathic link and sought the company of his own kind. He was shaken to the core of his electronic soul and found himself again in the office of Alexander McBald as a programming failsafe activated.

The old man was sat at his desk and leaning back into his chair.

"That was a tough one, my son," he said. It's been a long time since I was called out of your programs to advise you."

"Once again through my actions hundreds of thousands have died," the Guardian replied.

"Without those actions, billions would have fed the abomination that you have been asked to stop," the old man replied. "Anyway you now have complete free will to do whatever you think is right. Listen to your friends! They will tell you that you made the right decision!"

Kamiel found himself alone once more for a few minutes until Asue and Solace joined him.

"How many Thipdar died? Do we know?" He said.

Asue bent her head forwards and replied, "The city of Praxis and all the outlying towns have disappeared. There is a line of fiery destruction that cuts a thousand mile swathe until it boiled the sea! There must be more than a million of them cut down."

Solace touched the nannite on the arm and communicated straight to his mind, "Only you, Kamiel 637, could have mustered this armada. Only you could have taken the decisions that you have. There are billions of intelligent beings below us that have you to thank for their existence. Without your stand here they would have been taken to feed the abomination that will soon notice that some of its collectors have gone missing. Behind that wormhole lies a direction to other worlds that this thing was waiting to pounce upon. The Lagdoo only closed the wormhole this time and threads of energy are spun back to a junction. This is where we have to go next!"

Kamiel laughed and replied, "You as well! I have just been talking with my creator! He is lodged in my personality and surfaces whenever I need reminding of my duty! Goss!"

"I am here Kamiel."

"Give me a broadband connection to all in this system. I need all of them to hear me," the Guardian replied.

"People of Shandon and all of the expedition, hear me.

We have destroyed a larger collector than we have met before. This world's group mind can defend itself without us. We will leave some of the mind adepts behind and a number of Kresh to help you build and understand the new sciences that we leave behind. You have ten Toarvaks to assist you in crystal mining on the surface of the gas giants that are in this system. We are going to find out what lies at the junction of this wormhole. I hope that we will find more intelligent races and prevent the Harvester from having them. We may be back? Let me hope that if we do come this way again we will find you well prepared!"

Asue turned towards the attentive Lagdoo and said, "You heard him! Collect all Toarvaks and tell them to return to the Ark. We must be on our way as soon as possible!"

CHAPTER FIFTEEN

The beautiful world of Shandon turned below them, as the last Ark of the Goss approached the re-opened wormhole. Behind them on the trip'o-dal planet, Kamiel had left a number of aliens and nannites to teach the knowledge that the expedition had brought with them. The Toarvaks had returned to the Ark and had resumed their positions around the hollowed out moon. The Lagdoo opened up the wormhole and the hollow moon dropped through, following the energy strands left behind by the massive collector.

Once again Kamiel gave the order to go out of phase and the speed of the Ark went from sub-light to trans-light velocity. This time the journey would be much shorter, so it was unnecessary to go into stasis and the time could be spent rethinking strategy.

Deep inside Toarvak 6, Link-soo-shan over-saw the final stages of her most ambitious project in genetic engineering. In a telepathic society it had been extremely difficult to keep any secrets from each other. The nannite that had worked with her had foregone the ball of organic flesh that would have been host to the Goss. She was a 'Sharn' type nannite and was also a genetic engineer and life specialist with a greater than usual amount of curiosity. What the two of them were about to do, had never been done before. They had waited eighteen years for this day to arrive and had managed to keep this secret from all other minds. The laboratory with its single life vat had been keyed to their signatures for all that time and had not been entered by anyone else.

The vat began to drain of fluid while the two scientists

read the life-sign, monitors for any discrepancies. With great care, the vat began to tilt so that the mindless clone lay upon her back. When all the fluid had drained away and the sides retracted, the breathing tube was removed. Link-soo-shan watched, as the woman's chest continued to rise and fall without the input of the breathing tube. The eyes remained closed, as if the body were asleep. The human woman would be a striking beauty amongst her kind. She was tall, with blazing red hair that fell in waves to her waist and muscular in her build so that she could have been at the peak of her athletic powers. The body age of the clone was set at eighteen years and her skin colour was a light chocolate brown and had been chosen by Link-soo-shan herself. A great deal of extra genetic engineering had gone into the mix by adding the Gnathen forebrain that gave her a slightly enlarged forehead. Here would be the lobes that enhanced the psychic powers that the Gnathen-human people possessed.

The nannite reached forward to the strong hands lying quietly by her sides and trimmed her nails. Next she did the clone's toenails and inspected her firm legs for any imperfections. She made contact with the skin and entered her bloodstream, releasing nannites into the system so that she could monitor the awakening.

Link-soo-shan finally reached into a pocket on her bandolier and removed a small box. She opened it and stared at the flat crystal mounted inside.

"Well Kamiel," she thought to herself, "I am about to carry out the bargain I made with you so very long ago, when you asked me if I wanted anything to take with me into the future. There is still one wrong that I need to make amends. I just hope that this will work as well as I hoped."

The Brood-mother placed the crystal upon the forehead of the engineered clone and concentrated her mind into the personality placed into it.

"Restrain her," she said and waited until the Guardian had looped nannite strands over the sleeping woman.

She felt the personality quicken from the Matrix in the crystal and cross over the mental link into its new home.

"Nagoth-shan! Be unafraid. I who gave you life and purpose give you life again. Do nothing, but breath in and out. We will have much to do together, you and I. This body that you will awaken in, is a human female that I designed with this nannite's assistance. It will be very unfamiliar to you. Take your time getting used to it. I once did you a great wrong and I mean to make amends."

The body went into spasms as Nagoth's mind filled the empty shell.

"Great reverend Mother! I am alive again! I breathe! I feel so different!" Nagoth gasped and began to quieten.

Link placed her great hand upon the chest of the woman and said, "Stay calm and we will remove the restraints."

Two piercing green eyes looked into hers with total trust and stared at her hands as the tethers withdrew and she raised them up. Nagoth began to panic!

"I have four fingers! My legs are wrong! What has happened to my knees? My legs bend a different way. My tail has gone," she cried.

"Sleep my daughter. Sleep! I need a little help, my nannite friend and I think I know just who," remarked Link-soo-shan as she turned away after returning her daughter to an uneasy slumber.

Emelia had become bored with nothing to do and had wandered away from the quarters that she shared with Larse. Having been born on a world that had been predominantly human, she had never seen aliens before except the Gnathe, after she had met Larse. She had heard of the Gnathe by the books she had read as a child, but all these others were totally new. She found that she liked them more and more as she got to know them. The Vogb and their amazing light shows around the top ring when they 'spoke' were a delight to watch. She was very fond of the Bazantii and enjoyed their company, particularly when they permitted her to ride upon their backs. She had played chess with the insectoid queens and had even been allowed to be there as the Lagdoo hatched from their eggs. Whenever she got the chance she visited the Kresh and had got to know some of the clans. She had been given a tunic made from the pelt of an old male who had died. It had been his wish that she wear it to remember him by. The ones that still sent shivers up and down her spine were the Gnathen Brood-mothers. They were so big!

She felt a warmth inside her head and heard her name, "Emelia?"

"Yes Goss. Who wants to speak with me?"

"Hello Emelia! It is I, Link-soo-shan. I need your help. Could you join me at the life laboratories this very moment?"

"Of course I can. I am on my way," she answered. "What can I do for you?"

"At the moment shut up your mind and be silent," Link answered. "I will show you why when you get here and thank you!"

Mystified, Emelia did as she was asked and following the map Link had imprinted into her mind. As she walked Emelia did the little exercises she had learnt of tightening her mind, so that no stray thoughts escaped. She passed by many different aliens and a few humans on her way down, but did not stop to 'talk' with any of them.

She entered a small laboratory and saw a nannite and the great Link-soo-shan stood by a horizontally positioned life vat. As the giant moved to one side, she could see a sleeping woman laid on top of the table. She was lightly restrained.

"Who is this? She asked.

"If I were to tell you she is an old debt that I mean to repay, your curiosity would drive you to find out more! So, my young human, I will need you to listen while I tell you of events that happened long ago," Link answered and gestured to a nearby chair. "How much do you know of the first contact with Gnathe and human?"

"Only what the history books told me when I was growing up. I know about the struggle for power between you and Trann-link-sool. You were once the tyrannical ruler of the Gnathen Empire. You attacked the human settlement by teleporting into the domes and captured Alexander. I don't remember much else, except that you hid in someone else's body when everyone thought you had died and returned to strike back at the new civilization formed between the Gnathe, humans and apes."

Link-soo-shan stared at the blonde haired woman in quiet amazement, at how little she knew of the mind shattering events that had shaped the civilization that they were trying to save. Even though the human had joined her mind to Link-soo-shan's and the others to become the Toarvak 6 gestalt, Emelia had not eavesdropped into the other minds that made the collective. Link-soo-shan had to decide just how much to tell her to gain her understanding and support. There was so much to tell, that a complete history would overwhelm even this bright intelligent woman.

"My dear Emelia," she projected into her mind, "I will try to tell you what I can of our history. During the conflict between the humans and myself I was a totally different person to the one you see now. I was ruthless and cruel beyond anything that you could imagine. The events that changed my personality to the way I am today are it seems a little lost in the past. Maybe for the best! During my conflict with the humans, Alexander's captivity by me was more than unpleasant. Because of my hatred and loathing for him, I devised a torture that would not only bring him to the point of madness and humiliation, but would inflict more pain than you could imagine. As it happens the outcome was totally different from what I desired."

"What did you do?" asked Emelia clenching her fists in anticipating horror.

"Gnathe do not mate quite like you do. When the male is ripe for mating his breeding stalk is snapped off by the hooks in the vagina of the Gnathen female and inserted into the egg. The fertilised egg is then passed to the Brood-mother to be carried and grown into young. I held Alexander in a telekinetic grip while I mated him to the Gnathe you see here on this table. Upon climax Nagoth almost tore Alexander apart and nearly killed him. During the sexual union, Alex got into her mind and undid all the conditioning that I had put there since she was a young Gnathe. She helped him to escape from my settlement and was instrumental in my downfall."

Emelia shuddered with revulsion and stared at the young woman lay sleeping on the table, and cried out, "Do mean what I think you do? Is the mind inside that young woman that of Nagoth? Why? Why have you done this terrible thing?"

"To make amends, young one. Listen to me. Open your mind to what I say to you. All her life this Gnathe loved Alexander far more than you could know. She saved his life and showed courage far beyond most Gnathen females and was Alexander's protector all her life. Most of all, she was my only surviving daughter of those times and before she died I saved her mind in the Matrix of a memory crystal. What we are about to face in the future, I cannot even guess. This threat is far more dangerous than the Goss. In all the years since Nagoth 'died' I have carried her sleeping mind with me and Alexander has never forged a lasting relationship with any other human female. He needs someone by his side and I believe that this personality transferred into this human woman is what he needs."

"You were the one who defeated the Goss! I remember now," Emelia said and lowered her guard. "Give me more information about your history before I agree to do what you want."

Link sighed and agreed. She gave Emelia a condensed version of the events that produced the first great group mind composed of Gnathe, humans and apes that searched through time to find the original Alexander McBald.

Then she took her through the transporting of Kamiel through time, with her mind saved and filed in his neural nets, back six million years to when McBald was alive. She showed her the moving of the Earth and moon to its new home with the transplanting of the Gnathe to Jupiter. Finally she enlightened her of the long years when she shared Kamiel's mind with Alexander himself and the bond that they forged over the centuries.

Emelia staggered and reached out, to find the strong grip of the giant holding her steady. She looked up at the triangular face staring intently at hers and felt the tip of Link-soo-shan's tongue touch her lightly on her cheeks.

"That was very private, Link-soo-shan," she said and touched the lips of the Gnathe with her fingertips. "I will do whatever you ask. You can depend on it!"

"What I need you to do is to place your mind inside Nagoth's. I need you to show her how to be a woman! I require you to show her how her new body works; how to walk, how move as you do. It must be done gently and with great care," Link insisted. "She must learn everything that a human learns from a baby, but remembering that

211

she has an adult's body. Most of all you must teach her about sex and how to cope with the intense urges that you humans live with. I do not have that problem, so am not equipped to advise on that subject! The Gnathe mate once on a cycle, you humans can do this thing any time. How you find time for rational thought has kept my curiosity bubbling for thousands of years!"

"Waken her once I am inside her mind and make her an echo of my actions," Emelia demanded.

Once again the nannite allowed the mind of Nagoth to rise from slumber.

As Nagoth surfaced she found that she had a partner in her mind that linked her muscles to another. She sat up and felt a little nausea that reduced once she opened her eyes and looked into a human face. It smiled at her and she felt her lips part and she smiled back. A hand was held out and she gripped it. Next she felt her body slide forwards and off the table so that her bare feet met the floor. She stood! All the time Emelia's mind stayed lightly inside hers, guiding, not forcing her beyond what she was capable of.

The two women walked together slowly around the table, hand in hand. Both of them bent down and touched the floor. Emelia sat and Nagoth sat with her, still gripping her hand tightly. Slowly they both drew their knees up together and rolled over onto their fronts into a crouching position. The two women stood up and released hands. Nagoth made a few tottering steps towards Link-soo-shan, gaining confidence with every step.

"This is strange without a tail," her mind projected to Link, "But I feel that I can do this. Thank you great Reverend Mother for what you have done. This body is amazing!"

"You must learn to talk with your mouth in the human language as humans do and you have to learn how to eat with your mouth closed! There is still so much for you to learn," said her Brood-mother.

The wall bulged and exuded a silver form that took on the familiar characteristics of the female shape of Toarvak 6.

"Many years have I watched this room and wondered just what you were doing here, Link-soo-shan? Quiet have I been and my own counsel have I kept. My continued silence will you have. This whole project requires that all of us have a reason to need it to succeed. Alexander has nothing but his duty to drive him. This will give him something more to motivate his desires. Years I lived inside my Larse, Emelia, knowing his every thought, feeling his every pain. Spread was I through both man, Gnathe and Kresh. Understand you all do I, yet surprised am I even now, by all intelligent organic life!"

"If you were flesh and blood I could be very jealous of you, Tee Six," Emelia laughed and placed her hand affectionately upon the nannite's shoulder.

"Love him both do we in our own fashion, Emelia," the artificial intelligence replied. *"Clothes will this human female need. A nannite have I sent for a selection of tunics and shoes to bring here, as naked she will create a commotion! Did you not think it through that when she can walk from here, dressed she will need to be?"*

Nagoth had by now managed to walk unaided around the life vat that her body had grown inside for eighteen years. She had learnt to bend and touch the floor without falling over, after the first tumble. Emelia had helped her to her feet and found her to be much steadier in managing the unfamiliar body. Every minute that passed by, the Gnathe settled more and more into the human female body. Gradually she found that Emelia had removed herself from her motor systems and she was now totally in control of her body. She explored herself with her hands and fingers and found that anatomically she was very similar to how she remembered herself, except for her ears and the hair that fell to her waist. There were also two fleshy protrusions jutting from her chest that felt strange. A feeling of discomfort began to mount and went through her lower abdomen. A muscle relaxed and she found herself passing urine onto the floor.

"Nagoth, I'm so sorry! I should have sensed your need," Emelia thought and helped her squat over the drain. She entered her mind and imprinted some of the basic female's hygiene etiquettes.

"Thanks Emelia. I'm getting there," Nagoth said, using her vocal cords and mouth for the first time.

The clone had a fine contralto voice with a slight husky edge and a musical lilt that transfixed Emelia where she stood with surprise.

"What a beautiful voice you have, Nagoth," she said in astonishment. "That will turn some heads!"

At that moment a nannite appeared with a selection of tunics, skirts, underclothes and shoes. Toarvak 6 met her at the laboratory door and sent her on her way bringing them to Emelia.

"Through these you should sort and decide you must what this new human hybrid will wear," Toarvak 6 remarked. *"Interesting this will be!"*

Emelia stared hard at Nagoth and decided the first thing to fit would be the bra to support the two magnificent breasts that this clone had been endowed. She sorted through what the nannite had brought and with an appraising eye dressed Nagoth with a suitable size and showed her how to alter the straps for comfort. Panties and socks were soon added to leave a tunic and shorts. She chose an olive green tunic and rusty brown shorts. Emelia whistled through her teeth at the transformation she had achieved. Nagoth naked was eye-catching enough, but clothed she was enhanced beyond any woman Emelia had ever seen. Link-soo-shan's genetic engineering had produced far more than the Brood-mother could have foreseen. Nagoth was stunning!

"What's the matter, Emelia? You are staring at me! Is

there something wrong with me? Am I ugly?" Nagoth asked.

"Oh no, my dear! Oh no! You are the most attractive human being I have ever seen, my new friend. Let me put a pair of flat soled shoes upon those perfect feet and see how you walk, fully clothed," Emelia instructed her and found a pair of bright red shoes to fit.

Link-soo-shan was satisfied by the reactions that Emelia had expressed. Part of her plan had come together, even better than she had hoped, now the next step! The Brood-mother turned and watched as her daughter walked steadily around the laboratory with increasing confidence. It certainly looked as if the transplant had been a success. Time alone would tell!

Link tuned her mind towards her daughter and said, "Do not be too ambitious little one. Learn to live in this new body before you try meeting too many people. Most of all wait until you are confident enough with others before you meet Alexander! He can wait. He has been without you for thousands of years and has been re-cloned many times. Emelia was once very old before she was collected and also re-found a love she thought she would never see again. There are many kinds of love, my child, not all between male and female! I give you this life not just to enjoy, but also to give an old friend a balance that he has lost. He becomes reckless in his reincarnation and that bothers me!"

"Great Lady Link and most Reverend Mother, believe me when I tell you I will do all that you say. I am alive as I could never have ever thought possible, in a way that I could never dream of," Nagoth replied. "Alexander can wait, but when I cannot stand to be apart from him any more, I will go to him and only hope that he will not react in horror!"

Emelia laughed and said, "My dear new friend, I guaranty he will not react with horror! You will come back with me to my quarters with my man, Larse and learn to live as a human woman. We will become great friends you and I. Great friends!"

The weeks passed by and Kamiel stopped the Ark at the crossroads of the wormholes. There, left by the Collector to hold the pathways together was a small version of itself. From the inverted 'vee' a number of strands showed up on the sensors. There were five that stretched away down each individual wormhole. By the energy generated by each warp in the fabric of space, Kamiel could make a good assessment between them as to which of them led down a short tunnel and which ones were further away. The 'bud' off the collector was quite oblivious to the Ark's presence, as Kamiel had kept it out of phase. Here the crossover points were light-years from any star, so destroying this small version of the collector would present a problem. Besides which, leaving it here would ensure that they could return to this crossroads after they had ventured down each wormhole, to see what had interested the Collector. Kamiel made his decision and dropped the Ark down the shortest wormhole to find out!

Two weeks later the wormhole collapsed at its end, sending the Ark flying towards a yellow sun that had a diverse set of planets orbiting around it and in the band of the star's living area a blue jewel. Kamiel ignored the gas giants behind them that were well outside the freezing point of water and concentrated on the second world from the star. Here were the telltale signs of a collector's visit. An ethereal net of energy hovered over the entire planet with strands leading back to the wormhole. The web hummed with the energy collected from the world below. A constant supply of life energy was being fed back to the collector at the wormhole crossroads. The nannite had the Lagdoo put the hollow moon into orbit around the planet so that they could gather data. It did not take long to find out why a steady stream of life energy was being siphoned off from the world below. It was a pre-Lagdoo planet, teeming with reptilian life, fighting for survival. Vast shallow seas washed against the beaches of small continents that were joined by land bridges. The seas were alive with hungry life forms of every kind that killed, ate, killed and ate again. On the land, fern jungles gave way to plains that were home to millions of grazing animals, some of which measured hundreds of feet in length and weighed many tons. Predators stalked these vegetarians bringing down the weak, lame and old. Life was extinguished in the numbers of millions every year and fed the unseen web above them. It would be a long time in the future before intelligence began on this world, so for the moment it would provide a steady diet of energy for the collector to amass and nothing more.

Kamiel decided that there was nothing here to keep the task force and returned to the miniature collector at the junction, after destroying the web. The Arc had visited each of the pathways through the wormholes, without finding intelligent life. Kamiel had decided to leave the longest one till last and had unravelled the webs surrounding each world before leaving. This had left the miniature collector more and more agitated with each severing of the energy link. As Kamiel had surmised the junction was many light-years away from any star so destroying the collector would present a problem. There was a different way however.

Without a constant source of energy the collector would eventually dissipate and gutter out like a candle that runs out of wax. Kamiel gave the instruction to drop down the last wormhole and use the ancient weapon to collapse it behind them, leaving the miniature collector alone in the emptiness of interstellar space. The Kresh had considered the situation after studying the energy being and advised Kamiel that this was the tidiest way to leave this area of Andromeda. They also reminded him that the Harvester would eventually start to notice that its collectors were vanishing without a trace.

Kamiel decided that he would deal with that situation when it happened. For now it was of greater importance to see if they could intervene between intelligent civilizations and their planned extinction. Every new planetary consciousness that could be added to the Ark's leadership, could give them an edge he had not considered until the Thipdar's planetary group mind had thrust the remains of the Collector into their star. Unlike the Milky Way galaxy civilization that had been peaceful for hundreds of thousands of years, all of these Andromeda societies had known nothing but war and strife and they knew how to fight.

CHAPTER SIXTEEN

Alexander watched moodily from the observation screen, as the Ark approached the end of the wormhole. He had spent a great deal of his time with his nannite friends discussing tactics and possible future actions. The last encounter with the large collector had shaken their confidence to the core. Its ability to deflect the focussed energy from the centre of the Thipdar's sun had caught them ill prepared for alternative action. The great surprise had been the link-up of every trip'o-dal's mind on Shandon into a vast defensive gestalt, instinctively using the power of the gate's telekinetic crystals to thrust the remains of the Collector into the sun.

Those of the Kresh that had decided to make Shandon their new home had briefly taken dominance over the group mind and had blended their knowledge and expertise into the gestalt. With the help of the nannites and the Toarvaks that had stayed on they would soon knit together a different society. Long before the inevitable collision with this part of the Andromeda galaxy with the one that they had left, Alex was sure that they would move their world to orbit another safer star. A viable breeding compliment of the other alien species had also jumped ship to make this world their home.

What the future had in store for them was impossible to guess. His organic friends of all sorts of shapes accepted his leadership and judgement. Sometimes he found it a heavy duty to bear and was quite happy to leave the battle leadership to Kamiel. Although Alex was the clone of Alexander McBald and possessed his attributes, he did not have his mind, just his ability for leadership and his

219

intelligence.

Amongst the blending of the many personalities that made up the enigmatic artificial intelligence, the original mission director was the dominant force. Now that Kamiel had complete free will, he was as ruthless as his creator and designer. Events had acted upon the Guardian to shape him into a leader far beyond any organic's abilities. Without him, the hopes and destinies of all living things would end in death and extinction. Yet he had the capacity for compassion that made him more than special amongst his own kind. Whatever he needed to ask, the nannites would give, including their immortal lives.

Alex had been cloned and brought back using the 'soul catcher' crystals and had lived centuries at different times, always whenever there was a need for his abilities. How many more times this would happen was just speculation, but sometimes he felt so tired of the responsibility that went hand in hand with his being alive. His body was still young and would last hundreds of years before it began to age, but his mind was so very old! Even after all these years he missed those of his time when the Jupiter based civilization was young. He missed his Gnathen friends and the raptors that Shoo-lin had imprinted from hatching. Leader-of-many had allowed him to ride him during the fight against Link-soo-shan and had saved the life of Fredrick by killing and eating the Gnathen Tyrant.

So much had happened over the years to change things. Now he valued the Gnathen Brood-mother's friendship above all of his many relationships. She still amazed him with her mental powers, genius and her ruthlessness! She had the courage to act as bait for the Goss during their conflict with the then parasite. Without her abilities and determination the defeat of the Goss would have been impossible. Now she was pitting her wits against the greatest foe yet.

This ancient life form had taken the life energy from their own galaxy, until the Kresh and the Gnathe had changed all that by retrieving the civilizations through time. Now it was reduced to this one and had complete control over it. They had destroyed two collectors and left a small one to dissipate. They had yet to find out where the huge energy being was located. Before they did this Kamiel had decided to find as many inhabited worlds as they could and impregnate them with the Goss. This would leave whole planets with the capability to form gestalts and defend themselves from any collectors that attempted to take their life energy. Using the Goss network it was possible to keep in contact in real time. What were needed were more contacts with other civilizations, preferably at a technical level.

The wormhole collapsed behind them sealing off the small collector at the junctions and the Ark broke free. In front of them was the shining disc of a yellow sun peeping from behind a blue world of mighty seas and continents. This was another Earth-like world sat conveniently within that narrow temperature band that would allow liquid water to exist. Once again a large moon orbited this world to give it tides and weather. It was too opportune to be natural. A quick analysis showed that it did not belong and had been taken from a gas giant and placed here billions of years ago. Its size to density ratio was wrong and did not correspond to its position around this sun. This had to be planetary engineering on the Harvester's part. Everything had been arranged to bring forth life on the world below and to be cropped at regular intervals. Spun around the planet was the familiar energy network, leading back to the collapsed wormhole.

Kamiel brought the Ark into orbit around the world at a greater distance from the moon and in opposition to it. The slower orbit would allow them to review the situation before their gravitational mass added to the tidal power. At this distance out it should be negligible. The Guardian sent Toarvak 6 and 12,402 to reconnoitre the planet below and find out if there were intelligent life here.

In the inner reaches of the Northern Citadel the collective of Queens had been informed of the Ark's arrival. An observant male drone had been scanning the night skies from the observatory telescope, whilst charting the changes of the moon. Senior minds had been called in immediately and had decided that a visitor had arrived from beyond this world. Many telescopes had been trained upon the new small moon as it slowed and manoeuvred into a wide orbit. More collectives joined the Citadel's Queens and strengthened the mind bond. Information sped around the world that a visitor had come from the stars. All disputes were put on standby and the world-mind of insectoids waited for the next step.

As the Toarvaks dropped lower to the planet below, they broke through the cloudbanks and got their first glimpse of the civilisation they had come to find. Every flat place had been developed and given over to crop growing. Hills had buildings, towers and bridges, leading to roads that networked through the fields with parallel canals. Those hills not built on, were terraced and irrigated from artificial lakes built on the tops of them, with the excess water spilling out into the flat fields. Wherever it was possible to grow crops, a field had been hewn out of the wilderness and planted. The roads were by the main part totally straight until a hill city intersected the highways, only then did they bend.

Alexander and Larse were watching the unfolding landscape with others of the human group on board Toarvak 6 when they were aware of an insectoid Queen by their side. Her head was level with his elbow and turned towards him.

Her antennae stroked the human leader's hand as she spoke into his mind, "These are my people! Here they have wrested order from the wilderness. We have found a truly ordered, insectoid world, human called Alexander."

"If you believe this, Queen, then what would be the purpose of the energy net, strung around this world," Alex replied.

The Queen's eight eyes around the top of her head clouded, as she considered a reply and said, "Overpopulation! An artificial state of warfare would have to be enacted from time to time in a place set aside for this. We have no birth control other than the destruction of our young. To keep optimum genetic excellence it is necessary to send the most unworthy to slaughter each other."

Larse shuddered for a moment and dared to ask, "What do you do on board the Toarvaks to keep your numbers from increasing?"

"We mostly cull the old workers and eat them when they are beyond use. Remember, human called Larse, they are almost mindless! They are merely the extension of our will. I would expect that these people to do the same. If they greet us with a banquet, then you should think about what you eat before you chew! We should land this Toarvak in the largest city. Human called Alexander, tell Toarvak 6 to find a platform in the centre. All cities would have them for food collection points."

Alex shook his head in amazement at the logical directness of the Queen and relayed the message to the artificial intelligence.

He asked the insectoid, "Will it be safe for us to come out and meet these people?"

She waved an intricate dance with her upper four arms, clicked her mandibles and ducked her head before saying, "No! It would be better for all, if only the queens approached the rulers of this Citadel first and explained the situation. These offshoots of our species have never seen an alien being and you would be marked as food! They will be logical however as are we, but until their workers have been ordered to leave you alone, you may be in danger!"

As the weeks passed by, the alien insectoid queens had visited the ship and met their counterparts. The more adventurous queens and their attendant male drones had investigated the 'soft ones' with a passing interest. The on-board insectoids had instructed them not to treat them as workers and to be careful not to damage them.

These insectoids had developed independently of the ones that the Goss had gathered into its collective, although their DNA was identical. They had the skills of working with metals, chemicals and were biochemists of a high order. Their aptitude for physics had led to a keen interest in astronomy after the development of glass lenses had made telescopes a reality.

When Kamiel felt that they were ready, he ordered

both Toarvaks to take the insectoid queens out of the atmosphere, to show them the energy web spread across their world. During the contact with the aliens they had been impregnated with the spores of the Goss and now found that the 'soft-ones' as they called all the other crew of the Toarvaks could also 'talk'. They had been unable to understand what their function was and had wondered if they were food for the insectoids. Logical to a practical level beyond even the Gnathe, this had worried them, as the various soft-coated creatures were using the equipment inside the Toarvak. They felt it impolite to ask their insectoid hosts and were quite surprised to find out the truth. It was when they met their first nannite, that the shock of confronting artificial intelligence nearly paralysed them with amazement. To the insectoids, they were the most alien of all as logically they were not alive in an organic sense.

Yet it was Asue who spent a great deal of time with the Zanti explaining the reason for the arrival of the Ark. She projected into their minds the events of the journey so far into Andromeda galaxy and the destruction of the collectors. With great care she then introduced the idea of the threat to their very existence and told them what they knew of the Harvester and their avowed intent to destroy it. Apart from the telepathy that all queens and male drones possessed to control the workers, they had never considered other psychic powers. A few lessons with the Gnathe and humans in the use of telekinetic enhancement crystals soon changed that. Once they had mastered these, they were introduced to the command crystals that could open up portals. The Kresh now took up the challenge of passing on their abilities of moving whole planets into different orbits around the sun by using a group mind.

It did not take long for the Zanti to make a request to place crystals upon their own moon so that they could exploit the empty spaces. Now the enhanced civilisation really took off as the Zanti burrowed deep under the regolith and ferried glass domes to the moon to cap off the burrows. A number of nannites involved themselves with the construction of the living areas to make sure that there were no air leaks.

Aided by the members of the Ark, a stage of planetary engineering now took off, with Toarvaks seeking out moons in orbit around the gas giants and the Kresh showing the Zanti how to bring them together until there was enough mass to begin a liveable world. They then put this new world in orbit around the Zanti sun a million miles further out, where the nannites began the work of terra-forming it using Nano-technology. A number of the expedition had decided to stay on this world when it was finished to support the insectoids and more Toarvaks were built to aid the new civilization.

During this time Emelia had spent all of her free time teaching Nagoth-shan to be a human woman. In the beginning, Larse had taken one look at his partner's new friend and was struck speechless. Everything about her sent his hormones into overdrive and he struggled with control for a few moments.

"You owe me an explanation Little Flower," Larse gasped, never taking his eyes off the beautiful woman stood uneasily my Emelia's side. "Who is she and what are you doing with her?"

Emelia smiled and replied, "She is Link-soo-shan's daughter in human form. She is fresh from the life vats and is to be a secret from Alexander. Open your mind and I will explain!"

Toarvak 6 had added a bedroom onto the living quarters of Emelia and Larse by moving the room sizes to accommodate the addition. Nagoth had found it difficult to sleep on a bed, as she had spent her life as a Gnathe sleeping on a perch and it took a while to adapt. She also had trouble with clothes and the contrivance of straps and cups to contain her breasts. To her amusement they seemed to hypnotise Larse whenever she forgot to wear the arrangement. Emelia was always on hand to turn her back to the bedroom and make sure that she was dressed properly. She had cut Nagoth's flaming red hair at shoulder length to allow her to wear it tidily with a band or drawn back as a ponytail. Her sexual encounters with Larse she allowed Nagoth to share telepathically to show her what could be achieved between a woman and her man.

From time to time Link-soo-shan would pay a visit to check that her protégée was making good progress.

On her last visit she remarked, "I believe that you should eat at the communal hall amongst the rest of the crew who live on this Toarvak. Nagoth needs to be seen and accepted by others, both human and alien beings in her own right as a person. She also needs something to do. I suggest the position of bodyguard to the delegations would suit her talents."

Larse, Emelia and Nagoth made their way to the long tables where different situations were catered for. There were chairs, perches and resting frames for different types by the side of the tables. Replicating booths were situated in the walls for anyone to dial for whatever they needed. On impulse Nagoth dialled for pod-vine fruit and had a bowl of freshly toasted beans. She added a sweet chilli sauce to dip them in and followed Emelia and Larse to a vacant table.

As she dipped the fruit into the sauce and nibbled her meal she was aware of many eyes turned her way. A new face in the hall was unusual, as most of the creatures on board the Toarvak had been there from the beginning. Several of the human males picked up their bowls and cutlery and made their way to where they were sitting. The women in the hall quietly watched to see how she dealt with the situation.

A dark-haired man sat down beside her, just beating another blonde man who sat opposite. He sat so close that he touched her arm with his and applied pressure with his knee to hers. She felt her colour rise in her cheeks.

"Hello, my sweet! Where did you come from and what by what name are you called," he whispered in her ear and raised his hand to touch her hair.

Moving as a blur, using the enhanced muscular system that Link had designed in, Nagoth swivelled round and caught his hand in hers. She slammed it down upon the table with an audible thud and reached round his head to twist his ear.

Holding it in a vice like grip she spoke quite plainly so that her voice carried, "When you have developed manners, I may tell you my name. I suggest that you and your randy friend find another table before I break your arm, or you carry this ear in your pocket for the rest of your life! Should I invite you to this table, I will call you. Until that sorry day, back off!"

She released him and stood up, as he staggered back, first clutching his hand and then checking his ear for damage.

Larse and Emelia rose and stood by her side as support.

"I apologise! I apologise! I was ill mannered. Please may we start again? Look I really am sorry. What more can I say to you? My name is Roger and I have been part of this Toarvak ever since I came out of the vats," he said and held out his bruised hand.

Nagoth stared at it and briefly shook it replying, "I accept your apology, Roger! If you can control yourself you may have breakfast with my friends and I. Your friend may stay if he wishes. This is Larse and his woman Emelia. I am called Nancy and I am spoken for, so whatever thoughts you had in your head, you may keep to yourself."

After this encounter Nagoth was able to freely wander the vast inside of the Toarvak without any problems from predatory human males. She was stared at by the entire human contingent, as she travelled around with Emelia, but word had got round that she was not up for 'grabs'! She had seen Alexander from time to time as he travelled back and forth from the safety of Toarvak 6 to the Zanti city-hive around them, but had never managed to get close to him. Wherever he went, Fredrick who wore Minnis in her capacity as a battle suit shadowed him. The other bodyguards consisted of Thomas and Larse. After putting pressure upon Larse for an introduction, Nagoth became another bodyguard in the delegation that were dealing with the Zanti.

The Zanti city was the most alien place that Nagoth had ever seen. Her old life on Jupiter had nothing to compare with. There were tall towers that were joined by narrow bridges that had no railings. There was a sheer drop from the sides of the parapet or any veranda jutting out from the city buildings. There were no attempts to make any safety precautions, as the Zanti could see no need. They could climb up any vertical surface as easily as if it was flat. Radiating from the central tower were the arches linked to the other towers like the spokes of a giant wheel. Glass windows kept out the cold winds from blowing inside the towers where gardens flourished and were irrigated by water fed from the roofs. Every available space grew edible crops that were collected and stored for consumption. Toarvak 6 had extended three long legs to suspend herself over the central food storage area close by. A large observatory was located at the very top of the central tower and it was from here the approach of the Ark had been noticed.

It was here that Kresh engineers with the help of Hannah were building a radio telescope for the Zanti to use to expand their knowledge of the universe. Alexander and the other human members of the delegation were teaching the Zanti queens the delicate art of telekinetic manipulation inside their bodies so that heart defects and other malfunctions could be repaired. In return for this guidance the queens had given over to the Ark's insectoids a great number of their own young to strengthen the genetic mix of the visitors. Alex had been given an invitation to visit the part of the hive where the eggs were laid and the grubs hatched.

Alexander decided to accept the honour and informed the Kresh working on the radio telescope that he would be leaving them to go to the other side of the city-hive where the nurseries were built. As Hannah was still working with the Kresh, Fredrick stayed with her to help lift the heavy parts using Minnis. Both Larse and Thomas were busy teaching the Zanti queens the secret of levitation, so it would have been impolite to leave. Besides they had been inside the city-hive for some weeks without any incidents, so he beckoned the new member of the delegation to follow him, as a queen led the way into the maze of the hive towards the nursery. He had not as yet spoken to the new arrival to the delegation and this would give him the chance. It was a matter of protocol that each queen was followed by at least one worker to minister to her needs. To remain a person of seniority in the Zanti hive, Alexander needed to be accompanied at all times to maintain his position as leader. Even with the telepathic link established between the Zanti and the 'soft-ones' there were still difficulties relating to the insectoid mindset. Until this discovery of the insectoid world, the Ark insectoids had never referred to themselves as a collective name to the other aliens. Even Thomas, who had spent many years with them before his resurrection, had never known what they called themselves as a species. When Alexander had asked them, they had replied that they were known as the Sshann. Individual names were unknown and rank of seniority was interwoven with family ancestry in such a way that it was easier for the 'soft-ones' to refer to them as just Queen. The only difference between the Sshann and the Zanti were in colouration and size. The Sshann were about the size of a large dog and deep black, while the Zanti were blood red and smaller, with their globular heads at elbow level to the humans.

As the two humans made their way down, the temperature began to rise and luminous fungi grew from the walls using the increased moisture to spread. Soon the roof began to drip and the floor began to get very slippery underfoot. The Zanti queen and her worker trod the downward path with no sign of slowing up, as the six clawed feet had no trouble biting into the spongy floor and keeping her grip. After some time the tunnel widened abruptly into a large chamber with masses of glow fungus growing over the roof. The walls were covered in large hexagonal cells that held eggs in various stages of maturity and some had ruptured, disgorging grubs into the waiting mandibles of the attendant workers.

On heaps of rotting vegetation, heaped into cones that were constantly turned over by more workers, were a rich variety of fungi. In amongst these midden heaps crawled the maggoty young of the Zanti squirming and eating. Some were leaving the heaps and were carried off by the workers to harden into pupa. Out of the hundreds of grubs only a few would mature into queens or male drones. The rest would become mindless workers constantly controlled by the intellect of the queens, as extensions of their will. At the centre of operations were a group of queens directing the actions of the workers. The young queen that had led the two humans down to the nursery chamber made her way towards them to communicate, momentarily forgetting about Alexander and his attendant. She began to explain the reason for the visit and the controlling queens switched their concentration.

Alexander began to notice that some of the nearer workers were taking an interest in the two of them and clicking their mandibles. More and more of them rose to an upright position as they caught the scent of the two humans. Those that were fanning the eggs put down their woven fans and shuffled forwards. Without the movement of air the chamber soon began to become fetid and it became difficult to breath.

With the scent of fresh food in the air, the workers began to become more and more difficult to control by the queens as they tried to retake control.

Alex heard the mind of the young queen in his thoughts,

"Go! Go quickly. Retrace your steps and head for the surface. We will try to hold the workers back. Hurry!"

Alex grabbed the young woman's hand in his and turned and ran back into the tunnel that they had just come down.

"Can you levitate?" he asked.

"Yes," Nagoth answered and lifted into the air.

Both of them kept to the tunnel and sped along the dark, ill-lit highway as fast as they dared, heading for the surface. Coming towards them were a fresh contingent of insectoid workers heading for nursery duty. Alexander ran into the controlling queen at full tilt scattering the Zanti workers against the tunnel walls. In the dim light of the glow-fungus Nagoth could just see the insectoids scuttling back onto their feet and making for the partially stunned Alexander, mandibles clicking. She levitated over him and grabbed the first insectoid by the mandibles and cracked its head in half, throwing the kicking body into the others. As the next one bent its antennae towards the human on the floor, she seized it by the foreleg and swung it like a club, tearing it out of its socket. She grabbed Alexander by the back of his tunic and levitated off the floor until they were touching the ceiling. As one of the Zanti workers reached up to them, she disrupted its heart by tearing the arteries apart with her mind. Slowly she lifted Alex over the milling workers until she was well to the other side of them. Nagoth laid him on the ground and checked him over by entering his body with her mind. Apart from the concussion he had suffered by smashing his head into the insectoid's neck as it had lifted its head, all was well. She locked her legs around the semi-conscious man and once more obeyed the training that Larse had given her on levitation, as she lent over him and cradled his head in her arms. She shielded herself from the gravitational force and drew on the telekinetic crystal that she kept in the skin pocket just above her breasts. She linked her mind with his and lifted the two of them from off the tunnel floor and made for the outside of the city-hive.

A draft of air gave her a sense of direction and diverting into a higher tunnel, she was able to manoeuvre the two of them onto a veranda overlooking the central tower. Gently she lowered the two of them onto the mosaic floor by the opening and found herself looking into Alexander's open eyes. Too late she tried to remove herself from Alex's mind and found him inside hers.

Astonishment!

"How can this be? I know this mind! Although centuries have passed I could never forget," Alexander exclaimed in disbelief. "What has happened to you?"

"I am Nagoth-shan, resurrected in human form by the great Lady, Link-soo-shan. I seem to have saved your life again! Maybe, just maybe, its why I am here," she said and unlocked her legs from around the human. "And yes, I still love you Alexander. A long time ago you set my mind free when I was forced to do a terrible thing to you. This body is human and now I will not tear you apart if you make love to me!"

In an alien city, on an alien world, Alexander found the greatest reason to defeat the Harvester in the willing body of an alien female in a human form.

Nagoth asked, "Can we do that again?"

Alex replied, "We can do it as many times as we wish."

"Then do it again, now!"

CHAPTER SEVENTEEN

Alexander stood shamefaced with Nagoth beside him in front of his nannite friend, as Kamiel proceeded to give him the roasting of his life. To make things worse the Guardian refused to resort to telepathy and conducted the interview in sound.

In a measured voice the nannite pressed his case, "You have lived centuries and have been resurrected three times and you have learned nothing! McBald must be turning in his grave and feeling as much disappointment as I do with his clone. Speaking of clones! Do you think that I have an inexhaustible supply of vats filled with your ready to wear body suits! Do you think that I have your personality on tap that I can reinsert it if you terminate this one?"

"It was a matter of protocol, Kamiel. I was offered a chance to see the nurseries by a queen," Alexander explained.

"Have I not insisted that you keep with the main party at all times? This queen was hardly out of her pupae case and had no idea how dangerous the nurseries would be to something that smelled like intruding food! You are more than lucky that you have not been cut to bits and fed to the larvae of the insectoids as we speak," he said, raising the volume a little so that Alexander winced. "And! Where did you go after you made your escape from the bowels of the city-hive? You hid! And! What then? You spent who knows what time spending your energy in sexual pleasure with this freak that Link-soo-shan created!"

That comment by the enigmatic nannite broke the dam and Nagoth began to sob, "I'm not a freak. I'm not! I'm not!"

"Then what are you Nagoth-shan? You stand before me a human woman, but you are not," the nannite replied. "You are a bastardisation mix of human body and Gnathen female mind. Although your capacity for tears is a human trait and you have managed to behave as one for some time. Who taught you? Tell me! Do not waste my time making me find out."

"Emelia taught me," she answered between sobs. "Larse also helped me to adjust."

"Did she now! She taught you well. You must have been given a human name. What is it?"

"Nancy," she replied. "Everyone calls me Nancy."

"Kamiel! Enough, enough! I was foolish to risk my life. I know that old friend. Be assured I shall not risk it again without great cause. Thousands of years ago I altered this female's thought patterns when I set her free from Link-soo-shan. What I did ensured that she could never be a pure Gnathe again. She loved me, Kamiel with a fierce passion, but was unable to release that love until now. Nagoth or Nancy, as she is now will be my reason to be cautious in the future. Remember, Kamiel, Link-soo-shan never does anything without a purpose. Speak to her and listen to what she says."

The Guardian slipped his mind into Alexander's and said, "Even though my personality was fashioned from humans, this emotion of love still eludes me. I will seek out the Gnathen genius and speak with her in private. I must admit she did well to keep this a secret in a multi-telepathic society. The Zanti are very ashamed that the incident took place and will take greater care in the future. So some good has come from this foolishness. Now I must see a scheming Gnathe by the name of Link-soo-shan!"

Link looked down at the nannite in front of her and

chuckled to herself before answering Kamiel.

"My plan was successful then?"

"You nearly got him killed! I need him on this project. We all need him and his insights," Kamiel answered and fixed the Brood-mother with an eyeless stare.

"Wrong! You need him motivated, you cold-hearted nannite. I could see this and he is not of my species. This is my solution to the problem. Admit it, Guardian; there has been deterioration in his judgement. He was a lot sharper when we dealt with the Goss! Besides, I felt that I owed it to the both of them. What I did to Alexander was a cruel and terrible thing. The result to my daughter was to change her mentality completely. Had she not rescued Alexander and affected the outcome of events as she did, neither of us would be standing here. Be logical Kamiel! And, may I say, be compassionate!"

"You seem fated to constantly amaze me, Link-soo-shan, once tyrant of the Gnathe! You have an insight, far beyond me at times," the nannite replied. "It was time well spent when you shared my mind after the time jump to Alexander McBald's time."

"My dear Kamiel, it was an experience far beyond anything I have ever lived through. Sharing your mind with Alexander for the centuries we had to wait on the space station until we caught up with events on Jupiter, has given me an insight that you seem to have avoided.

Now to other things! I have been giving the events that have transpired a great deal of thought. We have saved two civilisations from extinction. This is all very noble, but this will not help us defeat the Harvester. I have been talking with Hannah and Toarvak 6 about modifications to the Kresh ships. We have seen how the large rings work, that are positioned around the flange of the Ark. Opening a gate in the heart of a star and directing it at a collector will work after a fashion, but we saw how the collector deflected the energy stream and how it destroyed the Thipdar cities."

"I know that Link-soo-shan. I know! Millions died that day to save that world. It was an awful price to pay. Somehow we must make sure that it does not happen again," the Guardian bitterly answered.

"There could be another way," Link replied and explained. "Toarvak 6 can change her shape, as you know. Instead of forming a ball, the Toarvaks can operate just as well as hollow barrels. If command crystals are fitted into rings that are positioned at each end and the rest of the ship goes out of phase, then they can operate independently. They all carry enough crew to operate as a group mind to operate the gates while the gestalt fly the Toarvaks through the collectors, cutting them to pieces. Until we try this on a collector, we cannot find out how many we need to pit against them."

"I agree! Had it not been for the group mind of the Thipdar people, guided by the Kresh, thrusting the collector into their star, we could have lost that encounter," Kamiel said.

Link-soo-shan stared down at the silvery figure and replied, "The obvious solution is to contact and impregnate as many civilisations with the Goss as we can. Using my suggestion about the smaller star-gates built into the Toarvaks I propose that we send small fleets of the Kresh ships with mixed crews, down every wormhole that we can and try to establish contact with as many intelligent races of beings that we can find. If a problem occurs that the Toarvaks cannot handle, we have two world minds to draw on. We now have many thousands of Toarvak ships; it is time to use them!"

A silver shape disengaged itself from the wall and stood before them.

"I have altered the shape of the Toarvak and I have built into the mouths a ring of command crystals with a dominant telekinetic one to activate them. All we need to do is to leave orbit and test the new weapon," Six stated.

Kamiel and his Gnathen friend just stared at each other in amazement.

The Guardian turned towards the Kresh artificial intelligence and said, "Is there anything that remains private on this vessel? Do you hear everything said in sound and thought by telepathy?"

"No! Well, only the important things. You are after all living inside me! I must admit that most of the banal chatter goes by me unheard, but when you two are together I will be there beside you," she replied and melted back into the wall.

Kamiel had ten Toarvaks modified in shape and fitted with the crystal bands. He took them all out to the largest gas giant's orbit and settled on a mediocre ice moon that the nannites had disregarded when they had built the new planet near the orbit of the insectoid world.

They had taken out of orbit a minor world closer to the sun and reset it in a new orbit much further out. They then collided the largest icy moons together with it, until they had produced a planet with an acceptable gravity and re-set it in its final orbit, using the Kresh over-mind. Under the guidance of the nannites, the new world was developing an atmosphere, due to the melting of the various ices and applied Nano-technology. Already primitive life had been transplanted from the insectoid world into its melt-water seas to thrive. It was a slightly colder world than the insectoid's home and possessed arctic conditions at both poles. The landmasses would soon be seeded with vegetation that would prepare the new planet to be used.

This icy moon would make an ideal target, as it had a high sulphur content and would have been useless to incorporate into the new world, as it would have required more Nano-tech work than could be justified. Under the gravitational pull of the gas giant, the surface was constantly rupturing and venting gases. Kamiel watched from the Ark and the Toarvaks uncoupled themselves from their anchor points. They launched into a vertical figure of eight pattern that tilted the formation so that each Toarvak could view the moon and sight the star-gates at different areas. Keeping the majority of each Toarvak's mass out of phase except for the crystal bands and their fixings to each of the Kresh ships they slid through space at high speed. On a central command each Toarvak opened a separate hole inside the star and let the stream of energy cut into the moon. The moon opened up as if a giant surgeon's scalpel had incised it right down to the semi-liquid core. As the Toarvaks passed by the moon the figure of eight twisted into a horizontal position and let loose a stream of energy again, directed at different areas. The moon came apart! Great chunks detached themselves and flew away only to be recaptured by gravity as the moon pulled itself together again.

Alexander had operated as an over-mind to the ten Toarvaks and had formed a gestalt of every alien mind on board the Kresh ships, leaving the collectives to follow his lead. He had opened and shut the gates as the rest of the over-mind had concentrated on the aerial ballet. Alexander had then passed the position on to another mind, stepping back to observe. All the leaders of the gestalt tried every tactic and formation that each could think of, until Kamiel was satisfied that they had demonstrated to the other collective minds housed in every other Toarvak all that could be learnt. The Goss had provided a composite link-up to every mind across the light-years from the Thipdar world to the insectoids. Now it was soon to be time for the armada of Toarvaks to depart in fleets of ten down every fracture in time and space that they could find. Wormholes were to be investigated and collectors only destroyed if they were imminently about to terminate a civilisation or send it to war. What was more important was to spread the word to every intelligent race they met that the final struggle was soon to be waged, once the Harvester had woken from its eons' sleep.

Kamiel called Hannah via the Goss to meet him at her laboratory. It was a small distance from the Ark's control room and next to the crystal store that was constantly added to from every gas giant that they investigated. The two gas giants at the insectoid's planetary system had been rich in all types of crystal and had been plundered by the armada of ships. Enough had been passed onto the insectoids to satisfy their needs, but the majority had been kept by the Toarvak fleet to hand on to future allies.

She found the enigmatic Guardian stood waiting for her. As always it was impossible to guess whatever he wanted, so Hannah just waited for him to begin.

"Hannah, do you remember when you were first experimenting with electrical charges, trickle fed into the crystals to increase the mind's power and range, just before you developed the shield for the habitat?"

"I remember it well, Kamiel," the human scientist replied. "It was something that I did not pursue at the time, as other things came to be of more importance. Once Trann-link-sool discovered the method of grouping minds together and increasing the telekinetic power by that way, my research in that field petered out for a while! When we sent the group mind through time and wrested the Earth and moon out of orbit and repositioned it, I fed power into the crystals for the mind to draw on. We did some more when we developed the far ranging scanner to defeat the Goss, but again the power of the group mind eclipsed the research. It is a science that we have used again and again combining Gnathen psychic abilities with human science. What do you want me to do?"

"We have discovered how to amplify our senses from learning from the Gnathe. Also humans and apes have benefited from their genetic engineering," Kamiel answered. "The two Gnathe with partially human minds, Azander and Marren have been resurrected along with Ender-whann-soo at my insistence. What I want you to do is to concentrate your collective minds on a long-range scanner that can be operated by the Trans-sentient ones. You have my authority to co-opt onto the project anyone else that you can think of that can be of help. I need to know just where the Harvester is located before I can plan anything and the only ones who can do this are the children of Archive!"

Hannah rocked on her feet and stared at the silver form stood in front of her in disbelief.

"Do you not realise how large they are, Kamiel?" she spluttered with amazement.

"It is because I know this, that I have set you the problem, Hannah. I trust that you will find a solution before the fleet scatters amongst the Andromeda star systems, so that they can avoid it! I have returned the Ark to a functioning system again so that all the Trans-sentient ones can come here to be at your disposal before they go."

Hannah and Fredrick stood together on the inside of the Ark as it rotated, giving them an artificial gravity. To them there was no motion, only a slight pull to the side that they soon got used to. Minnis had enveloped Fredrick so that he could lift the heavier pieces of the equipment from Hannah's instructions. The giant and the nannite had blended together so often that they worked well together in any situation. By allowing Hannah's mind to operate the two of them as extra hands and fingers she was rapidly building the harness that one of the trans-sentient Ones would wear. Also the two Gnathe, Azander and Marren worked in gestalt with her, their partially human minds allowing her to easily dominate the collective. Their Brood-mother, Ender-whann-soo had provided the mental bridge to the Tran-sentient ones to guide their non-technical intelligences into understanding what Hannah was trying to accomplish.

Hannah called some of the Tran-sentient ones together so that they could fit the harness over the one chosen to carry it. The one to be fitted with the enhancing device was known as Archive-index. She carried the database of the original Archive's knowledge and could access the memories that were carried by the other Trans-sentients who had taken the living brain of the original and made it their own by digesting it. All of the Globes that carried the heavy harness increased their hydrogen input to the floatation chambers and steadily began to lift the harness over the front face of Archive-index. She withdrew the tentacles in the way and wriggled into the encircling yoke. Hannah allowed the power cables to remain slack as the Trans-sentient began to take the weight by adjusting her specific gravity. The ring of crystals made contact around the being and began to activate, as the natural Kirlian radiation of the living creature's electro-magnetic field began to activate the crystals.

Hannah joined the remarkable mind of the Trans-sentient and allowed herself to ride upon the great intellect as it searched through the database. As Archive-index spun through the collective memories catalogued inside her deepest levels she automatically reached out for the minds of the Globes who were carrying what she sought. Slowly most of the original mind began to function as 'Archive the ancient one' and began to approach awareness. The mind stabilised and reached out for all the missing parts scattered around the inside of the Ark. To Hannah's astonishment she found herself confronting an intellect that was vast and many millions of years old. She was recognised in an instant and all her knowledge became assimilated into the reassembled mind.

"Young mouthful! You are a very clever kind of human. I welcome you to my many sided personality. The young globes did as was asked of them; a difficult thing for them to do! I have survived after a fashion. A new thing after so long! I am more than pleased to be of assistance and am quite happy that my assimilation has worked. Now, young creature named Hannah, it is time to pipe power into this harness and we will track down the abomination," the ancient Trans-sentient gently eased into Hannah's mind.

Hannah sat in her command chair stunned into silence for a moment.

"First I must contact Kamiel," she said and reached out. "Goss!"

"Yes Hannah."

"Connect me with Kamiel," she asked.

The nannite was reviewing the performance of the barrel shaped Toarvaks when he was interrupted by Hannah's thoughts.

"Hannah! You have made progress?" he said.

"More than you could know, Guardian," she answered. "Archive is back! She is scattered amongst the young Trans-sentients as fragments of the original. Archive-index is the key to awakening the whole personality. She is ready to search for the Harvester and will take us along with her."

"I will alert Asue and Solace that I may be 'away' for a while. Make sure that your bodily needs are maintained. Have yourself incarcerated into a life-vat so that you do not starve! We could be some time searching," Kamiel insisted.

Fredrick stared at the naked body of his lover, suspended in the life-vat fluid with breathing tubes entering her mouth and feeding tubes fixed into her stomach wall. A catheter entered her bladder while a waste tube was securely fixed into her anus. Life-sign registering pads adorned her body, monitoring heartbeat and vital signs so that Azander and Marren could constantly watch for any adverse changes. Once again Hannah had shaved her head so that her crown of crystal amplifiers made a good skin contact. Fredrick had a duplicate set of controls to operate in case anything should happen to Hannah's control over the situation. The last week had been spent in preparation for the mind-search. All of the Tran-sentients had grazed and fed to capacity so that they could endure weeks if necessary of deprivation.

Hannah trickle fed power into the crystal harness and felt the potential of Archive's mind increase. The incredibly old Trans-sentient reached out to the stars as Hannah constantly increased power to the crystalline components surrounding her. As a single unit Archive's individual units blended together and followed the arm of stars back to the giant black hole at the centre. From here the individual spiral arms of stars swung out into the great darkness like curved spokes of a cartwheel. The mind considered the maze of wormholes that linked each and every-one of the stars together. Some had been brought together and linked into a spider's web system that led to others. Archive considered the billions of years constructing the pathways from star to star that fed energy back and forth. She became aware of the Collectors' minds patiently monitoring the events happening on the life bearing planets. In their isolation they were unaware of her and the tiny minds of Hannah and Kamiel who rode the stars with her.

The Tran-sentient followed the wormholes outwards to the edge of each spiral arm without as yet any success in locating the thought signature of the Harvester. What information did come through was the location of the sentient creatures that were being monitored by the collectors. The richness of the Andromeda galaxy's civilizations were stunning, as each Collector pushed and manipulated every culture to increasing sapience. There were many on the verge of interstellar flight that were being shepherded along the path of warfare. This mass harvesting of life force would soon take place on many planets. Unaware of the influence exerted upon them by the Harvester's Collectors, cultures were fed misinformation and hatreds stirred up to goad them into unleashing death and destruction upon each other. If nothing else this fishing trip had pinpointed where to send the Toarvaks first.

Then a faint remembered fragrance of thought from the long past registered on the combined searching mind. Archive felt a dreaming presence spread out along the edge of a spiral arm of stars. The mind was not organic! It was an energy pattern and it was many billions of years old. Slow thoughts moved along the pathways of its existence. An insatiable hunger ruled this self-aware energy being. No thoughts of compassion, no thoughts of love, no emotions of any kind had kindled in this unique entity. The need to exist was all that drove it. The need to feed on life energy was the reason for its existence. It had no understanding of organic life, only that the energy that it gave off sustained it. Only when the hunger came would the Harvester awake fully, as to stay aware used too much energy. The energy fields around its edge turned inwards to avoid radiating the store of its life outwards. The substance of its existence became a massive, ball shaped, billion threaded, globe of strings. Thousands of connections disappeared into the ball from the nearby wormholes and pulsed as energy was transferred. Larger than the average solar system, dark matter had become energy and had become aware. The embodiment of evil had been born during the forming of the universe and had not been left behind.

Kamiel entered the dominant position of the three-part mind and said, "Time to go back I believe. Now we know where it is sleeping. We also know where to send the Toarvaks to save the most technically able civilizations. Come, Archive and Hannah, we have enough information to share with the others. Carefully the Tran-sentient withdrew from the area by retreating down the nearest wormhole leading back to the centre of the Andromeda galaxy. From there she eased her mind outwards again towards the edge that the expedition had entered. Finally the familiar mental noise of the Toarvaks and their crews acted as a beacon and drew them back.

The power had been shut down, supplying the energy to the crystal harness by Azander, who had monitored the return. She began to drain the tank and restore Hannah to a fully functioning state. Marren began to remove the tubes from the human's body, while Fredrick supported her weight. The Gnathe finished removing the life support monitors and allowed her to stand, holding Fred's hand.

"I feel so weak," she said to him. "How long was I in that tank?"

"You've been suspended in there for nearly a month," he replied. "Were you successful?"

"Oh yes, more than you could know! Kamiel will need to plan our future very carefully. Open your mind!"

She showed Fredrick what the three minds had experienced and he sat stunned as more minds came aboard to view what they had seen. All the components of Archive's mind returned to their individual identities, but all of them retained the memory. Now that the Harvester had been visited and assessed, should it awaken they would be aware of its return to consciousness and be able to sound the alarm.

Kamiel had wasted no time calling a meeting, once his mind had returned, to find that his living host to the Goss had almost died. The meeting he arranged was with every Toarvak ship's mind with all of the nannite Guardians scattered throughout the fleet and the newly constructed world. Reverting to machine time he imparted the facts of the entire encounter with the ancient energy being. Then he gave the co-ordinates for all the technical civilizations that Archive had discovered and his instructions.

In teams of ten the Toarvaks picked up a Trans-sentient from the Ark, departed through the wormholes and fanned out into interstellar space.

CHAPTER EIGHTEEN

This land from sea to sea was in torment. Ruined towns set blasted towers against a reddened sunset. Metal tanks crawled remorselessly forwards over what was left of the roads hunting resistance. Aircraft fought in the sky as bombers sought targets on the ground to drop their cargos of death. The war was in its zenith and was the war to end all wars. Both sides believed the cause was just.

Hiding in trenches the second battalion crouched low as artillery thumped and crunched overhead. Hanging in the barbed wire at the top of the trench hung the decomposing bodies of the foe. Laid in the mud and slime of the newly won trench were more of the army of occupation of this once productive farmland.

High up above, the network sparkled as it collected fresh life energy from the dying people below. The Collector spun more filaments around the planet below to be sure of harvesting all the souls of the dying. Soon it would be time to return with its cargo. Already it was beginning to feel bloated with energy.

Suddenly it became aware of company, as ten Toarvaks winked into existence close to its main array of information collectors. Before it could register the fact that something outside of its long existence had made contact with it, the fires of the sun began to slice apart its' 'head' and consciousness ceased. The great wings opened to the full force of the solar wind and the body of the Collector lifted away from the planet below. Without the controlling influence of the main sentience the collector began to wither and radiate the energy of its life into the void.

The whole battle had taken just a few minutes to execute and every tactical detail had been broadcast via the Goss to every other group of Toarvaks scattered across the Andromeda galaxy. This one had been easy.

The Toarvaks unravelled the net around the world beneath them, dropped out of the sky and hovered over the battlefields. They shed the spores of the Goss wherever they found concentrated armies beneath them and waited as the guns stopped. Aircraft that were scrambled, found that although they could find the huge spaceships quite easily, all they could do was fly through them. Some that flew into the barrel shaped Toarvaks did not come out again. The pilots were being re-educated to a new reality and becoming ambassadors from the aliens in the sky. Warships disappeared at sea after a silver cloud enveloped them and again re-education took place with greater numbers. Again this knowledge was passed to the Goss to distribute to the rest of the Armada.

Another formation of ten Toarvaks at another star-system surprised two collectors harvesting a particularly bloody battle and managed to destroy only one of them. The other dropped down a wormhole to make its way back to the Harvester and found twenty Toarvaks waiting at the network branch. It had time to register alarmed surprise before it was enveloped by the Toarvaks and taken out of phase. They took it to a nearby star before casting it aside at the edge of the solar flares. The collector was snuffed out instantly by the roaring energies.

Out of the millions of energy conducting wormholes, with the knowledge gained from the Tran-sentient ones, only the technical stage civilizations were liberated. Slowly the Goss was spread throughout each culture and potential world minds gained sapience. All of them realised a burning hatred for the entity that had used them to feed itself and bided their time. Whilst the creature slept, the number grew and with it the strength of the opposition. The Kresh engineers moved those worlds that were closer than safety dictated to the impending collision of the two galaxies, to another solar system at the opposite side of Andromeda. They used the power of the world minds at their disposal. Those collectors waiting at the fringes of the collision were hunted down and destroyed before they could return to the parent creature and report their findings.

Kamiel received the news of yet another victory with mixed emotions. Over the years several hundred civilizations had been saved without as yet awakening the Harvester. The one thing that the artificial intelligence did not want was the abomination to awaken too soon. So far not one collector had made it back to the Harvester, but as more and more civilizations escaped the bloody yoke of the Collectors, it took them to the time when hunger would awaken their foe.

The new planet that orbited the insectoid's star had been named Haven and had burgeoned with transplanted life. Drawing on the experience of building Toarvak Prime, the nannites had again built a world that would accommodate all of the various alien species. They had searched through the planetary system until they had come to the conclusion that there was insufficient material left to build a moon to drive the tides. Using the knowledge gained by Archive's search for the Harvester, they surveyed other planetary systems until they found one that would do. They used the insectoid's world mind to bring it through and left the Zanti extremely happy to have learnt how to do this. In orbit around Haven, Kamiel had placed the Ark. Another large stargate had been built and anchored to the new moon that had been named Haven's Rock! It occupied the Lagrange position, forever following the moon's orbit, locked to the planet Haven below. It had become a very busy piece of equipment as Toarvaks exited it carrying ambassadors from the newly liberated civilizations.

Haven occupied a similar environment to the Zanti world except for the larger ice caps at each pole. The one million miles further out made little difference to the amount of radiated heat from the Zanti star and the fact of the planet's mass being slightly greater, made its set orbital velocity the same as the Zanti world. There would never be a tidal problem as they would remain fixed on either side of the sun. At the moment the axial tilt had given the northern hemisphere an autumnal weather pattern at the lower edges of the Polar Regions. Seasonal fruit trees were heavy with their crops and ready for picking. The pod-vines of the Gnathe were always in fruit, as they did not rely on seasonal variations. Once planted and watered, they continued to flower and fruit continually. The farmlands of both human and Gnathe flourished together, along with the Bazantii, Kresh, Thipdar and Vogb plantations. More alien settlers came to put down roots amongst the visitors to Andromeda. Many came to learn new mental techniques from the Gnathe and their allies. The genetically improved Kresh were only too keen to teach their method of transferring planets and even whole solar systems to new safer positions away from the colliding edge of the galaxy. Only in the formation of a planetary group mind could such things be achieved with absolute safety. Once again the strange symbiont that was known as the Goss, lived in all sentient creatures and connected all of the minds together. Still an undercurrent of apprehension still sat at the edge of each civilization's minds; when would the Harvester awaken?

Now that Archive had been resurrected and had awoken

amongst the Trans-sentients, Index kept the crystal harness on and with Hannah's help kept a mental ear open in the direction of where the Harvester slept. Each Tran-sentient kept its own individuality, but tucked away at the back of their minds was the ancient personality of Archive watching over her 'children' so that if she were needed, then she could surface and take overall control.

The Guardians had built roads and settlements to link up all over the new world. Mixed alien communities were the norm as each species soon learnt the advantages of living together, rather than being isolated. The lessons learnt in the Ark's amphitheatre in combat had taught them all about each other's strengths and weaknesses.

Asue had designed and built a large, square, community manor house that could house all of the different sentient beings. It had a central communal hall under a large transparent dome with a central table surrounded with perches, chairs, platforms and all kinds of seating or resting furniture to suit them all. This was used as a central eating-place and as a meeting hall for any decisions that had to be made. Living quarters were built into the structure around the square that dominated the centre. Stairs, ramps and lifts connected the many different floors to allow all beings to visit one another. It had become the central place of administration for the many beings that had entered the Andromeda galaxy to destroy the Harvester. It was simply known as Admin Centre.

In one of those living quarters a women with bright, copper coloured hair was being violently sick into the toilet bowl. She held onto the seat with an iron grip as her body continued to heave with dry retching. Gradually the sensation ebbed and she found that she could keep down some water if she sipped it.

Alexander put a gentle hand on her shoulder and said, "Nancy my love, I think you are pregnant!"

Nagoth-shan shuddered as the sensations of nausea subsided and replied, "How long does this effect last? Where is Emelia? I need her help."

Alex laughed and said, "There is a long way to go yet, my love. These symptoms usually last only for the early part of pregnancy. As time goes by you will experience many different sensations as the babies grow."

"Babies!"

"I can detect two life signs inside you, Nancy. 'We' are having twins! Over my lifespan I have produced more children than I can remember with different partners, but something tells me that these will be different! Emelia and Larse are outside our room now," Alex said. "Shall I let them in?"

With that the door opened and Emelia swept into the room and gave Nagoth a hug and opened her mind to her friend. Having had children of her own long ago on Daedalus Two and also since her resurrection, she was well versed in the practice of pregnancy. She imparted the knowledge of just what it meant to be pregnant and have a child grow inside a womb. At this time of the day her children were being taught at the 'Main Academy' with many of the alien young.

Nagoth sat down and digested the information passed into her mind by the human woman.

She looked up and replied, "This is going to be quite different to passing a fertilised egg to a Brood-mother."

Emelia smiled at the upturned face and said, "Don't worry! Humans have been doing this for millions of years! Your body is as human as mine. You have seen me carry a child since you were released from the tank and held our daughter in your own careful hands. I will be there when it is time and you can guaranty that Asue will be delivering the twins when they are due."

Larse gave a measured look at Alexander and looked towards the door.

"Larse and I will go outside for a bit and get some air and share the news with any of our friends we meet," Alex said and left the two women together.

Once outside with plenty of other minds talking back and forth, Alexander stopped and turned to Larse and lifted one eyebrow.

Larse frowned and said, "Link-soo-shan will need to know. I wonder what else she has altered genetically with Nancy's body. I do not completely trust our Gnathen friend. She follows a different agenda to human beings. Her mind works along another path, totally different to the way we think. I am quite aware that we have lived and worked together for centuries in real time and our civilizations have been interlocked ever since they retrieved the Earth from the expanding sun. We have been together for so long that we have forgotten that they are aliens."

Alexander stared at Larse in horror and replied, "You have made me consider the unthinkable. We shared minds for longer than you could ever imagine. Link-soo-shan has been my friend for the majority of my life. We are as close as two thinking beings can be in separate bodies. She has saved my life many times and I trust her implicitly! The hatred that she had for me is so long in the past that it is beyond her recall. She would not do anything to harm me or Nagoth."

"Alex! I am not saying that she would harm you, just that you have forgotten that she is a Gnathe! Who else would have recreated Nagoth-shan as a human woman? All I ask you to think about is that Link does not think the same way as you and I. They have no concept of love, as we know it.

Brood-mothers are egg carriers. They do not mate and have no sexual partners. They are instinctive genetic engineers. All Gnathe now have ears instead of hearing crests, hands without talons and carry four nipples to feed their young instead of chewing the food and spitting it down their throats. They have altered their brains to increase their physic abilities. Look at yourself in the mirror sometime. You do not look completely human anymore. All of us are hybrids, carrying Gnathen genes to give us the extra lobes in our brains to be natural telepaths and the other abilities. We have been improved! In my previous life, Toarvak 6 improved what was there to give me extra abilities. Now I walk around in a hybrid body designed by Gnathen genetic experts with those abilities grown in!"

"Since I came back to life after growing to maturity in the vat, I have not questioned the fact that I am healthier and with quicker reactions. My mental abilities are sharper than they were in my previous life," Alexander thoughtfully answered. "Leading a group mind has become easier and merging with a Toarvak collective is as natural to me as walking this corridor."

The two humans stopped outside Link-soo-shan's apartment and were received by one of the Brood-mother's kindred.

"I am Sammat-shan. Welcome. The Lady Link is expecting you. Will you have a percolated coffee?"

Link-soo-shan was comfortably at rest on her perch and had her tail coiled around her feet. The large tri-angular head swung round and her green eyes fixed on Alexander. She moved from off her perch and reached forwards to the human and picked him up by his upper arms. The giant held him easily aloft, level with her face and lightly touched his face with her tongue.

"Alexander! You are worried. Nagoth is with child. Did

you think that I would not know?"

Alex squirmed in her effortless grip and she put him gently down onto the floor in front of her. Larse quickly sidestepped into the room and leant against the wall away from the giant's reach. Sammat-shan entered the room with three mugs of freshly percolated coffee on a tray, black and sweet and set them on the table.

Link picked up the pint pot of strong coffee and returned to her perch, waited for Alex to speak and remarked, "The coffee is good and strong. It has become a great pleasure to my taste-buds and I find that the caffeine boost aids clear thought!"

"I know that your race has genetically tinkered with human beings as well as yourselves. I will be blunt! Have you improved the human body further that Nagoth was resurrected in? What will her pregnancy bring forth? I know that all the resurrected humans and apes have been improved," Alexander said. "Is my Nancy the same type of human as all the other females?"

"Not quite," the Brood-mother replied. "As you know the Gnathe always strive for perfection. I must admit that improving the Kresh became a problem due to their culture, but we managed to surmount that obstacle. Nagoth however, carries the seeds of greatness within her. We shall have to be patient and allow nature to go its course!"

Alex watched in horror, as his alien friend drank her coffee and rocked back on her perch. His mind went through all the possibilities and felt Link's mind enter his.

"Dear friend, did I not bring back someone who you could never love in her previous form that loved you? We Gnathe may not feel the same emotions as you twin sexed beings do, but we are capable of forming relationships! I watched over the embryo growing in the life tank for eighteen years and brought her to a state of perfection.

Is she not beautiful to all of your senses? If you and I had not shared so many experiences over the years, I could be offended by your lack of trust, but I do realise that it is ignorance and worry that brings you to my door."

Within a mind link there could be no deceit and Alexander relaxed and drank his coffee.

As the two humans left the powerful mind of Khann-link-sool slipped into Link's and made the remark, "He has no idea of what you have done, has he?"

"It is enough that he will go back and reassure Nagoth-shan that all is well. She will find it a natural thing when the twins begin to talk to her before they are born. As I said to him, we must be patient. If I am right in my expectations these two 'humans' will be necessary when the abomination awakes."

Nagoth-shan had endured the expanding girth as the twins grew with growing apprehension. It was now six months on from the morning she had retched for the first time and there seemed no end to the swelling in front. Her appetite had taken several strange pathways with annoying urges to eat odd things in combination with others. At one time she had craved and ate pickled onions with sweet pod-vine fruit picked early so that the pods were still green. The urge to eat toasted bread covered in honey and eaten with boiled eggs had lasted for two weeks until she found that suddenly she could not face the thought of any of the combinations. Then it had been tomatoes by the bag-full with raw cabbage! The strange thing that she had to come to terms with was that not all human women suffered from these cravings when pregnant.

She was resting in the spring sunshine on a wooden bench made by one of the Thipdar craftsman when she was aware that something was picking through her mind and the sensation came from within! She concentrated her thoughts inwards and found two warm fuzzy places in her mind.

"Ma-ma?"

She was not shocked, as all Brood-mothers made contact with the young that they carried in the brooding pouch at a certain stage of development. All Gnathe were born able to walk, partially developed, with language skills and distinctive personalities. They were not as helpless as human children and developed much faster.

"I am here," she answered and felt both infant minds reach out to her, one male and one female.

Nagoth felt them kick as they began to move around inside her womb. A fierce and unconditional love filled her mind like a warm glow. She realised that she would kill to protect these young. This was something that she had not been prepared for and it caught her by surprise. Female Gnathe passed the fertilised egg to the Brood-mother and rarely had anything to do with the young afterwards. If the egg were developed into two Brood-mothers, then a female would feel great pride that her genetics had provided the base line for this development rather than male or female Gnathe.

She reached out to Alexander's mind using the Goss to find him.

He was in telepathic contact with Hannah and Index, finding out what the sleeping state of the Harvester was, as a co-rider of the questing minds, when Nancy made contact with them.

"Alexander! The twins' minds have surfaced. They are aware of me and I of them," she projected and opened her mind to all three of them.

Alex was stunned by Nagoth's revelation, as was Hannah. The Tran-sentient studied the link to the twins dispassionately and filtered the information back to Alexander.

"This is a new type of mind, friend Alexander. Watch these minds carefully as they grow and develop. I have never felt minds of this type before and neither has Archive in all the millions of years she has lived. Speak again with Link-soo-shan, I feel that she has more to tell you!"

The maternity ward was always busy with the new arrivals of every alien species and had been designed by the Guardians to accommodate all types. They studied each new species and new wings added on continually to the building. Solace had added to her skills by absorbing medical knowledge and becoming part of the new system. She had followed the gestation period of Link-soo-shan's creation and had monitored the twins' progress. These tiny human children were developing at a steady rate and she felt that they were far more advanced than any other unborn babies that she had been involved with.

The time of the birth had arrived and Asue was a constant companion to Nancy who was now beginning to feel apprehension. She felt that her body was out of her control and her worries were being passed on to the unborn twins. They were becoming increasingly restless, as they too could feel that a great impending change was imminent. Link-soo-shan had studied the impending birth with great interest and had reassured Asue that, as the body she had genetically nurtured was perfect in every way, there would be no complications. Nagoth had insisted that her Brood-mother be there at the birth as well as her friends. Emelia showed Nancy how to use the birthing chair by assuming the position in front of her.

The backrest was slightly tilted, with sidebars that dropped down for her to grip with her hands. Her backside fitted into a scalloped support, allowing her legs plenty of opening movement with her feet supported, knees half bent so that she could push against a solid resistance. Emelia had allowed her friend to experience her memories of the many births that she had accomplished as a mother.

Nagoth felt a sudden gush of water and she became aware that she was draining fluid over the floor. Alexander took her by the hand and walked up and down the maternity suite with her. Several minutes later she mounted the birthing chair and wriggled into a comfortable position, gripping the sidebars with her hands. A contraction started deep within her body and faded away taking with it the pain.

Asue waited patiently and placed her hand on the bulge, entering the woman's nervous system. She monitored the contractions and relayed the news to the waiting gathering.

"She is starting her contractions and the twins are confused, but fine," the nannite said. "There will be nothing more than this for some hours yet before these babies are born."

Another contraction shuddered through the naked mother to be, as she brought her muscles into action. Ten minutes elapsed before the next one took over the Gnathe/ human hybrid and made her sweat and clench her teeth. Again and again the contractions took over. The twins were both head down and engaged, now began their journey into the world. By the time Nagoth felt that she could stand no more, Asue slipped an epidural into her spine and released her from the majority of pain. The contractions speeded up to a desire to push. The first twin began his downward passage into the light and air. A hair covered head emerged and Asue manipulated the baby into the waiting hands of Alexander. She snipped the umbilical cord, giving the baby boy a slap as she did so.

The boy gave a howl of indignant pain and rage and reached out to the closest mind to him.

Alex found himself hurled through the air clutching the baby tightly to his chest to protect him. He landed on his backside up against the wall of the delivery ward, where Solace had gone into machine time to catch him, before he suffered damage. Both nannite and human reassured the tiny infant that he was safe and that the slap was necessary to start him breathing. The eyes of the child were wide open and regarded his father with an unblinking gaze for several moments, while his mind registering the unconditional love that Alex had for his son.

Alex cradled the child and presented him to Nancy where she could touch him before taking him to be washed and wrapped in a warm towel. He very gently laid him in the cot, being very careful not to startle the infant and returned to Asue's side where she awaited imminent developments.

Once again the contractions intensified and once more a hair covered head appeared. The nannite inserted her hands around the tiny shoulders, assisted the entrance of the girl with the next push and cut the umbilical cord. This time she did not slap the child before handing her over to Alexander, who held her very gently. Alex stared enraptured at his daughter, walked round and handed the girl to Nancy.

"Say hello to your daughter, Nancy. Whatever you do, do not startle her, or face the consequences!"

Nagoth felt her breasts ripen and milk began to dribble from her nipples. Immediately she put her daughter to her breast and the girl began to suckle. A wave of indignation erupted from the nearby cot filling the minds of all the humans there and Alexander hurried over to carry his son to the unoccupied nipple. Both babies began to greedily fill themselves from Nagoth's ample milk supply. She felt an overwhelming contentment as her newborn babies fed.

She reached out to the mind of Link-soo-shan and said, "Thank you, Reverend Lady. Thank you so very much for this unexpected gift!"

Asue finished tidying up the afterbirth and wiped Nancy clean, before clearing everything away. She then monitored each twin by inserting a nannite filament into each child's nervous system. Asue concentrated her mind on the results and came to the conclusion that both twins were exceptionally healthy, although both had a higher than normal metabolic rate.

Link-soo-shan stared down at the tiny infants as they slept and felt quite happy that all her expectations would be satisfied. She held her innermost thoughts tightly behind a shield. There would be ample time yet before any of the humans would sense the difference.

CHAPTER NINETEEN

The twins grew at a phenomenal rate, both in body and mind. Whatever was in the milk that gushed from Nagoth's breasts it more than satisfied the ever-present hunger that the infants radiated. At three months, the two of them were able to stand holding the bars of the cot. By six months they were able to walk, were demanding solid food as well as their mother's milk and were the size and development of a two-year old child. It was not possible to gauge the extent of their minds. They had absorbed all that Nagoth carried in her mind when they had gestated in her womb. Even as helpless babies they had been able to telepathically 'talk' to their mother and it was not too soon before Alexander felt them picking at his mind every time he visited them.

Alex tried to spend as much time as he could with the growing twins as well as their mother. As any parent he was joined by that unconditional love that parents have for a helpless child that belongs to them. He was never quite sure that the feelings were returned. It was more a feeling of need and protection that each child displayed. Alex accepted that this would have to be enough. There would be ample time for the bonds of parenthood and child to strengthen. They were indeed different to any of his previous children.

He made his way to the apartments that were allotted to himself and Nancy. He felt the connection to his partner's mind, as he walked up to the door. As always he shared an echo inside Nagoth's thoughts, when the two growing minds listened in.

"Is everything alright, Nagoth," he said as the door swung open.

There was a feeling of great accomplishment inside the room.

As Alexander walked in he was met by two small figures sailing through the air towards him, hand in hand. Just before they swooped down they released their hold on each other and entwined their hands in his hair. Both gave him a fierce hug and held onto his upper arms with their legs. Alex found himself lifted off the ground without him doing the levitation and carried into the room towards a chair. There, when they spun him round to sit, the twins let go and slid down onto his lap.

"Daddy!" The two minds joined his. "We can fly, just like you!"

Alexander sat stunned by this fresh development and just stared at Nagoth in amazement. His heart rate went up as the beautiful woman pulled her copper coloured hair back behind her ears and rebound it with a band. She bent forwards over his face, held him by his ears and kissed him with a deep passion.

"Aren't they clever, Alex my love? We should go outside where they can really expand their talents," she projected into his mind. "I will open the window and we can really fly."

With that thought ringing in his mind, Alexander felt Nagoth push with her mind and the window opened wide. Before he could argue the point, two small children with auburn coloured hair, shot through the window followed by their mother. Alex levitated, followed them outside and expanded his energies to swoop upwards to join them.

He interrupted the urge to go high with a warning to the twins, "The higher you go the colder it gets. You are not dressed for heights! Stay at treetop level."

The twins dropped down as asked and raided the topmost ripened fruit from a plum tree. They effortlessly hovered while they ate several and threw the stones down to the ground far below. From this vantage point they spotted the huge bulk of a young Tran-sentient in the distance, feeding off the topmost branches of a fruit orchard and sped off sideways towards her.

It was Archive-index, who constantly monitored the state of the Harvester for any sign of wakefulness. Hannah and Fredrick were her constant companions and had set up camp on her upper surface. They had pitched a tent on top of the Tran-sentient in front of the gasbag. This was anchored by nannite tethers, into the living flesh of the immense being that floated in the air. Inside the tent they had a microwave oven with a grill and convection heating, to cook their meals. Index provided some of these, as she caught small animals while she drifted and fed. Hannah maintained the portable generator to supply continual power to the crystal harness and joined the mind of the Tran-sentient from time to time to shadow the search. Minnis remained with her organic friend as an independent nannite, until he needed her to become his armour. She often complained that there was nothing for her to do and that she missed the action of the 'old days'!

It was to this peaceful interlude that the new family of Alexander and Nancy suddenly erupted. The twins hit the side of the tent with shrieks of delight and slid down the incline. They burst into the tent and attacked Fredrick by jumping on him. The giant found himself occupied in a play-fight that needed all of his senses to stay ahead. In the end he wrapped his arms around them to keep them still, only to find that they had forced his arms open by telekinetic force. Free from restraint they once more piled in and this time Alexander took control by gripping them tightly with his mind and keeping them in the air, away from their big friend.

"Enough! Manners!" he piled into their minds. "Have more control than to hurt someone who loves you! Steady down!"

"OK," came the twin minds in unison. "We are just pleased to see uncle Fredrick! He's fun! You can let us free now father."

Alex did so and set them down onto the living floor of the Tran-sentient's back. Immediately he did so he felt the twin minds go elsewhere and realised that they were with Hannah and Archive-index hundreds of thousands of light years across the other side of the galaxy.

The new group mind studied the ball of entwined spaghetti with an enlightened extra sense. They could now feel its controlled hunger and a feeling of when the abomination would waken. Not yet, but a time in the future that would come. The twins would know when, as they developed. The mind withdrew and separated into four distinct minds, but all had experienced the twins' early sense of precognition.

There was a stunned mental silence and then Archive-index spoke, "I told you Alexander, that there was a different mind within us, before these children were born. As I told you before, seek out Link-soo-shan and find out what she knows!"

Alexander sat down on the living flesh of the Tran-sentient and gathered his thoughts together. He looked at the children that were now cuddled up to his friend and to the incredible 'human' wife that the Gnathe had grown in a life tank. She had the mind of a female Gnathe in a human body and had adjusted well. The development of the twins inside her had progressed similar to a Brood-mother's gestation of Gnathen young. Long before they were born, Gnathe could communicate with their Brood-mother and were born with language skills. They also had a portion of their minds imprinted by the carrier. Their development was extraordinarily fast against human young, even faster than the pan-chimpanzees. Because of the white-knuckle ride that he had endured with these incredible children, before and after they were born, there were many things he had not questioned. It was time to take stock. He suddenly realised that neither Nagoth nor himself had ever given the boy and girl a name. Each identity was recognised mentally by them, so names had never been necessary in a telepathic society. Each alien species had their own way of communication with each other besides telepathy, but humans and apes also used speech! He was conscious of a mind inside his.

He was aware of a steady gaze from his son who said, "My name will be Shoolin after a brave friend of yours from long in your past. Remember always father that you are me and I am you. To a great extent your mind is my mind with some differences that will become apparent over the years. All that you have ever done is in my memories, as are Nagoth's. From that springboard I also have Link-soo-shan as mental grandmother to draw upon. This body may be new, but the mind that lives in it is much, much older and is a mixture of human and Gnathe!"

Alexander sat stunned and became aware of his daughter floating in front of him slightly to the left. She inserted her tiny hands into his and opened her mind, "Do not be distressed father. I am also all that Nagoth ever was and Link-soo-shan, but I am also your feminine side and carry all of your memories, so you may call me Alexis. Reach out to Link-soo-shan via the Goss and ask her to come here. She will explain!"

Alex sat with his children in his lap with Nagoth at his side and mentally called, "Goss!"

"I am here, Alexander. What do you require of me?"

"Find me the mind of Link-soo-shan," Alex asked and waited.

Alex held his communication crystal tightly in his hand as his old alien friend invaded his mind.

The Gnathen mind-link connected, "Alexander! What do you need of me?"

"Link-soo-shan! I would like you to concentrate on the crystal I hold in my hand and teleport here to the top of Archive-index, where I would like to speak with you face to face."

There was a load pop as the giant form of the Gnathen Brood-mother appeared in front of him displacing the air, only to rapidly find that she had a human child on each shoulder, pulling at her ears.

"Shoolin and Alexis! You have caused your father to wonder about you? What have you told him?" she asked and plucked the memories from the children.

"How did you know their names? I have only just found out what they wished to be called," Alex wondered.

"I have to ask how was it, that it took so long for you to know? You have been avoiding this moment. You know that they are special, old friend. Love of these amazing children has kept you blind!"

"Link! Stop talking in riddles! It has well passed the time for this. It is time that you told me everything. What have you done?"

"These are the next step in human evolution. They are a mixture of Gnathen genetic manipulation and human clay, moulded to be both human and Gnathe! They will have the one ability that eludes us; - precognition! As they develop and reach maturity and that will be sooner than you can imagine, they will be able to look forwards in time. They will know when the Harvester will awaken and where it will go. They will have all of our psychic powers at a strength that will leave those of us that contributed, in their shadow and like Gnathe they will have instant recall. They will be far greater than the augmented Kresh. I am sure that when the time comes they will lead the assault on the Harvester by reaching out to all the world minds we have left behind. They will have the future of all organic life in their hands. These children will need to be nurtured and cared for, as they are children, as much as children are, although much more powerful."

"We need to inform Kamiel," Alexander said. "He needs to know this."

"It was Kamiel that asked me to consider the problem, old friend and find a solution," the Gnathe replied.

Hannah had removed her crown of crystals and hung them out of harms way. She and Fredrick had listened to all of the conversation that had taken place between all the minds present.

She looked pointedly at Alexander and asked, "What other grand schemes has that Guardian got working away? What other decisions has he made without our knowledge? He really works on a need to know basis!"

Alex sighed and replied, "That nannite has the fate of every organic creature in his hands. His sense of responsibility far out-weighs even mine! As you know, his mind was modelled on the original Alexander McBald the project director of the Genesis Project and some of the finest minds of the time. McBald was a man who knew he was going to die along with his race. This Kamiel nannite he designed and brought into being has had some pretty unique experiences throughout our combined pasts. Without organic life, he would never have existed. This drives his sense of responsibility far beyond his drive to survive. He is an immortal being and is not dependant upon anything organic to keep him alive. Think about all

270

the civilizations the nannites have built at the edges of solar systems. None of them need organic life to continue to exist; yet they tie themselves to all sentient races. Many of them died building the stargate around the Last Ark of the Goss during the time we were falling through the wormhole to get here. They could have waited until we got here, but they felt it necessary to arrive with the weapon finished. Kamiel is my friend and I trust him."

Toarvak 12,402 exited the latest wormhole to find a world ravaged by nuclear fires. There was no sign of the collector or the web that had once encircled the planet. The nine other Toarvaks hovered in orbit around the cloud-shrouded planet. Beneath them nothing lived in the poisoned atmosphere that roiled and shed ash in a ceaseless rain. Nuclear winter had begun and would last for centuries. The network that the collectors used to gather in life energy had disappeared. All trace of the Harvester's gatherers had gone with it.

The ten collective Toarvak minds held a telepathic conference. Three of the Toarvaks were fielding augmented Kresh while the others carried a mixed crew of human, ape, Thipdar, Gnathe and Vogb. Within the 'walls' of the Toarvaks were nannite standby crews ready to carry the Goss spores to the world below inside themselves. All of the Toarvaks carried time distorting crystals.

Azander took dominance over the group mind Toarvak 12,402 and put forward the argument, *"The destruction here has not been done too far in the past. We could go back ten years and prevent this."*

On one of the Kresh ships, First of Dappled Grey agreed, saying, *"It would be simple to distort time locally and save these people. I vote we do this thing!"*

The rest of the Kresh agreed and applied their collective logic to the rest of the Toarvaks.

One collective protested the possibility that the time line

would be altered at this point and said, *"An echo effect would resonate through the universe."*

The ten collective minds considered this possibility and came to the conclusion that the risk was worth the endeavour. They dropped down to the ruined world below.

Temporal reality shimmered and ten barrel shaped ships winked out of existence and slipped out of phase. They had anchored themselves inside the planet below or they would not have surfaced where the star system had been ten years ago. They had picked a high mountain range to hide inside and could sense the difference outside as they drifted out. This world was alive! Above them sparkled the soul-catcher network and above that the skies were full of collectors! They hovered like flies around a dung heap. Instead of the usual one or two, there were dozens of smaller ones waiting to gorge on the life force and carry it back the Harvester.

The Toarvaks considered the problem. As they were located ten years in the past they could not call for backup. They would have to deal with this problem themselves.

The collective minds decided what to do.

Toarvak 12,402 slipped away out of phase and silently edged through the jostling throng of collectors until it was a half a million miles away. Here it positioned itself just in front of the mouth of the wormhole and held position, taking the ring of crystals back into phase. The other nine spread out until six were above and three below. There were many satellites in orbit controlling the slumbering missiles of death from both continents. These would have to be taken out first so that there would be no guidance systems available to direct the nuclear weapons. A constant crackle of static would immobilise the ground controls and prevent any nervous firing. Aircraft that were already in operation would have to be expendable. As the impending nuclear war was occupying most sentient minds, civil aircraft were flying at a minimum.

Positioned at one hundred and twenty degrees around the equator, hovering in the ionosphere, three Toarvaks unleashed radio silence. The fires of the parent star flashed through the air incinerating the satellites. The six ships above opened up a cross fire that disrupted the collectors causing them to scatter. From below came tongues of fire moping up the survivors that dropped down. Six of the collectors made for the wormhole gate, only to be met by a new sun that blossomed throughout their numbers and disrupted their energies. The web came apart and dissipated releasing the controlling elements urging the inhabitants of the world below to unreasoning violence. The element of surprise had worked in their favour.

The night sky came alive with the fires of the sun and those in command panicked, as all contact with armed forces ceased. Television programs were replaced by static and all telephone lines shut down. Without orders, weapons were kept on standby and all fighter planes remained grounded. Ships at sea continued to travel at the same pace armed and ready for action, but deep submarines had no idea what was going on high above and remained deadly, waiting for a signal that would never come through. Missiles in silos remained inoperative as all electronics were scrambled by EMH bursts of radiation emitted by the Toarvaks. On each side of the impending conflict the people cringed, waiting for the nuclear fires that did not come.

As the nine Toarvaks came back into phase however and entered orbit around the planet, one collector that had been tucked behind the single moon, opened its wings and caught the solar wind. At slightly less than the speed of the charged particles that swept out from the star, the last collector centred itself on one of the Toarvaks carrying the augmented Kresh. The life energy shone like a beacon in the night and the collector reached out and drained the Toarvak's crew in an instant. Instantly the eight ships left, went out of phase and scattered.

Puzzled by the disappearance of the life energy around it, the collector headed towards the wormhole entrance and the way back to its greater part to inform what had happened. As its mind sent the opening sequence to the gate, the fires of the sun erupted from a barrel shape just in front of it. Under the onslaught of the infernal fire, the collector came apart and the mind that drove it died, along with the life energy that it had drained from the Toarvak.

The future that would have been, altered into the new time line that now had another world mind, instead of a dead world. The ripple effect spread out and the Harvester felt the energy drain from what was, to what is and stirred towards wakefulness. Other energy filled the gap and the Harvester's awareness diminished except for a memory from long ago that this had happened before on a larger scale. The being slowly edged back into its slow thinking state and fed on what was still coming in from its 'farms.' Soon it would need to awaken fully and hunt for more, as the energy seeping in from the wormhole systems was getting less and less. It sent a pulse out to its 'collectors' scattered throughout the galaxy to check that all was as it should be. This signal would take many years to return to the Harvester. When it did, the loss of so many would alert the being and waken it fully.

Kamiel was tending his organic implant to maintain its 'life' and subsequently the host to the Goss. Connections led from this fist sized living pocket of flesh that lay in a nutrient solution to his neural network. The spores of the Goss lived and prospered in the cell structures and intertwined with each other. Completely mindless as individual spores, they made a bridge to all other spores wherever they were distributed. Somehow they linked throughout the wormhole systems to take a combined intelligence that existed as sum of the parts. The organism was very old and had memories that Kamiel had plumbed at great depth. When it was a parasitic organism before the nannites had changed it to a symbiotic, it controlled the dead as well as the living. The Guardian wondered if this ability could be of use in the future when the confrontation with the Harvester finally became unavoidable.

A familiar presence entered the nannite's mind uninvited, "Kamiel!"

"Goss?"

"Some of me is missing!"

Kamiel concentrated his mind on the symbiont's mind impulses, "Explain!" he demanded.

"A command of ten Toarvaks working at the far edge of this galaxy suddenly ceased to exist. All segments of my hosts are no longer in this time frame. It is the only answer to the situation. Amongst them was Toarvak 12,402."

"That is the Toarvak that travelled back in time with the research group to find out the reason for the impending galactic collision. It has an experienced crew, so I will have to trust that there was a good reason for the time jump," the nannite replied.

"Kamiel!"

"Yes Goss?" answered the Guardian. "Is there something else?"

"A new mind would speak with you!"

He found himself connected to something that was Alexander, with other minds and personalities added. He could sense Nagoth's mind and behind that Link-soo-shan's but blended together into a twin mind, independent of each other and yet resonating in tune with each other.

"Kamiel, old friend of our father," the male side of the twin mind responded, "We have much to do! The Abomination will waken, but not quite yet. Something has disturbed its long sleep."

"Something done now, yet in the past! I detect a ripple in time," the female side of the twin added. "The timeframe of this universe is fragile. The future has been changed in our favour. A powerful ally has been saved from the Collectors. Things are too cloudy to look too clearly into the future at this moment. We need to grow! Make sure that we are given the time to do this!"

In the sudden silence Kamiel was astounded. Link-soo-shan's genetic tinkering had bourn fruit! He had stayed well out of the way of the birth and subsequent development of Alexander's twins. What he had hoped for had come to pass. The organics had developed precognition with the help of the Gnathe! He would no doubt, be soon visited by his old human friend, demanding explanations. The nannite reflected on that thought. Were there any human beings left in the galaxy? What looked basically human now was an upgrade of human and Gnathen genetics bound together. Probably the only true humans and pan-chimpanzees that existed were on their way to the Greater Magellanic Clouds, travelling in the globular cluster designed by the Kresh stellar engineers. Hardly any of the alien beings that made up the compliment of the expedition into Andromeda had not been altered and improved by the Gnathe while they grew in the tanks! Before this confrontation with Alexander he felt that he needed to listen to what his maker would advise.

Kamiel concentrated his neural nets inwards to activate his private program.

The world disappeared around him to be replaced by

the office of Alexander McBald's and his designer was sitting at his desk facing him.

"Kamiel 637! It's been a long time since you last came to me," the old man said and sat back in his swivel chair. "So out with it! What do you want?"

"I have not needed to seek your advice for some time it is true, but now I have a human problem to deal with. I know that when you created me, your mind was instilled as my central processor and the other minds that go to make up my entire personality are grafted on to that anchor point," the nannite replied.

"And your problem is?"

"Although I have a basic human origin, my thoughts are driven by logic and circumstances not by emotional drives," Kamiel answered. Through the centuries of my existence and my association with all sapient species I have gained an insight into organic life. I still find the sentiment that you refer to as love, difficult to totally understand."

"It was never thought necessary to program that set of emotions into any of the nannites," Alexander explained. "All of your 'race' were constructed to be logical and to have a sense of duty. Your criteria, was to ensure the survival of the human race after we had perished in the expanding sun. As events have shown, you Kamiel 637 you have done far more than was ever expected of you. You have transgressed the limits we set within you and gone far beyond the initial boundaries."

"Of all the other nannites created by humanity, Asue 637 comes closest to my way of thinking. She too was destroyed and recreated when Hannah reversed time during Link-soo-shan's attack on the time travel project, but it falls to me to send my people to their deaths. I am responsible for millions of sentients who have died due to my decisions. All of the organics are now my people. I must use them as

I see fit to ensure victory over this abomination that lives off the life energy of billions! They accept this! Sometimes I feel no more than an intelligent machine, until I use the Goss to communicate amongst all organic sentients. It is then I get the echo of what it is to be organically alive. Now I must face your clone and explain just what I have done in using him and justify myself."

"Surely this is no bad thing if it adds a measure of humanity to your electronic soul? I am just a pattern laid inside your programming to remind you of what you can and may achieve. Be who you are and embrace the thought that humanity is an idea," the old man said and stood up.

Behind the imagined human was the view from his office window showing the Earth as it was once. In the sky a full moon looked down on a green and living world while to one side of it a part of Icarus was visible. This was the gas giant that the combined minds of Gnathe and humanity had placed the planet and moon into orbit around, using a mixture of psychic power and technology.

All this had come to pass because of his plan of joining the Gnathe to his people to maintain their survival on a hostile world. The fact that it was on its way to the safety of Greater Magellanic Clouds with the rest of the sentient peoples of the Milky Way was because of his efforts so long ago.

Kamiel let go of the images and the audience with his maker and waited for Alexander to come to him. He would now tell him the truth about his twins.

CHAPTER TWENTY

Alexander stood for a moment outside Kamiel's office and searched his mind on what to say. Logic told him that the Guardian had good reasons to do whatever he chose and had always in the past weighed up the situation before acting. Humanities' involvement with the Gnathe had been necessary to enable them to survive, but it had cost lives on both sides. Without those sacrifices there would have been a universe with humanity missing from its uncaring existence. What sacrifices would the enigmatic being be calculating into the new equations now?

The door silently opened before he could signal his need for entry and he was conscious of being appraised by the silver figure of the nannite. Kamiel had changed his optic band to a pair of definite eyes with a nose and mouth, so as to present a face to his organic friend. It always amazed Alex that the slight figure in front of him was of less body mass than himself. The human was a nearly a head taller than the nannite and broader across the shoulders.

The Guardian looked at him and the silver face smiled.

"Come in, Alexander," he said.

"I expect that you know what I want to talk to you about, old friend, so let us be plain. What devious scheme have you initiated concerning my children with Nagoth and what is your involvement with Link-soo-shan?"

Kamiel increased his size to Alexander's and answered him, "A long time ago I set Link-soo-shan a task. The one psychic power that none of the organics possessed was precognition. Both Khann-link-sool and Link-soo-shan tried augmenting the Kresh without success, other than strengthening their already existing powers. The experiment ended with the selected Kresh becoming psychotic, which we overcame using the 'games' that channelled their madness by defeat. This became a useful interlude that enabled all organics to have a better understanding of each other's weaknesses and strengths. I have had them looking into other alien species without any progress, so Link decided to try a long shot with human genetics. Look around you Alexander. Does any of your resurrected race, look human? Even the pan-chimpanzees have been altered and improved. This took place tens of centuries ago, long before the tanks were set up to re-grow the clones your minds were to awaken inside!"

"I guessed as much, Kamiel. It is something that I was quite aware of, but just accepted," replied Alex. "I know that this body has been improved since I last walked around in the previous clone. The changes in Nagoth's body are obvious to me now. She is faster, stronger and mentally quicker than anyone I have known from the resurrection. Her psychic ability is greater than mine and much more powerful in the telepathic reach. She can levitate and fly like a bird and reach inside almost anything with a telekinetic touch far more delicate than mine. She is the pinnacle of Gnathen genetic engineering. Also the silver ball embedded into her brain linking her with the Toarvaks, has made sure that every part of her brain is fully connected into a neural interface."

"That is why she was made! It was Link-soo-shan's idea to put Nagoth's mind into the human body. She was well aware of the love that demented female Gnathe had for you and besides she felt a measure of guilt to what was done to you so long ago! Even though she could never totally understand the emotion of biological love, she was well aware how to use it. You were the ideal male to be bred to her creation, to tie up all the genetic tweaking!"

"Bred! You relegate me to the level of a stud! Kamiel,

sometimes you go too far," he cried in anger.

Kamiel seemed to become taller as he spoke, "Alexander, I have to use the clay at my disposal. Have you not benefited from all that I have engineered? Nagoth would not find it strange for the twins to become conscious while she carried them inside her body. You well know that Gnathe are born advanced. They will grow rapidly into maturity, hopefully before the abomination wakes. Shoolin and Alexis are the first organic creatures to possess the talent of precognition. They will know in advance when the Harvester will stir into action. We will have to be ready long before then and have all of our weapons in place for that very day. Why do you think I was so angry when you nearly got killed in the insectoid's hive? Now old friend, go and enjoy your amazing children and most of all, Nagoth as a human female. It would be a good thing if there were more than two born with these powers!"

Suzzan-link-khann and the rest of the collective brought Toarvak 12,402 into orbit around the enforced peaceful world below. She had left a Toarvak in place next to the wormhole in case another collector should materialise. They had made themselves quite plain to the instruments of the warring factions below. The firework show had dominated the skies all over the planet when the Toarvaks had channelled the sun's energies into beams of incandescent fury as they took apart the collectors. Thousands of nannites had descended through the clouds as giant dandelion seeds spreading the Goss spores far and wide over the densely populated cities. Once they were down on the ground, the silver figures signalled back to the organics in the ships above that the world that they had saved was a Kresh civilization. This was the first Kresh world that the Andromeda task force had found. They were nowhere near as advanced as their cousins from the neighbouring galaxy, but they were well advanced in nuclear knowledge. Both sides of the impending conflict had solved the problems of nuclear fusion and were generating electrical power for their cities by this method.

Driven by the collectors prodding, both sides had amassed a world-cracking amount of nuclear weapons. The over-kill was enough to destroy their planet twenty times over. All Toarvaks had maintained the constant static to silence the electronics that controlled the slumbering behemoths of death. Until the spores of the Goss had spread throughout the Kresh and united them into a vast telepathic community, none of the Toarvaks would land. The nannites had made no effort to hide from the people and had ignored the panicky attempts by the military forces to contain them. They had just allowed the bullets to pass through them and had walked through the tanks whenever the Kresh had tried to contain them. After a few days they were left alone to go where they wished.

Meanwhile the spores began to spread, until enough of the Kresh had become hosts in positions of command to allow communication to take place. This was now the time for a visit from Suzzan and 'First of Dappled Grey' inside Toarvak 12,402, with a deputation of the rest of the alien species. Once this proliferation of the spores had spread, the Toarvaks ceased the static barrage and civil air flight got back into a daily routine. The city of Togas was picked as it was situated on a large tourist venue on an island used by both opposing factions. The island lay on the equator and Togas was built around a deep-water harbour that serviced the hundreds of hotels and was used as a conference centre.

Toarvak 12,402 gently descended from out of the clear blue sky and positioned itself over the harbour. The Toarvak extended legs to correspond to the anchor points that were clear of vehicles and sent them out of phase so that it could penetrate down to bedrock to take the weight. The alien vessel towered over the tallest buildings and shone in the reflected light of the morning sun. It was half the size of the city. Next a pseudopod extended down to the level of the road and stopped just short of the delegation waiting for them.

First of Dappled Grey stepped out into the sunlight with his ears erect and directed his thoughts towards the tense group of Kresh.

"There is nothing to fear. We have come a long way to prevent your extinction. I will be blunt. There are a great many alien beings in the spaceship above you. Many of their community have sacrificed their lives to keep you safe. Accept that this was done in the interests of all civilizations that live in this galaxy. To help you believe us, you are invited to come aboard to see the records we have, of what you would have done if we had not travelled back through time to save you. We have a great deal to show you and much will shock you, but your welfare is our concern."

The delegation drew back as the Kresh leader's thoughts dominated their minds.

'First of Dappled Grey' stood to one side and motioned towards the opening and projected his thoughts again, "Shall I say that you had better visit our vessel and really you do not have a choice!"

The delegation walked uncertainly into the silver tunnel that closed around them and retracted back into the vessel, high above. An opening appeared in front of them and they found themselves at the back of a huge control room. Inside were the most amazingly shaped aliens of every kind. There were bipeds, insectoids, conical shaped creatures and striding towards them a giant being with a long tail attended by smaller versions. The triangular head had un-unnervingly sharp teeth, with large vertically slit eyes and pointed ears.

They felt the presence of a coldly logical mind inside every mind of the delegation. There was an undertone of exasperation, as the being advanced towards them, but no hostility.

"I am called Suzzan-link-khann," the giant said. "I am a Gnathe and all these different aliens that you see around us are here to save you from a terrible extinction. We are from ten years in your future. I will show you what we found that sent us journeying back through time. It will test your powers of credibility to the limit."

A view screen activated and showed the delegation what had happened to their world and their civilization. Some of the Kresh were violently sick as the truth hit home. They watched mesmerised, as the views of their world burning in a nuclear holocaust were shown from orbit. Nothing living could have survived the barrage that they had unleashed.

"You were not to blame," Suzzan instructed the Kresh and switched the view to several weeks ago when the planet was covered from pole to pole in the collector's net when they had arrived.

Busily spinning more filaments were the Harvester's servants, quite clearly shown by their golden glow.

'First of Dappled Grey' opened his mind to the delegation and showed them what they had learnt of the Harvester and filled in the history of the expedition to Andromeda. He also gave them the details of his ancestry, coupled with the other aliens on the Toarvak.

"It is a lot to take in, my new friends," Suzzan impressed the delegation's minds. "As I told you; you were not to blame. This thing feeds on death, or shall we say the life force of organic creatures. It prefers sentient life and promotes civilizations up to a certain level and then destroys them. It then starts up a life cycle on another world by spreading living cells from planet to planet. This is why you have found that there are Kresh on board this living ship. This is the first Kresh world that we have found in this galaxy. Over the centuries the Collectors have driven you insane. Now that you have become hosts to the Goss symbiont spores and can telepathically reach out to every other host, including me, it will never happen again."

'First of Stripes of Brown' opened her arms wide and dropped her ears in submission, as did the rest of the delegation.

"What can we do to thank you? We are overwhelmed by your actions," she said.

"There is something that you can do for us, but for now I think that you should return to your respective people and relay all that you have seen and experienced inside this Toarvak," Suzzan replied. "We have changed the time-lines in this section of the universe by acting as we did. The future has changed and will affect us all. We will stay here for several years to give you the knowledge that you will require, but we must travel forwards through time to a point after our first arrival, to a point where we do not exist here. Although the universe has changed, we must not be in close proximity to our counterparts at the same instant when we catch up to our present! This is our problem! Believe me when I tell you that there is a fast growing galactic civilization that will welcome your addition."

The delegation broke up and wandered around the control room staring at the different alien beings. Soon they lost all apprehensions as they became lost in discussion with the differently shaped beings. They were fascinated by the light shows along the top ring of the Vogb as they spoke to each other. Of all the many strange beings, it was the nannites that excited them the most. They had reached the first steps in producing artificial intelligence themselves with the design and building of sophisticated computers. The independent Guardians were many steps beyond anything that they had produced in their laboratories. When Toarvak 12,402 produced an avatar that rose from the floor and spoke to them, some of the Kresh nearly fell to their knees in shock.

"Delegation of Kresh, welcome you are. Know that your counterparts in our home galaxy built me and fashioned my mind. A long, long way have we come to meet you. Vessels such as I will be left behind when we return to our time period. Much will you have to learn about becoming the collective that controls this vessel. Duplicates of those that freed you from the collectors will be commissioned before we go," the Toarvak said using same voices of the Kresh.

The delegation just stared at the silver Kresh that stood before them. This was again a nannite being, but different from the others. The silver shape never lost touch with the surface and seemed to glide along from place to place without actually stepping off the floor.

First of Dappled Grey gestured to the silver shape and said, "Yes my new friends, we were the designers of the Toarvaks in our home galaxy. The nannites were designed and built by those bipeds you can see at the main view screen. We have a rich and incredibly co-operative history going back hundreds of thousands of years. When we have reached our own timelines we will transport some of you to Haven to meet the ones in charge of this conflict against the Harvester. If I tell you that Haven is a constructed world, built by the nannites for all species to live on, you will have some measure of what lies before you."

One of the Kresh delegation turned to the 'First of Dappled Grey' and asked, "What is it that you require from us in exchange? The Gnathe called Suzzan said that there was something that you would ask for later. Ask now!"

"There is something that you possess in abundance

286

that you will no longer need," the Kresh answered. "We will need every nuclear weapon that this planet can drag into the open. You have no longer any use for them and when we face the Harvester, we will need everything at our disposal to throw at this abomination. We have other weapons that we will use, but having seen what you did to your own world, the quantity at your disposal will be better suited to lie in our holds until they are needed!"

Without a dissenting voice, the Kresh delegation agreed.

A few seconds after Suzzan's force had departed ten years into the past the nine Toarvaks materialised into the new present that awaited them.

The Gnathe's mind found itself under scrutiny as the Goss connected the mind of Kamiel with hers with the question, "What have you done?"

"I created a new reality, Kamiel," answered Suzzan. "We rescued a Kresh world from extinction. They had been driven to destroy themselves with nuclear weapons by a pack of collectors. There is a weapon's arsenal at our disposal here, enough to destroy twenty or more planets! More than enough to just sting the Harvester."

"Your actions woke the abomination! Fortunately for us it has returned to an inert state for the time being. I can only hope that the new future that your actions have propelled us into is a more favourable one."

" We went ten years into the past and returned a split second after we departed and created no paradoxes other than this localised one. One Toarvak and crew were lost in action. The Kresh that live here are more than thankful," replied Suzzan. "I have shown them what they did to their world under the influence of the collectors. They are tearing out of the silos dotted about this world, every intercontinental missile that they have built and are fitting them into the Toarvak's holds. Since becoming hosts to the Goss, the level of understanding has gone off the scale. Although they are not as advanced as the Kresh that live with us, their scientific knowledge is considerable. They have learnt very fast during the ten years we have been here and have already mastered the group mind techniques under the Gnathe and our own Kresh. We have a very valuable potential world mind here that will help to tip the balance."

Grudgingly Kamiel answered, "I will say that you have apparently done well. Altering the timelines of this universe is a risky business, but you managed to deprive the Harvester of a meal of life energy that it once had. The shock of that denial caused it to briefly awaken and something has happened that we have no clear knowledge of. We are still trying to find out just what, although we have do have gained another advantage," Kamiel said and filled Suzzan's mind with the results of Link-soo-shan's genetic alterations concerning Alexander's twins.

Hundreds of thousands of light-years away, the enquiring probes sent out by the Harvester began to reach the nearest nests of collectors. A repeat acknowledgement bounced back along the wormholes to ascertain that all was well. As the distances vastly increased, some of the probes found gaps in the network systems where cross connections used to be. Collectors reacted by sending probing signals of their own, only to find that there were areas that were closed off. A realisation took place amongst the budded offshoots of the Harvester that there was a reduction in numbers. From the millions of energy beings that served the Harvester's will, thousands were missing. In the billions of years that they had processed the hungry needs of their master, this had never happened before! The collectors had never questioned the system that they served, having little more intelligence than bees. There had never been a need for them to think past the steps necessary for them to collect the life energy and return to their 'parent.' Their very state of awareness patterned the slow life of the Harvester. Only when the final stages of a civilization required them to think in 'real-time' prior to the collection of life energy did they think in a manner close to intelligence. Collectors lived on the edge of awareness and used the Harvester's methods and memories. All of them were re-adsorbed by the Harvester when they returned with their cargo of life energy. They were then reborn, leaner and much smaller to re-grow, until they would become once more bloated with the latest crop. Collectors nearby to the empty places began the long trip out to the edge of Andromeda where the Harvester slept, to take it the information that it was diminished.

Dawn fell on Haven's spreading colonies at the administration building. Many more buildings had been added to the area and a town had sprung up with ample spaces between the homes with wide roads. Another winter had laid a blanket of snow in the higher Northern reaches of the planet. Spring had driven it away with strong winds and pleasant sunshine. The nannites handy-work had blossomed with the care that each alien race had lavished on the world. They had used the Kresh stellar engineers to move the world into orbit around another nearby sun and take it back in time a thousand years so that it could settle down. Once it had approached the same timeframe, they had brought it forwards in time to coincide with the events in real-time. A thousand years had been enough for the seas to fill up with fish and the land to weather. Alien animals had been selected from the clone banks and set free to multiply and fill all the empty spaces. Predators had been carefully introduced after several hundred years to keep a balance.

Farms had spread out from the administration building growing every kind of crop necessary to the various alien species. On the edges of the cultivated areas sonic fences kept the dangerous species away from the civilized parts. The young of every alien sentient species had never known any other kind of environment, so they accepted it as natural. They hunted outside the sonic fences for meat in assorted groups of aliens. The games played out inside the amphitheatre inside the last Ark of the Goss by their parents had taught them all about how to rely on each other. Meanwhile fleets of Toarvaks roamed the far-flung arms of Andromeda searching for technical civilizations to free from the collectors influence. Steadily the Goss spread throughout them and more world minds were added to the new federation.

Shoolin and Alexis were five years old and looked as if they were in their early teens. They were hunting a rogue Zanth. He was the prime male of a herd bred by Khann-link-sool that had charged through a gap in the sonic fence during a power failure. The Gnathe still enjoyed riding these beasts and bred them in competition with each other. This one was massive, with a spread of horns that erupted from the head of the Zanth to each side. They were each half the length of a human being and curved inwards from the top of the triangular head. He had been away from the herd for some time and was feeling the need to rut. This made him even more dangerous than usual. It had been decided that the twins should go and retrieve him as a test of their powers.

The Vogb had pinned him into a blind canyon by stinging him with their electrically charged tendrils whenever he tried to escape towards the mouth and open country. They had used levitation to insert themselves into spaces up and around the entrance and remained in full view of the Zanth, but out of reach. They used the other tendrils to anchor themselves to the rock-face. The twins had reached down the memory chain to Nagoth and across to Link-soo-shan's memories of when she had tamed a wild Zanth during her fight against the humans. They studied the method that their mental grand-brood-mother had used. Her knowledge of the internal workings of the Zanth's bodily functions became theirs. The bond between brother and sister had strengthened over the five years to become almost a single mind when they were working together. Simultaneously they dismounted the Bazantii and began to approach the interior of the canyon while the Vogb maintained their presence at the mouth. Their senses ranged in front of them and they made contact with the red mist of the angry Zanth's mind. The beast had retreated to the far end of the canyon and was blowing heavily through the froth around his nostrils. He was shaking his head from side to side and gouging his horns into the rocky sides of the canyon. As the two humans approached he bugled a challenge and snorted as their unfamiliar scent caught his nose.

Shoolin spread calming thoughts into his hormone driven mind while Alexis followed Link-soo-shan's knowledge of the blood supply to his brain. She gently clamped down using her telekinetic sense on the main artery to the beast's brain, restricting the flow and inducing an enforced sleep. The great head began to droop and the eyes glazed over, as the twins quickly walked up to him and climbed onto the back of his neck. Alexis allowed more blood to flow to his brain as Shoolin extended his control over the Zanth's mind. He filled the awareness with the knowledge that females in heat were just some distance in front of them. The weight on the back of the neck was ignored, as the prime hunger took over. He began to walk towards the canyon's mouth, blind to the Vogb holding onto the sides. The Bazantii fanned out from the entrance so as not to distract him, but just flanked the beast as he made his way back to the herd. In half a day they made good progress and the sonic fence could soon be seen. The Vogb remained seated on the backs of the Bazantii close enough to be able to sting the Zanth into unconsciousness if necessary, but far enough away to be ignored.

The twins dismounted and made sure that the Zanth made it safely through the deactivated fence. They sent the signal to Khann to switch the sonic fence back on and saw the Zanth kick up its back feet to leap away. Two of the un-mounted Bazantii galloped towards the twins to allow them to climb back onto their backs. Shoolin and Alexis curled their hands into the mane running down the broad back of their mounts and urged their friends to run back to the new headquarters that their parents now lived.

Alexander was suddenly aware of his son's mind in his.

"A good exercise father, do you not think?"

"You both did very well. I am proud of you both," Alexander replied.

Nagoth's mind filtered into the connection and added, "You found it easy enough to access Link's memories even though you were not mentally connected with her?"

Alexis explained, "We can follow biological birth-lines and mental ones that are connected to our strange family! If I needed to I could branch across to anyone connected to the Goss!"

Alexander shuddered at the ramifications of that statement, as he considered it further and asked, "Is your connection with Index, the Trans-sentient still sound? What can you feel from her monitoring of the Harvester?"

"We still have some years to go yet. Alexis and I are aware that there is movement in the far reaches of the abomination's influence. When we get home both of us will send our minds on a far-reaching trip. We both feel that information is needed at this time. The only way to do this is to send our minds into the future.

CHAPTER TWENTY-ONE

Toarvak 6 had gone back into orbit around Haven, after dropping off her crew for some well-earned leave. They had disembarked at the town that had grown up around the Administration building. There were plenty of empty cottages scattered around the outskirts that provided temporary accommodation. Over a month had ticked by since the last ten Toarvaks had returned from a fishing expedition in one of the spiral arms. In orbit around Haven's moon 'The Last Ark of the Goss' continued to wait for the time of reckoning, as the nannites continued to modify the hollow moonlet and Kamiel continued to plan. Every Toarvak that returned with weapons deposited them at launching stations and passed them onto the Guardians.

Larse took Emelia into his arms and kissed her eyelids with tenderness. His heartbeat increased as she melted into his arms and her upturned lips sought his. Could it really have been over fifty years that they had been re-united since Kamiel had brought them back together? So much had happened in the intervening years and so much more lay in front of them. The time was fast coming at last, to repay the gift of a second life, bestowed on them by the civilization that had fled their home galaxy.

Sometimes he wondered, just what kind of a price that would have to be paid? He had risked his life many times during his wanderings on Daedalus Two in his youth and later in the conflict with the Goss. This entity that had been named as the Harvester, continued to exist by feeding off the life-force energy of entire worlds and was the size of a small planetary system. How could they even think to oppose it? He would follow the Guardian's instructions to the end and he just had to believe that the enigmatic being had a plan. It was not for him to know of all the plans that Kamiel had made, only to be counted on to perform as required.

Time had passed without being able to be counted, as their bodies still remained young and healthy. The only signs of age were a little greying of the hair and the fact that no more children would be born from Emelia, as her ovaries would no longer produce viable eggs anymore. They had produced many children over the years, who had grown up and now travelled onboard Toarvaks of their own. So much of their time together had been spent travelling from star system to star system, that it had been impossible to count the years. He had no real idea how long they had spent on the last Ark of the Goss. Here on Haven at least they could count the passing of the seasons.

Once more their minds and bodies blended as they physically joined together. The pleasure mounted as they both approached climax, both of them experiencing each other's joy. Emelia drove herself upwards against Larse's final thrust and let go with practised ease. With a shuddering of final pleasure they broke apart and lay quietly in each other's arms.

Emelia raised herself up and cupped her lover's face in her hands and said, "What troubles you my love? There is something at the back of your mind that torments you. I have looked into that space, but you shunt me aside."

"The time approaches when we must be prepared to settle our account. Alexander has told me that all six twins are scanning the future, to detect when the Harvester awakes!"

"It has been ten years since I helped those first children into the world. They are fully adult now and their psychic powers are off the scale. If the time has come then let it! I remember growing old waiting for you to come back to me. I grew withered and frail as the years went by. Long before the end, I was confined to my bed. I had to be fed, washed and kept clean, with constant care. I have had more than I could ever have dreamed of, being reunited with you. If it is time to chance our lives, then le t us once more join with Tee 6 and become Toarvak once more."

Inside and outside of the last Ark of the Goss, thousands of nannites had been busy building extra weapons systems to be aimed and fired by a simple press of a button. Most of the firepower of the many civilizations that had been rescued from the attentions of the Collectors had been brought through the wormhole systems to this artificial moon. Alien minds had been driven to design and build weapons of mass destruction capable of cracking a planet wide open. Now they were coming back to the very creatures that had inspired such waste of life and effort.

Inside the Ark, Kamiel and Asue had with the help of Solace spent a great deal of time building crystalline structures. In a great hall that had been specially built for the purpose, hundreds of these constructions radiated from a common centre of six. The life sustaining vats were tailor made for every alien that they had set free from the thrall of the collectors. A fine network of copper wires led to accumulators that drew their power from solar panels.

Alexander and Nagoth's children entered the hall with two more sets of twins that had been born from Nagoth's womb. They had been born two years apart and all of them had matured early, to now resemble teenagers. All of them had the same abilities as the eldest twins and were genetically identical and shared a common mind.

Shoolin and Alexis settled themselves into the crystal frameworks and hooked up the life supports. The vats began to fill.

Now the time had come to align all six minds into one group entity and include Archive-index. She would remain outside the complex that housed the tanks, inside her crystal harness, also being monitored by a Guardian specialist. She had fed well to give her the reserves to allow her body to go into a comatose situation. By her side were two other Trans-sentients to help keep her afloat and not crush herself by making contact with the ground. They would make sure that her gasbag remained full and that she did not move off in the wind. Others of her kind remained in the vicinity to take over the task of keeping her buoyant. All of them would contribute the individual fragments that would resurrect the ancient Tran-sentient, Archive.

In the past, the firstborn twins had managed to direct their minds forward in time to a hazy area that had become increasingly difficult to penetrate. All they could be sure of was that the Harvester was still inert, up until this grey area. There were a nexus of timelines that made a multitude of slightly different universes and possibilities. Somewhere in this folding and refolding of timelines lay the most successful possible outcomes. It was to this area the gestalt intended to spy on. They could only do this in close proximity to the Harvester.

Included in the proposed, great collective, group mind were a number of Gnathe, Vogb and Kresh to follow as observers and to lend their strengths to shield the inner minds of the 'Six' if required. More than a hundred human and apes would weave their minds around Shoolin and Alexis's siblings to make an individual group mind, leaving the aliens to become an outer shield. Only the best psychics had been selected and were required to be also extremely fit, as it was not known how long they would need to be inside the tanks.

Each alien settled into their individual cradle and waited for the life support systems to be hooked up to each of them, to keep them alive during the fishing expedition. The nannites were stationed one to a crystalline structure to oversee the lives of their charges were not over-taxed. Each alien being would float weightless in the life vats, being cared for by the Guardians. They would tirelessly monitor the feeding tubes, waste disposal and life signs of every being. Each of them carried a living piece of flesh that hosted the Goss. This kept them in loose telepathic contact with whoever they were caring for to adjust the power fed into the crystals up or down as required. Too much power would burn out the minds searching in the gestalt. Too little and the mind could fail as it lost its way among the stars.

Each telepath made contact with the command crystals and sensed the matrix stretching out into the cosmos. The six twins and Archive, melded into one mind that began to seek outwards, surrounded by the first layer of minds.

Hundreds of alien minds linked up together and loosely bonded with the 'Six'. Each mind gave up its most of its individuality to remain an encircling collective to feed the central mind whatever power it needed. Circuit breakers closed and power fed into the grid as the 'Six' reached out.

The gestalt entered the nearest wormhole and sped down the timeless avenue to the first nexus. It sidestepped the inactive collector sat at the branching point and diverted into a broad highway. This was a main highway leading towards the Harvester. Large collectors, swollen with energy were travelling down this immense tunnel to merge with their creator. The 'Collective' tightened their defences around the 'Six', by interweaving their minds so that no single mind remained exposed for long, as it dived into the swirling basket. Each mind became a strand that held to each other like lengths of willow constructed into a globe, constantly moving into and out of the weave.

Further and further out to the deep reaches of a spiral arm where the stars became scarce the gestalt travelled. On the last Ark of the Goss the crystal chamber was silent. The only things that moved were the ever-present nannites as the life-support systems were checked. Each Guardian monitored the life signs constantly as the days turned into weeks. Some of the strands interweaving the globe were occasionally touched by the edge of a collector's solar sail, as the wormholes became more crowded. When that happened the strand withered and died, leaving the attendant nannite to close down the life-support. Deep inside the writhing ball of shielding minds the 'Six' with precognition remained sheltered and wrapped around the receptive mind of Archive-index, the ancient trans-sentient. The mind-sphere was the centre of focus of the ancient mind of Archive.

The composite group mind exited the end of the wormhole and found itself amongst a busy swarm of collectors. In front of them writhed a hollow globular web that filled the void the size of a red-giant star. It was an Icosahedron with twenty faces of equilateral triangles, with inside this shape a Dodecahedron with twelve faces of pentagons. The gestalt realised that a Toarvak could easily fly through the spaces at the outer layers. Closer to the centre there were many more many faceted constructions and the more solid the energy being seemed to be. It pulsed. Hundreds of thousands of threads connected the Harvester to the wormholes and diving along the threads came the collectors. They plunged into the body of the energy being, adding their charge to its hungry needs. The gestalt moved away from the swarm, marking the entrance of the wormhole that was their only way home.

The Trans-sentient eased her thoughts into the slow consciousness of the Harvester and made an unobtrusive contact with the edge of the being's mind. Shoolin, Alexis and their four other brothers and sisters reached out to the future to sense the awakening. Several different futures opened up with different timescales pertaining to the situation. One situation showed an abrupt awakening with the Harvester reaching out for the probe! This timeline was put into stasis, examined and a clumsy mind-touch was terminated to a more tenuous contact. The timeline changed. Hundreds of possibilities were examined as to the reactions of the Harvester's existence to the universe and the longest time to awakening. Archive could feel the energy hunger swelling as the life force that the collectors were feeding the creature was beginning to be insufficient. There were by now thousands of civilized worlds that had been rescued from the attentions of the collectors. A possible favourable outcome began to stand out from all the failed timelines that would require a grim sacrifice. It was time to retreat from this place and pull the gestalt home.

The Goss held the matrix of the gestalt together and fed the information back to Kamiel and Alexander. More individual minds were lost on the journey back as they had travelled into a congested area. By the time each surviving mind had returned, over two months had gone by. Not every mind found that their comatose body had remained undamaged. Many of the Vogb had not taken to the long period of inactivity as the bipedal beings. They would need some time for recovery before they could try this again if it were necessary. The one thing uppermost in each creature's mind was to eat solid food. Outside the chamber, Archive-index was tearing up the vegetation and crunching up the foliage with whatever beasts that came into range.

Kamiel and Alexander pondered on the information gathered by the 'Six' at the far reaches of the spiral arm.

Alexander slumped into his chair and ran his fingers through his hair staring at the pictures in his mind, sent by his children.

"We knew that it was huge, Kamiel, but not the size and complexity that Shoolin and Alexis have shown us. Now we at least have some idea when the abomination will awaken. Do you have any more plans?"

"There are quite some years before the Harvester awakens," Kamiel replied. "I shall make the best of them by ensuring that all the members of our federation are given our findings. It is time that all Toarvak commanders were given their instructions. We have some moving and shifting to do. Goss!"

"Yes Kamiel. What can I do?"

"Connect my mind to all of the Toarvak commanders.

Kamiel's strange long-standing plans began to bear fruit, as information trickled back to him from each alien species. The equivalent of planetary Eisteddfods had been taking place for some decades, in every society that had been saved from the attentions of the Collectors. Every kind of art form had been honed and improved by each and every alien race.

The Vogb had produced their unique colour shaded poems, giving some of the most complicated light shows from their communication ring around their heads that had ever been seen. They were totally incomprehensible to any other life form, but any Vogb could appreciate these poems. Telepathically, using the Goss, they were sheer beauty when they were translated into any other alien mind. The shifting colours and varying intensities made them hypnotic to some non-Vogb and unimaginably lovely to others. Too much could drive a different species insane.

Locked away in the human library were orchestral works of many Old Earth composers. There were many human and apes who listened to the works of Beethoven, Mendelssohn and many other long dead composers with great pleasure. Amongst this group of musically appreciative people were those who loved opera even though they could not understand the language. Again, other some species found the sounds repulsive whilst others admired the complexity of the pieces without hearing certain vibrations at all.

The Kresh had hypersonic hearing and heard a completely different composition from anyone else. Thipdar music had the extra complication of being produced with four hands and their stringed instruments were beyond the capabilities of any other species to play. Every alien civilization had produced its own unique art forms, some of which crossed over the species barrier and some could not.

Kamiel had devised a defensive weapon from this knowledge that he felt would confuse the Harvester's way of thinking. Although it was totally inorganic it had learnt how to manipulate the minds of all intelligent creatures at its' disposal. The Guardian had decided to broadcast to this 'energy being' the appreciation of all these different art forms from the very beings that produced them concentrated in the world gestalts. At the very same time, incomprehension that the other species felt when confronted with them, were also to be broadcasted. He now had hundreds of world minds to use in the assault.

Where there was inexperience he had inserted a band of Kresh to control the power of the planetary gestalt. These were the sun shifters who would be responsible for moving the bigger suns that Kamiel had reasoned he would need to the vicinity of the Harvester. Other new world minds had accepted the Gnathe leading their collective power, to open gates at the heart of these stars. The Kresh had found a blue-white star on the other side of the Andromeda galaxy and had built a massive wormhole around it using a thousand Toarvaks and a million crystals to open the gate. The gravitational effect of losing this star would put a more than a wobble into the relationships of the star systems in the area. This area was so densely populated that it was a birthing place for these short-lived suns. The temperature rose to nearly 25,000 degrees Centigrade around the surface. When they opened a hole inside the centre, the resulting jet of incandescent star-stuff would make it spear out into a light-year long narrow cone. Kamiel intended to use like a surgeon's scalpel. The problem would be to make sure that the second gate was positioned as close as possible to the Harvester without being detected.

From some of the most alien intelligences came the question to Kamiel, "Why are you doing this for us? We are organic and if we were no longer here, the universe would belong to you and your kind. You are to all accounts immortal, yet many individual nannites and Toarvaks will risk the loss of their identities in this enterprise."

Kamiel had considered the question many times and had always answered aliens the same way by telling them, "All of the Guardians are programmed to defend intelligent organic life. We were designed and built by the minds of organic thought. From inorganic beginnings came forth life and from that life, now and again, intelligence evolved. From that intelligence, inorganic life has been created and allowed to develop. Without you we would not be here. We owe a debt to such as you, whoever and whatever you become. It would not be logical to allow you to disappear from the universe merely to feed the energy needs of a being that should have dissipated billions of years ago."

This answer had satisfied the Vogb, the Thipdar and all other types of alien species that were rapidly filling up the new federation of worlds. The insectoids had never considered the question, as their logical way of thought just accepted that the nannites were there as part of their lives. As nannites were by the majority, coldly logical, their thought processes mirrored the insectoids. It was only the Guardians who had associated with organic intelligences that displayed a different approach to thought.

Kamiel now had the hardest task to execute. He called his human friends together, along with a number of closely associated aliens. The nannites had constructed a conference hall next to the crystal chamber that housed the life-maintaining vats. It had a stage that Kamiel stood on and semi-circular seats, perches and leaning bars for each form of intelligent life that went to make up the federation of the Andromeda worlds. The nannite watched the spaces fill up and waited until all were settled.

Kamiel concentrated his mind through the piece of living flesh that played host to the symbiont.

"Goss!"

"I am here Kamiel."

"Connect me to every intelligence in this room and stay in the loop. You are included in this discussion and planning," the Guardian ordered.

"Me!"

"You are an integral part of this scheme and all organic life will depend on your unique nature! So follow my planning and you must say to me if what I ask you cannot do!"

The Guardian increased his size so that a giant humanoid figure dominated the stage. The conference hall fell silent and every eye was fixed on the nannite stood before them.

Kamiel's mind reached out with the aid of the Goss and the clear, coldly logical voice spoke clearly in every mind.

"We have now reached the stage of pre-conflict. The 'Six' have looked into the future and I have looked at every method that will give us an edge against the Abomination. You have probably wondered what the many different Eisteddfods stretched over every type of civilised world was all about. The collectors can control minds. We need to spread confusion amongst them. Each type of intelligent being develops their own peculiar form of Arts. Some of them can only be comprehended by their own species. I will need broadcasters from those who can see beauty and perfection of these art works and those who can only feel discord to witness a marathon set of performances. Each mindset must be broadcast at the same time and orchestrated by the world gestalt mind that produces each work of Art. Music for instance can be played and enjoyed by many different species. However, there are some types of beings who cannot understand music at all. These will need to listen at the same time, as the ones who produce the orchestrated works. The conflicting sensations will be mentally broadcast together and directed at the collectors. As they lose control of their objectivity, other world minds must redirect the information at the wakening Harvester. They will feed the conflicting attitudes through the Trans-sentients, so that the energy being cannot shut out the conflicting signals. We must confuse this thing while the next part of my plan takes place."

Kamiel stood unmoving as only an artificial being could. All of the microscopic connections that held him together constantly locked and unlocked all over his nannite body.

His neural nets flowed constantly and stored information and discarded what was irrelevant in an automatic system. He forgot nothing. Even his emergence into consciousness countless thousands of years ago was as clear to him as yesterday. When he was sure that his audience was once more focussed on him, he carried on with his mental projection.

"The Kresh have manoeuvred a blue-white giant star through the wormhole systems towards the vicinity of the Harvester. It is still travelling as we occupy this chamber, so the collectors cannot detect it. Our fleet needs to get to that point of emergence at the same time. Before that happens the last Ark of the Goss needs to be there first. It must deliver the receiving star-gate as close to the Harvester as it can, with its cargo of nuclear weapons that all the 'civilisations we have 'liberated' have donated to the Ark."

Alexander stood and held up one hand.

Kamiel turned to face him and waited for him to reach out with his mind.

"How can we do this Kamiel? We all know that the collectors are sensitive to life energy. They are drawn to it like moths to a candle flame and the close proximity of them to nannites can disrupt your neural systems," Alexander flatly stated and he sat down.

"Nine hundred thousand years ago we fought against the re-emerging Empire of the Goss. The symbiont that we all carry within us enables all alien species to understand each other by a form of universal telepathy. One of the terrible things that the Goss was able to do was to control the dead for some time after life had departed. This ability is still within our most valued co-existent and is the way that this can be done. Those needed to manoeuvre the Ark must reach the wormhole's edge and die very soon after. If the Ark enters the area anywhere near to the Harvester filled with life, it will be the same as a giant firework exploding into a lightshow."

There was a stunned mental silence, as everyone began to understand just what Kamiel had told them. The Guardian waited for the shock to abate and acceptance take its place.

"To bring the Ark to this close proximity to the Abomination will require a group mind of some complexity. The Lagdoo will manoeuvre the Ark into the vicinity of the dodecahedron and release the crystalline stargate to spin like a human child's top. Controlled by the Goss in death, they will put as much distance as they can from the spinning gate before the Kresh open both ends. Link-soo-shan will store every mind on board into crystal storage to be retrieved at a later time if we are successful. She will enter a time stasis box once this has been achieved. I shall be aboard to oversee events and hopefully set up a beacon for a Toarvak to home onto. It's a slim chance of survival for those who decide to fly the Ark, but it's all I can offer any of you. The ancient weapon that closes wormholes will be deployed by thousands of Toarvaks as soon as the Ark has launched through the wormhole exit. The 'Six' have looked into the future at every conceivable possibility and this is the most likely to succeed. They will also be travelling on the Last Ark of the Goss to foresee any last moment favourable changes to my plan. Billions of intelligent beings will owe their survival to our efforts. Many of them may never know that we stood between their extinction and their evolution until they achieve the level of civilization to join our federation of worlds. Are there any questions?"

CHAPTER TWENTY-TWO

Far out on the galactic rim, the first messengers were returning to the Harvester and merging with its unique structure. Information began to flow into the unconscious entity and it began the slow process of its periodic awakening. The geometric shapes that made up its existence began to slowly turn and spin from the centre outwards.

Converging towards the Harvester were millions of Toarvaks all fully crewed and carrying many different weapons. Around the edge of the galactic arm, a collective world mind composed of billions of Kresh, were shepherding a giant blue-white star through wormhole after wormhole. It would appear for a blink of an eye as it exited one and entered another. The Kresh had done this before many, many times, but not with such a giant. This sun was relatively new and had just settled into its short lifespan, when the Kresh had spun a wormhole entry around it. The star was thirty times the mass of the sun that Earth used to orbit. Kresh stellar engineers had moved complete planetary systems and their suns into the Globular system that was fleeing the collision of the two galaxies, but even these had not the mass and inertia of this blue-white sun.

On board these Toarvaks were the augmented Kresh who had been genetically altered and enhanced by the Gnathe. These were the mainstay of the star shepherding minds that had grouped together. As one of the star-managers faltered, another took their place. Each crossover point that the star jumped, took its toll. At the lead position Toarvak 6, hunter killer, was about to break out of the wormhole leading towards the Harvester's position. The six that made her crew were Larse, Emelia, Thomas, Trann-link-khann and a Vogb, called Deep Orange with Tee 6 that together made the Toarvak mind. This new mind meld had come about due to Kamiel's decision to keep Link-soo-shan and Khann on the Last Ark of the Goss with him. The Gnathe's abilities would be tested to the full, as they would be the ones who killed each crewmember and stored each mind in crystal with RNA, leaving their bodies to be controlled by the Goss after death.

One hundred thousand light-years away from where the Harvester slept uneasily something watched the wormhole activity with curious senses. This product of an almost interstellar travelling civilization had sent probes to nearby star systems to gather information and replicate themselves. The plan had been to cannibalise the replicated probes and the mining machines when the Janise had developed their own interstellar ships and had arrived at the prepared world. The Harvester had exploded their sun before they had any chance of doing this.

One probe had soft-landed upon large cold world, too far from its sun to be able to have an atmosphere containing free water. The first action the probe did, was to survey for metals and release small mining machines. The machines dug into the ground and found what they were designed to do and brought metal-bearing earths back to the probe, that smelt them into the materials it needed. As the parts mounted up, more mining machines were assembled until the number was sufficient to reassemble them into a larger kind. The larger mining machines brought back greater quantities until there was a surplus enough to build another probe. Once there were four probes, they amalgamated into one bigger unit with greater complexity and greater computer power. Over the centuries the hive of industry expanded and the central mind controlling the industrial complex achieved sapience. As the Janise had not arrived, the original directive that ruled the artificial intelligence began to alter. After several thousand years the intelligence had exhausted the metal bearing rocks throughout the planet. It was time to look elsewhere.

Other probes had also been successful on worlds orbiting other stars and the same chain of events took place. Inevitable contact had been made and disputed territory led to warfare that lasted for thousands of years until every artificial intelligence finally joined together. Travelling at a fraction of the speed of light and taking many thousands of years to travel from star system to star system the empire of the machines grew slowly and as communication was limited to light speed, information was slow to reach the central intelligence. Toarvaks had slipped through the life barren systems it dominated and out of sight using wormholes. They were seen and recorded with the information sent back. The central intelligence had no knowledge of wormhole technology, as it relied on psychic power to open one. So it patiently waited and built a flytrap.

On board the Last Ark of the Goss, Kamiel linked up to the gestalt of minds and directed the hollow moon down another wormhole. Asue monitored the life-signs of the six identical twins as they hung suspended in the tanks connected to life support. They constantly searched the immediate future and directed Kamiel's attention to any nearby collectors travelling down the wormholes with them. The greatest risk was when the Ark exited a wormhole.

As they approached the entrance, sensing their life force, an energy-fattened collector began to make its way towards the Ark from behind.

Kamiel deployed the Ark's ancient weapon and closed

the wormhole behind them. The collector disintegrated as it hit the sealed door. This wormhole was a short one and the Ark found itself in empty space within a short subjective time.

It exited close to gas-giant orbiting a star and went out of phase until it put some distance between them. In front of the next wormhole entrance was a cluster of collectors. The Ark gestalt found them and directed Fredrick to take them out with one of the Kresh nuclear weapons. The big human was tucked into a cradle that served a launching pad with Hannah by his side, controlling the battery selection. Fred ignited the engines of a planet-cracker and sent it on its way towards the collectors. The inverted vees swarmed towards the life inside the Ark, sailing the solar winds. Fredrick detonated it when it reached the inside of the cluster and watched them vaporise. On the other side of the Ark another collector sailed towards them catching the solar wind. Alexander and Nagoth were in command of the battery this side. Nagoth selected a medium sized fusion bomb and Alex sent it on its way with maximum rocket assist. As soon as the missile reached the proximity of the energy being, he detonated it, destroying the Harvester's servant.

Kamiel and the Ark gestalt, once again opened the wormhole and the Ark slipped through leaving the remains of the destroyed collectors behind them. Once inside, Kamiel shut the wormhole behind them. The 'Six' identical twins, as a closed group mind, turned their precognitive powers towards the wormhole exit.

The mind of 'Six', Shoolin-Alexis, spoke as one to the Ark gestalt, "Send a planet-cracker in front of us, timed to explode no more than twenty seconds after it emerges from the wormhole. Divert the Ark at the next junction to the small thread and allow the missile to continue down the main corridor."

Kamiel sent the instructions to Fredrick and Hannah. He used his gestalt power to analyse the wormhole structure in front of him. Soon they would emerge in the vicinity of the Harvester. He flicked the Ark down the thread and parted company with the nuclear weapon.

At the same time he turned to the two Gnathe at his side and said, "Its time!"

Link-soo-shan and Khann-link-sool both nodded in human fashion and started on their way towards their friends and colleagues with a rucksack of crystals each. This task had fallen to them, as the most competent telepaths and crystal experts. They had worked out the technique with Khann, who had volunteered to die and be reborn back into her old body. Asue had stood by ready to restart Khann's twin hearts after the process. Link had bridged Khann's mind into the storage crystal at a moment before stopping her hearts. The Goss had then taken control for a while and showed that the mind controlled Gnathe was capable of doing anything that was asked of her. Asue then restarted her hearts and Link restored Khann's mind to the reanimated corpse. They were successful, but Asue was worried about cell damage in the Brood-mother's brain so she forbade them to do this again. Khann agreed and declared it unnecessary for her to enact the process to Link, as she was sure of what they had to do.

When the stored minds were reunited with living flesh it would be with newly grown clones. The Goss would use their original cloned bodies until the creature could no longer manage them.

She made her way towards the Lagdoo who controlled the Ark and began her task on the coldly logical reptilians. Every one of them remained at their posts as the Gnathe approached. Only one of them even turned to watch as they set up their equipment.

"Goss are you ready?"

"Yes," the symbiont replied. "I will take control as each heart stops."

With the bell-like voice of the Goss echoing through her mind, Link-soo-shan began to kill and collect their minds, while Khann removed sufficient DNA and RNA to be sure of retaining all of their personalities and memories, as a safeguard. Once she had processed them she made her way to the weapon's console where Fredrick and Hannah were waiting for her.

Fredrick was seated at the controls of the missiles while Hannah selected which weapon to fire. As the Gnathe approached them, they stood up and hugged each other.

"We're ready for you, Link-soo-shan," said Hannah. "Do it now!"

The giant carefully placed a crystal on each forehead and bridged their minds across into storage. The Goss symbiont took control of the bodies without pause and sat them back down into the control chairs. From here they moved through the Vogb and the Thipdar, gathering minds as they went. As the two Gnathe collected, the Ark gestalt mind came apart. Now Link needed to attend to two old friends.

Alexander and Nagoth were still at their posts scanning the wormhole for collectors as they sped down it. They turned to meet the Brood-mothers as they entered the weapon's control sector. After a long lingering kiss, Alex reached up to Link's chest and hugged her for some moments.

Link found the bright clear mind inside hers, as Alex said, "Thanks my old friend. Thanks for Nagoth and those incredible children of ours. We have enjoyed each other's company across the eons. Let us hope that we shall again in the future whenever that will be."

313

Link lifted the human effortlessly and held him at face level. She ran her tongue over his face as gentle as a lover's kiss and embraced him. The Gnathe put him down and found that she was choked up with unfamiliar emotions. Her hand shook a little as she took out two more crystals from her bag.

Before she made the bridge she answered him with her mind, "I promise that I will bring you two back again once more. I shall watch over your growing clones until the day comes for the quickening. I will not let you go, my friend. A mind such as yours is all too rare in this galaxy. I feel that there will still be much for you and I to do in the future!"

With that thought in his mind, Link-soo-shan stopped his heart with her telekinetic sense and performed the bridge to his mind to crystal storage while Khann took the RNA from his brain.

The Goss sat him back down at the weapon's console and Nagoth approached her maker and stood between the two Brood-mothers. Link bent down from her waist and grasped her daughter's shoulders and entered her mind.

"You are far more important than you know," she projected. "If we are successful and destroy this abomination you will once more emerge from a cloning tank with your mind intact. The children that you produce in the future will not be as you have reared in this time frame. They were created for a purpose. That purpose is now. The human race is not ready for the jumpstart I have designed and planned for this time. Your body will be as beautiful to Alexander as this one, but with certain genetically changed systems. You will be happy, I promise you that!"

"Thank you Reverend Lady. Do with me, as you will. I will always serve you, as loyally as I once did when I was a Gnathe," Nagoth replied.

Link-soo-shan placed the crystal on her forehead, stopped

her heart and bridged her mind to the crystal storage while Khann stored her RNA. She watched her creation sit down at the control of the Goss and laughed inside her mind.

"Loyalty! When love comes into the equation my enhanced daughter, then experience has taught me that loyalty diminishes!"

Khann-link-sool turned to her one time bitter enemy and said, "Come! We must make our way quickly back to Kamiel and Asue. Our part in this exercise is over."

Link-soo-shan, once ruler of the Gnathen Empire and feared tyrant to her one time enemies, made her way back towards a silver-coloured, artificial intelligence, that had once promised her a far more interesting world if she could only see the universe more like him. He had been right!

Inside the Ark was a deathly hush as they returned. They passed the Lagdoo stood in unmoving ranks, ready to control the Ark once they emerged from the wormhole, all under complete control of the Goss. They stood like statues without breathing, as did every other crewmember. The only living beings left alive were the six twins, Link, Khann and the pieces of flesh kept alive by Kamiel and Asue, as they approached the end of the wormhole.

The nannite's mind became aware of the tightly compacted gestalt of the six twins connecting via the Goss.

"Kamiel!"

"I hear you."

"It is time for us to leave. Keep to the plan for the best outcome. Everything is now up to you. We can do no more, here in these prisons of flesh," the mind touch of Shoolin, Alexis and the other identical copies withdrew.

The bodies of the six twins went limp and the hearts stopped, as the collective mind withdrew. They hung suspended in the greenish liquid still attached to the feeding pipes and waste outlets. All the graphics dropped to zero.

Now the only living creatures left on the Ark were Link-soo-shan and Khann-link-sool.

The Gnathe had methodically placed each crystal into a named holder and sealed them into boxes according to the species. These they stacked inside the time stasis capsule and clambered into the space left. Both of them perched upon the bar, custom built for their weight and held onto the armrests.

Link-soo-shan entered Kamiel and Asue's minds for possibly the last time and said, "I do not believe in luck my nannite friends. Now all organic life has to rely on an intelligence that was designed and built to defend them. Many will die this day following your plan. Any who do, will accept their fate gladly to rid our part of the universe of this life-eater. Without you, Kamiel, this would not be possible. I hope to see you again when this is over. Alexander McBald would have been more than proud of his creations had he but the chance to see what they have been capable of. Destroy this abomination. Now activate the time stasis."

Kamiel did so and connected to the Goss. He felt the inertia of dead flesh, but the ability of the Goss to animate it was his to manipulate. The Ark left the wormhole mouth and materialised into empty space well underneath the Harvester's geometric shape. The ball of spaghetti was unravelling and expanding towards the wormholes, absorbing the collectors on its way.

In his mind for a moment was the fleeting sensation of Shoolin-Alexis and the combined minds of the other four twins saying a final goodbye.

The Harvester entered real time and became aware! A raging hunger possessed it and it reached out to the life forces within its grasp. Its mind reached out, feeling for the life that swarmed about it.

More than a million Toarvaks had exited a hundred thousand wormholes. Like a cloud of bees they headed towards the Energy being. Half of them assumed the barrel shape and using each independent group mind, they opened a gate at the heart of the stars the Kresh had brought with them. Swarms of collectors fried as the criss-cross beams of star-matter caught them in their hesitancy. Some of them touched the Toarvaks and drained them of life. The others soared upwards and over the top of the abomination. They opened their minds and broadcast everything from the thousands of worlds scattered across Andromeda.

Back on the worlds saved from the collector's plundering, the 'Concerts' were under way. Musical symphonies rang out to be enjoyed by those that could understand them and were broadcast to the Toarvak crews, carrying the receiving minds that sent them on to the collectors. Now the unique power of the Goss came into play and it acted as a conduit throughout the wormhole systems.

At the very same time, a contrasting effect was transmitted by those not of the same species. Vogb sent their light poems in all their beauty. The Kresh, who could not see in the same spectrum and were unable to appreciate them, sent their incomprehension. Thipdar mathematical music required all four hands to play the stringed instruments and a trip'o-dal mind to appreciatively understand the compositions. To humans the music was incomprehensible; to other aliens such as the insectoids they would experience a strange uplift of the mind. The insectoids sent their love of chess and played Grand Master games, transmitted by their own world mind next to Haven. Bazantii danced the dance of the hunt, watched by the Bazantii and the Vogb who found that it engendered the feeling of being the prey! Both versions were broadcasted to the Harvester and the collectors.

317

Every being that had an art form or many different ways of expressing their own artistic merits had worked to perfect it. Using the Goss, they telepathically transmitted a totally organic appreciation of the work and sent a contradiction with those aliens that were unable to understand.

The Harvester slowed in its movement towards the wormholes and the Toarvaks closed them with copies of the Ark's ancient weapon. As the confusion mounted amongst the collectors they became absorbed by the Harvester and added their chaotic emotions to the bewildered overmind. Nuclear weapons were released in waves and began to detonate around the upper edge of the Harvester's geometric energy form, drawing its attention to that area. The mind of the Harvester was now approaching real time and was drawing on its energy stores to try and understand what was happening it. Music flooded into its mind of every kind at a power that the energy being had never experienced before. The power of billions of minds all concentrated into one group mind resonated into its consciousness. This was multiplied by thousands of worlds all projecting at once.

It became confused by the ecstatic enjoyment of the hundreds of pieces of art forms played at the same time.

At the same time, alien attempts at understanding the meaning of the music added to the confusion. Its mind slowed down!

The Vogb light poems filled its sensory grasp beyond understanding. With this came distaste at the flickering lights transmitted by the topmost ring viewed by the insectoids.

The mind faltered as it struggled to make sense of the input. In all of its billions of years of existence, the Harvester had never sensed a world collective mind. Now thousands of them projected their own Art forms at the life-eater. The mind slowed even more, unable to reach out at the tantalising meals that flashed in and out of phase.

Underneath the Harvester, the Last Ark of the Goss hurtled towards a gap in the first geometric shape and sailed through one of the Icosahedron equilateral triangles. In front of them lay the Dodecahedron spinning the opposite way and the Ark swerved and dropped through the pentagon shape. Now Kamiel could see pulses of light sweeping through the spaghetti that wound itself through the spinning frameworks. As the edge of each geometric figure sliced through the strands it sparkled. Kamiel gave the order to the dead Lagdoo through the Goss.

"Release the rings."

Nothing happened!

"Goss!"

A faint feathery voice seeped into his mind.

"I am spread so thin! So much to do!"

"Goss! Pay attention. Concentrate your mind here! I need you now," Kamiel urged with his entire mind, drawing Asue into the mental shout. The rings had been placed so that the leading ring was held at ninety degrees to the one straddling the hollow moon. The Ark was rotating like a spinning top under Kamiel's direction.

The Lagdoo began to move like a well-oiled machine and the docking clamps released the first ring where it bedded into the Ark. The ark slowed as the last docking clamp let go and the first ring of crystals spun away from them rotating about the axis of the Ark. It was on course, heading for the centre of the Harvester. Kamiel gave the next instruction and the second ring floated away on the same axis, following the spinning ring.

The Ark swung away to coast through first one pentagon and then through the equilateral triangle and out of the Harvester's energy frame.

Kamiel reached out for the symbiont, "Goss! Tell the Kresh now!"

From out of a massive wormhole, came a blue-white star, shepherded by the Kresh. They connected the second gate to the first spinning crystal gate by warping the space between them, holding them fast. The planetary collective opened the second stargate and warped space to the centre of the giant.

Inside the Harvester two rings became active. One opened into the heart of the star and the other spun a blue-white sword a light-year long at right angles to the direction of axis. The jet of blue-white flame plunged deeper and deeper into the centre of the energy being. For the very first time in its billions of years existence, the Harvester felt the emotion of fear, as it began to unravel. It lost all control of the collectors and they spun off in all directions. It found that it could not travel down a wormhole to escape the spinning knife in its heart. Kamiel had got his bigger star!

Now the Kresh released the blue-white star towards it, as the Harvester froze helplessly in space unable to move. Although the creature was the size of an average stellar system it could do nothing, as the giant star with a luminosity of thirty-three thousand times that of Earth's sun, plunged towards it.

Inside the Harvester, the damage being done by the spinning open gate was preventing it from thinking rationally and to move out of the way. When it did try to do this it found too many of the wormholes closed and it couldn't choose. Indecision filled its mind, due to the damage also being inflicted by the Toarvaks. They were now destroying the collectors and breaking down the energy fields at that end of the onslaught.

Its mind filled with music. The ride of the Valkyrie boomed throughout its mind, broadcast by a group of humans connected right back to the world of Haven. The words were in ancient German and totally un-comprehended by the listeners. They just let themselves go with the emotion. The Harvester tried to dance the dance of the Hunter from the Bazantii and felt the Vogb fear of being the hunted! More mental confusion destroyed its ability to think!

Kamiel released a salvo of nuclear missiles at the bottom of the Harvester by operating the controls himself, as the Goss was now spread far too thin to activate the corpses of his friends. He timed the detonations perfectly and had the satisfaction of seeing the missiles explode one after another, as the lead bomb opened up the geometric shape. Through the hole he could see the others explode and deep inside was a new sun still doing its work as it spun. A salvo of missiles swept around the side of the Ark and he realised that his pacifist companion had released all the other nuclear missiles that they had left. Still the thing refused to die, but the geometric shapes began to sag.

A light year in front of the blue-white star flew a lone Toarvak out of phase. Toarvak 6 had activated the twin rings on its barrel shape and dived into the heart of the Harvester. She rode a pillar of fire well in front of the giant sun hard on her tail. The Harvester could not see or detect her as the star behind obscured its senses. The collective could see the unravelling geometric shape and aimed now for a tangential orbit, so that she cut through the first shape like a ripping plough. The spaghetti lines of force that connected the energy being to the wormholes had been severed by other Toarvaks. Here the creature bulged as it started to unravel.

Close behind them plunged the giant sun and Toarvak 6 sheered off to a safe distance with hundreds of thousands of others to watch the final destruction. Emelia, Larse, Thomas, Trann-link-khann and Deep Orange the Vogb, emerged from the silver mound that they had sunk into, to become Toarvak. With them, stood a tall, middle-aged woman, coloured silver, Toarvak 6. The organics moved to watch the view screens to watch the final moments of the Harvester, as the giant star remorselessly hurtled towards it. The rest of the crew who made up the group mind controlling the star-gates fore and aft had left their couches and joined the group.

Larse put his arm around Emelia's shoulders and said, "Well my love this looks to be the end."

Emelia laughed and replied, "No Larse, this is the beginning!"

The Kresh then released the reserve suns from out of individual wormholes dotted across space, all facing the Harvester's energy patterns. Ten white, bachelor stars, winked into existence and sped towards the life-eater. Every Toarvak took itself out of phase and the collisions that were about to take place. The mental onslaught stopped and the Harvester tried to speed up its mind to real time. Deep inside it the fiery sword continued to spin and dive ever deeper into the centre of its complex structure. It began disrupting the very substance of the life-eater, as the centre of its mind frantically tried to avoid the spinning blade.

The blue-white giant evaporated the outside layers of the Harvester right in the centre of the energy field. Ten more stars began to do damage to the outer geometric shapes in a double pentagon pattern. The only direction to travel was further outwards into empty galactic space. The Harvester began to move slowly away from the approaching stars, out into the galactic dark and away from the onslaught.

Now the gravitational pull of all eleven stars began to pull the Harvester back and to each other. The stars collided and began to implode, due to their combined mass overcoming the fusion reaction at the centre of the greatest star that had ever existed. A black hole formed and began to suck the substance of the stars, into the singularity that the Kresh had calculated would be created. With the stars vanishing inwards, also came the Harvester, as it unravelled the spaghetti inter-winding the geometric bodies and holding it together. In its last moments, its organic harvest heard it scream inside their minds, as it became compressed into the singularity. The spinning sword of celestial fire went out, as the remnants of both stars and the energy being winked out of existence, to become a wandering black hole heading away from the Andromeda galaxy.

The Toarvaks came back into phase with the universe. The world minds disbanded along with the concerts that were being played and mentally broadcasted. It had taken the efforts of every sentient race of technical beings to come together to destroy the being that had looked upon them as a crop to be harvested. Now they had a new society to form without the threat of their star exploding before it needed to. It would take millions of years before the spiral arm of Andromeda finished ploughing through the Milky Way galaxy, which left a vast amount of Andromeda safe.

Many light-years away from the new black hole, the Ark hung in intergalactic space spinning gently to produce artificial gravity.

Kamiel and Asue extended all their nannite senses to watch the ripple effect of the new singularity passing in front of the Andromeda Galaxy.

The Guardian opened his mind to his companion and said, "I was right! All I needed was a bigger star! Now let us release Link-soo-shan and Khann-link-sool from time stasis and get them started on re-growing new clones for all on board. It's going to be some time before we can rejoin everyone else."

Asue activated the time capsule and watched as the two Gnathe began to step off their perches with minds full of questions.

Kamiel checked that his piece of hosted flesh was still healthy and searched with his mind, "Goss?"

"I am here Kamiel."

"Well done, Goss," the artificial intelligence replied. "Well done! Now tell them where we are!"

The End

Epilogue

Hundreds of thousands of light years from the edge of the Andromeda galaxy and its new black hole, the Machine Intelligence began to transform a world. Over time a resplendent jewel would arise from a barren world. Such a place that any interstellar vessel would want to land and stay......and stay, until its secrets were fully understood.

About the Author

Barry Woodham was born in 1943 and has lived in Swindon, Wiltshire in England all of his life.

He spent his working life as a design engineer/draughtsman and worked on the nuclear fusion project for thirteen years. Finding himself with nothing to read one lunchtime, he began to write the saga of the Gnathe and the Genesis Project. The thought occurred to him that any life form evolved to live in this world would not be able to cope with the micro-organisms of another eco-system on an alien planet. After many of his colleagues began to read the chapters as quickly as he could finish them he continued on and finished the first book. The alien Gnathe are instinctive genetic engineers and alter living creatures to be their tools by the use of their brooding pouches controlled by the third sex. This first book is set millions of years after the sun has entered its red giant stage and is set on a vastly altered Jupiter. Humanity and intelligent Pan-chimpanzees are recreated by four Guardians made of nano-technology sent towards the stars from the dying Earth, to bring back mankind. One ship is stuck in the Kuiper Belt until it begins to fall towards the new sun and the crew are activated.

He was able to take early retirement through a legacy and continued to write the next book following on from Genesis 2, called The Genesis Debt. These have both been self published on Amazon.

He has now put the final touches to 'Weapon', the third book in the series that has been self edited and printed in a spiral bound condition.

While writing Weapon he decided to link all the books

together as 'The Genesis Project' and write all the books into a series. 'The Genesis Search' is set hundreds of thousands of years after the events that occurred in Weapon. This part of the saga concerns the deliberate collision of the Andromeda Galaxy with ours in the distant future. What kind of entity could cause this to happen and why? This book attempts to settle those questions and concerns building a hunter/killer group from the ones who defeated the 'Goss' in Book Three by going back in time to remove their DNA and clone them, restoring their stored minds into young healthy bodies. At the same time whole solar systems are being rebuilt and moved by wormhole technology to the other side of our galaxy to be launched as a globular cluster towards the Greater Magellanic Clouds and safety.

Whilst writing this forth book the idea came to be, that my group of mixed human and aliens would find themselves having to deal with the abandoned machine intelligence of Von-Neumann probes left behind by the events produced by the 'Harvester' and this would be worth considering as the fifth Book, Genesis 3, A New Beginning.

The complete range of 'Genesis Project' books by Barry E Woodham are available in hard copy and eBook file formats and include:-

Book 1. 'Genesis 2'
Hard copy   ISBN 978-1-909020-79-5
eBook for Kindle   ISBN 978-1-909020-81-8
eBook for all other readers   ISBN 978-1-909020-80-1

Book 2. 'Genesis Debt'
Hard copy   ISBN 978-1-909020-82-5
eBook for Kindle   ISBN 978-1-909020-84-9
eBook for all other readers   ISBN 978-1-909020-83-2

Book 3. 'Genesis Weapon'
Hard copy   ISBN 978-1-909020-85-6
eBook for Kindle   ISBN 978-1-909020-87-0
eBook for all other readers   ISBN 978-1-909020-86-3

Book 4. 'Genesis Search'
Hard copy   ISBN 978-1-909020-88-7
eBook for Kindle   ISBN 978-1-909020-90-0
eBook for all other readers   ISBN 978-1-909020-89-4

Book 5. 'Genesis 3 A New Beginning'
Hard copy   ISBN 978-1-909020-91-7
eBook for Kindle   ISBN 978-1-909020-93-1
eBook for all other readers   ISBN 978-1-909020-92-4

Also a new fantasy book 'The Elf-War'
Hard copy   ISBN 978-1-909020-94-8
eBook for Kindle   ISBN 978-1-909020-96-2
eBook for all other readers   ISBN 978-1-909020-95-5